TWISTED TIES

HANNAH HAZE

FOREWORD

This book is a 'why choose' bully paranormal romance with one female main character and more than one potential love interest. These love interests are ruthless and at times brutally unkind. There are scenes that some readers may find uncomfortable including violence and gore. For more detailed content warnings, please visit my website.

If you spot any typos in this book, please drop me a line so I can make it right: hannahhazewrites@gmail.com (Or just drop me an email anyway. I love to chat!).

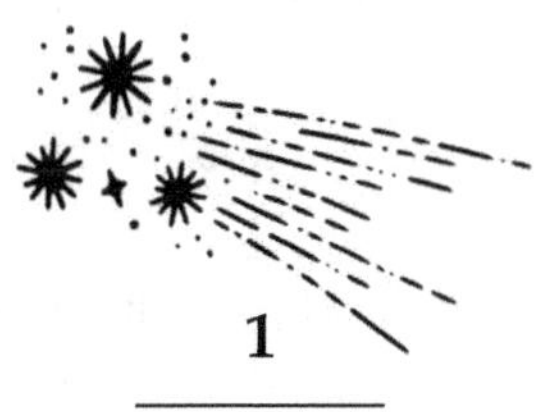

1

S tone

I STRIDE out of that alley and into the dark back streets down by the docks, white sea mist swirling in the dim light of the overhead lamps.

I'm going to find him. I'm going to find him and I'm going to kill him.

That man – that bastard fucking man – was going to kill her. To end her life. To take her from us. And for all my talk, for all my pretense that I don't give a damn about the girl who's stumbled into our lives and shaken everything upside down with both her hands, I'm lying.

I do care. I care so much it makes my heart ache in my chest and I can't stand there and look at her crumpled on the ground in pain.

I need to kill the man that did this to her. I need to make him pay for it. I won't let him live. No way am I going to let him live to strike again. Because he will. Renzo Barone is as relentless as he is disturbed, and his boss doesn't accept failure. They won't stop until the job is done.

So I'm going to find him and I'm going to kill him. And I'm going to do it right now.

I may not be a tracker like Azlan. But I have my skill, my ability – reading minds. And – what only my friend knows – is that if I try hard enough, if I concentrate with every fiber of my being, I can read them over distance. And Renzo's? Well, it's like a fucking siren – a chaotic, noisy mess blaring out there in the darkness.

His thoughts are too rambling, too many voices jabbering all at once for me to make any sense of it. Although there's one theme, one topic, repeating over and over again. The girl. Like he's obsessed.

Yeah, well, he can get in line.

I follow that crackling noise through the empty streets, my eyes flicking from side to side, watchful for any unseen strike, my hands raised and ready.

There's no one else out here. I suspect they heard that fight back there in the alleyway and have tucked themselves away and out of danger.

I know the kind of people who live here. Hell, I spent my childhood among them. They know to keep their heads down and to stay out of trouble. See no evil, hear no evil, speak no evil. That's the way to survive.

The noise of Renzo's mind grows louder, and I pick up my pace, until I spot him in the distance, sitting astride his motorbike, tying a tourniquet around his arm, the eerie mist lingering around his feet, making him appear ghostly.

I launch a cascade of my most violent magic towards him and his head snaps my way. He can't see me hiding in the shadows and he's forced to duck low, twisting and turning to avoid my onslaught.

I curse myself. If I held my temper, if I'd remained calmer ... but I'm too damn angry, rage curling through my body in hot, hot flames. Flames that don't want to listen to caution or logic. Flames that want to burn him to ashes.

I send more magic crashing his way, but I've lost the element of surprise now and he meets mine with his own, the bolts slamming into each other and exploding so fiercely, I'm forced to raise my arms and shield my eyes.

"The Enforcer and the Professor," he cackles with an amusement that sounds unhinged. "I haven't seen you fight together in a long time. This has almost been fun."

Fun?

Fun?!

The sicko nearly killed my girl. My mate.

I growl, stepping out of the shadows and firing rapid bolts straight at him.

He sweeps his arm through the air, creating an impenetrable shield, the bolts exploding against its surface but traveling no further.

"And out to save the girl? Curious ..." He kicks up the stand of his bike, wheels it around to face me. "Want to tell me why?"

"I'm going to kill you," I hiss, running at him. I don't give a shit about magic. I want my hands around his throat. I want to punch my fist against his skull. I want to feel it splinter into a million pieces.

His magic streams past me as I run, but I block it all, and then I'm on him, grabbing the front of his shirt and dragging him off the bike.

A sick grin spreads across his face.

They say the assassin has a love of blood, a love of

getting his hands dirty. That he likes to make his killings as messy as he can. No silent bolt of magic through the night, striking his victim in the back of the head. No, he'd rather break every bone in their body first.

Is that what he was going to do to her?

"You don't speak of her," I say, pounding my fist against his face and hearing both my fingers and his cheekbone crack. "You don't think of her. You will regret ever coming for her. Because I'm going to kill you."

"You're not," he says, smiling even though there's blood in his mouth. "Because you're not who you used to be, Phoenix Stone. With your smart suit and your comfy fucking job in the academy. Sitting all day, pouring over your books. I've seen you."

"You have no idea what I'm capable of," I hiss, swinging my arm back to hit him again. This time he ducks, landing a punch of his own on my ribs.

I grunt, the pain sharp below my aching heart.

"I've seen you watching her. Seen you looking at her. You know it's funny. When you watch someone like I have, you notice all the other people doing the same. And there are so many of you, aren't there?"

I don't know what the hell he's talking about. The man is insane. The noise from his head still loud in my ears, distracting me, attempting to drown me in its madness.

He tries to hit me again, but I grip him around the waist and throw him to the ground. He pulls me with him and we scrabble around, first me on top of him, then he on top of me, the road cold and wet beneath us, seeping through my clothes. I kick at him, zap him with my magic, hit at him, and then I have the upper hand again. My hands tighten around his neck and I squeeze and squeeze.

"I'm going to kill you," I snarl, the rage so all-consuming, all I can see is the amusement dancing in his eye, everything else fading away.

"Nah, not today, Prof.," he says. His manic eyes twinkle – one brown, one green. He winks at me and then he's gone. Just like that. One minute pinned on the ground beneath me, my hands tight around his neck. The next gone, nothing but thin air, my hands hanging redundantly.

How the fuck did he do that?

I twist around, scramble to my feet, searching for him.

There's nothing but mist and darkness and his bike.

I kick at the ground, swearing.

I failed.

I failed her yet again.

2

R^{hi}

THE ROOM IS DARK, the clinic still and quiet. I can hear the man in black's breath whistle. I can feel his presence, feel it deep down in the very pit of my core, a core that spins and swoons uncontrollably.

I screw up my eyes. Is he awake like I am? Awake in the dark, trying to make sense of everything that's happened. Or is he there, sitting in the chair beside my bed regretting everything that's happened.

He says he had no choice. He says he did it to save me. That if he hadn't given me his power, his magic, I would have perished in his arms. And those actions have led to this. The sealing of the fated bond – something irreversible.

Does he regret it? Does he wish he'd let me die? Because if we are what they say we are – a fated pair – it's not like he greeted me with open arms.

My heart aches in my chest, knowing the truth of it. He didn't want me. He didn't choose me. No, fate did the choosing. Fate gave him a mate like me. Stupid, ignorant, weak, pathetic.

A girl who has no idea how this complicated world works.

I open my eyes and stare up at the blinking light on the ceiling. On. Off. On. Off.

Why does it hurt so much?

The nurse had floated around me yesterday as if I was the luckiest girl on the planet, muttering about the blessings bestowed upon me, how fortunate I was to find my other half, how happy I must be.

"He saved you," she swooned, "it's so romantic."

Lying on the hospital bed with a broken leg and the memory of the agony his absence had caused still fresh in every cell in my body, I don't feel lucky or fortunate or happy.

It doesn't feel that way to me at all.

Mostly I feel sadness, a sadness that morphs to anger as the long night drags on. An anger that starts off lukewarm and simmers hotter and hotter, till I'm boiling over with it.

Where was my choice? Where was all my say in this? What does this mean for me now? Chained to the side of a man who clearly doesn't want me. Fated to be dragged around after him wherever he chooses to go.

No, no way. There has to be a way to undo this.

As the morning light filters through the clinic window, the blackness fades to a charcoal, then a murky gray and I see he is awake. Awake and watching me.

"You didn't sleep," he says.

"No," I say.

It's harder to stay angry at him when I can see his face.

Because, damn, it is a beautiful face, and his eyes, his eyes possess a power all of their own, making every part of my body tingle with anticipation.

"How do you feel?"

I chew on my lip. How do I feel? Angry, yes, but also tired and confused.

He leans forward, and that hook in my stomach grows stronger, the tingles across my skin more rampant. He lifts his hand and, after a hesitation, touches my cheek.

I gasp, closing my eyes, because I don't want him to touch me and yet I do. It's all I can think about. His touch on my skin. His touch everywhere.

He slides his fingertips down my cheek, and the pulse in my throat leaps.

"They're going to fix your leg this morning."

They didn't want to do it yesterday. Not after the draining of my magic, not with the newly formed fated bond so raw and ... I blink my eyes open and stare up into his face. How had the doctor described it? Unstable.

"Will you be here?" I ask, because I can't bear the agony I felt yesterday when he stepped out of the room.

"They're going to give you something for the pain, Rhi," he reassures me. "But ... I'll stay if that's what you want."

I glare at him. I don't know what the hell I want.

"I want to be alone," I snap. Do I? The sensations in my body say otherwise, but I'm so damn angry with him. "I want my pig. I want to see my friend. I want–"

A knock sounds on the door.

The man in black, Azlan, turns toward it, then back to me. "Come in," he says.

It's the nurse from yesterday. Her gaze swings between us with a sort of awe, like we are the most amazing thing in the world.

"Good morning," she says, brightly, "I've come to get you ready for the procedure." She walks towards the bed. "How are you feeling?" Before I can answer, she leans in to whisper, "Do you need to use the bathroom?" I nod. "Do you want him in or out for that?"

I blush so hard, I'm pretty certain the nurse must feel the heat from my cheeks. "Out."

"Would you mind waiting right outside the door, Sir?" she asks.

His eyes dart to mine and anxiety flickers across his expression. Does it hurt him as much as it hurts me when we're apart? Somehow I doubt it. Somehow I suspect that lucky gift is reserved entirely for me.

"I need to pee," I say.

My fated mate stares right back at me. "I'm not leaving."

"And you are not watching me pee."

"I'm not leaving you in agony again."

"The pain shouldn't be as intense today," the nurse reassures him.

"But it will still be there."

"Not if you're right by the door."

"You're not watching me pee," I say again, more firmly.

The man in black ignores me and addresses the nurse. "If she shows any signs–"

"I'll call you straight back in, of course." She smiles at him fondly as he rises to his feet and leaves the room.

Instantly, the hook in my belly pulls and I grimace at the sensation.

"Okay?" the nurse asks, hand on my shoulder.

"Yes," I say through gritted teeth. "You're right, it's not as bad as yesterday."

"Well, let's get you sorted quickly anyway, shall we?"

She turns to her trolley and lifts out what looks like a potty. I groan, wishing they'd sorted my leg after all, wondering if that doctor, the one who treated Azlan like an old friend – a close, old friend – is delaying it deliberately, just to make me suffer.

"It's very sweet. He cares about you so much," the nurse says as she helps me.

"Sweet?" I scoff.

"And he's so handsome. And tall and strong."

"Hmmm," I say. He is all those things. But he's also a liar. A big fat liar.

When I'm done and the nurse has helped me wash a little, she calls the man in black back into the room. He comes striding through, the pain in my gut alleviating immediately.

I sigh with relief and sink back into the cushions.

"The doctor will be back here shortly, to help prep you for the procedure," she says, wheeling her trolley back towards the door.

"Can I have something to eat?" I ask.

"Not until afterwards," she calls, the door closing behind her and leaving us alone again. I stare at the door and not at my mate. I don't have anything to say to him.

THEY PUT me under for the procedure, even though I tell them I can handle the pain, and I don't emerge again until several hours later.

The electric lights glow above my head and as I pull myself out of unconsciousness, I realize it must be evening.

"How long was I under?" I ask, sensing the man in black by my side, his presence making that hook in my belly hum.

"Six hours,"

"Jeez," I groan, my head fuzzy and my mouth dry.

"It was a complicated break. Took Lucinda a lot of work to fix it."

Lucinda? I frown.

"You were there?" I ask.

"Yes, I wanted to make sure they did a good job."

"Yeah, you wouldn't want a lame mate as well as a stupid one, would you?"

He's silent, but something in the air tells me he doesn't like what I just said.

I twist my head, even though it makes sickness swim through my stomach and find him frowning.

"You're not stupid," he says.

"If that were true, would we be in this situation right now?" He doesn't answer me. "Besides, Stone seems to think I am."

"Stone doesn't think that."

"He said it." I remember clearly. Every painful word.

"He was worried about you."

I snort. Stone worried about me? That crush was strictly one way, and now ...

"Does he know?" I whisper. "Does he know about our ... situation?"

What will he think? Will he laugh at us? Will he feel sympathy for his friend? Will he care at all?

The man in black keeps staring at me, only a muscle in his cheek twitching.

"No. I haven't told anyone. Only the staff at the hospital are aware."

I twist my head away from him. What will everyone think? What will they say? Especially the Council? Will they make me go to school anyway, even though it will rip the guts straight from my body to be away from this man? Will they expect him to stay with me?

The thoughts swirl in my head like a whirlwind. It's all so complicated, so entangled and twisted up.

"I'm tired," I tell him, "really fucking tired."

"We'll work this out, Rhianna," he whispers as I feel sleep pulling me down. "I'm going to fix this for you."

But as the blackness descends, I'm really not sure he can. Not even the man in black.

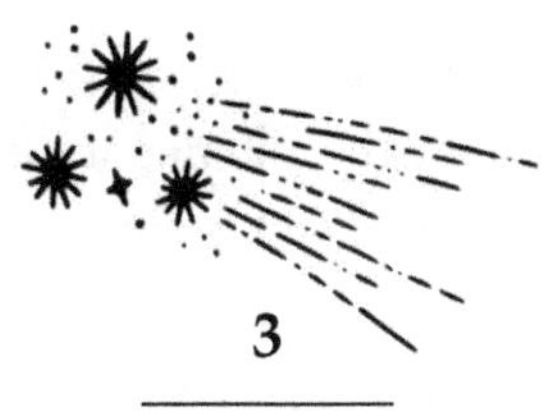

3

zlan

I WATCH as her eyes drift shut and her chest rises and falls in the rhythm of sleep. I wait until I know she's truly in deep, and then I flop back against the chair.

I know I won't sleep again. My mind's too wired. My body is too. Despite the depletion of my powers, it hums with an energy. An energy that stems from the bond. The hook deep in my body drags me towards her and all I want to do is touch her, taste her, claim her as mine.

But I can't. And not just because she's injured, healing, delicate. But because she doesn't want it. She doesn't want me.

She can barely look me in the eye. And when she does, I can see the hatred and disappointment spitting there.

A hatred and disappointment I know will be echoed in my best friend's eyes. In my father's too. Hell, probably in the Chancellor's eyes as well. He won't understand it. My father won't either. Only Stone would. But Stone has fought this from the beginning.

I know sooner or later, I'm going to have to tell him. Better it comes from me than someone else.

I send him a message. Tell him to come meet me at the hospital.

He knows it's about the girl. Of course he does. Which means he's here in less than an hour.

I wait for him outside the door to her room in the dimly lit clinic corridor.

The pain in my gut has me grinding my teeth, wanting me to plow straight back there, to sit by her side like a faithful dog.

I pull against it and turn to my friend.

His face is full of curiosity.

"What is it?" he says.

I look him straight in the eye. Invite him to see everything.

He stares at me, his jaw slackening in disbelief, and then he takes a stumble backward.

"No," he mutters.

"Yes."

He opens his mouth. Then closes it. Shaking his head as if he can't believe what he's seen inside my head.

"You ... you sealed the bond."

"Yes."

"Why the fuck–"

"She was dying, Phoenix," I say, my voice cracking despite my best efforts, "in my arms." Phoenix rubs his hand all over his face, as if trying to wipe away my words. "And don't say, I should have let her," I growl with a menace that has his hand freezing.

He tilts his head to one side. "Don't tell me you have feelings for her?"

Like he doesn't? I'm not stupid. Not blind.

"She's my fated mate," I say out loud for the first time. I've known it for all this time. But never, not once, have I allowed myself to think it, to say it, too afraid if I voiced the thought it would make it real. What a fool. What a stupid fool.

Stone frowns, following the thoughts in my head.

"How much does she know? What have you told her?"

"Nothing," I snap. "We've barely talked. She's not exactly happy with the decisions I chose to make."

Stone smirks at me. "The girl's a brat. What did you expect?" I take a menacing step towards him, and he lifts his hands in surrender. "So all those new mate instincts are true, huh? You want to punch my lights out?"

"I want to stuff your tongue down your throat for talking about her like that," I growl out between my teeth, knowing it doesn't make sense. The girl *is* a brat. I still don't want him saying it.

Stone nods, understanding.

"Your father?"

"Is unaware."

"York? Stermer?"

"Have not been informed."

Stone plunges his hands in his pockets.

"Barone?" I ask.

His shoulders slump and he looks away from me as if he's ashamed.

"Gone."

"You're sure?"

"I went after him ... I had him ... I was so close ..."

"And?" I ask, sensing there's more.

"He just vanished. Into thin air."

"Vanished or made himself invisible to the naked eye?"

"No. He was definitely gone."

"He can travel through space?"

"I presume so."

"I didn't know he had the power." It makes the assassin even more dangerous.

We stand in silence. For once, my oldest friend has nothing to say. The one person who has always understood me. Who has always stood by me. Who has always had my back.

"Can you forgive me?" I ask.

"I'm not the one you need to convince to forgive you."

I glance towards the door. "I had no choice."

"She understands fuck all about this world. About how it works. She won't understand. All she'll know is that you did this without her consent."

"Shit," I mutter. "This is a fucking mess."

"Yeah, good luck with that," my friend says, turning around and walking away. He's more angry than he cares to show me. But I know. I'd feel the same way if the roles were reversed. I'd hate him for it.

I turn back to the door, hand resting on the handle. I'd feel the same if I were in Rhi's shoes too. I'd hate my very guts.

But what's done is done. It was perhaps always inevitable. Fate is a far more powerful force than any magical would ever care to admit. Pulling us together. Twisting and entwining our lives. Sooner or later, we would have collided. Sooner or later, I would have made her mine. Or perhaps she would have made me hers.

I just have to make her see that. Have to make her understand.

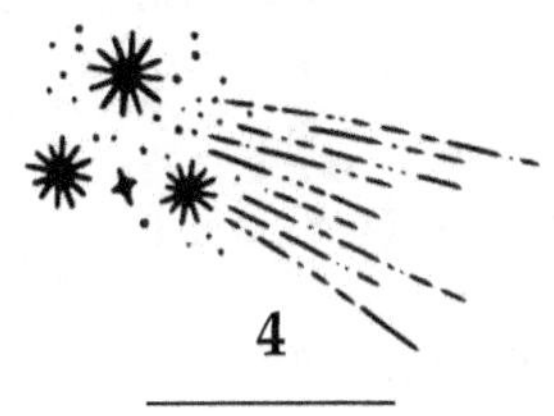

4

R enzo

I STARE DOWN at the knife in my hand, flicking up the blade and letting the fading light catch its sharp edge.

This knife killed Joey Lowsky, brother of Marcus.

He wants his death avenged, wants it avenged at all costs.

Lowsky is like that. All or nothing. Quiet, calm, calculating one moment, erupting with rage, raw and uncontrollable, the next. Apparently, it makes him fucking terrifying.

Not me though. I'm not like that.

Hey, I'm not like anyone else I've ever met.

My brain works in a different way.

My mom told me that long ago. Yelled it at me too when she kicked me out of her house.

Lowsky calls me his hunting dog. Says that because once

I pick up a scent, I'll track that thing down until it's ripped to shreds and lifeless in my hands.

And yeah, I'm like that too. Some call it ruthless. Some call it obsession.

I just know it's the thing that keeps me alive. The buzz in my brain, the thrill in my blood. I need it. It's like a drug. Like an addiction.

I tuck the blade into the handle, the metal cool to the touch, despite the warmth of my hands. I let my vision haze over, search through space and time, find the picture, a young woman's hand, fingernails chewed, gripping the hilt of this knife.

Her hand.

I think of the rest of her too. Small yet strong. Soft yet hard.

I pocket the knife and gaze up to the window.

I should be heading back to Lowsky. He's expecting me. Expecting to hear I've killed the girl.

But I'm lingering in the city. I can't help myself. I can't help but stand and look up at that window. Behind the glass I can see the dark figure of the Enforcer and somewhere in that room she's there too.

Fuck, I can feel it in my stomach. I know she's there.

I click the knuckles of my right hand, then the knuckles of my left, all the time my eyes locked on that window. The Enforcer is pacing. He's been pacing like that for two days. Does that mean she's hurt, dying?

I catch myself frowning.

I touch my fingers to my brow and tilt my head. Puzzling.

Dying is what I want. Dying is mission complete. Return to Lowsky and learn who the next victim to face their fate is, the next person to have crossed paths with Lowsky and the Wolves of Night.

But I don't think dying is what I want. My eyes fall down to my stomach. Curious …

The professor – the one who had fought me alongside the Enforcer, the one who came for me a second time, the one who said he'd kill me for attacking the girl – has only come to the clinic once. And then only for a brief amount of time.

I peer up at the window, watch as the man in black moves away from the glass.

He hasn't left her side.

What is his interest in the girl? What is the professor's?

An unregistered, hiding out in the wastelands. Nothing extraordinary about her.

Except …

I peer down at my stomach a second time.

If he leaves, I'll make my way to her room.

Not to hurt her. To pet her. To stroke that soft hair of hers. To suck in her sweet scent. Would she let me? Or would she scream and fight me again?

I smile. I like the way she screams. Like music. I can hear it in my mind. It makes me hard.

Curious again.

My eyes lower to the road and I watch as a car parks up and an elderly man climbs out, a bunch of daisies in his hands. A gift for some patient.

A gift. I liked sending my little rabbit gifts. Liked the idea it frightened her, had her shivering with fear, shaking on the soles of her feet.

I want to get her another gift. Not to frighten her. To remind her I'm thinking of her. To ensure she's thinking of me. To reassure her, we'll be together – her and me. It's meant to be.

The man reaches the clinic doors and they slide open.

Flowers.

I scoff.

I'm not gifting her flowers.

I'm going to give her a piece of me.

A lock of my hair?

Too fucking pathetic.

A drop or two of my blood?

Too much.

I examine my hands. Slide the littlest ring off my pinky fingers. It might be too big for her, but she can wear it on a chain around her neck. In fact, I like that idea better. My ring resting against her heart. A leash around her neck.

I pinch the ring between my forefinger and thumb and examine the silver skull. I stole it from some kid in our neighborhood. Took it from his hand, finger and all.

Fun times.

I smile.

I peer up at the window again. The Enforcer is still there. He's not going. It pisses me off. I won't be able to give my gift to her myself.

But I find another way, creeping up on some nurse smoking a cigarette round the back of the clinic.

I pull out the knife. I stroke my fingers along the hilt, feeling the carvings with my coarse fingertips.

Never used a knife before. Never plunged one into a gut, sliced one through a neck.

Wonder what that would be like. How it would feel.

Not tonight though. I need the nurse alive. Otherwise he can't deliver my gift.

"Hey," I say, and the nurse jumps a foot off the ground,

his cigarette tumbling from his fingers and singeing the front of his uniform. The smell of burned fabric pierces the air.

"Fuck," the man says, flicking the cigarette away and flapping at his shirt.

I get tired of waiting, and spin the knife in my hand.

The movement catches the man's attention, and he freezes.

"I don't have any money," he says quickly. "But you can have the packet." He shakes the cigarette box in his hand. "It's almost full."

I step closer. I can see the blood pumping in the man's throat. Bet he'd make a fucking fountain without me even trying. Just the touch of her knife through his skin. Skin really is shit. So thin. So weak. So pathetic.

"You want to help me?" I ask, coming closer still.

He nods, his eyes wide with terror as they look up at me.

I love that.

"Shame," I sigh. Guess, I was hoping for an excuse to kill the dude after all.

"Wh-what?" he stutters.

"See this ring," I say. I open my palm. His eyes dart down to look, though he's watching my knife hand out of the corner of his eye. "I want you to give it to the girl."

"What girl?"

"The one who looks like she fell out of a fairytale."

"What's her name?"

"Rhianna Blackwaters," I say. I like her name.

"I'll give it to her," he says, holding out his hand, eager to end this conversation and get away. "Who should I say it's from?"

I grin. "Her other half. She'll know."

A little nervously, the nurse pinches the ring from my palm and scuttles backwards.

"Hey Richard," I say, reading the name on his badge, the letters leaping about like jumping beans. "Don't let me down now, will you?" I smile at him, spinning the knife so quickly it flashes in the security light.

He nods again and races away.

I watch the knife spin some more.

She wanted it back but I'm glad I have it. Glad it's mine now.

I gaze back at the window.

Funny, I'm not sure I want to kill her anymore. My little rabbit, slipping from the fox's jaw.

No, I want to own her.

Own her like this knife.

5

———

R^{hi}

I WAKE the next morning to a kerfuffle outside the door.

My eyes flick open and I meet the eyes of my mate, before both our gazes dash to the door.

"What's going on?" I ask. Is that grunting I can hear?

Azlan shakes his head and lumbers to his feet, striding to the door. I notice the way his clothes are all creased, his hair a tangled mess and dark circles ring his eyes. It's not surprising. He's been sleeping on the tiny plastic clinic chair for the past two nights. He's had no opportunity to wash or shower. I almost feel sorry for the dude. Except I don't. Not one bit.

He opens the door and steps outside and immediately that pain splinters through my gut. It's not as painful as that very first time, but, goddamn it, it's still agony.

I swing my legs off the bed and, with an intake of breath,

test my weight on my feet. To my relief, the pain remains in my gut, no shooting spasms in my calf or my thigh. In fact, as I wiggle my toes, I have to admit that the doctor seems to have done a pretty good job.

However, my leg may be working but it doesn't stop me swaying on my feet and gripping the mattress. I haven't eaten a decent meal in several days. When the dizziness subsides, I hobble carefully towards the door, determined to discover what the hell is going on.

There've been enough secrets. If this is anything to do with me, I want to know.

Out in the corridor, I find Winnie and Pip arguing with the doctor, two nurses and the man in black.

"Winnie!" I cry barging through the small crowd and wrapping my arms right around my friend's neck.

"Rhi!" she says, squeezing me tight as Pip bumps his snout against my bare ankles.

"Animals are not permitted in the hospital," the doctor says, the look on her face reminding me of the snooty girls at school. "He needs to leave immediately."

If Pip understands, he doesn't care, licking my leg and squealing for attention. I release Winnie, and bend down, ignoring the man in black's intake of breath as I wobble slightly on my feet. I open my arms and Pip launches himself at me, licking my face and burying his snout under my chin.

"This is unhygienic and – it's licking her mouth! Azlan, I can't permit this. I've already bent rules for you, but this! She's not even meant to have human visitors, let alone farm-yard ones."

I scoop Pip up in one arm, take Winnie's wrist in the other hand, and lead them both through to my room, slamming the door behind us.

"Were they stopping you from coming in?" I ask angrily.

"Yep."

"And I suppose the man in black was trying to help them?"

Winnie frowns as I flop down on the bed and Pip plants himself in my lap, butting his head against my hand and demanding ear-tickles.

"No, he was trying to reason with them." I snort. "The man in black was the one who told me to come," Winnie says, "and bring Pip too."

I look up from Pip and stare at my friend.

"Really?" She nods. "What did he tell you?"

Winnie lowers herself down on the bed next to me.

"Oh, Rhi, he said you were in a terrible accident and that your magic was drained and you broke your leg really badly. I wanted to come to the clinic right away. I've been worried sick." She strokes her hand down my arm. "But this was the first time they'd let me and I didn't know what hospital you were in and–"

"It's okay, Winnie."

The raised voice of the man in black bellows behind the closed door and we both peer that way.

"Has he been here the entire time?" Winnie asks with a confused frown.

"Erm, yes," I say and at my tone she twists back round to examine my face. "I'm guessing he didn't tell you everything, then."

"Everything?"

I screw up my eyes. I'm not sure if Winnie is even going to believe this story. It sounds so utterly incredible.

"I was attacked."

"Attacked?" I wave my hand at her, indicating that isn't even the incredible part of this story.

"I tried to defend myself and ended up draining all my energy. I thought I was going to die," I add quietly, remembering that moment of both terror and acceptance.

"What happened?"

"Stone and Azlan showed up–"

"Azlan?"

I point to the door.

"I didn't know that was his name."

"Join the club."

"They saved you? Stone and ... Azlan?"

"Yep, and then ... then ..." I inhale, feeling Pip vibrate with pleasure in my lap, "my powers were so low, almost gone. Azlan ... he gave me his magic. He kept me alive."

Winnie blinks at me seven times in a row. It was a reaction my words generated a lot when we first met. More recently, I haven't been as adept at shocking her. She's grown used to my madness. But this, this leaves my best friend utterly speechless.

"Winnie?" I say, shaking her arm gently as she continues to stare at me, dumbfounded.

"That isn't possible, Rhi," she says, shaking her head, "One magical can't give their magic to another, not unless they are ... not unless they are ..."

"Fated mates?"

"Yes, and you're not ..." she trails off, her eyes growing so wide they look like two full moons in her face, "are you?"

I open my eyes. "We are."

"I didn't ... I mean I had no idea."

"Again, me too!" I say.

"Did he know?" she says, frowning.

"Yep, seems so."

"But he didn't tell you?"

"Nope."

"But there are signs, aren't there?"

"Yes, if you know what they are. I guess I just thought that's what a crush felt like. I didn't know it was more than that. And now ..." I shake my head, feeling tears pooling in the corners of my eyes. "I don't know anything, Winnie. I don't know what this means, how it works. I'm clueless and," perhaps my best friend is the only person I'd ever admit this to, "scared."

"Oh, sweetie," Winnie says, lunging across the bed to wrap me in another hug despite Pip's protests.

I sob onto her shoulder and as I do the door flies open.

"What's wrong?" the man in black says, his voice full of concern.

"What's wrong?" I spit. "What's wrong?"

"Are you hurt? Is it your leg?"

Winnie pulls away and spins around on the bed to face my mate. "No, it's you, you lying toad."

The man in black scowls at her, and oh my lord, that look would have most people quaking in their boots. However, my usually nervous friend takes it in her stride, waggling her finger at him as if the giant facing her is simply a naughty little school boy. "You lied to her."

"I never lied."

Winnie harrumphs. "You have some serious making up to do."

"I know," he says, meeting my eyes.

"But," Winnie adds, "you did save her which I am very grateful for. Just know, this girl means a lot to me – she's awesome and beautiful and smart and brave–"

"I know," he says a second time, still staring into my eyes and making my body thrum with energy.

"And if you hurt her in any way, if you so much as make

her shed one tear, then I am coming for you Mr. ... Mr. ... Mr. Enforcer. I don't care who you are."

For the first time since this all happened, I feel a sense of relief and happiness hovering in my heart. I am so lucky to have Winnie; Winnie and Pip. I'm not alone in this. I know I'd do anything for this girl and it seems like she'd do anything for me.

"I understand," Azlan says gravely.

"Right," Winnie says, lowering her finger, her cheeks flushing beetroot. "So if you'd give us a little more privacy, please."

The man in black looks to me. "It isn't hurting you too much?"

I shake my head and he steps out of the room.

Winnie lets out a long puff of air. "Ahh Rhi, the man may be an idiot, but he is also damn hot."

"Yeah," I say, my skin still tingling from that look of his. "I'm so confused."

"I can help with that," she says, jumping to her feet. "I'm going to the library and I'm going to check out every book ever written on fated mates, then we're going to sit here together and stuff our heads full of information until we are the world's two leading experts on the subject."

I manage a laugh. "Actually, that does sound like a good idea."

"Of course it does. I'm full of good ideas."

"But I don't want you to go."

She smiles at me empathetically and bends down to kiss my wet cheek. "I'll be quick, I promise. I'll be back before you know it. And anyway, I think he wants you to himself." She points to Pip who is licking my fingertips.

✳.

I'm still waiting for Winnie to return an hour later, when a nurse knocks on the door. It's not the usual nurse, someone different this time. Azlan eyes him with suspicion.

"I've come to check your vital signs," he says, squirming under Azlan's gaze. "Would you mind leaving the room, Sir?"

"I don't need to leave the room," he says.

"Azlan," I say, "the man's only trying to do his job. Go wait outside the door."

Azlan glares some more at the poor nurse who seems to shrink before his eyes, then strides out.

The nurse sighs with relief. "He is pretty intimidating," he mumbles, reaching across to wind the blood pressure monitor around my arm.

"You're telling me!" I mumble back, watching the needle skid across the dial as the nurse pumps air.

"All good," he says, taking my wrist in his hand next and pressing down on my pulse point as his lips move. Finally, he sticks a thermometer in my ear and then adds all the readings to the notes clipped at the end of my bed.

"You're all done."

"Thank you," I say.

He collects up the equipment but hovers by my bed. He opens his mouth and closes it.

"Do you need to check anything else?" I ask.

"No." He maneuvers the equipment into his left hand and digs his right into his pocket. "There was a man outside. He wanted me to give you this." He holds out his hand, a silver ring with a skull head carved into the metal work balances in his palm.

I stare down at the ring. "What man?" I whisper.

"To be honest, he looked like trouble but I thought maybe he was your boyfriend or something. I guess not though considering ..." He motions with his head towards the door where the figure of the man in black hovers behind the frosted pane.

The ring is familiar. I shiver. The hand from my dream. The hand that tried to strangle me. Renzo Barone's hand I now realize. I shiver again, remembering both the creepy aura of the man and the strangely alluring magnetism.

"He is trouble," I say. "Big trouble."

The nurse glances at the ring in his hand as if he expects it to burn his skin.

"You want me to dispose of it?"

"Yes, please," I say. "It's most likely cursed."

The man's eyes widen in horror and he looks like he wants to throw the thing out the window. Instead, he returns it carefully to his pocket. "I'm sorry. It seemed harmless to me. Just ... if he ever asks, I delivered it to you, okay?"

I go to ask him what exactly Barone said to him, but then the door swings open and Winnie comes charging through.

This time no one has attempted to bar her entrance which I think is down to the man in black. However, she returns empty-handed, slumping into the chair by my bed with a defeated sigh as the nurse takes his opportunity to hurry away.

"Where are all the books?" I ask, confused.

"Gone," she says. "Not one book on the subject of fated mates in the entire goddamn library. Can you believe that? Someone checked them all out!"

"I guess it's a popular subject."

"But every book?"

"Maybe someone else is in a similar position to me."

"I doubt it, Rhi, fated mates are extremely rare."

"You said your cousin was one."

Winnie screws up her face. "That didn't work out."

"What?" I say with alarm. I thought it was meant to work out between fated mates. I thought that was the whole point. I assumed that when my anger for Azlan fades it would be all right, eventually, somehow.

"It wasn't the real thing. They got their bloods checked."

I shake my head. "I'm confused."

Winnie holds up her hand, then dives into the satchel she has slung over her shoulder. "I couldn't find books, but I did download and print everything I could find on the internet. I mean, some of it will be bullshit, but some of it will be accurate."

"Hmmm."

She dumps a load of printed pages onto the bed. "There are loads of people searching for answers on the internet, loads of agony aunts answering questions. I used to devour this stuff when I was a teenager," she says, staring off into space, "hoping one day ..."

"It isn't all it's cracked up to be," I point out.

"Not even the," she tilts her head, "you know."

"We haven't done the 'you know', which you know, Winnie."

"I just assumed ... in the last few days ... he certainly looks like he wants to get his hands on you."

I swallow, both terrified and turned on by that thought. "I've been injured, remember? And really, really damn angry at him." I push a napping Pip gently from my lap and drag a couple of the pieces of paper towards me. "It's been intense," I tell Winnie. "Every time he leaves the room, it's like my insides are being ripped out from my body. I mean, how am I meant to function like a normal person if I always have to be chained to his side?"

"I'm not sure I'd have a problem being chained to his side," Winnie mutters.

"Winnie, would you want Trent with you 24/7? When you have to pee, when you have to–"

"Wait!" Winnie says, lifting her hand. "I remember reading something on this." She rifles through the piles of paper until she finds whatever she's looking for, lifting it with an "uh huh."

"What does it say?"

"Hang on." She runs her finger down the text, halting and peering up at me. Her cheeks sizzle but there's a look of mischief in her eyes.

"What?"

"It says here that when fated mates bond, they are forced together by that newly cemented bond, making it painful to be apart."

"I told you that bit."

"But that force lessens considerably once the fated pair start ..." she clears her throat, "banging."

"It does not say that." I snatch the paper from her hand and read it for myself. "Shit," I mumble when I see she's right.

"It seems most fated mates get it on pretty darn quickly so they don't have this," she waves her hand about, "phase you're going through."

"Yeah," I say, lowering the page and glancing towards the door. I can see the dark, towering outline of the man in black outside the misted window, and my pulse jumps in my throat as well as between my legs.

I can't deny it. I may be angry as a hellcat with him right now, but I also want to rip the man's clothes off. And I suspect that would be true with or without the bond.

"This sucks," I say, half-heartedly.

"Yeah, sure, banging the super-hot dude really sucks." Winnie rolls her eyes at me.

"He lied to me, Winnie," I say. "And now you're saying the only way I can escape the dude is to start sleeping with him." I rub my thighs together at the idea and swear I hear a low growl from behind the door. Jesus Christ!

"No, I'm saying, once you do, this entire situation will get easier. It won't be as intense."

"Really?" I say, because sleeping with the man in black sounds like the very definition of intense.

6

R^{hi}

Winnie and Pip stay for another hour, the man in black, to his credit, waiting outside the door the entire time, giving me the space I requested. By the time she leaves, hugging me and battling with a struggling Pip who clearly wants to stay, I know a hell of a lot more about fated mates than I did. Okay, maybe not all of it is accurate, but it's a start.

There's one question I have unanswered though. One I'm far too embarrassed to ask Winnie. One I most definitely won't be asking the man in black either.

I don't know if it's even something I need to worry about. Whether it's something I've imagined. Whether I'm just confused right now.

Because that pull in my gut, that tug, the one everyone says is the sign. The sign you've met your fated mate. It isn't only Azlan I've felt it with.

But that can't be right, can it? I must be confused. Mistaking butterflies in my stomach for something more powerful.

I'm still mulling it over, when the doctor comes in on her evening round.

She's tall, slim and elegant; her hair carefully styled, her lips painted scarlet red and her suit designer. She looks more like a classic film-star than a doctor and I'm suddenly conscious about my most-probably scruffy appearance.

She spends several long minutes inspecting my leg, asking me to bend my knee and wiggle my toes.

"Is her leg healed?" Azlan asks, watching the doctor's every move intently.

"Yes, and there seems to be no damage. I was very careful to preserve the nerves. Wouldn't want her walking with a limp now, would we?"

"Thank you, Lucinda," Azlan says, resting his hand on the woman's shoulder. She leans ever so slightly into his touch in a manner that has my insides spinning.

"Anything to help, Azlan. You know I'm always here for you if ever you need me." She covers his hand with her own and I have the urge to kick her with my newly healed leg.

The man in black's phone buzzes in his pocket and he pulls his hand from hers to examine the screen.

"I have to take this," he says, strolling straight out of the room and slamming the door behind him.

Pain spirals instantly through my gut and I scrunch up my eyes against it, wincing. Is sleeping with him really going to solve this problem?

"Painful?" the doctor asks.

"Yes," I say, biting down on my lip, my body trembling.

"Well, what exactly did you think would happen?"

I open my eyes. She's frowning at me, any mask of

professionalism that had been hovering on her face, gone. Now I see something like hatred in her eyes.

"Excuse me?" I say. Is the pain twisting my mind?

"You tricked him into bonding with you, and now you have the audacity to bitch about the consequences."

"Tricked him? I didn't trick him." I stare at her with incredulity. "Look, I don't know what he told you–"

She scoffs. "You expect me to believe that Azlan would choose a *girl* like you for his life partner?" She spits out the word 'girl' like I'm some diseased creature and I wonder if she actually is related to my arch nemesis, Summer Clutton-Brock.

"He didn't *choose* me."

"Exactly," she says darkly.

"Fate did," I finish. "And I had as much choice in it as he did."

She shakes her head. "Fate wouldn't choose *you* for *him*. This is some kind of clever trick, some kind of deception, and when I find out what you did–" she grabs my wrist, squeezing it hard, "I'm going to tell him everything and then I'll watch as he tosses you like the piece of trash you are to the sidewalk."

"Investigate all you like," I hiss, "there's nothing to find. Hell, until a day ago I knew nothing about fated mates. I didn't even know he was mine."

She leans in closer, her eyes narrowing. "Everybody knows about fated mates. You need a better story. That one doesn't work."

"I don't care if it works. It's the truth. And it's none of your business anyway."

"He's a good *friend*. A very old *friend*." This time she leans on the word friend, taunting me with it. Why does she even care about this? The only reason I can fathom is jealousy. Were they sleeping with each other? Are they still sleeping with each other?

"What do you mean by that?" I ask sharply, realizing too late that she wants me to ask her exactly that. She wants to tell me.

"Azlan's taste in women is sophisticated. He likes grown ups with intelligence, elegance and who know what they're doing in the bedroom. Someone who suits his status."

"The man in black?" I laugh. "Are you kidding me?" She's obviously never seen him in his worn boots, out riding his bike.

"No, I'm not. Seems like you really don't know anything about him."

"Maybe I do. Maybe it's you who doesn't. But either way, it doesn't matter. He's mated to me."

"For now," she says, digging her nails into my wrist. "But as soon as I–"

I send a shot of energy through my arm and the doctor yelps, releasing my wrist and shaking out her fingers.

Azlan storms through the doors, his face like thunder.

"What the hell is going on?" he demands.

"She zapped me," the doctor says with a pout and a flutter of eyelashes, holding her hand limply against her body like I snapped every one of her fingers.

I wait for the reprimand. I wait for him to berate me. Instead, he grabs the doctor by the upper arm and drags her away from the bed.

"And what did you do to her?" He examines her shocked face. "What did you say to her?"

"Azlan! Absolutely nothing. How could you insinuate such a thing? This girl is–"

He turns to me. "Rhi?"

"It doesn't matter," I tell him.

The doctor laughs hollowly. "Oh, of course you don't want him to know."

"What?" he growls.

"She's playing you for a fool, Azlan. She's no more your fated mate than her smelly little pig is."

"You think I wouldn't recognize my own fated mate, Lucinda?"

"I think she's deceiving us all with some kind of complicated magic."

Now it's his turn to chuckle as he walks her towards the door. "We all know there's no such thing. And here I was thinking you were intelligent. Maybe you're the one who has been fooling us all."

The doctor scowls at him. "She's a scrawny little girl, Azlan. Ignorant, ill-mannered and ill-bred. You deserve someone better."

"Someone like you?" I can't help jibing from my bed.

"I was his first love, sweetheart," she calls back. "I'll always be special."

"It was never love, Lucinda. And it was a long, long time ago."

"Doesn't matter though, does it? You think your family will accept her? They wanted me for you, you for me, because we are suited."

"You know I don't give a damn what they want."

She turns on him. "Because you're pathetic, Azlan. Determined to throw your life away. Always so determined."

"And you are a cruel bitch. I'm beginning to wonder if it really was necessary to make Rhi wait for that procedure or if you just wanted to see her suffer."

The doctor smirks up at him and he starts to shove her out of the door.

"I'll be reporting you to your supervisor."

"I am the supervisor, darling."

"Then I'll be lodging a complaint to the medical board."

"And maybe I'll report this new *union* to the authorities."

"You promised me," he growls.

"And once upon a time you made me some promises, Azlan. Promises you didn't keep."

"I'm warning you, Lucinda. You breathe one word of this to anyone, if anyone in this clinic breathes even one syllable of a word, I'll–"

"What? What will you do?"

"You'd be sensible not to find out. Because you won't be alive to regret it."

His eyes are full of menace and fear suddenly floods the doctor's eyes. She knows he is serious.

"I'm warning you only once," he repeats, then pushes her through the doorway and slams it shut.

He stands there, shoulders heaving for several silent minutes. Then he marches to the bed, throws back the covers and reaches for me.

"What the hell are you doing?" I say.

He scoops me up into his strong arms.

"We're getting out of here and going home."

7

R^{hi}

"HOME?" I say, having no idea where he means.

Another doctor attempts to block his path as he thunders down the corridor, wittering on about the importance of monitoring me for another day or two.

The man in black simply glares at him and says through his clenched teeth, "Move before I blast you into next fucking week."

The doctor scuttles away and soon we're out of the clinic with its bright lights and sterile stench, and out into the warm light of day and the fresh air.

I inhale deeply, smelling my mate's scent in my nose, making me dizzy and light-headed.

He flags down a taxi and bundles us both into the back of the cab, barking some address I don't understand at the driver.

"Where are we going?" I say, shuffling away from him and folding my arms across my chest, despite the way my body keens towards him.

"I told you. Home." He reaches across my body, and my heart skips several beats. But all he does is take the seatbelt and buckles me in.

"I'm not a baby," I mutter.

He simply glares at me like that is debatable.

"Do you want to explain to me what that was all about?"

He frowns and turns his attention to the window.

I huff in frustration. "Is she your girlfriend?"

"Would I be here now if she were?"

"You tell me," I say in frustration. "I know nothing about you. You only deigned to tell me your name three days ago. No, wait, that wasn't actually you."

The taxi driver glances at the two of us in the rear-view mirror but I don't care. He can hear every last detail if he wants to. I'm not the asshole here.

"There's nothing to know." He turns his head slowly and meets my eyes. "And you haven't exactly been forthcoming yourself."

I change the subject. "Are you sleeping with her?"

"Are you jealous?"

Yes, yes, I'm fucking jealous. My guts are boiling with it, right alongside all the anger and rage and heat and ...

He pounces on me, slamming his mouth against mine and kissing me so hard I lose my breath.

A needy moan slips straight from my throat, a noise I've never made before in my life, and he presses me further into the seat, crushing me with his weight, his hand fisting in my hair, the other squeezing at my tit.

Then his lips leave my mouth and find my neck and he's sucking and biting up and down my throat as my chin tips backward. On instinct, I part my thighs, wanting the weight of him there, needing something there.

"I'm so angry with you," I say, my hands fisting in his shirt.

He snorts. Sucking so hard on my skin, my eyes slam shut and roll backwards in their sockets. His hand tugs at my top, pulling down the material and tweaking my nipple hard between his thumb and finger.

And oh god, I think I may burst into flames, actually combust. I'm so hot and so–

The taxi driver leans down hard on the horn, the blaring noise making me jump out of my skin.

The man in black growls with so much ferocity I almost feel sorry for the driver.

Perhaps he's used to it though, because he simply says in a bored voice, "We're here."

With a curse word, the man in black reaches into his pocket and sends a handful of notes fluttering in the driver's direction, then he's dragging me out of the car.

I wrap my legs around his waist and he kisses me all the way up the steps to the front door, waving his arm so it flings open, and stumbling with me inside.

We don't make it as far as any bedroom, he's dropping me onto a sofa and ripping at my clothes before the door is even shut.

My pulse races at about a million miles an hour and every part of my body is screaming out for his touch. Somehow, though, I manage to muster enough willpower to land my hand on his chest, pushing against his beating heart.

"I haven't done this before," I confess, my voice sounding all breathy and panty in my ears.

"I know," he growls, gripping my calf and bending my

leg up into my chest. "But I'm not going easy on you, little mate. I can't." His gaze drops down my body.

He's destroyed my panties and I'm open and exposed for him and it should be enough to have me blushing like crazy. Instead, I want him to touch me there so badly I'd be prepared to beg.

Holding my leg in place, he swims a thumb through my folds, ringing my clit and making me jerk with the sensation and then finding my entrance. He plunges his thumb inside and I groan, stars knocking across my vision.

"So fucking tight," he murmurs, giving me no relief as he pulls out his thumb and fumbles with his fly.

I barely get a look at him, but what I see is large and thick and something that is never going to fit inside me.

"Birth control," I mumble, and he waves his hand through the air, a rubber sheathing his cock.

"I'm going to have you now."

It isn't a question. Although, I'm certain if I said no, if I told him to stop, he would. And so I give him my answer anyway. I want to be angry at him. I want to hate him. But I can't. Because I want him and I want this more than anything I've ever known.

"Yes."

He groans like I gutted him and then he's thrusting inside me, my walls stretched wide and the wind whipped from my lungs.

"Oh god," I gasp, but he doesn't stop. He keeps going, deeper and deeper inside me until there's no more of me to give and no more of him to take. The hook inside me spins uncontrollably, light and energy singing in every nerve. And I know Winnie is right. This is what fate wants. For us tangled and twisted together like this. Combined and one.

"Good girl," he tells me nibbling at my ear. "Such a good girl. Going to open up for me now."

And I don't know what the hell he means but his words seem to have my walls relaxing around him and he pushes further inside me, reaching places I never have with my own fingers. I've never felt this full, this overtaken. I pant at the intrusion and, with a grunt, he bottoms out, our hips colliding.

"Shit," he mumbles. But there's no pause. He's sliding out of me in the next heartbeat. I whimper, I don't want him to go. I want him inside me. Deep inside me. Like before. I don't wait long. He slams into me, the sofa skidding along the floor with the force. And oh, somehow that feels even better – so damn good, I can hardly breathe.

He levers himself up, holding my leg to my chest and, taking my hand in his other, pinning that above my head. He stares down at me, his gaze so hot it's like fire, and then he does it again, grinding his way out, hitting every sensitive spot inside me and slamming back inside. I scream out but he wasn't lying. He has no intention of going easy on me. It's raw. Animalistic. Base.

And I don't want it any other way. Not soft. Not gentle. Just like this.

This has been growing between us for so long. Wanting each other. Fighting it. Fighting each other. Denying what we both wanted. What we needed. This. Him crashing inside me again and again. Over and over.

I can feel the sensations coursing through my body, building, spiraling, upwards and upwards, edging closer and closer, but just as I'm hovering on the cusp, he groans, all the anger, the tension, the passion draining from his face, replaced by something reverent. He holds my gaze and then he's collapsing down on top of me, crushing me into the soft belly of the sofa, our skin damp with sweat.

"Fuck," he mutters, into my neck, "fuck."

I lay there unable to move, trying to catch my breath, wondering what just happened.

He lifts his head. "I'm sorry."

I screw up my nose. "Don't say that. Don't tell me you're regretting it now."

He frowns. "Did it feel good?"

I frown right back at him. "Do you care?"

He snaps off the rubber, tying it and tossing it towards a trash can. "Do I care?"

I lean up on my elbows. "Yes, do you care?"

Another of those growls rumbles in his throat, his eyes morphing dark and then he's diving at me again, this time burying his face right between my thighs.

I gasp, the sensation of his mouth and his tongue on my most sensitive parts, like nothing I've ever known.

"Do I care?" he says again, lapping at my clit and making me squeal. "Of course I damn well care. So tell me. Was it good?"

"Yes," I moan, "but I didn't ... I didn't ..." I can't get my freaking words out. What he's doing to me makes it hard to think straight.

"Come?"

"Hmmmm," I moan as he circles me with his tongue again and again.

"Well, I'm going to put that right, right now."

He continues to circle my clit, agonizingly slow, round and round but not over, not on.

"You're going to come for me. Okay, pretty girl? I'm going to make you feel so good and you're going to come on my tongue. Come right into my mouth."

"Y-y-y-yes," I murmur, reaching for his head and burying my fingers in his dark hair.

"You taste so good."

I'm not sure I believe that, but I don't have the willpower to argue. I don't want to distract him. I don't want him to stop.

"More," I murmur, rubbing my pussy against his mouth, feeling the sharp sting of his stubble against me.

"More," he moans, his lips vibrating against me and making me jolt with pleasure.

He slides his tongue slowly over my clit and I cry out, my spine arching. He does it again, slowly and carefully, like he wants to taste every single millimeter of my clit.

"Oh god," I say, my hands fisting in his hair. I don't think I can take this. It's too much and too little, too good and too cruel, all at once. Tears slide from the corners of my closed eyes down my cheeks. My breath turns panty and needy, my legs shake around his head. My core tightens. The bond in my stomach fizzes with excitement.

He kisses my clit, kisses it like he kissed my mouth, and slips two thick fingers inside me, massaging the sensitive spot against my wall with precision.

I choke. The combination is so intense I can hardly bear it.

"Now little mate," he says, against my pussy, "come for me now like a good girl."

Then he flicks me hard with his tongue. Once. Twice. Three, four, five times. I writhe beneath him, begging for mercy and then I break. Pleasure rushing all over my body, so much of it, I'm drowning in it. Stars burst against my eyelids and my pussy clenches and convulses around his fingers.

I've never come so hard in my life.

It lasts for several long, long seconds and then I fall back down to earth, buffeted along the way by wave after wave of more ecstasy.

When it's over, I open my eyes and find him staring at me once again.

"Better?" he asks.

I nod, not sure I'm capable of words.

"Good. Good girl," he says in a way that makes me shiver with pride. "I like it better when you come." He licks his lips, eyes swimming over my wrecked body. "Now go pee."

"What?" I say in horror. This was my first time. My first every thing. It may not have been the most gentle romantic introduction into this stuff, but I'm not prepared to jump from that to ... That is too much. "I'm not peeing on you."

The man in black stumbles to his feet. His face glistens with spit and my mess and that should surely make me feel queasy and yet, it makes me want to drag him right back down and do that thing with his tongue all over again.

"You need to pee after sex or you'll end up with an infection. The bathroom's that way." He points over my head, before walking away, giving me a perfect view of his very toned ass.

Winnie wasn't wrong. The man is hot. And that was hot. So hot my body's still shaking and I'm not sure I'm actually capable of standing on my own two feet.

A door slams and for a moment I don't realize that the pain in my gut is lessened. Winnie was right about that too. Banging seems the answer to our problems.

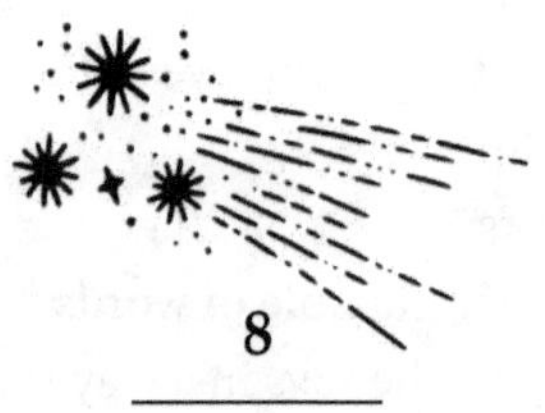

8

A zlan

SHE SPENDS the rest of the day curled up on my sofa watching TV. She's wearing one of my shirts and nothing else, her bare legs tucked up underneath her.

It has my pulse beating a drum in my throat and my palms damp with sweat.

I want to touch her again. I want to taste her again. I want to hear her moan in that sweet way she does when she comes.

Fuck!

I messed things up. It was her first time. I should have bought her flowers, rented out a hotel suite, littered the bed with rose petals and taken it a hell of a lot slower than I did.

I pace into the bathroom and splash ice cold water over my face, scrub my hand down my cheeks and stare at my reflection in the mirror. Like the sealing of the fated-mate bond, it's done now. It can't be undone.

Her gaze flicks to me when I reenter the room and I can't help but notice the way her angry eyes flitter down my form and she bites her lip.

It's too much and I'm weak for her.

I stroll over to the sofa and when I reach her, I take her hand in mine and pull her to her feet.

"What are you doing?" she says.

"Taking you to bed," I tell her, pulling her along behind me.

"Maybe I'm not ready for bed." Her voice is pissy.

"We're not going there to sleep."

"Oh."

"But if you don't want to ... if that was a one-time-only thing ..."

"I want to," she says quickly, sounding breathless and making me hard.

The blinds are drawn in the bedroom, the light dim, the room bare. I don't spend a lot of time in this house, I've never had cause to decorate it, to fill it with stuff, but having her in my room is like letting sunshine flood the place.

I find the hem of my shirt and slowly lift it over her head. Then I let my gaze swim over her naked body. It was all too rushed, too frantic before. I never got to soak her in like this. To admire the fullness of her breasts, the way her nipples stiffen towards me, begging to be sucked. The line of dark, soft curls between her legs. The curve of her waist and her hips. The swell of her ass.

But then there are the marks. The bruises. The grazes. The scars. Some new, some recent. Some much older.

I trail my fingertips over them, making her body tremble and my bond hum.

"How did these happen?"

"Let me see," she says, frowning. "This one here, that was you. Your magic. In the clearing."

Her displeased expression reflects onto my own brow.

"I'm sorry," I say. I don't know how many times I can say it.

"It's okay," she mumbles. "Besides, I bet I made my mark on you too."

I scoff. "Any you did, I healed."

"But I did mark you?"

"You've done more than mark me," I growl, tugging her up against my body.

"I have?"

"You've captivated me."

She scoffs again.

I take her chin in my hand and lift her face to mine. "You're beautiful." That doesn't seem to satisfy her. "Brave. Smart." She goes to argue with me but I get there first. "And you don't know when to shut up."

I kiss her and though all that anger still swirls through her, I can feel desire too, growing stronger and stronger the deeper, the more firmly, I kiss her.

"You're wearing clothes," she grumbles when we break away to catch our breath. "Which seems unfair."

"So do something about it," I tell her.

She waves her hands and my clothes vanish into thin air. She giggles at her little trick, although it soon dies on her lips, as she lets her gaze swim over me like mine had done hers.

"I hope you can return those clothes, sweetheart. The shirt was expensive."

She isn't listening to me. She's reaching out to touch me instead, letting her warm hands swim down the contours of my chest, over my abdomen, following the line of fuzz to my stiff cock.

"I'm going to make you come first, this time. It'll feel better."

"For who?" she says with suspicion.

"You."

Again she opens that mouth of hers, to speak her mind, but I grab her ass and walk her back to the bed, slowly lowering her onto the surface.

"You want my tongue again, sweetheart?" I ask her, sweeping around the shell of her ear. Her breath hitches. "Or my fingers this time?"

She doesn't respond and I decide I want to watch her face when she comes, so I open her legs and stroke my fingers through her folds. She's already obscenely wet, her heart thumping in her chest, her emotions scorching hot through the bond.

Fuck, this is addictive. She is addictive.

I circle her clit achingly slow until her legs tremble violently and she's pleading with me for more. I wonder where I find the restraint not to roll on top of her. But I find it, bringing her close to the brink, then denying her that pleasure. Doing it again and again, until her hands are tight around my wrist, her fingernails digging deep into my flesh and she's spitting at me like a little hell cat. Then I can't resist. I bend my head down and kiss her pussy, sucking on her until she comes into my mouth, my fingers sliding into her cunt and feeling the way her pussy convulses and quivers.

"Oh god," she screams, "oh god!" She hangs on to me for dear life and then it's her scrambling at my body, attempting to drag me on top of her. Begging for more. Begging for my cock. A cock she's only had once before.

"You want it, you come and get it," I say, flopping back on the mattress. She looks at me with a frown. "What are you waiting for?"

"I ... I don't know what I'm–"

"Come and sit on my cock," I growl. She glances down at it. Hard, stiff, waiting for her. Her eyes darken and she rolls onto her hands and knees and crawls across the bed towards me.

I let out a long, drawn-out groan. She's curvier than she was. All pink, soft, warm flesh. Her dark hair falling over one shoulder. She's far more delicious than she realizes. How the hell did I keep my hands off her for this long?

She halts alongside me and I half expect her to slap my face. Instead, she hesitates.

"Come on. Sit on me."

She leans over me, resting her hands on my chest and swings one leg over my body, her pussy hovering above my cock. All pink and pretty and wet.

I reach up and take her hips in my hands.

"Looks like we're back here," I say, thinking of that night in the clearing.

"I want you inside me," she says, sounding way more whiny than a girl who's only just been broken in deserves to.

I take my cock in my hand, and she wriggles her ass, lining herself up.

She goes to lower herself down onto me and I stop her.

"Slowly," I growl. "I want to watch."

She whimpers and it takes considerable strength to prevent her from slamming down; instead I guide her gently, watching as that precious cunt, my mate's cunt, swallows me up.

I groan. She's so tight. So warm. So soft.

She lowers down further until she's sitting right on top of me like a princess on her throne.

"That looks good," I say.

Her bottom lip trembles and color swims across her skin.

"Now you need to move, little mate. Up and down on my cock."

I guide her upwards and she squeals with the friction, her eyes rolling around in their sockets.

Yeah, fucking this girl is like nothing I've experienced before. The intensity of the sensations is amplified tenfold and coupled with her emotions through the bond. I can *feel* how good it is for her and it turns me on.

"Good girl, that's it."

I lower her back down and she cries out. I'm hitting that spot inside her. The one that made her come on my fingers. This time I'm going to make her come around my cock.

She starts to get the idea herself, moving herself up and down on my cock, and I lift my hips in time, fucking her from below, meeting her every time she lands back down on me.

I remove my hands from her hips and take her hands in mine, entwining our fingers together. I watch her body move – the bounce of her tits, the grinding motion of her hips, the hues of skin. Then I lift my gaze to hers. She's watching me with those bright eyes, her lip caught between her teeth.

"Come on, come again for me," I whisper.

She moans, a blush sweeping up her neck and into her cheeks. Her rhythm falters. Her thighs tremble.

When she comes, sitting on my cock, she's so damn beautiful it whips my breath right away.

✳.

WE MAY NOT BE TALKING but we are fucking. A lot.

It seems I've opened a Pandora's box and the girl can't get enough of me or it. Not that I'm complaining.

And at least it's lessened the tight bind between us. It's no longer painful to separate from her, although there's a constant pull, tugging me back towards her, and the connection too, allowing me an insight into her emotions and feelings. Emotions that are still boiling over with rage.

It doesn't matter how many times I make her come. She's still angry at me.

She's going to be angry again. Might as well get it over and done with.

"I have to go out," I tell her.

She's curled up on the sofa once more. Her friend delivered her pig to her yesterday and it's curled up in her lap. It lifts its head when I enter the room and I swear it glares at me. It hasn't been delighted about the times I've kicked it out of the bedroom. But I'm not having that creature watch while I ...

"You do? Where?"

I stare at her, not answering, and she frowns, more anger rolling through the bond.

"I need to get back to school."

"There's no hurry," I say, letting my gaze linger down her body. I don't want her to go. I want her close by, and not just because Barone is out there somewhere, waiting for her.

"Winnie says there are all sorts of wild rumors circulating about me." She frowns. "What exactly did you tell Principal York?"

"Same thing I told the Chancellor. That you were in an accident."

"Did you tell them I was attacked? Do they know about the Wolves of Night?"

"No. The only people who know about that are you, me and Stone."

"And Andrew, I'm guessing." Her brow crinkles. "And what did you tell them about ..." she chews on her thumbnail in that infuriating way she does, a way that has all my attention drawn to her mouth, "us."

"So far, nothing."

"But those doctors–"

"Won't speak if they know what is good for them."

"So, we're keeping this a secret?"

There is one person I would give anything to keep this secret from. Unfortunately, that is beyond my control. His spies and informants are far superior to the Chancellor's. And while the doctors in that clinic may be too afraid to spread rumors, there'll be more than one who will have been reporting to him as soon as I set foot in that clinic.

"Whatever you want," I say.

"You want to keep it secret?" I simply stare at her. She tosses her head in annoyance.

"Whatever."

"I don't know how long I will be. Stone is going to come and–"

"I don't need a babysitter."

"Barone is still out there, Rhi."

She grimaces. "I'm not frightened."

"You should be."

"Then if he's so terrifying why are you leaving at all?" She scowls at me. "Or maybe you're hoping this time, he'll finish the job."

I scowl straight back at her. Have I been acting like a man who wants her dead? I can barely keep my hands off her. If I had a choice, I'd be tossing her over my shoulder and into bed, not riding across the city for this damn stupid summoning.

Of course, I could, if I wanted to, simply ignore it, but I know that won't end well.

"Don't open the door to anyone but Stone. Don't leave the house. Don't even look out of the window."

"Am I prisoner now?"

"It's for your own safety. I'll be back as quickly as I can."

I lift my cloak from the back of a chair and fasten it around my neck.

She watches me, and I see the way her bottom lip quivers, along with her throat.

Does she want me to stay?

"I could come with you," she says.

"No."

"You can't just order me about like this. Just because–"

I stalk towards her, cutting off her words. Bending down, I whisper right by her ear, noticing the way she shivers, "Are you sure?" I lift her chin and kiss her mouth. She doesn't even try to fight it. She kisses me right back. "Stay safe, Rhianna," I tell her, and then I leave.

As I slam the door behind me, I curse Stone with every known swear word I possess. He said he'd be here on time. He said he'd be here to watch her. Okay, he was a hell of a lot reluctant. But he promised and I can't afford to wait for him.

I don't want to leave her on her own. But what choice do I have?

I peer along the street.

I've worked every contact I have for information on

Barone. Nobody knows where he is. The man has the ability to disappear into thin air. Slither away into the shadows, waiting to strike again. Maybe my connections do know where he is. Maybe they aren't telling me.

I find it hard to believe he's in the city. Hard to believe he'd strike again so soon. He'll want to wait until we've grown complacent, dropped our guard. That's what I would do. But I'm not Barone. The man is unhinged, unpredictable. It's why he's been so hard to catch all these years. Most people think they're making random choices, going places no one will ever think of. Most people are predictable. They have their patterns if you look hard enough. Not Barone.

I look over my shoulder at the house. I swear she's watching me from the window even though I told her not to. The girl doesn't know what's best for her. Stone's right, she's a brat. A brat I can't get enough of.

I close my eyes and mutter several protection spells. Stone will know how to infiltrate them. No one else. And if anyone does try to tamper with them, I'll know and I'll be back in a heartbeat.

With one final glance at the house, I whistle for my bike and jump on the saddle as it draws close, riding away across the wet streets of the city.

The journey is over far too quickly, my heart growing heavier and heavier as I slice through water, the bottom of my pants damp with it, leaving the busy commercial districts for the suburbs, out further to the edge of the city, where the land begins again, green and lush from the rain.

The dominating iron gates come into view first, twisted and molded together, keeping everyone away. As I draw closer, they part with a groan of metal, and slowly I weave my way inside, up the driveway, its dark borders neatly clipped, blood-red roses dropping their petals across the ground, and drive up the incline to the house. It towers above me, dark and foreboding. The place gives me the creeps. Would do even if it was occupied by some other family.

I park up outside the steps that lead up to the bolted wooden doors, and watch as they open, the figure of a man slowly revealed.

My uncle.

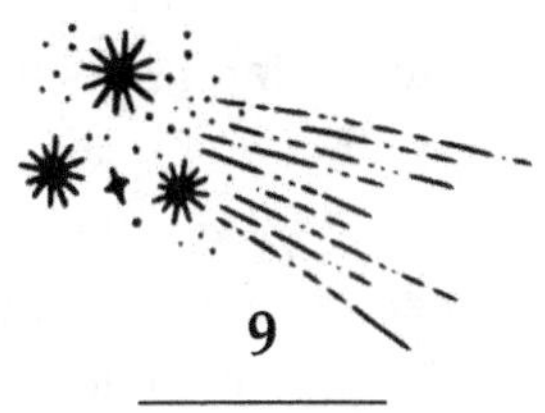

9

T ristan

MY COUSIN DOESN'T SEE me at first.

"You were summoned too?" I call to him.

He turns his head and spots me lingering halfway up the steps to the old family house.

"Yes."

He looks tired, older. Dark rings beneath his eyes, his face unshaven, his hair longer than it was. His role as the authorities' enforcer is taking its toll.

"Do you know what it's about?"

He looks up at the house. "Yes."

I sidle up to him, smacking him on the shoulder. He's thirteen years older than me, but these days we're the same height, same size, although where he is dark, I'm fair. You wouldn't know our fathers were brothers. "You going to tell me then? I'd prefer to go in prepared."

For a moment, he's silent, clearly considering whether to tell me or not. It never used to be like this. Growing up, he was my hero. He could do everything I wanted to do. He used to sneak me out to the forest, teach me magic I wasn't supposed to know at such a young age, show me things I wasn't supposed to see. I idolized the man, even more so when he gave our fathers the finger and refused to take the position in the authorities they wanted, opting for the role of enforcer instead.

He's been the black sheep in the family ever since. Not that he cares.

"I've bonded."

My hand falls away from his shoulder.

Bonded? He always swore he wasn't interested in a mate, in a family. It's what he'd fought most with our fathers about. They'd planned for both of us to find respectable, powerful, highly regarded mates and to continue the Kennedy line. Grow our influence and power. Azlan insisted he didn't want that. As an enforcer, he'd live a life alone.

I examine the side of his head. Despite the tired appearance of his face, his eyes have that glint, the glint of a man who has found and claimed his fated mate.

Without the family's permission or approval, I'm betting. No wonder the summoning. No wonder his haggard appearance.

"Who?" I ask.

He turns his head and meets my eyes.

"I doubt you know her."

I smirk. Yeah, the fathers will be pissed about that.

"Are you serious?"

"Yes."

"Who is she?"

His face remains completely passive, a blank canvas. "A young girl from the wastelands. An unregistered."

The blood in my veins runs cold. "What's her name, Azlan?"

"Rhianna Blackwaters."

I stumble backward as if he's punched me right in the gut. His brow furrows.

"You know her?"

Nausea swims in my stomach and my vision swoops in and out of focus. I inhale, forcing oxygen into my lungs, restraining my arms to my sides. Because if I didn't, I'd blow the fucking bastard apart.

Rhianna Blackwaters.

He can't be serious! He can't be!

"Of course I know her," I snap, "she's in my school, in my goddamn house, Azlan." I glare at him, trying to spy the hint that this is a joke, that he's teasing me somehow, like he used to. If he knows, if he suspects, has he chosen to taunt me like this? Or is this the fathers' doing? A way to wheedle the truth from me? "Her?" I spit.

My cousin takes a menacing step towards me. "Yes, her."

"Have you lost your mind? She's a nobody, a nothing."

"She's everything," he says, his words rumbling through the air.

"She's trouble," I take a step towards him. "What do you know about her? Are you sure you know everything?" My gaze flicks around his face.

His frown grows darker. "I know someone attacked in the forest, Tristan. Someone who couldn't be seen."

I match his gaze. Apart from Spencer, he's the only one who knows. The only one I ever told. The one who advised me to keep it hidden.

"The girl is mentally deranged and a liar. Whatever she told you–"

"Stay away from her," he snaps, turning his back on me and marching up the steps.

My fingers twitch by my sides. Darkness and rage swirl inside me, begging to be released onto him. I want to burn his flesh. I want to break every bone. I want to grind him into ash.

She doesn't belong to him.

I stumble back a second time, clutching my stomach. What the hell is wrong with me?

I let out an angry snarl and then I chase up the stairs, following my cousin.

Our fathers may have allowed my cousin some rope, but that will end today. There is no way in hell they will let this stand. They will snap that rope back faster than a rabbit in a snare. The girl will disappear from all our lives. *All* our lives.

Azlan's already disappeared down the long dark hallway of the house as I jog through the doors. I pace quickly after him, passing the ancient portraits of family members, most of them men, most dressed in stuffy old outfits. Most were warlocks who ruled these lands before the Republic was installed and the authorities took control. Some were even Chancellors themselves. Our family name is ubiquitous with power. It's only a matter of time until we rule like we used to.

When I open the door into the dining room, I find I am the last to join.

My father and my uncle sit at opposite ends of the table. My father's sister cowers on her chair, beside her weedy husband, and my mother and Azlan's younger sister flank their sides. I take a seat beside Azlan, unable to look at him, and wait for whatever this is to begin.

My father – the older brother, the one who has always been in charge – signals with a nod of his head to my uncle.

"We have been waiting for you, Azlan," my uncle says.

Azlan stares straight ahead. As usual these days, he has nothing to say.

"Did you not think it of utmost importance that you inform us of your circumstances?" my uncle continues.

Azlan remains silent.

"We had to learn this second hand, boy!" my father spits and I see he is as angry as I am, the wooden arms of his chair splitting under his grip.

He rules this family with an iron fist – something I suspect would have been the case despite birth order. He is more cunning, more calculating, more ruthless, more powerful, than his younger brother or sister.

My uncle glances at him nervously and my aunt, mother and cousin shift on their chairs. Only Azlan remains unmoved. He's faced my father's wrath often enough.

"This information should have been imparted to us as soon as you were aware," my uncle says. A heat crawls up my neck and I stare down at the polished tabletop in front of me. "The girl is unsuitable and–"

"Would have been disposed of," my father says.

Azlan's head whips towards him. "You will not touch her."

"You will not tell me what to do." My father jabs a finger in Azlan's direction, sparks hissing on his fingertips.

"She is a nobody, a nothing," my uncle continues, mirroring my words. My stomach rolls. "There is even talk that she was unregistered."

"She was. I was assigned to bring her in."

My father snarls, jumping to his feet and slamming his fists down hard on the table.

"Are you determined to destroy this family, our good name, our reputation?"

"You know I don't care about any of those things, Uncle."

"Leonardo!" my father says, glaring at his brother. "See what your leniency has led to?"

"He doesn't mean it," my uncle says. "He is newly mated to the girl, the fated bond freshly formed. He is–"

"Emotional," my other cousin, Azlan's sister, continues, eyes full of fear as she examines my father's furious face.

She leans across the table, to clasp her brother's hand. "She cannot be a nothing. Not if fate has chosen her for my brother. There must be something special about her."

Azlan's gaze falls to his hands and he swallows.

"Well, is there?" my father hisses.

When he doesn't reply, my father directs his attention to me. "You know of the girl, Tristan?"

"Yes, Sir."

"And is there? Is there anything remarkable about her at all?"

He glares at me with his piercing eyes, and my magic flares in my fingertips.

Is there anything special about the girl? Anything at all?

I think of the wound on Spencer's stomach.

I think about the way she's captured my attention.

I think about the way she has bonded to a man who swore he would live his life as a celibate.

"No," I say flatly, "nothing at all."

"Can it be undone?" my mother asks, sitting upright beside my father, her golden hair swept back in a bun, her manicured hands crossed on the table in front of her.

I hold my breath. There has to be a way. He can't have her.

"You know as well as I do, Cassandra, that there is no way to undo such ancient magic. The foolish boy has sealed the bond. Only death will part them now." Azlan leaps to his feet, but my father simply smiles that crooked smile of his. "It was merely an expression, Azlan."

"Gone are the days this family can murder and plunder without consequence," my cousin says.

"This family does not stoop to the actions of the criminal gangs. You have made your bed, nephew, you can rot in it with your whore." Azlan lifts his hand and it is only the pained 'no' from his sister that prevents him from blasting magic at my father.

My father smirks. He has always been the most powerful magical in this family. Something he still believes to be true. He let us know it frequently, testing our abilities, pushing us to the brink, exerting his dominance. But those days have passed. These days I would beat him hands down. I suspect my cousin would too. My father thinks he knows everything with his little network of spies, but he's wrong. There is much he doesn't know. That he never will.

"Lie in your bed with your whore, and know this family will never acknowledge her, will never accept her, will never even admit she exists."

"Uncle!" Azlan's sister cries.

"It is fine, Eleanor," Azlan says. "It is no great loss."

He strides from the room, slamming the door behind him and the silence is only permeated by my cousin's muffled sobs.

"You are banned from communicating with the girl, Eleanor," my uncle tells his daughter.

"And you," my mother adds, eyeing me from the other side of the table.

"She attends my school," I say lazily.

"Then I expect you to report back anything of interest to me," my father says. "Azlan was always a lost cause." My uncle hangs his head in shame. "But all is not lost."

He turns his gaze on me and I feel the weight of his expectations heavy on my shoulders.

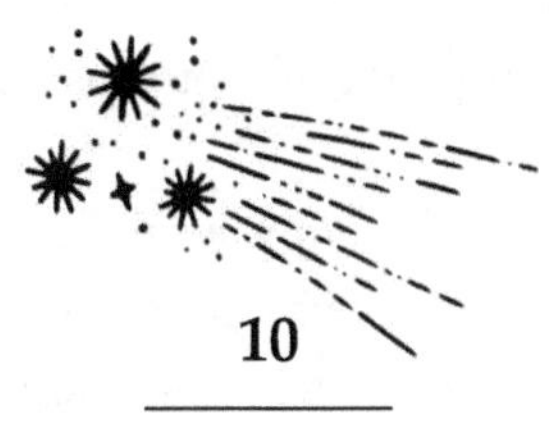

10

S tone

I HOVER outside Azlan's house, hands in my pockets, kicking at loose stones on the path.

I can't stand out here forever – even if it's far preferable to inside. I'm going to have to go in. I gave him my word. Why I gave him my word is a fucking mystery.

No, not a mystery. I'm as concerned about the girl's safety as he is. Doesn't mean I've forgiven him though.

I'm still fuming at him about this whole goddamn situation.

A situation that's one thousand times more complicated than it was.

Deep in my gut, I feel that familiar tug and glance up towards the window. The curtain twitches. She's there watching me.

I sigh and, dragging my feet, walk up to the front door.

My friend has cast a series of complex protection spells around the house, but I know him well enough to undo them all and knock firmly on the door. It's a minute and then I hear the light patter of footsteps and the door swings back.

She's standing in the hallway in what looks like Azlan's oversized t-shirt, her legs bare and her dark hair loose in waves around her shoulders. That hook twists deep and pulls me forward, but I dig in my heels and swallow. Her scent is sweet but different today. There's something ... something ... *masculine* about it. I frown.

"You shouldn't be opening the door without checking who it is first." She rolls her eyes at me in that manner that has my blood heating.

"I knew it was you."

"How?" I ask, and I swear a pinkness brushes across her cheeks.

She doesn't answer, spinning on her heels and taking off down the corridor, the stupid t-shirt barely covering her ass.

"Don't you own any clothes?"

"If you remember, you forced me out of my house with about five minutes' notice. I barely had time to grab any panties."

I swallow again. Hard. This is torture, especially when there's the scent of sex about the house. Azlan hadn't mentioned that bit, but it was inevitable. The fated bond is known to be impossible to resist.

"You've been at school weeks. Are you telling me you don't know how to buy your own clothes?"

"I don't have any money," she retorts, turning into the kitchen and striding to the cupboard. She reaches up on her tiptoes and that damn shirt slides up her legs even further.

I look away and curse Azlan for the millionth time.

Hooking out two cups, she places them on the counter. "Coffee?" she asks.

"Sure."

Her pig snuffles from the corner, all curled up and sleeping, and I see she's made herself at home.

"When are you coming back to school?" I ask, like a jerk.

She hesitates. "I don't know." She places the first cup under Azlan's ancient-looking coffee machine and presses a button. Black liquid chugs out into the cup and she passes it to me, her fingers grazing mine as she does. I swallow a third time, ignoring the tingles on my skin, the buzz in my gut. "But this situation is pretty damn confusing." She stares at her fingers.

"Yeah, yeah it is."

She turns her back on me to fill the second cup.

"Especially when your fated mate's best friend is an asshole."

Seems to me like that's the least of the complications here, but whatever.

"An asshole who saved your life."

"I thought that was Azlan."

"It was both of us," I say firmly.

"Doesn't erase the fact you tried to infiltrate my mind without my permission." She glares at me, blowing across the surface of her cup. An expression she manages to make damn hot.

I shrug. "You're keeping secrets."

"I'm entitled to."

"Not secrets about that, sweetheart." She bristles at that name and I can't tell if it pisses her off or turns her on. I need to get out of this damn house. "If Azlan knew–"

"If he knew what you tried to do."

I place my cup on the counter. "Let's get something

straight. I've known him far longer than you. Just because you've opened your legs for him doesn't mean you have some special insight into the man. Trust me, sweetheart, he has as many secrets as you do."

"Like what?" she says, unable to help herself, her mind buzzing with curiosity.

"Ask him, not me."

"You really are an asshole," she says, sending a barrage of revolting images my way.

"And you appear to have an unhealthy obsession with my asshole. Why is that I wonder?" I peer into her mind. What does she know about the bond? What does she feel?

But she slams down her defenses and I've no desire to break through them today. Because, no matter how many times I tell myself it was for her good, our good, the greater good – if she's wielding that kind of magic I need to know – the guilt has been eating away at me ever since. It's an unfamiliar feeling. I haven't cared enough about anyone to feel guilt for my actions in a long, long time.

For all my bravado, I regret what I did that night. No, it's more than that. I'm fucking ashamed of it.

I should apologize. That would be the non-asshole thing to do. But the girl irritates me, the fact she's fucking my friend irritates me, and I can't bring myself to do it.

"Your ass is of no interest to me," she spits and I stalk towards her, unable to help myself, the hook pulling me her way.

The pupils of her eyes swallow up that caramel color and she holds her ground, looking up into my face with determination written all over hers.

"You sure about that?" I ask, bending low.

"Never been more certain," she says, her shoulders rising and falling, her pulse jumping in her throat. She smells like him and fuck I've never been jealous of my friend before. He has a family, a family with wealth and name. He has unmatched powers and abilities. A position of respect. More money that I could dream of. I've never envied him for it. He's had his struggles, just like I have. But in this moment, peering down into her darkening eyes, the hook in my gut dragging me closer and closer, I feel jealousy and envy race through my veins.

The door slams open and heavy boots thunder down the hallway.

I take a step away from the girl and pick up my coffee cup. From the corner of my eye, I see the girl jump up to sit on the counter, her bare legs swinging. Her soft thighs on display. Soft thighs I have a strong desire to squeeze, to spread open.

Azlan marches into the room, tossing his cloak towards a chair.

"It went well, then," I say with a smirk.

"You know damn well it didn't. You know damn well it was never going to."

"What didn't?" the girl asks.

And I turn to look at her. "He didn't tell you?" She frowns at me and sends me the image of her middle finger.

"My family," Azlan says, striding towards her and taking the cup from her hands, helping himself to a gulp of her coffee, his hand resting on her hip, and a flush swooping up her neck.

I can't watch that crap. Not from the sidelines. That jealousy boils hot in my veins and the hook scrapes at my insides, painfully.

My body aches. My head thumps. I feel like I'm coming down with the goddamn flu. But it's not that. It's the bond. Unsealed. It's making me sick.

"You have a family?" she asks.

"Of course I have a family." He hands her back her cup and walks to the sink, slamming on the faucet and washing the city's grime from his hands and his face.

"Don't tell me," I say, shaking my head in mock disbelief, "you don't know who his family is?"

"I didn't know his name until six days ago," she says.

"Then you know who his family is, sweetheart."

"She doesn't," Azlan says, rubbing at his face with a towel.

Anger floods her mind. I can't blame her. Whatever fate might decide, it seems pretty fucking stupid to me to bind your life to someone you know so little about. Something I've been telling Azlan for months.

"My father is Leonardo Kennedy. My uncle, Christopher Kennedy."

She shakes her head. "Kennedy? You're a Kennedy? Are you related to–"

"Tristan Kennedy?" I venture. "They're cousins."

Rhi stares at us both, then tips back her head and laughs, her whole body shaking with it. "You're messing with me."

"I am not," my friend says.

"Have you been paying attention in your history lessons, sweetheart? Do you know who the Kennedys are?"

Her gaze flips from mine to my friend's. I swear I can almost feel the connection between them fizzing in the air.

"I'm not exactly interested in history. Who we are, where we get to in life, shouldn't be dependent on our last name, on who we are related to, on our blood."

"I agree," my friend says. "I've never been interested in my family's position."

"Unlike Tristan," she mutters.

My friend examines her. "Has he been causing you trouble?"

"She has an affinity for causing trouble for herself," I tell him.

"He's an asshole," she says, staring directly at me, "like everyone else at that school."

"Well, he's been forbidden to speak with you."

"Forbidden? By whom?"

"His father. In fact, he's forbidden my entire family."

"And your family just obeys everything he says?"

"Christopher Kennedy's word is law," I say. "If he says they can't talk to you, they won't."

"Including you?" she snaps at Azlan.

"If you may have noticed, sweetheart, Azlan doesn't exactly pay attention to what his family wants. If he did, he would have let you die."

She ponders on this for a moment, the thoughts swirling so quickly in her mind, I find it impossible to follow them.

"You're the authorities' enforcer–"

"Not what my family wanted for me. A path I chose."

"Why?"

"I don't believe in nepotism. What we make of ourselves shouldn't be dependent on our family name, on our relations or on our bloodline."

She chews on her thumb. "And they don't approve of me, I suppose?"

I scoff. "Rhianna Blackwaters you have no family, no real talents, and no abilities. Only a pig and a serious lack of clothes."

"Phoenix," Azlan warns.

"I assume it's what your uncle said."

He doesn't respond.

"I'm not a nobody," the girl says, sliding off the counter

and landing on her feet like a cat. "I'm my aunt's niece. And maybe I didn't spend years and years going to fancy schools like the two of you. But I'm learning every day. Which is why I'm going back to the academy."

An image of that mark on a man's torso flickers through her mind again and I catch her eye.

"You have powers, Rhianna Blackwaters. Powers a girl like you shouldn't possess." Azlan's gaze flicks to mine. "But who are you? Let me open those memories and–"

"I'm not letting you anywhere near my mind," she snaps, striding from the room, her little pig jumping up from her bed and trotting after her.

Or any other part of me, she says loudly in her head, and I try not to let my gaze trail down those bare thighs of hers.

"What powers?" Azlan says, when she's out of earshot.

11

R^{hi}

"YOU WANT to go back to the academy?"

I'm lying on his bed, tickling Pip's ears. He glares at the pig. He's already told me countless times: no pets on the bed.

"Yes, and I don't want you to try and persuade me to–"

"I think it's for the best."

Although I've convinced myself this is what I need to do, my stomach drops with disappointment, a feeling I know he can discern through the bond. I try my best to disguise it.

"Something we agree on at last." I manage a smile, one I doubt is convincing.

"It isn't what I want, Rhianna. If I had my choice, I'd never let you leave my bed." I wonder, if it comes to it, whether I'll be able to drag myself from it. "But I have a job and you have a madman out to kill you. You are safer at the academy."

"Safer than with my fated mate?" I can't help but spit.

"This situation is far more complicated than you understand. I have enemies. My family has enemies." He pauses. "You have enemies. The academy is one of the most guarded and protected places in the land. I want to keep you safe. And you will be safer there."

"So you want me to go?"

He sighs. "*You* want to go back."

I flop back on the bed, and Pip licks at my face.

"I do ... but I also ..."

"We will still see each other, Rhianna."

I lift my head to stare at him. "Really?"

"Yes," he says firmly. "But this will give us time. Time for me to find Renzo Barone. Time for you to learn, to grow your powers. Afterwards ..."

"Afterwards ..." I say, wishing I didn't sound so stupidly eager.

"We will be in a better position to determine our future."

That spasm of disappointment rockets through my stomach again. It's nothing. Only my pride wounded. That's all it is.

I thought I had a plan – perhaps not a very solid one – but I knew I had to learn as much as I could and then escape. Now, I'm more concerned with the thing Stone teased me with. My identity.

Because my mate is not only the authorities' enforcer, he is an heir of the Kennedy family. Strong, powerful, beautiful.

Why would fate bind him to me?

Is there something different about me?

I think about those memories locked in my mind. I think

about the scarlet magic I wielded against Spencer Moreau. I think about my ability to see magical fingerprints.

I think most of all about why my aunt was keeping me safe. From what? From whom?

Sometimes I wonder if she was keeping me safe from myself.

The man in black examines my face. "Then we're agreed. Once you're properly healed, you will return to the academy."

He paces forward, scooping Pip off the bed and depositing him outside the bedroom door. Then he stalks towards me with that dark look in his eye I know can only mean one thing.

Not yet. I'm not leaving yet.

Whatever comes next can wait until tomorrow. Because I'm pretty sure fated mates, bonded fated mates, aren't meant to live apart. I doubt it's sensible. I doubt it's what fate wants. Fate wants me in his bed, in his arms, pressed against his heart. Like now, the hook in my belly humming with satisfaction.

Going against fate. I doubt it's sensible. But when have I ever done the sensible thing?

However, a summons from the Chancellor to meet at the academy ruins all our best laid plans. It's something my mate insists cannot be ignored.

It's a week since I last stepped foot inside Arrow Hart Academy, and yet it feels like an age. So much has changed since then. My world once again twisted upside down and all the loose parts tumbling free. And yet, I'm here far sooner than I wanted to be, despite my declarations to Azlan.

"Let me do the talking," Azlan tells me as we enter the school through the old manor doors and make our way inside.

"Why?" I ask. It's pathetic, but I wish he'd hold my hand. I'm reminded of the last time I was paraded in front of the Chancellor to learn my fate. Only this time, I feel more nervous. Is it because I've grown fond of this place – despite all the assholes? Or is it because I'm growing fond of the man beside me?

"The Chancellor is a cunning man – perhaps not as cunning as my uncle," he mutters under his breath, "but we are better to keep certain pieces of information to ourselves."

"He's your boss. He employs you to keep the Republic safe. Shouldn't you be telling him everything?"

Azlan halts and I follow suit, glancing up into his face.

"He would use it against me. He would use it against you."

I shake my head. "Why?"

"My family has always been a threat to his position – a position my uncle believes should be his."

"Then why work for him?"

"I've no interest in politics, Rhi. But I do want to keep our people safe."

"From people like me?"

He frowns. "From the people trying to kill you. From the threat in the West." He rests his hand against the small of my back and my body practically swoons. It's like this every time. Every connection he makes, every touch, feels electric.

"But how about Lucinda? Or the other doctors at the

clinic? This is gossip, Azlan, and one thing I've learned from this school, gossip spreads like wildfire."

"They won't be talking."

"Because you threatened to break their necks if they did?" I roll my eyes.

"Yes," he says simply.

"But what if–"

"Unless we tell the authorities, they won't know."

"But your family knew."

"My uncle's spies are far superior to the Chancellor's or the Council's," he says darkly.

"But what if they have heard," I insist, worrying at my lip. "What will happen to us?"

"Legally, we've done nothing wrong, Rhi." He strokes his hand in soothing circles. "But the Chancellor won't like the fact I didn't tell him about this. He'll look to punish me for it."

Why didn't he tell me this before? Why didn't we plan this much better than we have?

"The labor camps?"

Azlan scoffs. "Ahhh, it won't be immediate and it won't be that obvious. But he'll find a way."

I really don't like the sound of that. I think of all the warnings my aunt gave me about the authorities. She said they were cruel.

"And me?"

He slides his hand up my back, cradling the back of my neck. "If, and Rhianna I don't think this is a problem, but if they have discovered our bonding, I will make it abundantly clear that you were ignorant, that you didn't know, that as far as you knew, there was nothing to tell."

"I didn't," I remind him.

"Yes," he says quietly. "I don't think you will be in any trouble for it."

"But why would he care? Why would the Council care?"

"You've been reading all those magazines, Rhi," he says, with a smirk. So he noticed that then? "Fated mates, bonded pairs, are rare. But according to some, they are also powerful."

"I don't remember reading anything about power."

"Probably not the sexy bit your magazines are interested in," he teases and I pinch his arm in revenge.

"They were the only research materials accessible to me."

"Right," he says, "sure."

I pinch him again. "Just tell me about the power bit."

"Some people believe that a bonded pair are more powerful together. That their magic is amplified by one another. But it's just a theory," he adds quickly. "Others have pointed out that happy magicals tend to be better at wielding their magic, and happiness comes with finding your fated mate."

"Hmmm," I say. Okay, the banging has definitely made me very happy, but the other stuff? We're far from a happy couple.

"Come on." He guides me forward, and together we climb the grand wooden staircase and pause outside the principal's office. Today the doors are open and I see the Chancellor and the principal in whispered conversation. As we approach, they turn and watch us and I examine their expressions: the principal's curious, the Chancellor's shrewd.

"Remember: keep quiet," Azlan whispers in my ear, before we step inside.

"Miss Blackwaters, you are looking better than I would

have expected," the principal says, to my surprise taking my hands in both of hers and squeezing.

"I am feeling much better," I say, Azlan bristling beside me.

"What happened?" the Chancellor asks, cutting straight to the point.

"Rhianna was caught in the crossfire as I tried to apprehend a criminal in the docklands area of the city. Her injuries were too great for me to heal her, so I took her to the clinic for treatment."

"And the criminal?"

"Escaped, Sir."

"Hmmm," he murmurs, eyeing us both through his glasses.

"What on Earth were you doing in that part of the city, Miss Blackwaters?" the principal asks.

"On my way to the pool hall."

"Alone?" the principal asks, her eyebrows leaping up her forehead.

"With Andrew Playford."

"Andrew Playford … you are aware he is missing?" She peers at the Chancellor and I shake my head.

The Chancellor strokes his chin. "You have been recuperating all this time?"

I nod, unable to help glancing towards Azlan, whose eyes are locked ahead.

"But not at the hospital. From what I understand, you have been staying at the enforcer's home."

The principal's jaw falls open and it's clear this information is news to her.

My heart pounds in my chest. Were we fools to believe we could keep this secret?

"Yes, she has been," Azlan says. "The hospital was not

secure, and as she is a known flight risk, I brought her back to my home."

The Chancellor's eyes narrow like he doesn't believe this.

"Rhianna is no longer a flight risk," the principal says simply.

Azlan turns his head to look at me. "That is not what I have been led to believe by Professor Stone."

The principal frowns at me, any brief affection that may have been hovering in her eyes, vanishing.

"You are aware, I believe, Miss Blackwaters, of the penalties if you disobey the authorities' orders and leave this school before you have graduated," the Chancellor says.

"The enforcer is wrong," I hiss. "I have no intention of leaving. In fact, I'm eager to return."

Azlan's jaw tightens. "She is not well enough to return to a school environment yet."

"I think Miss Blackwaters is a better judge of that than you," the principal says.

"Agreed." The Chancellor strokes his chin. "I apologize, Miss Blackwaters, for this unfortunate incident. But I agree it best you return to school immediately. The enforcer is a busy man and does not have time to babysit a young girl like you."

"Do you have any idea where Andrew Playford might be?" the principal adds. "There has been no word or sign of him."

"No," I say, "no, I don't. We were ... separated in the crossfire."

The principal nods. "Very well. You may return to your room. Lessons will resume tomorrow."

I turn, Azlan going to follow me out, but the Chancellor calls him back.

"We have more to discuss," the Chancellor says, landing a hand on my mate's shoulder.

Azlan looks at me with a pained expression that has my stupid heart cracking in my chest.

I bite at my thumb. "Would you bring me my pig?" I say to him.

He nods and I hurry away as quickly as I can, knowing if I linger I'll relent and refuse to leave his side.

But then I remember that he wanted this, wanted me to return to the academy. There was no pleading, no begging for me to stay with him. I'm not his choice. I'm not his family's choice either. Whatever I may be feeling for him, it isn't returned, no matter what my foolish imagination may believe.

The hook in my belly scrapes more viciously with every step I take. It's not like it was. The agony doesn't have me falling to my knees. But it is an ache, consistent and unrelenting, like a seriously bad period cramp. Am I making a big mistake?

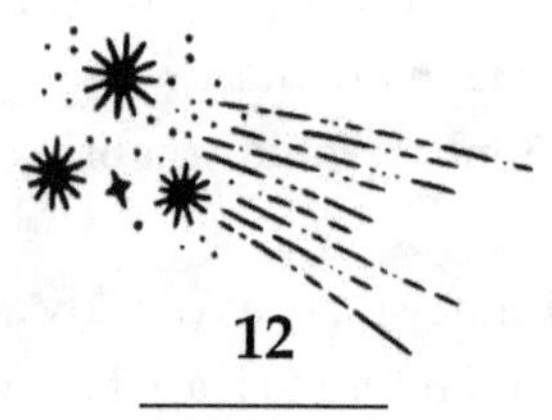

12

R enzo

"Hello," I say with a wide grin as I swing back the basement door and peer inside the dank apartment, a lone bulb swinging from the ceiling.

The boy is sprawled out on a bare mattress on the floor and at the sound of my voice, jolts upright in alarm.

His eyes land on me and widen with horror.

I like that. I like it a lot.

Slowly, I swing my legs down the steps, cracking my knuckles as I go, the noise making the boy flinch.

"It's taken me a long time to find you."

"I did what you asked," he says, "I brought her to you. That was the deal. You said you'd leave me alone and my debts would be forgotten."

I halt on the middle step and lean against the banister.

"You must be a giant dummy to piss off Lowsky." The boy doesn't say anything. Just keeps on watching me. These stupid rich kids, thinking they own the world and everyone in it. Thinking that the likes of us, we're the dumb ones. That we won't notice when they don't pay up, when they take delivery of the product but don't settle the bill. Yeah, maybe back in Aropia where this kid washed up from. But not here. Not the Wolves of Night. "You're right, the debt is repaid."

His shoulders slump with relief. A little color returns to his face.

Funny.

"What did you do to her?" he whispers. He looks thin, his hair greasy. Not surprising. He's been keeping his head down, keeping hidden. I've been looking for him in all the usual places. He's not as stupid as some of these idiots are.

"What did *I* do to *her*?" I chuckle, swinging my legs down the steps again, the boy practically shaking. "How about we talk about what *you* did to her?"

"M-m-m-me?" he says.

"You." I reach the hard floor and pull out the knife from my pocket. I like holding it in my hand. Like the way it feels, like the way it makes a fucker like this boy piss his y-fronts. Mostly, I like that it's hers.

A wispy cobweb hangs from one corner of the room and a spider scuttles along the ceiling, its silver eyes flashing for a moment. It's caught a fly and I watch it hurry towards its victim to deliver the deadly bite.

Things like that have always fascinated me. They say I'm cruel. But it's nature. Nature is cruel and bitter and doesn't give a fuck if you suffer.

I shake my head, draw my attention back to the knife, spinning the thing in my palm.

"I don't have friends. Never saw the point in them. But you were her friend, right?"

He cringes.

I snap my gaze in his direction and he jumps.

"Right?" I growl.

He hesitates, then nods.

"My mom was always saying," I rub my chin, chuckling at the memory, "play nicely, Renzo. Be kind to your friends. No pushing. No hitting. No ..." I chuckle some more, "strangling."

The boy's eyes flick around the room, looking for a way to escape. Something he won't be doing. He's like that fly in the web. More he struggles, more he'll be trapped, my magic already winding invisibly around his body.

"You're meant to be nice to your friends. That right?" He stands there dumbstruck. "That right?" I yell.

"Y-yes."

"Hmmm," I say, "then you weren't her friend." I take a step closer to him. He smells rank. Like someone who hasn't washed in days. Like someone afraid.

He should be afraid. I'm going to make this painful for him. It's what he deserves. My mom spanked me every time I hit one of those neighborhood kids. So it's only right. Only right I punish him too.

"You didn't give me a choice. If I hadn't done it ..."

He trails off as my expression grows fucking murderous.

"There's always a choice. And you chose you over her. You think you're better than her?"

He shakes his head.

"Nah, I don't think you are either." I smile to myself. "I think my little rabbit is fucking special. Really fucking special."

"She's a-a-a-live?" he says, amazed.

"Yeah, she is," I say with pride. "Told you she was special."

"Where is she?"

"Back at the academy."

He looks at me with disbelief.

"Yeah, she's there and you're here. Hiding. Hiding from me?"

"The authorities. For the moment. Until it's safe to return to my parents."

I laugh so hard my belly shakes and tears pool in my eyes. "Oh, you won't be going back to your parents. You won't be going anywhere."

"We had a deal."

"Ahhh, we did."

"You said if I did this, you'd leave me alone. That you'd forgive the indiscretion."

I take a step nearer. "I changed my mind."

"You ... you can't do that."

I spin the knife through the air, catching it by the hilt. "Can't I? You see, you betrayed my little rabbit. You handed her to the butcher to be slaughtered. And that ... that doesn't sit right with me."

"Please, I didn't–"

"You did. And now you will pay for it." I close the distance between us, loving the way he squeals and pleads, screams and moans. Like music to my ears.

I'm no different from that spider. No different from a wolf. Killing's in my nature because killing is nature.

He harmed my little rabbit and so I harmed him. Simple really. Not like those rules my mom was always trying to force me to obey.

When I'm done with him, I wipe the blade of the knife on that mattress and hold it in my palm.

"That one was for you, little rabbit," I whisper. "All for you."

I glance down at the body.

Should I send her his heart in a box?

Too much?

Probably.

I need to find some other way to tell her.

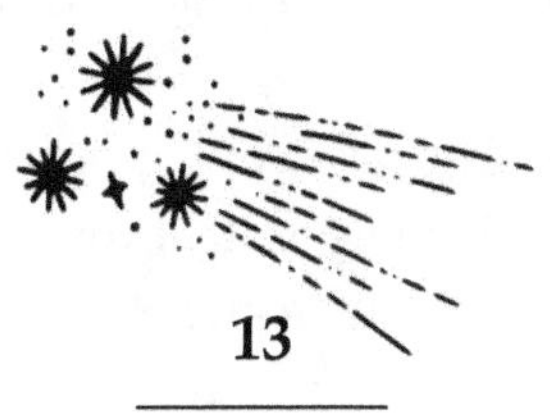

13

T ristan

I KNOW the moment she's back in the academy, can feel it in my gut.

I'd hoped this stupid thing with Azlan would keep her away. That apart from the family reunions – that, face it, are never going to happen – I'd never have to see her again. She'd disappear off to far-flung parts of the country, clinging to Azlan's side, as he hunts down the authorities' enemies. Perhaps she'd even get herself killed.

But no, she's back.

If I'm in luck, to pick up her stuff and go. If I'm in luck, I won't even see her.

Luck seems to have fucked me over these last few weeks, because I'm on the path with Spencer, Summer and the others when I feel her even closer.

I peer over my shoulder and meet her eye. Is it my imagination or does she look different? Taller, stronger, healthier. Her caramel eyes shine with determination and she refuses to look away from my gaze. Spencer lifts his head and spies her too.

"Pig Girl," Spencer says, rolling his eyes with exaggeration, "I thought we finally got rid of you."

"I guess you're not that lucky. Because I'm here."

"To collect your things, right?" Summer says with a smile. "Because you're leaving. Surely, York has discovered what a hopeless case you are by now and is kicking you out."

"No, sorry to disappoint you, Summer, but I'm definitely not leaving."

"Where's the pig?" Spencer makes a show of looking around. "Did someone finally turn him into a ham sandwich?"

The others chuckle and Spencer smirks at her

"No. He's at Azlan's. He's bringing him later." She meets my eyes again and I'm guessing he's told her. Some of it, anyway. The sanitized version. Even Azlan wouldn't be bitter enough to divulge the deep, dark secrets of our fucked-up family. Not unless he wants his fated mate fleeing from him in disgust.

Mentioning his name while she glares at me is a clear attempt to provoke me, though. One I'm not about to bite. I don't say a word.

"Who's Azlan?" Aysha says. Pig Girl smiles at her, an expression that has my jaw tightening. "Oh my god, he isn't your boyfriend, is he? Who is he?"

"Some loser, I'm guessing," Summer says. "Who would want a scrawny little scab like her? She smells and looks like a pig." Summer tosses her hair, then her eyes twinkle. "Maybe Azlan *is* her pig."

Spencer elbows Dan. "Pig Girl, are you finally confessing that you're in a relationship with that swine?"

The group bursts into laughter, all except me. The girl ignores them and rolls her eyes as if to say, "Honestly, is that the best you've got?"

"Come on," Summer says, tossing her hair a second time and beckoning to her friends, "we need to get to cheerleading practice before the polluted air gives us herpes." She catches my gaze and winks.

Summer and her girls file along the path, bashing into Pig Girl's shoulder as they go. She keeps her feet planted and refuses to move. I linger behind, watching as Spencer passes her last. As he does so, he grips her upper arm and hisses into her ear,

"Where have you been, Pig Girl?"

"None of your business," she says.

I watch with interest. Spencer blows hot and cold. It's like night and day with him. One minute the heart of the party, joking around like he just was; the next so fucking moody you'd think he had PMS. But I don't think I've ever seen the change come on so lightning fast, all the humor from a minute ago gone in a flash. Now he just looks pissed.

"It is my business. Everything that happens in this school is my business." She scoffs, and he squeezes her arm. "Tell me."

"I'd let go of me, if I were you," she says in a low dangerous tone.

"Why? You going to blast me again, piggie?"

"Maybe," she says.

"You're playing with fire," Spencer hisses.

"I'm not playing with anything. You're the one gripping my arm and demanding answers from me."

He huffs angrily and pushes her away.

"You would have been better off leaving, Rhianna," he says, then sprints off to catch up with our friends.

She watches him go, then spins around and jolts when she realizes I'm still here, blocking her path.

She holds my gaze for one long minute, her slight shoulders rising and falling, and I have the stupid urge to close the space between us, force her head back so she has to look up at me, so that she knows how much bigger I am than her, how much more powerful.

I don't care who her mate is. I could crush her in my hand like a little butterfly. Bend those fragile wings of hers all out of shape so she can't ever fly away.

She jerks her chin up at me. "Come on then, it's your turn. What you got? A lewd comment about my pet? A veiled threat? Demands I tell you my life story?"

I don't speak. I simply stare at her. There's a fucking hickey on her neck, hidden under her hair, peeking out from the collar of her shirt, but I can see it. It makes me want to destroy her all the more. That or press my lips over the bruise and mark her with my own.

My blood warms imagining it. If I did it, would she squeal and squirm in my arms? Or would little noises of desire bubble in her throat instead?

Unlikely.

She chose him. Not me.

She's his. Not mine.

"This is an improvement," she says. "Going for the silent treatment, huh? It's a vast improvement. In fact, I think this may be our most enjoyable conversation yet." She smirks at me in just the way Spencer had smirked at her earlier. "Maybe being bonded to Azlan is going to have its advantages."

"You should keep your mouth shut about that."

The smirk falls from her lips, and concern registers in his eyes. "No one knows that's his name," she says, a little hesitantly.

"You'd better hope that's true."

My father made it clear no one was to know of the bonding, but regardless, Azlan seems to be keeping his new status quiet. Judging by the discomfort on her face, I bet he's told her to as well.

The thought of all this is making my head ache. My body too. Like I just went twenty rounds with a grizzly bear.

I can't be here, this close to her, the hook in my stomach so violent it's torture, the breeze frisking her dark hair around her face, her lips wet and parted.

"He's going to kill me," she murmurs.

"I should be so fucking lucky," I mumble, walking the hell away, the hook straining to drag me back.

Is it worse? Worse than before? How can she stand there and act like she doesn't feel it too? Like it isn't destroying her from the inside?

Maybe she doesn't. She has her mate. She's made her choice.

I walk past the college buildings, out to the gardens and Venus common room. I need a distraction, something to stop the thoughts from battering my head, the pain from drowning my body. But when I reach the common room door, I realize the distraction on offer is not the one I want.

I can hear girls in there. Three, maybe four. They're talking and giggling amongst themselves curled up on the bed, but when I swing back the door, all that stops and they start pawing at each other, making out with exaggerated moans. Apart from Naomi, none of them are really into it, but they know I like a show like this, that ten out of ten times it will tempt me into joining them on the bed.

I watch them. All tits and ass and panted breaths. Naomi tugs down Sissy's top and sucks her stiff nipple into her mouth. So many tits.

Don't I love this shit? Isn't this the distraction I need after all?

Maybe all it will take is to fuck some other girl.

And here's not just one girl to fuck, but four.

I watch Summer's hand disappear into her panties as Naomi nibbles on her neck.

They haven't put on a show like this for me in quite some time.

"Are you going to join us?" Summer asks all breathy, like what Naomi is doing to her is actually enjoyable and not play-acting.

To be honest, I don't care if it is. The power thing has always been the appeal. Knowing they're doing it because I want them to and not because they like it.

Summer pushes Naomi away and crawls over the mattress, giving me an eyeful of her cleavage in her lacy bra. When she reaches the edge, she slides down to the floor and keeps crawling all the way over to me with a mischievous smile hovering on her lips.

Did *that* ever turn me on? Because today it leaves me cold. Stone cold. No heat in my body at all, just that constant aching thud.

I look back at the spectacle instead, hoping it'll do the trick as Summer reaches for me.

But I'm soft. Nowhere near hard.

I want to fuck these girls and forget about the pig one. I want to fuck her out of my system.

"For fuck's sake! Look like you actually want it!" I bark at them.

Summer glances over her shoulder at her friends with a scowl and they all start moaning more loudly, Aysha trying her best to fake a convincing orgasm.

"You want me to make you hard with my mouth?" Summer purrs, her hands wrapped around my thighs. I'd rather stuff my cock in a dead fish.

There's only one thing that would make me hard without fail. The last thing in the world I could have.

"Out," I say, unhooking Summer's hands and pushing her away.

The three on the bed, Aysha, Naomi and Sissy, pause, looking up at me. Naomi's hand cups Sissy's tit and her eyes are drowsy with lust. Usually that shit would have me hard in a heartbeat.

"Out!" I bark, louder this time, holding the door open in my left hand and pointing through the doorway with my right.

Sissy and Naomi jump off the bed, grabbing their clothes and racing out the door like two scared little rabbits. They can hear the menace in my tone. They're not prepared to hang around for a shitstorm. Aysha takes her sweet time skimming her top over her head and shuffling to the edge of the bed.

I tap my foot and she loses her nerve, sliding onto the floor and hurrying away.

Summer doesn't move from her position kneeling on the floor.

"Did you not hear me, Summer?"

"I heard you," she says in a bright tone, "I thought maybe you wanted some alone time, just the two of us."

"I don't."

"But it's been such a long time," she says, coiling a lock of hair around her finger. "I miss hanging out with you."

"You're sleeping with Spencer, Summer."

"Not any more," she says with obvious annoyance. "And anyway we were never exclusive, Tristan. Plus it's never bothered you before." She tilts forward onto her hands and knees. "We can do that thing you like, if you want."

"Not interested."

She scowls up at me. "You know, you and Spencer are turning into right bores lately. It's starting to get really tedious."

"Get out, Summer."

She huffs, rolling upright and padding closer to me in her bare feet.

She isn't scared of me like some of the other girls are. That's because she thinks her status as queen bee and her family's reputation means I'll never hurt her. She's wrong. I don't care who her daddy is. When your own father is a sick and twisted bastard, everyone else's look like fucking pussy cats in comparison.

She halts right in front of me. "It's ever since that pig girl arrived." Her gaze flicks round my stony face. "I've seen how you look at her."

I lean forward, getting my face right up and personal in hers. "Same way I look at you, Summer. With boredom. Now get out."

I grab her arm and swing her through the door, slamming it shut on her startled cries.

She doesn't know shit and she certainly hasn't seen shit ... has she?

I scrub my fingers through my hair, yanking the strands until my scalp screams.

Then I fling my arms into the air and seal the common room with an impregnable spell. I don't want anyone else coming in and I don't want anyone outside to see what I'm about to do.

I take a deep breath, letting the oxygen race down to my lungs, my hands fisting when I taste the sickly smell of perfume. Fucking girls.

Then with a yell, I swing both my arms out wide, hurtling magic across the room. It slams into a mirror on one side, and a window on the other. Both smash instantly, shards of glass crashing to the ground.

I hurl my arms above my head. Magic collides with the ceiling. Cracks fissure along the plaster, chunks fall to the ground.

I punch magic behind me, this time breaking the bed in two, feathers streaking high into the air.

I don't stop. Magic blasts through the air, hot and sizzling, melting everything it touches.

The beam above my head moans; the walls buckle.

I do it again, and again and again, growling and snarling, the magic hot on the ends of my fingers.

Until I'm standing, panting, sweat sliding down my face and my chest, in nothing but wreckage. Everything smashed and shattered to pieces.

I prefer it this way. I always have done.

There's far more beauty in the broken, in the damaged, than there ever was in the perfect, in the complete, in the whole.

Is that why? Is that why she was destined for me?

I stare at the damage as the light fades and my vision glazes. My breath gradually mellowing, those thoughts in my head settling like the swirling dust.

Then I sweep my hands into the air, more gently now,

and with attention and consideration I mend everything I've destroyed

And fuck, I want to smash her into a million pieces just so I can gather them up in my hands and mend her back together.

14

R^{hi}

THE DORM ROOM is empty when I reach it but fortunately, when Winnie returns an hour later, my welcome is a lot warmer than the one I received from Summer and her posse.

"Rhi?" she says, dropping all her books on the floor and dashing towards me. "Are you back or–"

"I'm back."

Winnie squeals, bouncing up and down on her toes before wrapping me in a hug.

"I'm probably being completely selfish given your current situation, but I am so pleased." She squeezes me, then stops. "Hang on," she mutters, taking a step back and swinging her gaze around. "Where is he?"

She peers under the bed and then stalks towards the wardrobe.

"He's not here." I giggle.

My friend swings around to look at me with a huge grin on her face. "Did you … bang?"

I roll my eyes. "Maybe … yes … quite a few times … actually pretty much non-stop."

I expect her to crow about being right – how all the banging has allowed me to separate from my mate. Instead, she takes my hands and lowers me to her bunk.

"Tell me everything," she says, eagerly.

"There isn't a whole lot to tell– Ow!" I yell as my friend pinches my leg. "I've only just recovered."

"From all the banging?" She pinches me again. "Don't hold back on me now. Come on, give me the dish, witch."

"It's been very … hot," I say.

"Uh huh." She nods eagerly, urging me to go on.

"He's very … skilled."

"Oh, I bet he is!" She waits for me to say more and when I don't she asks, "Is his dick as big as the rest of him?"

"Winnie!"

"Oh, come on, Rhi, I'm dying to know. The man is a giant. If I were you, I'd have been petrified that I could even fit his thing inside me." She makes a show of looking me over. "But you seem to be in one piece."

"You were the one encouraging me to sleep with him!"

"So, it didn't hurt?" she asks, ignoring me.

"No," I say, shivering a little at the memories. "Anything but."

"I'm pleased for you, Rhi. But, what happens next?"

"What happens next?" I ask, wondering if this is her way of asking me if I'm knocked up.

"You say you're coming back to school, but you can't seriously be away from your mate, as much as I want you here."

"We haven't exactly worked that out."

"You haven't talked about it?"

"No."

"On account of all the banging." She grins again.

"No, it's more complicated than that."

"Hmm, it shouldn't be, Rhi. You need to talk to him."

"He's coming tonight."

"Is he now!" She waggles her eyebrows. "I'd better make myself scarce."

"You don't have to."

"You've only just lost your V-card, Rhi. You are not ready to move onto sex with an audience just yet." I gape at her and she giggles. "It's fine. I'm meant to be seeing Trent anyway."

"And how is that going?" I ask.

"Well ..." she says, hooking her arm through mine and filling me in on everything I've missed.

I PACE IN MY ROOM, anxiously waiting for Azlan to arrive. Winnie has given me notes on all the lessons I've missed this week and it's clear I'm going to be even further behind than I first realized. Which means I really ought to use this time to concentrate on my work and catch up.

But I can't. I'm checking my phone every few minutes, eyes flitting to the window every other, and I can't sit still.

What if he doesn't come? What if he's too annoyed with me?

I chew on my nail until it's bleeding in my mouth. I swear, disappearing under the bunk for Winnie's first aid kit.

Of course that's when he arrives, as I'm wriggling out from under the bed, my butt thrust upwards in the air like a pig rooting for truffles. I swear a second time, rushing to open the door, aware my hair is a tangle about my head, my skin all flushed and blood running down my thumb.

I blow hair out of my face and hide my hand behind my back.

"Hi," I try to say casually, even though my heart is thumping at a million miles per hour.

His brow furrows. "What's wrong?"

"Nothing," I say a little too brightly.

He eyes me as he places a box on the floor, a box which snores loudly.

"Your pig. He's sleeping."

"Thank you," I say, lifting my thumb to start chewing on it again.

His eyes flick to my hand and his brow furrows even deeper.

"You're bleeding."

"It's nothing." I attempt to hide my hand behind my back again, but he snatches it in his own.

"You have to stop doing this."

"I can't help it."

He closes his eyes and the cut heals instantly. "I thought you learned that spell."

"I did. I guess I forgot. My mind has been on other things." Like him. Mostly him. But also the weird way my body reacted when I bumped into Tristan and Spencer on the path. Is that some strange side effect of the mating?

Azlan kicks the door shut behind him.

"Where's the roommate?"

"With her boyfriend."

He pulls me towards him. "What's been on your mind?"

"You," I say, rolling my eyes. Like he doesn't know that.

"Me? But you're nervous," he says, that frown not leaving his face.

"Nervous? I'm not nervous," I say, even though my legs are practically shaking. I'm pretty sure that's from anticipation, not nerves.

"Then why were you mauling your thumb?" He lifts my hand between us, then ducks his head and kisses it gently.

My breath catches in my throat.

"I didn't know if you were going to be angry with me," I blurt out.

"What about?"

"Wanting to come back to school so soon. It wasn't what we agreed."

"I got the impression you hated it here so I'm a little hurt you'd rather be here than with me."

"Most of the time I hate it here. But sometimes it's not so bad. And I want to learn. I'm fed up with being ignorant. Not knowing all the things I should know. It doesn't have anything to do with you, although living with you is pretty intense."

"Because I make you nervous."

"Because it's pretty extreme to go from never having had a boyfriend to living with one in a week."

"I'm more than a boyfriend."

"It doesn't make any difference. This has all been moving so fast."

He drops my hand and takes my place pacing around the room. "You're right. It has."

"I need some time to think."

"Me too." His words may be fair – an echo of my own – and yet I still feel like he just punched me in the gut.

Does he regret everything now? Or maybe he's bored with me already?

"Do you want me to leave?" he asks, staring with blank eyes at one of Winnie's posters.

"If you want to," I mutter.

He swings his gaze my way and his eyes have that heat blazing in them that doesn't just have my legs shaking, they have my knees buckling. "I don't want to go. But I will if you ask me to."

"I don't want you to go ... not yet."

We stare at each other. And if he doesn't lay his hands on me this instant, I think I might combust.

"Come here."

"Just because I'm your mate–"

"Come here, Rhianna."

I want to tell him to go to hell. That if he wants to touch me, he can freaking well move himself. But that hook in my stomach listens to him and not me and carries me across the room until I'm right in front of him, the heat of his body tangible.

He slides his hand roughly into my hair and tilts my face up to his.

"I don't like being apart from you. I don't like not being by your side, protecting you from danger. I don't like being able to sense your feelings through the bond with no idea what's causing them. I don't like the fact all I can think about is kissing you and making you moan my name into my mouth."

I swallow, my lips parting. "What's stopping you?"

His eyes dance with fire and then his mouth is on mine, consuming every one of those moans he'd promised as his other hand slides into my panties.

His fingertips spark with magic as he touches me, softly nudging open my folds and pressing against my clit. I moan some more as his magic vibrates against me, building in intensity and power.

"Azlan," I gasp, my legs shaking violently so that it's only his strong arm keeping me upright. I grip at his shirt, my own fingertips sparking with magic too.

"I love it when you come," he says against my mouth. He presses harder and I come easily on his fingers. Then he backs me towards the wall, my body still trembling with the aftershocks of pleasure.

I press my hand against his chest and shake my head. A frown brushes across his features and something that looks like hurt, but then I'm dropping to my knees and a flicker of excitement resides in his eyes instead.

We've done plenty over the last few days, but it's mostly involved his fingers, his mouth and his tongue on me. Or else he's had me in every position I could have imagined. I haven't done this, though. I've *never* done this. I'm a little nervous. I don't know what I'm doing but he's made me feel good innumerable times and I want to make him feel good too.

"Are you sure?" he asks me, sensing my hesitation through the bond. "You don't have to–"

I cut off his words with a determined scowl and pull down the zipper of his fly, reaching inside for him. I curl my fist around his girth. He's hot and hard in my hand. I hook his cock out of his pants and shuffle forward on my knees.

He groans a little, his eyes wide as he watches to see what I'll do next. For a moment I just stare at him. I may be pretty unfamiliar with male anatomy, but I've seen enough cocks now in the locker room to know he's big. No wonder I feel so damn full when he's inside me.

He's also beautiful in a way I'd never considered the

object hanging between a man's legs could be. Curved, girthy, solid.

Is it strange that I'm growing attached to his cock? It's not just the way it makes me feel. It's the way it looks too: big and solid like him, framed by a tuft of dark curls, a long protruding vein running his length, clear liquid dribbling from his head.

I lick my lips, thinking about how full he makes me feel.

"Rhianna," he says firmly, "I'm dying here."

A giggle that's half nerves, half incredulous at this entire situation, spills from my throat, and then I lean forward to kiss the tip of his cock. The skin there is as soft as velvet and I taste the tinge of salt on my lips. I kiss him again, then swirl my tongue around his head.

I wish I'd spent as much time reading about this as I had about fated mates. I wish I'd watched a video or something. I'm going purely on instinct here.

The man in black, reaches down to cradle my head in his hands, stroking the underside of my jaw.

"Little mate," he says, softly, "put it in your mouth."

My cheeks burn furiously, but I do as he requests, taking as much of him as I can between my lips. That taste of salt floods my senses and I feel him jerk against my tongue.

"Now suck," he says, his fingers moving to twist in my hair.

I hollow my cheeks and suck around his stiff cock.

He groans and I feel the intensity of it through the bond. I suck some more, moving my mouth up and down his cock so he's pumping in and out.

He grunts, his fingers stiffening in my hair, a stream of nonsense flowing from his mouth.

A sense of power cascades through my veins. It isn't magic, a fated bond or anything else like that. No, it's knowing I'm reducing him to this, the way he's reduced me so many times. And it may be me on my knees, but I'm in control here. I'm the one driving these sensations of ecstasy from his body.

"I want to come in your pretty mouth," he groans, and I suck him harder, feeling his cock throb on my tongue.

His hips jolt forward, and he thrusts into my mouth, his fingers pulling at my hair, and then warm liquid hits the back of my throat.

At first it takes me by surprise, and I think I might choke. Then I hear the deep command of his voice. "Swallow it down."

I do, letting it stream down my throat, some of it spilling over my lips.

When it stops, his fingers relax and I fall onto my backside, peering up at his face.

He stares straight back down into my eyes, the connection between us buzzing with energy.

Seems the damn fated bond doesn't only want us to bang. It also wants me to give him head.

I want to ask him if it was good. If I did okay. But I can't find the words and when he leans down to sweep his come from my lips, I feel my cheeks sizzle again.

"You missed a bit," he says darkly, offering up his fingers.

I should really tell him to go to hell. Instead, I find myself sucking his fingers, nipping at his fingertips and making him chuckle.

Then he's pulling me up onto my feet and kissing me again.

15

R^{hi}

I TOSS and turn on my bunk all night, my body not happy about being separated from my mate. It bitches about it as the owls hoot outside, the wind rushes through the trees and Winnie mutters in her sleep. I ache everywhere, my head pounds and the tug in my gut scrapes viciously. By the time I'm sitting in class the next morning though, I know I'm doing the right thing no matter what my body might have to say about it.

I've spent too much of my life dancing to someone else's tune. First obeying my aunt's wishes to stay hidden, then the authorities' command to come to this school and now I'm bonded to a man – something that wasn't my choice either, even if I am softening towards him, that anger chilling day by day.

It's about time I controlled my own life. And the start of

that begins with understanding who I really am and what I'm truly capable of. Arrow Hart Academy may be full of assholes, but it's the best place to be if I hope to learn.

And so I decline Mrs. Hollyhill's offer to head to the library in my Magical History and Politics lesson, asking as many questions as I can think of, ignoring all the snide comments about my ignorance.

"What's gotten into you?" Winnie says, elbowing me as we duck our heads to start composing an answer to the question written across the blackboard. "Oh, wait, I know what's gotten into you." She sniggers.

I roll my eyes at her. "You're becoming as bad as they are," I say, inclining my head to the bunch of bouncing bunnies and jocks occupying the back rows of the classroom.

"Hey," Winnie says, this time poking me with the sharp point of her pencil. "That is a low blow."

"Anyway," I change the subject. "Things have been crazy and now I'm more determined than ever to learn this stuff."

"Even history and politics?" Winnie asks, like I've lost my mind as well as my virginity.

"It's all useful, right?"

"Probably," Winnie says, before leaning in to whisper in my ear. "Your mate's family crops up quite often in these lessons."

My cheeks burn. "They do?"

"Yeah, maybe you'd better read up."

I nod, chewing the end of my pencil, then focus back on my blank piece of paper, determined to draft an answer even if I know nothing about the causes of the Dragonetti wars in the 17th century, and ignoring the intense sensation of longing residing in my stomach.

The lesson straight after is with Stone.

Despite my new-found enthusiasm for studying, I take my merry time packing up my bag, Winnie eyeing me with a raised eyebrow as I rearrange the books in my backpack for the second time.

"Anyone would think you're not that eager to get to our next lesson with Professor Hotness, Rhianna Blackwaters," she teases as we walk down the already-emptying corridors.

"That, Winnie Wence, is because I am not eager to spend any more time with Professor *Asshole* than I have to."

"Isn't he best friends with your mate?" she whispers. "Doesn't that mean you'll be spending an awful lot of your time with his hot ass?"

I groan. I haven't seen him since he was sent to babysit me at Azlan's house and that encounter left me more confused than ever.

Despite the fact he is an asshole – maybe *because* he is an asshole – I've always had a bit of a crush on the professor. Winnie isn't lying. He is easily the hottest teacher in this school. Handsome, with a body straight out of an action movie. Plus the way he teases me presses all my buttons in an entirely inappropriate way.

Urgh. It drives me crazy. He is the last man I want to have a crush on.

But maybe things will be different now. Maybe I won't feel the same way about him now I'm bonded to Azlan. Maybe I'll be immune to his good looks and assholey hotness.

Then again, it didn't feel that way at Azlan's house. I felt just as drawn to him as I always have. Almost like ...

I screw up my face as we arrive at the classroom door.

I rub at my forehead.

That can't be right though, can it? I have my fated mate. We're bonded for life.

Winnie pushes on the door, then peers at me. "He's locked the door," she says.

"What?" I say with irritation, shoving my shoulder against the door. It remains in place. I take the handle in my hand and rattle it. Definitely locked. "What the hell?"

"I doubt this is a good sign," Winnie says, straightening her blazer and then rapping on the door.

We hear heavy footsteps march towards us and then the door swings back. Stone waits on the other side, a disgruntled expression on his face.

"Ahh Miss Blackwaters, Miss Wence. So you *were* planning to join us today."

"Sorry we're late," Winnie mumbles, even though it's only a few minutes after the lesson officially started, nothing compared to the professor's usual tardiness.

"Ahhh Miss Blackwaters, the privileges of being a teacher." He emphasizes the word 'teacher', giving me a hard stare.

I stare back at him in response, not saying a word. I couldn't even if I wanted to.

It's that feeling. That feeling in my stomach. Tugging me his way. It's still there. I can't be imagining it.

Stone looks away and concentrates his attention on Winnie. "I'd expect this of someone like Rhianna, Miss Wence. But not you. I hope she's not proving a bad influence on you."

Winnie shakes her head and mumbles another apology.

I search the professor's face for any hint, any sign, he's feeling the same thing I am.

He looks tired, dark circles under his eyes, his face drawn. Other than that, there's nothing.

"In you go then, Miss Wence. We're reading the passage on page 969."

He steps to one side and Winnie hurries inside.

"Well, Miss Blackwaters?"

His gaze meets my eyes again and the sensation in my stomach pulls so strongly I nearly stumble.

"What?" I gasp.

"I'm waiting for my apology."

"*You're* waiting for *your* apology," I hiss, snapping out of my trance. I glare at him. "Don't you think you owe me one, *Professor*?"

"Do you want to come into my class or not?" he says lowering his voice, his tone full of threat.

"Depends. What are you going to teach me?"

His eyes travel down my form in such a heated way it makes my skin blaze.

"Get inside the classroom now, Rhianna!" he barks.

I roll my eyes at him in a way I'm sure would rival Summer and stride inside with my head held high. All the students duck their heads immediately and pretend to be reading from their text books.

I don't know why but I'm suddenly even more irritated with him than I was before. Irritated with him and this stupid sensation, this stupid situation.

I have a mate. A very hot mate. Okay, we may have our problems and things might not be as rosy as they should be, but when the man has his head between my thighs, I feel like I'm a princess. Like I'm special. Like he really means everything he's telling me with the movement of his tongue.

I shiver just thinking about it and sink into the only available desk right in the front row.

Stone comes stomping into the classroom after me, his expression even more thunderous and I realize he's probably experienced me thinking about Azlan eating my pussy second hand. That should make me feel less irritated and more embarrassed, but it doesn't and I glare right back at him.

The lesson is another boring one. Stone doesn't seem to actually want to teach us anything these days and instead has us reading yet more passages from books about the evolution of magic. The topic is actually pretty interesting, but the way it is written is so dry and technical it renders it duller than watching paint dry. And I should know. My childhood wasn't exactly full of crazy-ass entertainment.

The boring text and my lack of sleep, the warm temperature of the room and the strange buzz of my bond in my stomach start to get to me. My eyelids droop. Twice I jerk awake, shaking my head and trying to focus in on the words in front of me. The third time I jolt awake as my elbow gives way from under me and my head smacks against the desk.

I yelp, blinking my eyelids open. Everyone is staring at me, several giggling, one with their phone out.

"I wonder why you bother coming to my lessons, Miss Blackwaters, if you're going to miss a good chunk of the start and sleep all the way through the remainder."

I look up and find Stone sitting behind his desk, his boots resting on the surface, his hands clutched behind his head, a book balanced in his lap.

"And I wonder why you bother showing up to lessons seeing as you don't actually seem to want to teach us anything."

The room falls silent.

Stone swings down his legs and leans forward over his desk.

"See me after class, Miss Blackwaters." His voice is sinisterly quiet and it scares me a whole lot more than it usually does. Have I pushed him too far? Well, so what if I have? He's pushed me much further.

The bell rings a few minutes later and once again I take my time packing up my bag. I notice quite a few of the others doing the same. They're obviously hoping to over-hear me receiving a scolding from Stone. The people in this school really are twisted.

Stone continues reading his book, something that looks like poetry, and pays none of us any notice. Eventually, the last student runs out of ways to dawdle and the door shuts closed behind them, leaving just me and the professor.

He looks up from his book immediately and slams it shut.

"You think you're cute?" he asks.

"Do you?" I ask, resting my hand on my hip. His eyes flash and the hook in my stomach tugs. "I don't think I'm anything," I add quickly, then hesitate. "Except eager to learn."

He shrugs off his jacket and rolls up his sleeves, his strong forearms coming into view. Then he scrubs his fingers through his beard and I wonder how many students have fantasized about doing the same.

He screws up his eyes. "Can you not?" he says. Then he sighs. "Lots of students fall for their teachers. It's not uncommon. It's similar to a Stockholm syndrome situation."

"I haven't fallen for you."

"Did I say you had?" he says.

I chew on my lip.

"You can't turn up late, Miss Blackwaters. You can't fall asleep in my lessons. You can't give me backchat in my class. You think the principal's punishments are harsh, you have no idea what I'm capable of."

"I'm not scared of you."

"Maybe you should be," he whispers and I remember the pain in my head and frown. "Don't try my patience."

"Can I go now?" I ask.

"No," he snaps. "I think you owe me some lines."

"Lines?" I laugh. "That's your big scary punishment."

"It's only fair I give you a little warning. We all make mistakes," he mumbles. "Next time, I won't be so nice."

I snort and sink onto the nearest chair, pulling paper and a pen from my bag. It's lunch time and I'm not so used to skipping meals anymore. My stomach is already grumbling about it.

"What am I writing?" I ask, snapping the lid off my pen.

The professor smirks in that stupidly hot way and then swirls his right hand through the air with a flourish. A piece of chalk dances across the blackboard leaving a sentence of flamboyant writing behind.

I lean forward in my chair to read it, curious despite my best efforts.

I will show Professor Stone the due respect he deserves.

"I'm not writing that," I say.

"You are. One hundred lines please, Miss Blackwaters." He picks up his book and starts reading again, tugging off his tie as he does.

I swear under my breath and pick up my pen. This isn't a battle worth fighting. It's a relatively light punishment and the sooner I write the lines, the sooner I can eat.

I pick up my pen and hover the nib over the paper.

If I write quickly enough, I'm sure I can finish in thirty minutes which would leave me thirty more to rush to the canteen and hoover down some food.

I flex my fingers, and lower my pen to the page.

Then I halt, an idea forming in my mind. I drop my pen and wave my hand over the page instead. One hundred lines of perfectly handwritten sentences appear.

I smile.

"I'm done," I say triumphantly.

The professor looks up.

"It seems like maybe you're finally learning, Miss Black-waters." He holds out his hand. "Let me see."

I hesitate for a moment, then stand up from my desk, pick up the piece of paper and carry it over to him.

He takes it from my hand and his eyes glide over the page. The same sentence written over and over again. One hundred times.

Professor Stone is an asshole.

"Again the obsession with my ass," he whispers.

"You can kiss mine," I snap back.

He looks up at me.

"Don't ... fucking ... tempt ... me," he hisses, crushing the paper in his fist. He opens his hand and the ball of paper sets alight, burning vividly in his palm.

We watch it together, the paper curling, the flames dancing, the sensation in my stomach stronger than ever.

"I did your lines," I tell him. "Can I go now, Professor?"

"No, you didn't, Miss Blackwaters, so I advise you to sit back down and start writing."

I rest my palms on his desk and lean towards him. "Or what?"

"Don't test me," he growls.

"Why? What exactly are you going to do, Professor? You keep threatening me but you never actually deliver."

"What are you hoping for, Miss Blackwaters? That I'll bend you over my lap and spank your backside?"

He glares at me, his eyes darkening.

"Wh-wh-what?" I mutter. That's completely twisted, archaic, and sexist. And yet, I'm rubbing my thighs together despite myself.

"Don't play with fire," he says, "you'll only end up burned."

"I told you, I'm not afraid of you," I say, regaining my composure.

He pushes backwards on his chair, the legs scraping along the floor. Then he stands, walking around his desk and stopping right in front of me. He's bigger and broader than me but I hold my ground, tipping my head back to look up into his face.

"Are you sure?"

"Yes."

That sensation in my stomach hums at his closeness, and I can't help but let my gaze flit downwards. Down to where his shirt stretches across his muscular frame and the black lines of his tattoos protrude from the neckline of his shirt.

He feels impossibly close. The hook strains towards him.

I want to ask him. I want to know. But I'm too afraid.

What if I'm wrong? What if I'm just a confused girl who doesn't know a thing about men and sex and love? What if I'm just a horny mess for a man who should be out of bounds for more than one reason?

And what if he told Azlan? How would my mate feel if he knew his best friend stirred feelings inside me that he shouldn't?

The idea makes me sick.

"I'm not writing any more lines," I say, walking straight out of his classroom.

The last thing I want is for him to read all the messed-up thoughts swirling around in my mind.

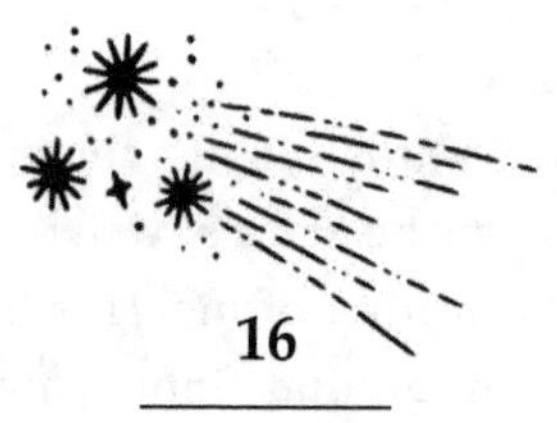

16

S tone

I PLEAD sickness and convince Jones to cover the rest of my afternoon lessons. It's not exactly a lie. I feel awful. My head dull, my bones aching, my muscles sore.

It was only a matter of time. Fate isn't a power to be messed with and, as my research is proving, a power you can damn well alter either.

I stomp back to my cabin and lie out on the bed, trying not to think about my run in with Rhianna. Trying not to think about the thoughts in her head. She feels it. Of course she does. And now she knows what it is. Has a name for it. But she hasn't asked me about it. She's too ashamed, too confused. I could change all that.

But then what ...

This won't end well. I've seen it in front of my own eyes. It will destroy me. It will destroy Azlan. It will destroy her.

Suddenly, I'm so damn angry. Fate is a fucker. A cruel and twisted fucker, hellbent on torturing us all.

Fuck, it's not like I even give a shit about myself. My life has never been sunshine and rainbows. It's been gutters and grime, sewers and scum.

But I don't want this for *her*. I don't want it for *him*.

I want to undo it. I want to take fate by its twisted throat and snap it in two. I want to scrub out every star written in our charts. Scorch away every crease in our palms.

I groan. I'm so tired. My body hurts everywhere.

I try to close my eyes. To blow away the anger and sleep.

But all I see is her. On the ground, lifeless, unmoving, dying.

The picture of it swims around and around till I'm so dizzy, so nauseous, I swing my legs to the floor and force my head between my knees, waiting for it to pass. Then I stagger up onto my feet. I can't stay here. I know Azlan wants me to. Wants me watching his mate for him. But I can't.

I'm going to see him.

I find him at his house, in his bedroom. There are clothes all over the bed – the bed that smells of her – and a rucksack resting on the floor.

"Are you running away?" I ask, leaning against the door frame and crossing my arms.

"Hello Phoenix," he says, without looking up. "The Chancellor's sending me West."

"West?" I say, straightening up and taking a step into the room.

"Yes, West."

"Why?" Azlan's missions take him all over the land, hunting down unregistereds and gang members alike. But the West? There are battalions of magicals stationed there, protecting the border. Azlan isn't needed.

"Apparently there are reports of Western soldiers infiltrating our lands. He wants me to discover what they are doing."

"Infiltrations?" I scoff. There have always been such stories for as long as I can remember. Azlan and I have always agreed such stories were cooked up by the authorities to keep the people frightened and obedient. "You don't believe those rumors?"

"I'm not sure. I intend to find out."

He shoves one last shirt into the neck of his rucksack and yanks the string to close the top.

"When do you leave?"

"In the next few days."

"And how about Rhi?"

He freezes, then rolls up to stand. "I'll be gone a couple of days. No more."

"You can't know that for sure."

"I can," he says, jaw tightening. "I can't be away from her any longer than that."

No, the bond won't allow it. He stalks towards me, resting his palm on my shoulder. "You'll watch her for me? Keep her safe?" he pleads.

I nod curtly. I would do it even if he didn't ask. He must know that.

"I don't like this," I say.

"Me going?" he says with a weak smile. "I didn't know you cared so much."

"You wish," I say. "No, the fact that the Chancellor is rattled enough to send you west. What does your uncle say? What are his spies reporting?"

"You know I'm not talking to my family right now."

"Even Eleanor?"

"She won't know anything."

"Maybe you should ask her anyway. This doesn't sound safe, Azlan. Sometimes I think you forget you're only one man. Sometimes I think the Chancellor forgets it too."

"You know I can take care of myself."

"But it's not only you now, is it? Not only yourself you have to worry about. If anything happens to you ..."

I stroll towards the window and gaze down at the street. I don't want him to see my face.

"Nothing will happen to me," he says gently.

"It better not, pal," I say through gritted teeth. "Because if it does, I don't care if you're already dead, I will wring your neck."

"You care about her," he says, softer still.

"So you keep saying."

"So you keep showing."

I scoff at him. But I can't deny it.

17

R^{hi}

I COULD REALLY DO without gym first thing the next morning. My body is sore from the separation away from my mate and I didn't sleep a wink again last night.

"You could probably plead with coach to let you off, considering the state of your leg only a week ago," Winnie says as we hurry towards the gymnasium.

"Nope," I say with resignation I try to feel. "I'm serious about learning. I'm going to focus damn hard on my studies and that includes learning everything I can in gym class, even if it's mostly going to involve being thrown on my back over and over again."

"A skill I'm sure you've found rather useful over the last few days." Winnie chuckles.

I can't help a smile. And I can't help feeling grateful for Winnie. For all my bravado, I'm not exactly looking forward to facing Spencer on the mat again. His black mood when I bumped into him on the path two days ago suggests he'll be as brutal as ever. Coupled with the way my body reacted to him when we last met, I have a feeling I'm going to be battered and bruised by the end of the lesson.

For once, I am in luck. No combat training this lesson. We're back to running laps around the field. Something I'm actually fairly good at and, compared to many of the other forms of torture Coach Hank likes to thrust upon us, relatively painless.

This luck doesn't last long though. I'm about to step into my uniform once gym class is over, when Summer and her little posse emerge from nowhere, forming a tight circle around me.

I go to sidestep them, but before I know what's happening; several pairs of hands have grabbed me, pinning my arms to my sides and pushing me towards the showers.

"What the hell?" I yell, trying to free my arms so I can defend myself. But there are too many girls holding me tight, their long nails pinching into my flesh. "Let me go!"

"Stop it!" Winnie shouts, and I peer over my shoulder at her as I attempt to dig my heels into the cold tiled floor. She's being held against the lockers by three of the cheerleading squad. "What are you doing?"

"I'm so fed up with this little pig polluting the air I'm forced to breathe with her stench. God, I can smell her a mile away," Summer says in a bored voice, her arms crossed casually over her chest ‍and something sinister brewing in her eyes.

"I don't smell!" I snap. In fact, I had already showered and dried myself. "If a smell's following you around, ever thought it might be yourself?"

"Aaah!" Summer screeches. "Get her in the stupid shower." I tussle as best as I can with the four girls holding me, but it's no good. With my hands trapped, I can't use my magic and they push me easily into the cubicle right at the back of the row. They force me under the shower head, two of them holding my head. I hear Summer click her fingers and a torrent of freezing cold water comes thundering down.

It's so cold it whips my breath away and I can't breathe, water running into my nose and my mouth and my eyes as they hold my face under the downpour. I choke on the water, trying desperately to spit it from my mouth but more and more of it pours into my face.

"Stop it!" I hear Winnie call through the gurgle of the water in my ears.

I start to panic, no oxygen reaching my lung, my chest starting to burn, my head beginning to spin.

Just when I think I can't take it anymore, the flow cuts off and I gasp for air, coughing and spluttering water down my front.

"What do we think? Clean enough?" Summer says. I blink up at her, water streaming down my face. My hands are still held and I can't wipe it away. "Hmmm," she says, with that stupid smile I'd really love to wipe from her face. "I don't think so."

She lifts her hand.

"No–" I scream but my words are cut off as she clicks her fingers a second time and more water pours into my face. Somehow it seems even colder than before. The water slides down my throat and I choke on it, the world fading away as I'm starved of oxygen.

But the water has also made my skin slippery, the grips on my arms loosening. I take my opportunity, jerking free my arm. For the briefest of seconds I consider blasting my magic at Summer. God, I really, really, really want to. But if I also want to be expelled, that's a sure-fire way to achieve it. Instead, I swing my hand upwards and shoot magic at the shower head.

The water stops dead and pipes and plaster tumble downwards.

The girls holding me scream and dive to one side, and I cover my head, debris raining down on my crown.

"Little bitch," one of the girls mutters, brushing plaster off her body.

Summer simply smiles. It's sickly sweet and I know we're not done here.

"Destroying and vandalizing school property. I think I'll have to report you."

"Waterboarding other students," Winnie snaps. "I think I'll have to report you."

Summer laughs. "You do have a wild imagination, Winnie Wence. I didn't see anything untoward. Did you?" she asks her friends. Ten girls shake their heads. "How about you?" Summer growls, turning to the other girls in the locker room.

Some drop their gazes to the floor and others mumble, "No, Summer."

Summer swings back round to Winnie with a grin, but her satisfied words are interrupted by the locker room door swinging open and Spencer barreling through.

"What the fuck was all that noise?" he says.

"Just Rhianna Blackwaters being clumsy with the shower equipment," Summer says sweetly. "Anyone would think the girl has trotters instead of feet."

Spencer swings his gaze towards me, his eyes swimming down my shivering form.

"Put some damn clothes on," he snaps at me. "Then

clean it up," he adds, before turning and strolling right back out.

"You heard the man," Summer says, sweeping her hair up into a ponytail. "Clear it up."

She bounces away and her troop of cheerleaders follow after.

18

R^{hi}

"I REALLY HATE THAT GIRL," I mutter to Winnie once we're alone in the locker room.

Winnie peers over her shoulder.

"I don't think you are the only one. In fact, I reckon more people hate her than they do love her. I bet none of her friends actually even like her. I almost feel sorry for her."

I stare at Winnie, my wet hair plastered to my head, cold water dripping off my body and onto the floor. "Are you serious?" I say.

Winnie considers me. "No. You're right. She is a bitch and one day karma will come for her."

"I'm not sure I can wait for karma to get her act together. I think I may need to step in and hand out some retribution of my own before then," I say, stepping out of the cubicle and blowing warm air through my hair and over my body.

"You could go tell the principal."

I shake my head. "You heard her. No one will believe me. She'll have at least ten of her cheerleading buddies queuing up to accuse me of lying."

"Hmmm." Winnie steps into her uniform. "Just don't do anything stupid."

"Me? Do anything stupid?"

"Yes, you, Rhianna Blackwaters. She is not worth getting expelled over, even if that would deliver you straight back into the waiting arms of your very hot mate." She tilts her head to one side. "You could always tell your mate what happened."

I can feel my mate's anxiety through the bond. I'm pretty sure he got a blast of my emotions during that shower ordeal and is obviously not very happy about it.

I reach into my locker, pulling out my phone and finding three missed calls and five messages from him.

"He's definitely concerned," I mumble.

"I bet he'd put an end to Summer's mischief," Winnie says darkly.

"I'm not having Azlan fight my battles for me."

"Seriously? Because if I had a six-foot-five giant of a mate, I'd let him fight every single one of my battles."

"Nope, I can take care of myself. He already saved my neck once, and look what it cost him."

Winnie frowns.

"Cost him an amazing, beautiful mate."

I roll my eyes and tap out a reply to Azlan.

RHI: I'm fine. Just a disagreement with one of the girls in my class.

. . .

I ADD two smiley faces in the hope he'll believe my bid to downplay the incident. I bet the man in black never uses emojis. I bet he doesn't even know what a smiley face means. Then again, I'm not sure I do either.

Immediately, my phone rings in my hand, but I decline it.

RHI: I'm about to go into class. I'll call you later.

I SHOVE my phone into my bag before he can call again and tug on my uniform.

"Come on," I say, beckoning to Winnie, "I don't want a lecture from Dr. Johnson for being late. Let's not give Summer that satisfaction as well."

PRACTICAL MAGIC with Dr. Johnson should, in theory, be one of my favorite lessons; a chance to test my actual magical abilities and stretch my wings. However, Dr. Johnson's obvious infatuation with Summer has always made these lessons painful. The entire lesson often seems to be devoted to worshiping her favorite student, while torturing me. More often than not we're forced to watch the head cheerleader perform for us and then made to clap whenever she demonstrates yet another magical skill. Plus the doctor has a great knack for turning a blind eye to Summer's cruel remarks and mean behavior.

It's the last thing I need.

Today's lesson, however, turns out to be different. Dr. Johnson meets us at the classroom door and tells us we'll be heading to the meadow at the far side of the academy's gardens.

"We need outside space to practice this particular magic, boys and girls," she says, her eyes straying to Summer and lingering on the neck of her shirt.

"What do you think we'll be practicing?" I ask Winnie as we follow the line of other students along the pathway and through the gardens, the heady aroma of blossoms hovering in the sunlit air and bees buzzing eagerly from flower head to flower head. Flowers that wouldn't be here if it weren't for my labor in the gardens.

"Hmmm," Winnie says, twisting her braids around her head and pinning them in place as we walk. "Could be defensive or battle magic? We'd definitely require space for that."

"Battle magic," my spirits lift, "I like the sound of that." I grin at my friend. "Especially if it means I can get a little revenge for all those smutty comments."

"Smutty comments? Me?" Winnie says, with a feigned look of innocence.

I giggle and hook my arm through hers, relieved to be back in her company. The man in black may be hot but he's also intense. I feel on edge in his company. With Winnie I can be myself – and not worry about saying the wrong thing, or having food stuck between my teeth.

However, any hopes that I might be paired with my best friend for this assignment are quickly squashed.

"You'll be working in pairs," Dr. Johnson says as the last student filters through the hedgerows and into the mead-ows. I've only been here once, when out searching for Pip and that day, low clouds had hung in the air, blocking the view. Today, the bright blue sky drags on forever and so do the endless fields and countryside. For a moment I'm mesmerized by it and almost miss Dr. Johnson's next instruction. "Listen out for your names please."

She starts to reel off names in pairs, several students either groaning their displeasure or thumping the air in triumph. I don't know why. Dr. Johnson hasn't even told us what we'll be doing in this lesson. Of course, Summer is paired with Aysha and the two rush into each other's arms like they've just been reunited after years apart. I throw Winnie an unamused look and she waves a little apology, already standing beside her partner, Andrew's friend, Dane.

When my name's called my gaze flicks away from the view and back to our teacher. The name that follows has most of the class gasping and then whispering behind their hands.

Tristan Kennedy.

I glare at him. A look he returns tenfold.

Was this his doing?

Because it's clear Summer's not happy about it from the way she folds her arms across her chest and starts to protest. Dr. Johnson doesn't notice, already on to the last few names.

"Right," she says, looking up from her list and cowering slightly when she encounters Summer's death stare. "Today we'll be practicing the art of combining powers to amplify and increase them. As you will know, this practice is especially useful in battle or in self defense. If you can work with another magical in tandem to combine and increase your powers, you can prove an unstoppable force."

"I don't think Pig Girl should be paired with Tristan Kennedy, Diana," Summer says to the teacher. "They are nowhere near matched. I think I'd be a better match for him." She throws Tristan a knowing look. He responds with a yawn, finding his fingernails fascinating.

"I don't *want* to be paired with him," I snap. "I'd happily swap."

Aysha frowns, obviously not happy that Summer is ditching her for Tristan, leaving her with me.

"I would tend to agree with you, Summer," the teacher says, making me hate her ten times more than I already do. "But it was the principal who picked the pairs, not me."

"Principal York doesn't know us as well as you do," Summer says with flattery that has the doctor's cheeks glowing a rosy color.

"That she may not. But the pairing was based on some assessment of compatibility that I am not privy to." I meet eyes with Winnie who is clearly as surprised as I am. "Now, let me explain how this works. Summer, if you wouldn't mind." Summer flicks her ponytail over her shoulder and sashays towards the teacher. "We need to link hands," the teacher says with obvious enthusiasm, taking Summer's in hers. "Then we need to attempt to tune into the frequency of the other person's magic. It requires patience and peace of mind. You must clear your thoughts. Give your full attention and devotion to the other person."

I twerk an eyebrow. There is no way I'm giving Tristan Kennedy anymore of my attention. He's had far too much of it over these past few weeks.

"Ahhh," Dr. Johnson says with a sigh that almost sounds erotic. "I can feel your magic, Summer."

Summer grimaces and shuffles on her feet, obviously uncomfortable.

"Can you feel mine?" the doctor asks.

"No, sorry, I can't," Summer says, snatching back her hands.

Dr. Johnson opens her eyes, her face utterly crestfallen. "Oh, well." She clears her throat. "If Summer had been ..."

she clears her throat a second time, "able to feel my magic too, the next step would have involved the two of us working together to entwine our magical powers. It's almost like weaving. Again it requires concentration and patience."

"Then how is this useful in battle?" someone asks from the back of the group.

"Once you get the hang of it, the process becomes quicker and easier. Skilled magical pairs can combine their powers with little thought and almost instantaneously."

"And," I say, raising my hand, "is the same process involved when one magical gives their power to another?"

All the pairs of eyes in the meadow swivel my way and several people chuckle.

"That's not possible, Miss Blackwaters. A magical can't give another magical their power."

"I thought it was," I say.

The teacher shakes her head, and I'm about to get snarky when Winnie steps in to my rescue.

"Between fated mates it's possible, though, isn't it?" she says. "In fact, isn't it the process for sealing the fated bond?"

"That or boning," someone yells out.

The teacher looks longingly at Summer who is studying Tristan.

"Well, yes, technically it is possible between fated mates. But obviously those are rare and becoming rarer."

I stare down at my sneakers, a bee buffeting against my yellow laces. That hook in my stomach strains and I peer up into the sky-blue eyes of Tristan Kennedy.

I can't be feeling that right, can I? Maybe it's just his power. I hate to admit it, especially to the smug bastard himself, but he is far more powerful than anyone else out here in this meadow. I can sense his magic thrumming in the air. Raw. Brutal. Kind of entrancing. Is that what I'm feeling deep in my core?

"Find a space in the meadow, away from other pairs. It really is better if you don't have any distractions. And let's get started. This really is a case of giving it a go." Dr. Johnson waves her hands at us and most pairs head off eagerly to find a spot in the meadow, whispering about why they've been picked for each other.

I sigh and peer Tristan's way. He's still glaring at me, although he doesn't move. Neither do I.

"Come on, you two," Dr. Johnson says, giving my shoulder a nudge. "Off you go. Look there's a spot down there, by the edge of the meadow. A perfect spot."

"This is a load of–" Tristan begins. But, unlike Summer, Dr. Johnson seems to be one of the few teachers who doesn't think the sun shines out of Tristan Kennedy's ass.

"Very essential knowledge that a magical like you will find extremely beneficial one day, I'm sure. Your father and his brother are extremely skilled at this practice as I'm sure you are aware."

Something flashes in Tristan's eyes and then he's trudging down to the far side of the meadow.

I watch him go.

"Miss Blackwaters, if you want to avoid ending up in detention with me again, then I suggest you move your heinie!"

Reluctantly, I follow Tristan through the long grass and wildflowers; by the time I catch up with him, he's already lying out on the ground, his left elbow resting on one bent leg. He looks like something straight out of an aftershave commercial.

He refuses to look at me, twisting a blade of grass around his fingers instead.

I cross my arms and peer around the meadow, looking at all the other pairs linking hands, some enthusiastically, others with hesitation.

"You know, this is a big improvement, the not-talking-to-me. I think my quality of life is going to be greatly improved. Your father has done me a massive favor."

He snorts, winding the grass ever more tightly around his fingers, bleaching his fingertips white.

"Although I have to say, I'm surprised. I didn't take you for the type to obey orders."

His gaze leaps up to mine. "You really do talk a lot of bullshit, piggie. I don't know what the hell you're talking about most of the time."

I smirk at him. "If Daddy knew ..."

He lumbers to his feet and takes a stride towards me. "My father doesn't think you're worthy of my attention. I happen to agree with him. You're a speck of inconsequential dirt. I don't know what crap you pulled with my cousin, but I won't let you ruin our family name, the way you are going to ruin his life."

"If Azlan heard you speak like that to me ..." I whisper, the bond – that hook – yanking in my belly. Through the bond, I feel Azlan awaken once again, like he's aware of all the emotions this conversation is stirring in my mind.

Tristan throws back his head and laughs, a noise that causes the people nearest to us to look away from one another and towards us. "Azlan said as much to my face, Blackwaters. You think he's happy to be mated to a magical like you?"

His words hit me like a slap to the face.

I swallow it all down, not wanting him to see how much they smart me. But it's too late. He's seen. And now it's his turn to smirk at me.

"What? You seriously thought he was pleased?" He takes another step towards me until he's close enough that I can see the pulse jumping in his throat and the myriad of blues in his eyes. "You're a nobody," he hisses right into my words.

"I'm Rhianna Blackwaters," I hiss right back, and to my surprise he grabs my hands in his, electricity sparking from his skin to mine and my magic rearing up from the pit of my stomach to meet his.

"What are you doing?" I try to yank my hands away.

"Let's see what you've got then, Blackwaters."

My magic practically fizzes in my veins at the challenge.

"I'd rather eat shit than combine my magic with yours."

"Really?" he says, with another of those lazy smirks, "because I can feel your magic. It's practically salivating at the opportunity to touch mine." He closes his eyes.

"You're delusional," I say, except I can feel his magic too and as my eyes drift shut, I can see it as well. Blue like his eyes and swirling in the air. It's vivid and distinct, powerful. I screw up my brow. I don't understand how I can see this.

"Fuck," he mutters and I wonder if he's seeing something similar or whether I've somehow pissed him off just through the power of my existence.

My own magic reaches out to touch his, just as his does mine, and it's not something I'm controlling. It's something happening all by itself. As the prongs of mine collide with the throngs of his, my entire body shudders with pleasure and his hands shake in mine.

"What the fuck are you doing?" he growls, but he doesn't pull away.

"I'm ... I'm not doing anything," I whisper as our magic curls into one another, twisting and knotting together. His magic feels different to mine. Stronger, just like it looked.

But spikier, less stable, less steady. Like it might combust any second.

"What does mine feel like?" I ask. Because I want to know. I want all these questions about myself answered and maybe here is one he can.

"Dark," he whispers back. "Naïve."

"Growing," I say, the corners of my mouth tugging as my magic soars up into the air and his chases after. "Growing."

"You need to learn control," he says, gripping mine with his and dragging it back down towards the Earth.

I frown and attempt to shake him off, but his grip is tight, vise-like, and so are his hands.

"You're hurting me," I gasp.

"You think you're something special, Rhianna Blackwaters. Because Azlan Kennedy followed his dick instead of his brain. But you're not. You're weak. You'll always be weak. I could crush you if I wanted to."

I furrow my brow and with all my might, push back at him, tugging at the fingers of his grip. It starts to loosen, and he redoubles his effort, pushing with so much might, I yelp and sink to my knees.

"Stop," I plead, feeling my magic wane. "Please stop."

It grows weaker as his grows stronger and it's in that moment that it happens. A single drop of his magic leaves him and seeps into my veins.

I gasp and he throws my hands away, stumbling backwards so quickly, he trips before regaining his footing.

He shakes his head wildly, the neat locks of his fair hair shaking around his face. His eyes are wide, almost terrified, the blood drained from his skin. He's more moonlight than golden now.

"No!" he says.

I stare down at my hands. It was the merest of drops.

Tiny. Yet I can feel it swirling through my body like delicious poison, heating my blood, spinning that hook in my belly, causing my bond to reverberate.

I hear Azlan's voice loud in my ears.

Rhi?

What? Am I imagining it?

I bring my hands to my ears. Am I losing my mind?

His voice rings out again. My name over and over again.

Then I hear a different peal, the peal of laughter. I look up to find Summer and Aysha towering over me.

"See Aysh, I told you it would end in disaster." She adopts a look of feigned sympathy. "Did he fry your brains, Pig Girl? What do you expect when you play with someone a thousand times more powerful than you?"

I glance over to the spot where Tristan had been. He's no longer there. Flattened grass the only signs that he had been.

A thousand times more powerful? No he wasn't. He was stronger, but not for long.

Not for long.

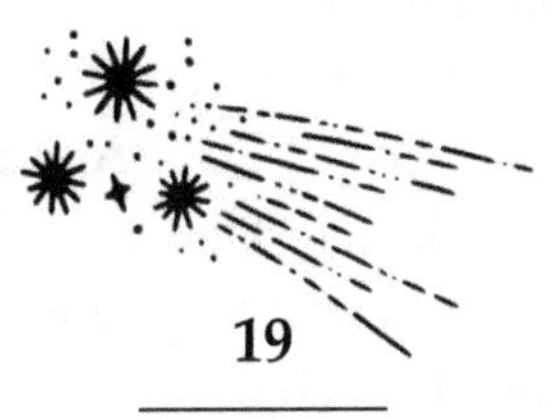

19

S pencer

SOMEHOW I MAKE it through another day, leg jigging uncontrollably all through class and dinner, my guts rolling and my insides churning, my bones aching with the desperate need to break free.

Afterwards, I stumble to my room, spilling my guts in the toilet bowl, my limbs shaking, my skin damp with cool sweat.

I force another pill down my throat. I stare at my stomach. I try to reason with my mind. Try to hush the turmoil building and building inside me.

My heart beats faster, louder, thumping against the confines of my skull. Loud like a war beat, like a warning of what's to come.

It's all useless. All fucking useless.

Why the hell did she come back?

I shouldn't have kissed her. Shouldn't have tasted her mouth. It's made everything worse. A million times worse. And I'm barely containing it all.

What the fuck was I thinking?

I don't even remember. I don't even recall the distance closing between us. Just my mouth on hers, her breath tangled with mine, my hand clasped around her throat.

It's haunting me. Obsessively. Making my gut spin.

I'd hoped with her gone, it would diminish. That slowly it would all fade. That I'd regain my fucking control on this.

But now she's back and it's worse than ever.

It's her scent. Her scent is different. And that smell – fuck, that smell – has everything inside me raging.

Because there's a masculine hint to her scent now. Something that doesn't belong to her.

She hinted at a boyfriend. But it's more than that. A lot more than that.

Fire and rage and flames burn.

I can't ... I can't handle this.

It's been too long and I can no longer control this. Can no longer hold back what lurks within.

I'm going to unleash it. I don't care about the rules of this college. Or the restrictions the authorities have placed on magicals like me. I don't care about any of the consequences.

The pills aren't working and my ability to fight this weakens day by day, hour by hour, fucking minute by minute.

If I don't stop fighting it, it will rip me apart.

As soon as darkness envelops the grounds, I'm out the door, wearing just an old pair of sweatpants and my sneakers, sprinting as hard as I can. The sweat soon pours down my brow and into my eyes. My arms and my legs burn. My lungs scream. I don't stop. I'm already losing it. Losing the control. The darkness inside me far blacker than the darkness of this night. And I haven't even reached the cover of the trees.

My path takes me right past her dorm, her scent hovering in the air like a goddamn tease, her shadow floating past her window.

I want to crash straight through the wall and taste every inch of her, hunt for the source of that goddamn scent.

It's too dangerous.

I'm losing it. Losing the control.

I need to get away.

I push on, towards the looming trees.

As I run, my bones crunch, my skin stretches. I force myself deeper into the forest, swerving left and right, then falling to my knees as the pain overcomes me.

My body is no longer my own.

Pain streaks through me, my vision flashes white. I dig my fingernails deep into the dirt, bite down hard on my tongue, force myself not to scream.

My skin rips, my bones grind, harden, reform. I snarl. My fingernails now claws, scraping at the ground, my feet now paws. My skull snaps as it lengthens and I lose it all. My mind plunges into a blackness I won't wake up from for hours.

I only hope I'm far enough away.

I RIP out from the boy's body. Free at last. No longer confined by a prison of flesh and sinew.

I land on four paws, stretching my limbs, tight and stiff from the months of ill-use.

The boy has grown stronger, better adept at holding me back, even though it brings a cost to himself.

He does not trust me. He fears I am the monster I most certainly am.

I curl my long tongue around my lips and taste the air: dank, wet, organic matter.

I drag my tongue over my fangs and my incisors, the edges as razor sharp as they have always been.

I lift a paw, then another and another, shake out my thick dark fur from the crown of my head to the tip of my tail. Then I flip back my head and howl. A noise that will have them shivering in their beds. As they should do.

I have no constraints like the boy. No concerns for the feeble lives of humans. I would as easily snap my jaws through the neck of a child as I would a rabbit's kit. Why should I care? It is they who keep me bound. Hidden away. Causing the boy a misery he can't describe. A burden they won't let him release.

It should not be this way. It was not this way in the past. We should be as equals, flicking between our two forms as day flicks to night and night to day. Two halves of the same globe. Dark and darker still.

The sound of my howl knocks against the ghostly trunks of the trees, alert and trembling in my presence. The sound amplifies, echoes, warning all the living creatures that I am here now.

I listen for a response. A call in return. And as always there is none. There are fewer and fewer of our kind now. Constrained and incarcerated. Hunted and persecuted. Wiped from the Earth.

He does well to keep me hidden. Even though it costs him dearly.

I prod at the ground with my front paw. Soft and doughy

from the rain. I sniff the air and there is the faintest trace of it. That scent. That of the girl's. The one that has driven both of us to distraction.

I growl lowly. The noise so sinister even the leaves on the trees, far above my head, tremble and fold in on themselves.

Then I run, racing through the forest at the speed of lightning, the fur on my head and my shoulders whipped back with the force, my paws barely pounding the ground as I speed through the trees.

I am going to find her.

I care not what the boy thinks. What he believes.

I care for none of it at all.

20

R^{hi}

BY THE END of the day I feel like I have a raging case of PMS. My skin is irritable, I can't sit still and I snap at Pip when he starts slobbering all over my leg when we return to our dorm after dinner.

Winnie side eyes me.

"What?" I say, hand on my hips.

"Nothing," she says, reaching down to tickle Pip's ears. Pip throws me a disgusted look, then busies himself lavishing Winnie with licks instead of me.

"I just don't feel like having pig slobber all over me tonight, okay?"

"She doesn't usually mind, does she?" Winnie says to Pip, scratching the spot under his chin that makes him dribble with delight. "And she doesn't usually throw a hissy fit when the meat is overdone and the potatoes soggy."

"It tasted like shit."

"It always tastes like shit."

I kick at a pair of balled of socks Pip must have snuffled from the wardrobe. "I'm in a bad mood, okay?"

"Because?"

I glare at her.

"Why don't you call him? Tell him to come over."

I consider insisting that the man in black is not the cause of my foul mood. But who am I kidding? And the incident with Tristan in the meadow has made everything worse. I don't know what any of that meant.

And what I think it does mean can't be right. It just can't be. It is another case of me misunderstanding. Of not knowing what I should know.

However, what I do know for sure is that the pull of my bond in my gut is driving me half mad.

"Firstly, I'm pretty sure he isn't allowed to 'just come over'," I say with even more irritation. "Secondly, it would start every tongue in this school wagging. Thirdly ..." I throw my hands up in the air.

"Tongues are already wagging. And since when did you care?"

I shrug. "I don't want to get him into trouble."

Winnie snorts. "I don't think the man in black worries about things like that. If you want him here, I'm pretty sure he'd break every rule and every door to get here."

I bite my lip. The idea of that making my insides turn hot.

Can he feel that through the bond too?

Oh jeez.

"You know," Winnie says, letting Pip climb onto her lap, "it's like this at the start regardless of whether there is a bond involved."

"What do you mean?"

"I mean when you're first with someone – first in love–"

"I'm not in love."

Winnie gives me a cynical look. "When you're at the start like this, you're so hot for one another you can't stop thinking about each other, can't keep your hands off each other. It's kind of addictive."

"Is it like that between you and Trent?"

"Rhi," Winnie says with a coy smile, "did you really think I needed that bathroom break in the last period?"

I stare at her. "Oh my god, Winnie, you are way more devious than I imagined."

"I can't help it," she says, sighing. "Like I said. It's addictive."

"It is," I say. Then I glance at my friend. "But ..."

"But?" she says, making kissy faces at Pip.

"Does it ... do you ..."

"You know you can ask me anything here, Rhi. I'm pretty sure I'm beyond shockable now."

"You're in love with Trent, right? And really hot for him?"

"Yeah."

I decide to just come out with it. "Doyoustillfeelhot-forotherguystoo?"

Winnie strokes Pip's ears, considering her answer. "Are we talking about Stone here?" she says.

"I just want to know. Is that normal? To be with one person, and still have feelings for someone else? Or am I a giant bitch?"

"You're not a bitch, Rhi. Everyone finds Stone hot. Even those of us in relationships. Even those of us with really, really hot fated mates."

"Hmmm," I say, sinking down onto the floor beside her. I

consider telling her about the sensations in my stomach. I consider telling her about what happened with Tristan. But I'm still not sure I didn't imagine it all. Or misread the sensations. Or misinterpreted what happened.

I go to stroke Pip's head, but he jerks it away and turns his back on me. "He's really good at holding a grudge," I say.

"No, I think he just loves me more than you now."

"I thought you hated having a pig around."

"We bonded while you were in hospital."

"Be careful, you'll end up with a name like mine."

"Can't be any worse than metal mouth. Or bean pole."

I laugh. "I've never heard anyone call you that."

"They used to. Then they found you to pick on instead."

"Terrific."

I groan, and tip my head back onto the bed behind me. "Do you think there is magic to stop me feeling this way?"

"About Stone?"

"About Azlan. I want him here so badly I could scratch my own eyes out."

"Was there anything in those articles?"

"No. I'd bet there'd be something in those library books though. Because I don't see how I'm meant to function like this and some clever magical must have come up with a solution."

"Maybe," Winnie says skeptically.

I jump to my feet. I bet those books would have some explanation about my encounter with Tristan too. About why the bond in my core hums sometimes when Azlan is nowhere to be seen.

"I'm going to see if the books are back, and if they're not, try and find out who took them. Wanna come, Pip?"

He snorts dismissively.

"He's my baby now," Winnie says, bending down to kiss him.

"Humph," I say, stomping out of the room.

The long summer nights have passed now, and though the air is warm, the grounds are dark, the path barely lit by floating bulbs along their edges, the full moon hidden behind whispery clouds. Behind the dorm building, the forest is eerily quiet, not even the wind whistles in the leaves, and the crunch of gravel under my feet sounds especially loud, the pounds of my heart in my chest even louder.

Is that the bond too? Sending my heart erratic?

The sound grows louder, the hook twisting and turning in my gut, and I consider reaching into my pocket and dialing Azlan's number. Or could I reach him through the bond? Beg him to come.

My ears fill with the pounding. Like a drum.

Thud thud thud.

Then, too late, I realize it isn't my heart at all. That thud, that pound, it's not coming from my chest, it's coming from the path behind me.

I spin on my toes, raising my hands, and I'm knocked clean off my feet, landing down hard on the path, the immense weight of a creature pinning me to the ground.

I try to scream but terror seems to freeze the sound in my throat and I stare up into a pair of glowing chestnut eyes, a huge snout, teeth like blades in a strong jaw and endless mounds of thick black fur.

The creature looks like a wolf, only it's easily three times the size, and though its face is that of a wolf's, there's something human about it too – the curve of the cheek, the intelligence in the eyes.

The creature snarls in my face, its teeth extending, drool

streaming from its mouth onto my face and its claws piercing the skin on my chest.

I can't move, my arms pinned by the weight of the creature, and if I attempt to shake him off, it'll have its fangs in my throat before I've even summoned my magic.

It continues to growl, the noise becoming angrier, then it lowers its snout, its warm breath brushing over my face. Its black nose quivers as it draws in breath. Then its eyes darken.

"You," it snarls.

And I'm not sure if I'm imagining the sound in my head. Or if the words really were said by this beast.

"Get off me," I say as calmly as I can. "And I won't hurt you."

"Hurt me?" The creature's lips curl in amusement, and it huffs through its snout. Then it lowers its jaw to my throat.

Now. Now I need to fight back, I have nothing to lose. It's going to kill me anyway. I squirm under its weight, its body immense and muscular, far larger than mine. It's hopeless. The thing pins me still, drawing the sharp points of its teeth down my throat.

"So pretty," it says. "So young, so delicate. No wonder you're driving him to distraction."

"Let me go!" I yell, not understanding the beast's words, hoping someone might hear me.

The beast's tongue hits my skin next; wet and warm, it glides up the column of my throat. "You taste so very good, little pet. Could lick you everywhere." The tongue slides higher over my chin and up my cheek. "Would you like that?"

I close my eyes. The beast's voice contrasts to its appearance. Silky and velvet in my ear. More magic? What is this thing? And how the fuck can it talk?

My magic sparks in my fingertips, ready, and the hook in my belly spins around and around. I search for something, anything. A way to free myself.

"Going to eat you, little pet."

I gasp in horror but then a force slams into us both and the beast is knocked off me. It whines, landing on its side and skidding across the gravel. As quick as a flash, it springs to its feet, though, standing up on its hind paws and growling in the direction of the assault. I scrabble backwards, trying to find my own feet, searching the darkness for whoever has come to save me.

No one. Nothing. Only darkness.

The wolf beast snarls, then launches itself forward, meeting something solid in the thin air. It snaps its jaw and magic flares in the air.

I hear a man groan, breath panting.

More magic sparks and I lift my hands to fire my own. But where? At what?

"I know you're there," the beast snarls, whimpering as magic singes the fur on its back, then running and locking its jaws around something I can't see.

Another groan. More magic.

My eyes flick around the scene, straining in the darkness, trying to make sense of the nonsense in front of me.

The wolf howls as magic hits its back leg. And then it's spinning, snapping, howling and growling, magic the color of blue swirling and sparking around it.

Then more pounding. I turn, arms raised ready for another attack, but it's Stone, sprinting towards me. He skids to a halt beside me, eyes swimming from me and then the beast as it continues its dance, dragged and cajoled towards the dark trees.

"Are you all right?" Stone pants, eyes darting over me. I nod and then he's following after the beast.

"Stone!" I scream.

"Get out of here, Rhi! Go to my office and lock yourself inside. Don't let anyone in but me."

"But Winnie? Pip?" I yell.

"Are not in danger. You are."

And then he's gone, swallowed by the trees, only the sparks of magic and the howl of the beast confirming I haven't imagined this whole episode.

I watch the sparks for several seconds but then I hear the sound of doors opening, people calling to one another.

I pick up my feet and run towards the looming shadow of the mansion, more and more lights switching on as I approach. I see Principal York and some of the other staff rushing from the door, and I step back into the shadows and let them pass. Then I dash inside, climbing the stairs two at a time, and race through into Stone's classroom and his office, slamming the door behind me, and casting a locking spell.

Then I drop into the chair at his desk and attempt to catch my breath.

What the hell just happened? What the hell was that thing? Another assassin sent by Lowsky?

I try to recall the creature's words. But they'd all been nonsensical to me, like a riddle that I'd never be able to solve.

My cell phone buzzes in my pocket. Winnie.

I answer the call.

"Rhi, are you okay? There's something going on in the woods."

"There is?" I feign innocence. I'm not sure I want to alarm my friend. "What's going on?"

"I don't know. Probably just two students taking a fight too far. It happens sometimes. There's staff everywhere."

"Maybe I'll stay here in the library then."

"Yeah, if I find out anything more, I'll let you know."

I hang up. Then check my messages.

One from Azlan. Sent several minutes ago.

Are you in danger?

I'm safe now, I reply, but no further messages are forthcoming, and I slump back in the chair and try to collect my thoughts. As I do my eyes stray to the books on the table.

Many of them.

All on the theme of Fated Mates.

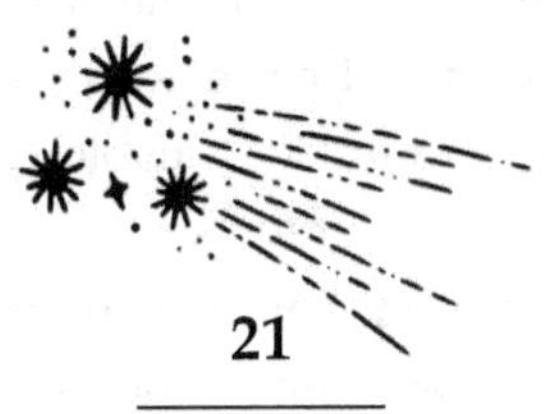

21

___

S tone

"Professor Stone!" the principal calls to me as I come striding out of the trees. She's surrounded by a line of staff members, stopping the students, many dressed in their pajamas, from entering the forest.

I walk towards her and she steps away from the others, not wanting our conversation to be overheard.

"What did you discover?"

"Nothing. Gone."

She straightens the collar of her jacket. "What was it?"

"A werebeast. It attacked Rhianna Blackwaters."

The principal peers out towards the trees. There have been attacks on the school before. It is nothing new to her. You can't house the children of the Republic without such threats. I doubt she's ever encountered a werebeast before, though. They're rare, deadly, restricted in many parts of the country.

"How did it get in?" I ask the principal. The school grounds are patrolled and protected by all sorts of security spells. A werebeast would be unable to wander in, even from the direction of the forest.

She doesn't answer, and her thoughts are securely protected behind a wall – one I could break if I wanted to, but not without a fight.

"We had better gather the students up. Ensure everyone is accounted for," she says eventually.

"I'm going to go and check on Miss Blackwaters."

The principal nods, already turning to the staff members behind her.

I stride quickly along the path, breaking out into a run when the voices behind me fade. By the time I reach my closed office door, I'm out of breath, my brow damp with sweat, my t-shirt clinging to my chest.

"Rhianna!" I shout, thumping on the door.

"Stone?" she says, her voice slightly muffled by the panel of wood that separates us. "Is that you?"

"Yes?"

"How can I know for sure?"

I swear under my breath. "Just open the goddamn door."

"Not until you–"

"Remember when I chained you to the bed the first night–"

The door swings open. "That was a dickhead thing to do."

I smirk at her, eyes darting over her body. Thin red lines scrape down her throat and she stinks of dog.

"You smell disgusting," I say, grimacing.

She scowls at me. "You're not exactly smelling like roses yourself, Professor."

I push my way inside, eyes straying to my books on the desk.

"Are you hurt?" I ask, closing the book that lies open behind my back.

Her eyes flick to my desk too.

Crap! She wants to ask me about the books. She also wants to know about the beast.

"It was a werebeast," I say, diverting her attention away from my books. "I'm assuming you don't know what one is."

She shakes her head. And I sense her frustration.

Another thing to add to the list of stuff she knows fuck all about.

"It looked just like a wolf – a giant wolf – but it seemed ... almost ... human."

"Because a werebeast can shift between human form and beast form."

"It spoke to me."

"What did it say?"

She shakes her head. "How could it speak?"

"I told you, it's half human."

"Who was it? Was it ..."

The image of Renzo Barone glows in her mind and my hands clench into fists.

"Renzo Barone is not a werebeast."

"But that creature was sent by the Wolves Of Night. Another assassin from Marcus Lowsky."

"The beast said that?"

She frowns. "No, but it attacked me."

I land my hand on her shoulder and tilt her head to one side, examining the scratches on her throat. They aren't deep, but they glow red in the dim light of my office.

"Are there more?" I ask.

"Yes."

"Show me."

She shakes her head. "I'm fine."

"This was a werebeast. Any wounds need treatment and healing."

"I can go to the infirmary."

"No."

"Or Azlan can–"

"Show me. Stop wasting my time."

She gives me another of those scowls, all furrowed brow and spitting eyes. The kind of bratty look that has my guts spinning and my cock – fuck.

"Fine," she huffs, shaking off my grip and reaching for the hem of her shirt. Carefully she pulls it over her head and then she's standing in my office in only her denim shorts and her fucking bra.

I swallow. There are puncture wounds across her chest, over her collarbone and her rib cage. One by her right shoulder. A shoulder that lifts and falls with her breath, her fucking tits doing the same.

I try my damn hardest not to look. But, fuck it, even Azlan fell. A man one hundred times more respectable and restrained than me.

And so my gaze trails down her form, over the perfect curves of her breasts. The bra she's wearing is white and lacy and see-through, the pink of her nipples clear through the material.

I drag my eyes away and stride towards the far cupboard in my office.

I can hear her breath loud in the space between us as I search through bottles on the shelf, finding were-weed and tugging off the stopper. Then I search for cotton wool, finding some in an old first aid kit I suspect the previous owner of this office left behind.

"It's going to hurt," I tell her, tipping the bottle right over, so that the vivid green liquid sinks into the waiting cotton bud.

"What is that?"

"Were-weed to ensure the werebeast curse does not enter your bloodstream."

"What?! What curse?"

Her eyes widen with shock, and I shake my head making her feel small and stupid again.

Shit, I don't like doing that, my stomach aches every goddamn time. But it's necessary. For the best. It's better if she hates me. We don't belong together. Fate is cruel. It would end in disaster.

"Werebeasts were normal humans once, until they were cursed, cursed to live their lives half human, half beast. The curse can pass from generation to generation or it can afflict a magical if it enters the bloodstream."

"Why the hell have I never heard any of this before?" she asks, reaching out to take the swab from my hand.

"You don't know the words for the spell," I say, shooing away her hand. "Werebeasts are extremely rare these days. And the few that remain are restricted and controlled."

"How did one get into the school, then?"

"I don't know, but I intend to find out." My hand hovers above her skin. Pale like moonlight. "Ready? It's going to hurt."

She bites down on her lip, her eyes steely with determination. She nods.

I press the cotton wool against the wound, whispering the old incantation, my eyes not leaving hers. She tenses, bites down harder on her lip, pinching it between her teeth. But she doesn't cry out, doesn't complain.

She's harder, stronger than she looks. I should know that by now.

"Okay?" I ask when it's done. Relief floods her face and I dab tenderly at the wound with the cotton wool, watching as it heals. "Next one," I tell her.

She takes a steadying inhale, then nods, and I press the cotton wool against the puncture wound on her chest, right above the curve of her breast. I can feel her soft skin quivering beneath my fingertips, can hear the whistle of her breath between her teeth, can smell the sweet tinge of her scent beneath all that dog.

She was a skinny thing when we first picked her up. All skin and bones. There's more meat to her now. A lot more meat. My fingers twitch as I say the old words. I want to touch more of her.

"Done?" she asks when my mouth stops moving.

I jerk out of my reverie, checking the wound is healed and moving to the next one.

When I've healed all the wounds on the front of her body, I make her turn around slowly for me, checking there are no more, seeing that there is plenty more fat on that ass of hers now, those denim shorts of hers grown tight and frankly, obscene.

"There are no more," I say, dragging my gaze back to her face. Her cheeks are all pink, her lips pink too and wet. I stay the hell away from her thoughts, even though I'm curious as hell. "Let's do the scratches on your neck. They are going to hurt the most."

"Shit," she mutters, and I take hold of her arm and bring her closer to me. Automatically she looks up into my face, tilting back her chin and it would be so easy to kiss her right now. So easy, like stepping off a ledge and falling. I sweep her dark hair away from her face and her neck, tucking it behind her ear, the small shell littered with three silver stars. Her body is still and for once she holds her tongue, holds her breath too. Gently, I tilt her head to one side. She swallows.

I examine the wounds on her neck. The red scrapes were not made by claws.

"What caused these?"

"Its teeth."

Teeth. It dragged its teeth down her throat. I swallow. Imagining it. Imagining doing the same.

Fuck!

I hesitate. Then press the new piece of cotton wool against the start of the wound, trailing it down the long column of her throat, over the place where her pulse dances. She winces, closing her eyes.

"You're all right," I tell her softly. "Nearly there."

I mutter the words, my magic humming in my fingers, on my tongue, the proximity of her making my blood sing.

The red lines fade, disappearing into the pink of her flesh, and I can't help brushing my fingers down the place where they were. Checking, just checking. She closes her eyes, and sighs.

My grip on her arm tightens.

"Rhianna, I–"

There's a thump on the door. Loud and insistent.

"Rhi! Stone! Are you in there?"

Azlan.

I drop my grip and she opens her eyes, gazing first at me and then the door.

"Yeah, we're in here," I say, my voice back to its I-don't-give-a-shit tone. "No need to break the fucking door down."

I wave my hand and the door springs open. Azlan comes crashing through the doorway. Eyes half-wild.

"Are you hurt?" he asks her, then turns to me. "Is she hurt?"

"Not badly," I say. "A few grazes. I've already treated them with were-weed."

Azlan's shoulders sag. "Thank you." Hesitantly, he steps towards the girl, reaching for her hand and linking his finger through hers. It's the most intimate thing I've ever seen my best friend do. A man who is usually all coldness, efficiency and professionalism. It's too much and I have to look away.

Fuck, I knew this would be hard. But not this hard.

"What happened?" Azlan asks.

"I was heading to the library–"

"Alone, after dark?" Azlan growls.

She rolls her eyes and I'm glad I'm not the only one treated to that bratty behavior.

"This school is meant to be the safest place for me. Remember? Anyway, it came out of nowhere, knocked me off my feet and pinned me to the ground."

"You fought it off?" Azlan asks, sounding proud.

"No, I couldn't, it had my arms pinned."

I scoff. "You can't use your magic with your hands pinned?"

"Most magicals can't," Azlan says, jumping to her defense. "How did you get away?"

She hesitates, shaking her head slowly. "Something helped me."

"Something?" I say.

"I couldn't see what it was. It knocked the beast off me and then they were fighting. I couldn't see what it was."

"Because it was dark?"

"No, because … it wasn't there."

Azlan stares at her.

"It doesn't make any sense," I mutter.

"I know," she snaps. "But there was this other time, before, in the forest. Something I couldn't see attacked me then too."

We are all silent.

"I'll look into it," I say, peering at Azlan.

"How did a werebeast get into the school?" Azlan asks.

"I don't know. But I will find that out too," I say.

"Come on, Rhi. I'm taking you back to mine," Azlan says. The girl frowns. "It isn't safe here."

I snort. "She's safer here than anywhere else."

"A werebeast just broke into the grounds and attacked her, Phoenix!"

"I'm not leaving the school," she insists. "It's gone now, hasn't it?"

I peer at my friend. "It hasn't been found, but York will be doubling security as we speak."

"I'm not leaving you here with that thing still out there, especially if we don't know whether it was sent to kill you or not."

Rhi's gaze falls to the floor. "I don't think it was going to kill me. If it was going to, I don't think I'd be standing here with my throat intact."

I think of those scrape marks on her throat. I see the beast's face in her mind's eye.

"Does Marcus Lowsky have weapons like werebeasts?" I ask.

"Lowsky has all sorts of weapons," Azlan says dismissively. "I'm not leaving you here alone and unguarded."

I try not to bristle at his words. I was there, right there, saving her neck. I healed her wounds. I am looking out for her, despite my own best goddamn interests.

"I'm not leaving," she says again with even more force this time.

"Then I guess I'm staying," Azlan says, glaring right back at her.

"I thought the Chancellor is sending you out West?"

"West?" Rhi says.

"Not yet."

"Fuck," I say. I've never known Azlan be so dismissive about an order before. "Did you not hear me say the principal will be doubling security? York won't let you stay, Azlan."

"She doesn't have to know about it."

"You don't exactly fade into the background, man."

Rhi giggles and goddamn it, if that cold-hearted bastard doesn't smile right back at her. I might actually vomit.

"Stone's right," she says. "You don't and I'm in enough trouble as it is."

"This isn't a negotiation," Azlan says.

"And you don't get to tell me what to do."

I sigh. "You can stay with me, Azlan." My friend nods, then opens his mouth to speak. "No, Miss Blackwaters cannot stay at my place too, so don't even ask."

I frown and march towards the door. I may be his best friend. I may be prepared to do a lot of things for that man. But listening to the two of them going at it in my guest room, no. No way.

22

R^{hi}

WE FOLLOW Stone out of the mansion and onto the path. The campus is eerily quiet and I'm assuming everyone has been ordered to their rooms.

When we hit the gravel path, we part ways, Stone walking on alone and Azlan and I walking towards my dorm.

"You're really okay, Rhianna?" he asks, when we reach my building. My name in his mouth sounds oddly tender, like maybe he really does care about me, and isn't simply bound by some fate of fortune.

"I'm okay," I say.

He slides his ungloved hand into my hair in that way that has my knees buckling and my insides spinning.

"I don't like this. I don't like being apart from you.

Feeling all your emotions through the bond, not under-standing what they mean."

I sigh. God, I don't like it either. Every fiber of my body wants us to be together. But I need to understand who I am and I need space to do that.

He strokes his thumb over my cheekbone. It's rougher, more calloused than Stone's – the thought of the professor's touch on my skin making my heart beat even faster.

It's so confusing, all of this. I have a fated mate. A fated mate I am damn hot for. So damn hot I'd get down on my hands and knees right here on the path for him if he asked. And yet, minutes ago my body was shaking with anticipa-tion, hoping the professor would kiss me.

I am one hell of a bitch.

"What's wrong?" he asks, sensing my unease through the bond.

"I'm just keen to get back to my room to check if Pip and Winnie are okay."

He examines my face. Does he believe me?

I don't know but he kisses me nonetheless, a kiss which contains as much tenderness as his tone. I'm not used to such tenderness from him. From anyone but Pip.

"Be careful," he says as I pull away, my head and my heart even more confused.

"Me? How about you? You're meant to be going on a mission to the West, not staying here with me. The Chancellor–"

"It'll be fine," he says stiffly, but I don't believe him. I don't think the Chancellor is a man who takes kindly to disobedience. "You don't need to worry about me. You need to concentrate on keeping yourself safe."

"You think Stone was wrong? You think that werebeast was meant for me?"

"I don't know but either way be careful, Rhi, and if you need me–"

"I'll be fine," I say, striding away before I change my mind and beg him to take me home with him.

I try not to think of him or Stone as I walk into the dorm, the werebeast and his words entering my head instead. Was it really just a coincidence that it was me it attacked? Because my life has been full of coincidences like that and I'm not so sure I believe in them anymore.

The room is dark when I return and find Pip curled up on the end of Winnie's bed, both sleeping peacefully like there isn't some deranged beast on the loose.

Winnie stirs as I undress.

She yawns. "Jeez, have you been in the library all this time?"

"Uh huh," I say, wondering if I'm doing the right thing lying to Winnie like this. Probably not. I resign myself to come clean.

"Wow, it must have been a really good book. You missed out on all the fun down here."

She yawns and rolls over, promptly falling back into sleep.

I guess I'll have to tell her in the morning.

I climb up on my bed and try to ignore the gnawing hook in my belly. It's impossible, the sensation only growing worse the longer I lie there. My thoughts become entangled. The werebeast, Stone, the man in black, Tristan. That nagging feeling that everyone knows more than me. Especially Stone and Azlan.

It's then I remember those books in Stone's room. The missing books. The books on fated mates. I'd barely had time to flick through them before Stone had returned to his office, but I could see the pages he'd marked and the notes he'd made.

Why the hell would Stone be studying up on fated mates? For Azlan? For himself?

Azlan knew about the bond long before me. Has Stone known that long too? And what the hell was he looking for in the pages of those books?

I decide I'm fed up with secrets. There were so many questions I should have asked my aunt while she was alive. I'm not making that mistake again.

If this is more than a crush with Stone, I need to know. I need to understand what it can mean.

I throw back the covers, and in the dark pull on my jeans and a hoodie.

Outside, the dark and the silence are even more oppressive, the forest still quiet. I half expect the werebeast to jump out at me from the shadows again.

Well, let it try. Because I am pissed off and bristling for a fight.

If York has upped security, it's pretty ineffectual, because no one spots me on the path through the dormitory buildings. No one stops and questions me as I pass through the gardens, the Venus common room dimly lit from within, and duck though the line of sycamore trees. I've never been to Stone's room before but I've heard him and Azlan describe it as a cabin on the edge of the grounds and there's only one of those marked on the map.

As I emerge from the trees, I spy the outline of it through the gloom and then the low tenor of voices. I pause, squinting through the dark. Some kind of decking runs around the small cabin and Stone and Azlan sit together talking, one lone candle flickering by their feet.

Something makes me stop. I don't call out to them, don't

let them know I'm there. Instead, I hug the shadows of the trees and creep closer, listening.

Maybe it's really stupid listening in to their conversation. Maybe I know deep down in my heart no good will come of it. But my damn curiosity gets the better of me. Especially when I hear my name.

"This situation is fucked up and freaking unbearable," Stone says, his feet resting on an upturned crate in front of him.

"You think it's easy for me?" The man in black looks out towards my direction, rubbing at his stomach.

"I can see inside the girl's head, dickwad. I'm aware there are some considerable upsides to your current situation."

"I'm more than ten years older than her. I feel like a pervert every time I lay my hands on her."

"And yet you keep laying your hands on her," the professor growls.

Azlan doesn't respond to that, simply drags his hand over his face.

"Let's just agree not to discuss it, okay?" Stone says. "I don't actually want to know. Tell me something else instead. Tell me you've found out more about her mother."

I smother a gasp with my hands. My mother? What the hell?

I want to crash through the clearing and demand answers from them, but I know they won't give them to me. I know they'll claim they know nothing. So I keep myself hidden.

Azlan shakes his head. "Only as much as I told you. The file in the Chancellor's office wasn't a complete one. I need to search the archives, but it's bound to be classified."

"Even for the Enforcer?"

"Even for me."

"Your father? Your uncle?"

Azlan chuckles bitterly. "For my uncle probably not. But do you think he'd seriously help us?"

Stone considers this for a moment. "No, he'd use it against us."

"Exactly. If, as we suspect, her mother was some kind of asset, sought after by both sides, he'd be after Rhi. Just like Lowsky."

"Just like the Chancellor," Stone says quietly.

"We don't know that for sure. We don't even know if he is aware of the link between the two women. They look alike but–"

"You were sure though?"

"I've had a lot of time studying her face. It had to be her mother."

I don't hear any more because my ears start to buzz with the words I have heard, so loudly I clench my teeth together against it.

Azlan looks up towards the trees again.

"What is it?" Stone asks, peering my way as well.

I turn and run, not caring if they hear me, not caring if they see me.

More lies. More secrets.

Stone tried to break into my mind.

The man in black forced me from my home.

I should never have trusted them. Ever.

Fate may have chosen Azlan as my mate. But fate can go to hell.

I'm at my dorm, bursting through the doorway before I know it, hardly aware of the journey I just made, a million thoughts crashing through my mind.

"What is it?" Winnie says, sitting up in bed and cracking

her head against the bunk above, Pip waking up too and snorting loudly.

"I'm leaving," I say, pulling my bag from the wardrobe and stuffing my clothes inside.

"Leaving? You only just got back. Where are you going?" Winnie asks, swinging her feet to the ground. "Back to the man in black's house?"

"No, back to mine," I say, stuffing my phone and some books into my bag for good measure and beckoning towards Pip.

"Your home? Back in the wastelands? Why on Earth–"

"I need answers, Winnie. I need to know who the hell I am. I need to know who my mom was. Who my dad was. Why the hell my aunt was so determined to keep me hidden. I'm sick of knowing nothing about myself."

"And you think you'll find those answers back at your home?"

"I know I will," I say, thinking of my aunt's locket. The more and more I consider it, the more certain I am there are answers waiting for me inside. I was just too dumb to think of it before.

Winnie tiptoes over to me cautiously, placing her hand on my shoulder. "I understand, Rhi. It must be awful having all these unanswered questions." I nod, wiping hot tears from my cheeks. "But can't this wait until the morning? It's the middle of the night and there's a werebeast out there somewhere."

"It has to be tonight," I say. "If I wait until the morning, they'll try to stop me."

"Who will?"

"Azlan. Stone. York. The freaking Chancellor."

Winnie squeezes my shoulder. "Okay, okay, but how are you going to get there?" I know what she's doing. Trying to make me see reason. But I don't want to. I want answers. And this time, no one – and no thing – is going to stop me from having them.

"I'll steal a bike. I'll steal Azlan's bike."

"It's two days' drive away. They'll catch you before you get half way."

"They won't," I insist, crouching down and opening my arms to Pip. He peers up at Winnie, clearly unsure what to do, but he's my pig and he's damn loyal, and so he trots over and lets me scoop him up into my arms.

"Rhi, are you even aware of the reputation of your mate? If he wants to catch you, he will. Wouldn't you be better off waiting and talking to him about this? I'm sure he'd take you if he knew how much this meant to you."

"He's keeping secrets from me, Winnie," I say, more tears cascading down my face, tears Pip licks away with his tongue. "He never told me we were fated mates. And he knows stuff about my mom he's keeping from me too."

"Oh," Winnie says, squeezing my shoulder, "oh sweetie, I'm so sorry."

For a moment, I almost succumb to the temptation to let her hold me in her arms while I cry on her shoulder. But I sniff, blowing hard through my teeth.

"Please don't talk me out of this, Winnie. I need to do this."

"Okay," she says, "I won't."

"Thank you."

"And I'm coming with you."

"What?" I say, nearly dropping Pip in my surprise.

"I'm coming with you. We'll take my car."

I gape at her in disbelief. My friend who nearly fainted from fear when she was summoned to the principal's office is prepared to break a load more rules to help me out.

"I can't let you do that, but seriously, what? You have a car?"

"Yes, I have a car. How else did you think I got to college? Flew on my broomstick?"

"You never mentioned it before," I mutter.

Winnie strides over to the wardrobe, wheeling out her little overnight case and tossing clothes inside.

"Winnie, you can't come with me."

"I can," she says, sounding determined. "I'm not letting you go alone."

"Winnie, even if I let you, there's even more chance of being caught in a car than on a bike. The bike can travel at least five times as fast."

"Not this car." She snaps her case shut. "It's had certain ... erm ... magical upgrades. Upgrades that may not be quite ... technically .... legal."

"Winnie Wence, who are you and what did you do with my best friend? You own an illegally-tampered-with car?"

"It was my cousin's. My mom doesn't know about the upgrades."

"Your cousin sounds like he is a badass.

"*She* is."

"And how fast can this car go, then?"

Winnie shrugs her shoulders. "I don't know. I've been way too worried about getting into trouble to go anywhere near the upgrades."

"Then maybe–"

"But now I have an excuse," she says, holding out her hand to me.

"What about Trent?" I say.

"I'll message him. Come on, are we doing this or not?"

I look down at her outstretched hand, thanking every god and every lucky star that I've made a friend like Winnie.

"Yes, we're doing it."

We set off down the path, Winnie hauling her suitcase into her arms because the wheels are damn squeaky. Halfway, we hear boots crunching gravel and duck behind a bush, waiting until Dr. Johnson and another teacher pass us on the path. If they're meant to be undertaking centurion duty, they're not making a very good job of it. Both of them are too engaged in their conversation to spy us crouching in the dark. When they're out of sight we hurry on.

"Where's the car?" I ask Winnie.

"There's an underground parking lot underneath the gymnasium."

"There is?"

"Yeah," she says, "it's mostly full of pretentious sports cars and owned by the rich kids. My car looks pretty pathetic parked among them. But hey," she elbows me, "my car can go a hell of a lot faster than theirs."

I smile at her through the darkness. Maybe a bit of rule breaking is proving a good thing for Winnie.

When we reach the gymnasium, she points to a side door and then to the road that curves round towards the mansion.

"You wait here, ensure the coast is clear. I'll go fetch the car," Winnie says.

"Shouldn't we both go get the car?" I ask, peering around.

"You need to keep an eye out for any patrolling teachers." She strokes her hand down my arm. "Will you be all right? Are you worried about that werebeast? I think that–"

"I'm not worried. You go. I'll buzz your phone if there's any danger."

"I won't be long," Winnie says, inputting a code on the door and disappearing inside.

I lower Pip to the ground and swing my gaze around in the darkness, my ears alert for any sound.

"What are you doing out here, Blackwaters?" a voice says from behind me and I nearly jump out of my skin.

Tristan Kennedy.

Crap.

I turn to face him and at first I can't find him, not until he steps out of the shadows and then his undeniable form emerges through the gloom.

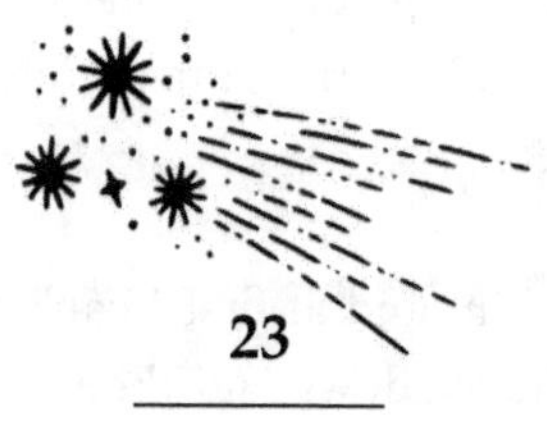

23

T ristan

"ARE you dumb as well as stupid?" I ask her as she stares up into my face.

"Neither," she hisses back.

I snort. "There's a werebeast on the loose and you're out of bed. Alone. In the middle of the night. Do you have a death wish?"

"The only wish I have is for you to leave me alone. Go away, Tristan. Daddy said you weren't allowed to talk to me, remember?"

"I'm your head of house and I have a right to know what you're doing and where you're going."

"Who says I'm going anywhere? Maybe I'm just enjoying a midnight stroll."

I jerk my head towards the door her friend just ducked inside. "You leave the campus, they'll expel you."

"Isn't that what you want?"

"I'm just informing you of the facts, Pig Girl."

"Why? Are you planning on snitching on me again?"

Probably not, but I haven't decided whether I'm going to let her go either. It isn't safe. And I don't know what she is up to.

What the hell does she think she's doing? And where the hell is my cousin?

I take a step towards her and the dim light from the moon overhead falls across my face.

She gasps, the indignation and hatred falling from her features as she stares at me in horror.

My face must be pretty bad. It feels pretty bad, but I haven't exactly had the opportunity to look in the mirror.

"Your face!" Without even realizing it, she takes a step towards me, like she's being pulled there by some invisible force. She reaches up to touch my cheek and I duck my head away from her. Suddenly aware of her own actions, she frowns and snatches her hand back to her side. "Why haven't you healed it? Do you want me to–"

I snort. "And end up with a deformed face, no thank you. I'm on my way to the infirmary to have it looked at."

"Can't fix it yourself?" she says. "The all-powerful Tristan Kennedy. I thought it was a simple spell."

I grab her arm and tug her forward. She squeals, my fingers tight on her arm. The connection causes sparks to run down my fingers and I can feel her energy again, like I could in the meadow. Only this time, hers far surpasses mine.

"You really are an ignorant, little pig. Some things you shouldn't play with yourself."

"Like your beautiful face?" she says, her voice dripping with sarcasm.

I smirk at her. "You think my face is beautiful?"

"Let go of me, before I blast another hole in your face."

Her pig appears from nowhere and starts to butt his snout against my ankles.

"What the hell?" I yell. "Get off."

I go to swing my foot back, and the pig girl punches me right in the ribs. Usually, her feeble attempts would hardly register. But my face wasn't the only thing to take a pounding and I wince in pain.

"Don't you dare drop kick my pig, you asshole," she says.

"Then tell it to stop dry-humping my leg."

"You wish," she spits.

I glare at the creature and make a thing of swinging my foot back again. The girl growls, attempting to hit me a second time as I hold her at bay. The pig whimpers and scurries to hide behind her legs. Some guard dog he is.

When my ankles are safe from sexual assault, I swing her back around to face me.

"Where are you going?" I say. She grinds her teeth together and doesn't answer. I scoff. The girl really is growing too big for her britches. She needs to be brought down a peg or two, be reminded of who she is talking to. "What? You think you get to ignore your head of house when he's talking to you? You think you're special now just because you're sucking the Enforcer's cock?"

She flinches and her cheeks sizzle in the moonlight. It was just some shitty line. I've been trying my fucking best not to think about the two of them together. The girl had virgin practically written across her forehead. And now ... Seems I hit a raw nerve. Seems sucking his cock is exactly how she's been spending her time.

My stomach swims with nausea, ties itself in a fucking knot.

Am I jealous?

Of her? Of him?

No.

"Don't congratulate yourself. I doubt you're any good at it, little Pig Girl. You should have taken the opportunity to suck cock in the locker room while you had the chance. Then maybe you would be good at it."

"You are such a sexist–" She peers down at the small animal cowering behind her legs.

"Pig?" I say, with another smirk.

Her phone chirps in her pocket and we both glance down at it, reaching for it at the same time. My hand lands on her hip, the denim tight, my fingers grappling at the curved flesh there. Her own hand lands over mine.

It has that knot twisting harder.

"Tell me where you're going," I say, my voice dangerous now.

"I can feel it," she says, her voice low and sinister too, the tone making my pulse leap with excitement. "How low your magic is." She tilts her head to one side. "How about a trade? I'll tell you where I'm going, if you tell me what happened to your face and your powers?" My jaw clenches. "Yeah, I didn't think so."

Then without warning, she grips my fingers and sends a blast of energy at me. I curse, too weak to block it, and the force causes me to stumble away.

The little pig grunts in satisfaction and the girl lifts her hands in front of her body.

"You want a hole in your stomach like Spencer, come at me again. Otherwise leave me alone. It's none of your business what I'm doing or where I'm going."

She's right. It isn't. It shouldn't be. But I've never wanted to know anything so badly.

"You're going to regret this, little pig."

She shrugs one shoulder and hooks her phone out of her pocket. "Probably," she says to me, before bringing the phone up to her ear. "All clear," she says, into the cell.

I clench my jaw hard, my molars straining. My fingers twitch. But there's not enough in the tank. And she knows it.

I could raise the alarm. I could call my cousin. I'm certain he has no fucking clue his mate is sneaking away in the middle of the goddamn night. But I'm not going to do any of those things.

I'm going to stand and watch as a red car – that looks like it's held together with sticky tape – comes crashing out of the underground garage. I'm going to stand and watch as the girl picks up her pig and dives into the passenger seat, the car revving, the headlights cutting out.

I'm going to stand and watch as the girl waves over her shoulder at me and then the car is gone. Just like that. One second there, the next second, poof.

I stare at the place it occupied.

This isn't my concern. None of my business. My father said to stay away from this girl.

This is my cousin's mess to sort, not mine.

I stalk towards the mansion. I need to see the matron. I've already wasted vital minutes dealing with that girl. I can't waste anymore.

I peer up at the principal's office as I draw closer to the mansion. Her light shines through the window. I could go tell her what I've just witnessed.

But I'm already going to have enough questions to answer. Enough trouble to deal with.

I don't need to add to my shit. The girl can look after herself.

And that knot in my stomach? It can go to hell.

24

R^{hi}

I CLING TO MY SEAT, Pip burying his face in my stomach as the car hurtles along, the scenery blurring into one continuous dark line outside the window.

"Jeez, this car really can go fast," I say, gulping down a scream as we career round yet another bend.

"I know. Isn't it awesome?" Winnie says, her eyes and her face both wild with excitement. "Now I understand what Clem meant. This is nearly as good as sex."

"I don't know. I never felt like my stomach was being dragged five miles behind me during sex."

"Really?" Winnie says, eyes darting from the windscreen in a manner that has me closing my eyes and praying to the gods. "Not even with that huge dick of his?"

"Winnie," I wail, "please look at the road."

"Relax, Rhi," she says cheerfully, tugging hard on the gear stick. "I know what I'm doing."

"Tell that to the squirrel you nearly hit several miles back."

"I was nowhere near it," she tuts. "I never took you for such a drama queen, Rhi."

Pip moans and I pat his head in a manner I hope he finds reassuring. He stops quivering but refuses to look up from my lap. I don't blame him. I've never been on a fairground ride but I bet this is what it's like. Only those rides last a matter of minutes. We've been driving for five hours straight, the faintest hint of dawn now crawling over the horizon in the distance.

"How much further do you think it is?" I ask, examining all the symbols and lights on the dashboard, all of them meaningless to me. I glance out at the lightening scenery instead. But everything is too blurry for me to determine if I recognize anything yet.

Winnie peers at the display. "It says we're still an hour away."

"Okay," I say, squaring my shoulders. I can do this. Besides, we're going to make it here in half the time it should have taken. That gives us a head's start on the man in black, and anyone else who tries to follow us.

Exactly an hour later, when I'm just about thinking I'll never be able to dig my fingernails out of the seat cushion, the car slows dramatically.

"What's going on?" I ask Winnie.

"I think we're here," Winnie says as we both stare out of the window.

The sun is hovering well above the horizon now, making the light all hazy and golden. The road ahead lies empty and beyond I can make out the first few run-down buildings of my home town.

"Does this look right?" Winnie asks.

"Yeah, this is it," I say, sliding down low in my seat.

"What are you doing?" Winnie asks.

"Hiding," I say.

Winnie frowns. "Why?"

"There's a price on my head, and I don't trust the people in this town not to shop me in."

"A price on your head? My God, Rhi, what did you do?"

I peek up at my friend. I've been hiding too much from her. It's about time I came clean. On most things anyway. I just hope she's still willing to be my friend when she learns the truth.

I explain everything to her as we weave through the town, just as desolate, just as crappy, as it always was, and drive out to the forest, plunging into its green depths and on towards my home.

"Wow," Winnie says, as we bounce down the old track, the clearing so close I can almost smell it. "That is a ... lot." She's quiet for a moment taking it all in. "How come you never told me all this before?"

"Just admitting I was unregistered nearly gave you a stroke, Winnie."

She grimaces. "Yeah, you're right. I'm sorry about that."

"You don't need to be sorry. I'm the one who's been less than liberal with the truth."

"I understand why you weren't."

"You do?" I say, amazed my best friend can be so understanding all the time. I wish I could be more like her.

"Yeah. There haven't been many people you could trust in your life, Rhi." She slows the car down as the track narrows and I point out the thinning in the trees. "I'm kind of touched that you trust me enough."

"You're my best friend, Winnie." I chuckle. "Well, actually you're my only friend–" Pip snorts loudly. "My only *human* friend."

"You're my best friend too, Rhi."

"How about Saskia?" I say with a little jealousy.

"You know, she hasn't messaged me once since she left school. I guess we weren't as close as I thought."

"Here," I say, as we pass through the gap in the trees and out into the sunlit meadow, my old house crouching in one corner.

The beam above the door is still broken, several of the windows smashed, and the chicken-run trampled to pieces. But to my surprise – and yeah to my relief – the place is still standing.

"It looks cute," Winnie says, pulling up outside, "and homely."

"It was," I say, opening the door and letting Pip scuttle out to do his business.

I don't follow him. Instead, I feel through the air for any magicals, but the only presence I can feel is Winnie's. Then cautiously, I step out of the car, my muscles and bones sore from the long drive. I roll my shoulders and my neck, not walking up to the front door, but circling around the house instead, observing the damage done to the old place.

There are no signs of any chickens. Only a few brown feathers are floating around the yard. The back door has been kicked in and my bike is a burned-out husk at the back of the place.

Winnie follows me, tutting and sighing as she surveys the damage too.

"I'm sorry, Rhi."

"It's okay. It's better than I thought it would be."

At the front door, I hesitate, then step inside. It doesn't smell like it used to. No incense curling its way through the house. No herbs simmering on the stove. None of my aunt's floral perfume floating through the rooms. Instead it stinks of damp, mud and men. There are dirty footprints running up and down the hallway, all different shapes and sizes.

Pip barrels through our legs, darting all over the place and grunting unhappily at all the damage.

"Do you think it's safe here?" Winnie asks, her bravado from the car fading fast.

"Probably not," I confess. "But I'm guessing those looking for me think I'm long gone and unlikely to return. I'm probably safer here than in Los Magicos."

"Hmmm," Winnie says, observing the way the couch has been slashed and all its stuffing pulled out. "Who would do that?" she mutters.

"Assholes," I say.

"Yeah, assholes." She follows me through to the kitchen. "So what are we looking for exactly?"

"My aunt's locket."

"Right. Is it in a jewelry box or something? Or would she have hidden it somewhere safe?"

"She's wearing it," I say, walking towards the larder.

Winnie is quiet and when I peer over my shoulder at her, I see the color has drained from her cheeks and she's doing that blinking thing.

"Wearing it?" she mumbles.

"Yes."

"But ... but ... she's dead."

"Yeah, she was buried wearing it."

"Oh jeez," Winnie says, slumping onto the nearest chair. "Are you proposing we ... we ..."

"Dig her up?" I say, casually, pulling out all the tins and jars from the larder shelf. I didn't search this place thoroughly enough after she died. It never occurred to me that she might have left me information. I was too busy surviving and grieving to consider anything other than how I'd feed myself, Pip and the chickens each day. Now I'm going to check every single hiding place I can possibly imagine. "No, she's buried in the cemetery on the edge of the town. I think if we turned up there with shovels and started shifting earth, we'd draw too much attention to ourselves."

"You don't say." Winnie picks up one of the jars from the table and holds it up to the light, examining the contents. "This looks like Trixie leaves. It's really difficult to grow. My grandma tries every year."

"Take it, if you think it will be useful. Take anything you think will be useful."

Winnie nods and starts dragging the other jars towards her.

"So, how are we going to get the necklace then?"

"I don't know." To her credit, Winnie doesn't curse at me this time. "But there must be a way."

"She's buried. Underground. And I assume she's in a casket."

"Yeah."

"Then I don't see–"

"There must be a way, Winnie." I grin at her. "We're witches, bitch."

"Not the best though, are we?"

"Bullshit, Winnie. That security spell you did on our room was amazing. And I've seen you in class. Holding back when you know the answer. Pretending to make a mistake when you've already completed the task like half an hour before anyone else."

Winnie blushes. "Summer doesn't exactly like competition."

"Summer is a bitch."

"And the other kids don't like smart alecks."

"Yeah, well, what I'm saying is I know you're a good witch. Maybe I'm not that–"

"You fought off Renzo Barone and killed that man in the woods. You are strong and brave and incredible, Rhi."

I laugh. "If that's the case, then, bestie, between the two of us we must be able to work this out."

Winnie sits back in her chair, spinning a jar around absent-mindedly in her fingers.

I turn back to the tins and jars, emptying them all until I hit the back of the shelf. I feel along the wall that lies at the back, searching for a loose brick or a hidden hole. There's nothing so I return the jars and tins and start with the next shelf.

"We could try a summoning spell," Winnie muses.

"What does it do?" I ask her.

"Exactly what you'd imagine. Summons the object you're looking for. My mom used to use it all the time when we were kids and we couldn't find our school shoes or our raincoats or our lost teddies."

"And it worked?"

"Yeah, but whether it would work through six feet of earth and a wooden casket ..."

"It's worth a try," I say feeling along the back wall of this shelf.

"We could try enhancing it." Winnie pulls out her phone and starts typing. "Urgh, no signal."

I laugh, replacing the jars and crouching down to the final shelf. "Welcome to the backend of nowheres-ville, Winnie."

"Seriously, how did you live with no signal? Is there Wi-Fi?"

"No, there's the old laptop upstairs in my bedroom but you have to plug it into the cable if you want to connect to the internet."

"It's like living in the middle ages," Winnie mutters as I show her up to my room, Pip trotting along behind us.

It's even more trashed than the other rooms in the house. The pictures are all smashed, the pages ripped from all my books, the bed sheets slashed and the stench of urine strong in the room.

Winnie clutches my arm. "Oh Rhi, I'm so sorry."

I swallow. "It doesn't matter, Winnie. This isn't my home anymore."

Winnie glances at me with concern, then waves her hand through the air, the smell of urine disappearing and replaced by something citrus.

I march to my desk. The drawers have been emptied of course, but the laptop is still there. Probably because they couldn't get the old thing to turn on and believed it to be dead. I place it on the desktop, switch the on button, then give it a helpful thump. It takes a good second but then it whirls slowly to life, the screen flickering and eventually settling into a grainy picture. I connect the wire and dial up to the internet.

Winnie watches on in disbelief.

"All yours," I say when the web page finally loads.

Winnie takes the seat, Pip curling up by her feet – obviously having forgiven her for the car journey – and I return downstairs to complete my search of the kitchen.

My foot is on the bottom step of the stair, when I feel it for the first time. That awareness. The tingling of the air. There's another magical here. Nearby. As I tune into the awareness, a shiver of fear curls down my spine. They are close. Really close. I was so busy chatting to Winnie, I wasn't paying proper attention to my surroundings.

"Hello, little rabbit," a voice calls out from the kitchen, low and sinister. A voice that has me freezing on the spot. "I've been hoping we'd meet again."

25

R^{hi}

I AM PARALYZED, unable to move, struck by indecision.

Do I run? Do I call out to Winnie and Pip? Do I fight?

Or do I step towards him? Step closer like the pull in my gut demands.

It's that magic of his again, weaving through the air, ensnaring me like a sinister web.

It has to be his magic, doesn't it? Because it can't be anything else.

I peer through the gap in the door to the kitchen and I can see him sitting there, on the chair Winnie vacated only moments ago, his tattooed arms resting in his lap, his legs kicked out in front of him and crossed at the ankles.

For a moment, I'm stunned by how striking the man is. Something I never appreciated in that dark alley in Los Magicos. Here, in the sunlit kitchen, I see him more clearly.

His brown skin glows almost golden in the light and his frame is even bigger, even more muscular than I remember. Hard, solid. Yet, even with the scars that criss cross his face, there's something boyish about it, emphasized by his strangely mismatched eyes.

"What?" The corner of his mouth lifts in a half smile and those eyes twinkle with malevolence that has my blood running both hot and cold. "Not pleased to see me?" He rests his hand over his heart and pouts at me. "I'm hurt. Here I was believing we were such good friends now."

"We're not friends," I say coolly.

He nearly killed me last time we met. If it hadn't been for Azlan, I would be dead. I can't let him strike first this time. Not with Winnie and Pip upstairs.

Could I blast at him through the gap in the door? Could I strike him first? Would I be strong enough to take him out?

What am I waiting for?

"Look at all those wheels spinning in your head. It is adorable. You don't want to die, do you?"

"I'm not going to die. You're the one who is in danger here."

The corner of his mouth twitches a second time. "You actually believe that, don't you? But little rabbit, there's no one to save you this time." He lumbers to his feet, like this whole conversation is draining or boring or both. He tucks the chair back under the table and takes a pace towards the door.

I try to step backward, retreat up the stairs, but I'm frozen in place, those invisible twines of his twisted around my body like last time.

"It has been a challenge to get you on your own again," he continues, "to find this private time for us to talk – because I have been very keen to talk with you again. But he's always been there, hasn't he?" His face twists ugly as he paces through the door, his movements like a jaguar stalking its prey. "Only now ... he's not." He grins, all sinister, his mis-colored eyes manic in their intensity. An intensity which would be almost mesmerizing if it weren't focused on my destruction. He waves his hand through the air. "Maybe he's not the man for you. Maybe you need someone more," he walks closer, "dangerous." He flicks his tongue over each syllable in that word and despite myself, I shiver.

His face lights up in delight. "You like that idea, little rabbit?" he whispers eagerly.

I watch him, my body itching to step towards him, straight into the snare I'm sure he's setting for me.

I shiver again, this time from fear, but I'm not as frightened as I was the last time we faced each other. This is my home, my sanctuary. And I'm realizing his insanity gives me an advantage. He could have killed me already. Struck me as I walked down the stairs. That would have been the efficient thing for an assassin to do. But he's not efficient, he's wasteful. He wants to play. And playing gives me a chance. One I intend to use. I just need to keep him talking, talking as I carefully unfurl the magical binds he's wrapping around me. I won't make the same mistake I made last time, won't blast through these ties and waste all my magic. I need to conserve it, conserve it for the fight.

"How did you find me?"

He grins at me. "I'm not giving away my secrets that easily. But if you want to trade ... I reckon there are one or two things you could do for me."

My brow crinkles. Isn't he here to kill me? Has he changed his mind? Does he think I have information worth hearing?

Except that dark look of his doesn't suggest the thing he wants to trade is information.

"Why do you want to talk?" I ask.

He cocks his head to one side. "You've sparked my interest." I glare at him and my expression seems to delight him. "You've obviously sparked *his* too. What is it about you?"

"I don't know what you're talking about."

"You're fucking him." He frowns, a more genuine expression, and comes nearer, slowly drawing in breath, his nostrils flaring. "You don't smell so innocent anymore. Not like you did." His eyes flick over my face. "But it has to be more than the sex that's tempted him. Don't get me wrong, you are pretty." I frown despite myself, trying to concentrate on unwinding his magic and not letting myself become diverted by his mad ramblings. "Pretty but not exactly ..." He smirks and his gaze meanders down my body in a way that doesn't seem disdainful. In fact, there's a heat in it. A heat that warms my blood and has me edging forward. More fucked up magic? "Then again ..."

"You've been watching me?" I say, scrambling around for a way to keep him talking.

"I have." His eyes find mine. "I like watching you." He takes another step nearer. He's close now. I can smell the masculine scent of him. The sensation in my belly hums. "You're such a strange little thing. And you sound so delicious when you scream. You know, I bet I could make you scream twice as loud as he can."

I glare at him some more.

"Little rabbit," he chuckles. "This is unfair. You don't mind when he makes you scream. You rather seem to enjoy it."

He can't possibly have heard us together ... That isn't true. Is it? It can't be. He's messing with me.

"More wheels spinning," he says. "You do like to think a lot. Fucking and thinking, thinking and fucking."

"You're sick," I spit. For the briefest of moments, he looks genuinely hurt, like my words have wounded him. That can't be right either, can it? Why would he care what I think of him? Then that amusement returns to his face.

"If you want," he says, licking his tongue slowly along his bottom lip in a manner that has my pulse jumping, "we could find out just how sick and twisted I can be."

"I don't want to play your games."

"If I'm honest, I'm not one of those guys who's particularly bothered by consent, little rabbit." He takes another step. We're just a foot apart. "But for you, hey, maybe–" His words halt mid-sentence and he shakes his head suddenly, swiping at his ears as if annoyed by an irritating thought. "This isn't what I wanted to talk to you about," he mutters. "I have another gift for you."

"My knife? I want it back."

"No, you left it behind and it belongs to me now. All mine." He halts, peering down at my hands. "You're not wearing it."

"What?" I say, struggling to follow his rambling thoughts.

"My ring, little rabbit. You didn't like it?"

"Why would I?" I say in disbelief.

"Because I gave it to you."

"I don't want anything from you," I hiss.

He smiles at me. Those eyes of his draw me in and I hold my breath.

Why aren't I fighting him?

He bends closer, gaze traveling over my face. "You sure about that, little rabbit?" he growls, a sound that seems to travel right through my body. He reaches into his pocket and

I flinch ready to receive an attack, but all he pulls out is his closed fist. "Because I think you'll like this gift." Slowly, he uncurls his fingers and, despite myself, I can't help looking with curiosity at what rests in his palm. Three or four small white objects. "I wanted to bring you his heart, but it would have been fucking messy."

I gasp and then the bedroom door on the landing above creaks open.

"Rhi?"

I go to warn Winnie, to call out, but I'm too late. Barone's head snatches her way, and before I can raise my hands to stop him, he's sent a blast of magic at her. Winnie screams as the magic hits her stomach and she flies backwards through the open doorway. I hear her crash into the wall.

"NO!" I yell, shooting a torrent of magic his way. It smacks him on the shoulder, and he hisses, stumbling backwards. Before he can react, I volley more his way, and he lifts his hands to shield himself, my magic crackling and splintering around him.

"I don't want to hurt you, little rabbit," he calls out. I snarl, stalking forward, feeling that dark magic sizzling in my fingers. "I want you to come with me."

I don't answer him, simply let that dark magic fester until it's so rabid, I have no choice but to launch it across the small space between us. It hits his shield, the thing splintering and shattering into a million pieces and Renzo tumbling to the ground.

His eyes go wide with wonderment, and a wild smile pulls across his face.

"Crimson magic," he says with awe, like he's seen something truly angelic. "Fuck me."

"I'm going to fucking kill you."

"You are?" he says, that smile even wider as he stares up at me.

His obvious delight has me hesitating. Do I want to kill him? I think of the man in the wood. I remember how that felt. Something dark shimmers in my belly.

"Use it, little rabbit," he says from the ground, his eyes glittering. "Use it all."

The magic burns in my veins, scorches my fingertips. And I want to. I want to use it. I don't want this man chasing me. I don't want to live in fear the whole time that any moment he's going to leap from the shadows. I don't want to feel this strange pull to a cruel murderer like him. I don't want him hurting the people I love the most.

The thought has me lifting my eyes to the landing. Winnie? Is she okay? Is she – my throat constricts so that I can't breathe – alive?

As if my thoughts summon her, she steps through the doorway, Pip at her heels. She lifts her hands and the man on the ground is too entranced by me, his eyes locked on my face, that he doesn't see.

Winnie's lips move, her hands dance through the air and Renzo vanishes from sight.

26

R^{hi}

I STARE DOWN at the space Renzo Barone occupied only moments ago. Did I see that right?

I step forward, squinting at the ground. Only those white objects remain on the floor where he'd lain only moments ago.

"Come on," Winnie shouts, hobbling down the staircase as she clutches her stomach. "That spell won't have sent him far. We need to get out of here."

"Wh-wh-what did you do to him?" I say as Winnie pushes my shoulder, forcing me down the remaining step. "He's gone."

"It's just a stupid spell. Me and my sisters used to mess around with it all the time. Drove Mom mad."

"I don't understand," I say dumbfounded as she grabs my wrist.

"It just sends the person someplace else. My little sister used to do it all the time to my middle one – just as she'd be lifting her dessert spoon to her mouth, she'd shoot her upstairs to the bedroom."

"So where is he?"

"I don't know exactly. I sent him as far as I could, but the spell is limited. He won't be far. Which is why we need to move."

"Wait!" I say, tugging on her arm and pulling her towards the objects.

Teeth. They are teeth. Two white molars and a canine.

"Are they human?" Winnie says, her voice quivering.

"I don't know. He said ... he said they were a ... gift." I swallow down bile in my throat.

"Oh my god!" Winnie says, sounding equally sickened.

"Should I take them?" I ask.

"NO! They could be cursed!"

"But shouldn't we hand them over to Azlan or something? Have them work out who ... whose they were?"

"Rhi, no!!" Winnie yanks on my arm, pulling me away towards the door.

Outside, she sprints to the car, Pip chasing after her. I swing my gaze round the meadow before ducking into the car.

Winnie jerks the vehicle into gear and shoots us out of the meadow.

"Are you hurt?" I ask her, noticing the way she rubs her stomach.

"It's not too bad. Grandma's protection spells are pretty hardy things."

"Your Grandma placed a protection spell on you?"

"Yeah."

I peer at Winnie's midriff. I'm sure that blast should have torn her in half.

"Do you think she'd put one on me?"

Winnie smiles with sympathy. "It only works on blood relatives. It has to be interwoven with love by a blood relation."

I sigh and sink into my seat. "Maybe my aunt placed one on me."

"Maybe. But they only last a couple of months at a time." Winnie wipes at the windscreen. "So, are we going back to Arrow Hart?"

I chew on my thumb. "No, the cemetery. I'll know if Barone's there."

Winnie glances at me but doesn't argue and I direct her. I won't let myself be so stupid a second time. This time I'm staying tuned into that sense, even if Winnie's proximity has bells ringing in my head, the noise making it ache. It's better than being attacked again by that man.

"Was he–"

"Renzo Barone, yes," I confirm.

"And you knocked him to the floor? Woah, Rhi, that's ..."

"You were the one who blasted him away."

Winnie grins. "Sometimes the simplest spells are the best. That's what Grandma always says. She says people are too quick to overlook them in search of more complex, powerful ones. That they dismiss the spells so often used by mothers and their children, when really they can be the most effective."

I nod. Only the magic I'd used to bring that man to his knees wasn't simple. It wasn't complex either. Crimson magic. It had his eyes gleaming, gazing at me like I was a goddamn angel.

The memory has me shifting on my seat with unease.

Was I going to kill him? I had every right to, didn't I? And yet
the idea of it makes me sick.

I stare out of the window, watching as my home town
thins and the old cemetery, perched on the brow of a
dusty hill, comes into view. A permanent wind sweeps
through the place, wearing away the few gravestones that
litter the plot, so that it's impossible to know who lies
where.

Not that I'd ever forget where she rests. Even though I
haven't been back since the day she was buried. The image
of it is sketched into my memory. Not something I'll ever be
able to erase.

"Can you feel him here?" Winnie asks as we draw up
into the small parking lot at the base of the hill. A rusty sign
announces the cemetery, and there's one other car parked
up beside it. I don't recognize the make or registration
number. I don't think it's anyone from town, but I can't feel
any magicals other than Winnie.

Gingerly, we climb out of the car, locking Pip in the back
despite his angry squeaks, then follow the path up the hill,
both on high alert.

We pass a new grave, the earth still disturbed, the grass
having not yet reclaimed the space. Another has fresh wild
flowers resting in a vase against its stone and a third has a
string of plastic ones draped over a cross. All the other
stones are unloved and clearly unvisited. Guilt swims in my
chest. I should have come sooner. I should have left flowers
every chance I had.

"Where's her grave?" Winnie asks and I point to the far
side of the plot. We weave our way through the stones and
as we draw closer, I stop in my tracks.

I'm wrong. There's a third grave adorned with flowers, a
bunch of red roses, resting next to the stone. A stone which

only bears her name because I couldn't afford anything more.

"What is it?" Winnie says, her voice strained.

"Roses. On her grave."

"From Barone?" Winnie frowns.

I shake my head. "I don't think so."

"Then maybe they're from one of your aunt's friends."

"She didn't have any friends, Winnie. It was just her and me."

Winnie gulps and swings her gaze around. "You want to leave?"

I shake my head again. I want that locket.

I march ahead, that wind agitating my hair and blowing into my face.

What a crappy place to end up. Here, alone, on this hill, ever tormented by this stupid gale.

I should have buried her in the meadow. Under the trees. With the wild flowers.

I stop by the edge of her grave. The roses are fresh. Only a day or two old. There's no note with them. I touch them anyway. No magic fingerprints, although perhaps, maybe, the faintest trace of magic.

I sink to my knees and let my hand rest on the earth. It looked like that other grave before. Now there's grass. Yellow and grizzled, dust curling with the wind.

Maybe that trace of magic is hers. Still lingering. Still here.

The wind rushes past my face and whistles in my ear and I swear it's like her voice, whispering to me.

"Rhi?" Winnie says. I peer up at her. "Are you okay?"

She's still clutching her stomach and I wonder if it hurts more than she's letting on. I should be trying to heal her. I should be getting her home to a doctor. Not insisting she trails after me on this mad quest. Shame swoops through my body.

"This was a stupid idea. We should go."

"Don't you want me to try first? The summoning spell."

"It's not going to work."

Winnie tuts and sinks down to her knees beside me. "What did the locket look like, Rhi?"

"Silver, oval, small, with swirling patterns engraved across its surface. I never saw her open it so I don't know what was inside."

"Okay," Winnie says, resting her hand next to mine. "I'm trying really hard to focus on lockets and not dead bodies." She screws up her nose, then her eyes and I see her lips move as she whispers something silently.

"Anything?" I ask, after a few minutes.

Winnie shakes her head, her eyes still closed. "It could be the distance but I can't ... feel anything. Usually you can sense the lost object even though you don't know where it is. But this ..."

"It must be the earth." I rock back onto my behind. "Damnit!" This entire trip was a waste of time. I didn't even get started on searching the house and we don't have enough time to try other spells in the hope of obtaining my aunt's locket. We need to get out of here before Renzo Barone tracks us down.

"Are you certain she was buried with it?"

"Absolutely," I say. "I was there when they closed the lid. I saw them lower her into the ground." And I stood in the wind, the dust making my eyes stream, as they'd covered her coffin with earth and buried her.

"I really can't feel it."

"Never mind," I say, resting my hand on her shoulder. "I appreciate you trying."

"Hmmm," Winnie says, opening her eyes. "I could try something else. Maybe–"

"No, it doesn't ..." I freeze. On the edge of the periphery of my awareness, I can sense something. "Another magical," I whisper.

"What?" Winnie says, peering over her shoulder. "Renzo Barone?"

"No, not him. It's not powerful enough." Winnie's gaze flicks to mine.

"Let's go," she says.

We race down the hill, slipping and sliding on the dry grass, and dive into the car, Pip squeaking at us and trying to lick at my face as Winnie switches on the engine.

"Arrow Hart?" she asks.

"Arrow Hart," I confirm.

She floors her foot to the gas and I swing my gaze around searching for the magical who's there somewhere.

It's not until we're flying down the road that I spot them.

An older man, long gray hair tied back from his face, hands in his pockets, face wizened, watching as we fly past. A red rose in the buttonhole of his old jacket.

"Winnie," I say, "stop the car."

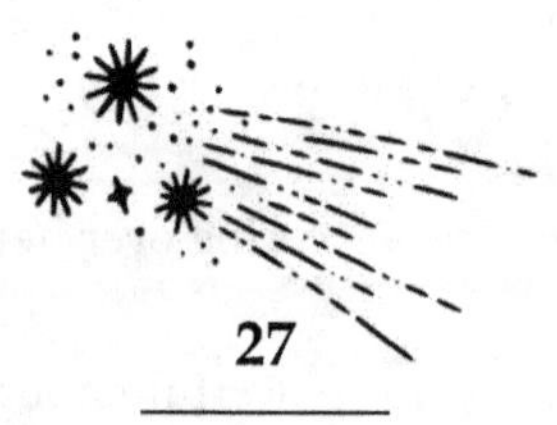

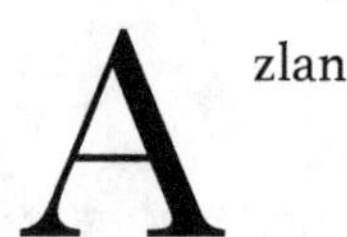

27

Azlan

I THOUGHT the bond was meant to weaken over time. Become more bearable. Something eventually I'd hardly notice.

It isn't the case. The gnawing in my stomach grows stronger as each hour of the night passes, so I'm tossing and turning on Phoenix's spare bed, unable to sleep.

By the time the day is dawning, I can't bear it any longer. I'm going to have to see her.

Damn the consequences.

She's mine and perhaps this separation, perhaps this creeping around and keeping it secret, is a foolish idea.

She should be by my side, in my arms.

In my bed.

I tug at my laces, tightening my boots until they cut into my skin.

My mind is turning into a sewer. Thoughts and ideas I've never entertained swirling through my head. Ideas and thoughts the other teenage boys used to obsess over that never interested me before. Never occupied my every waking moment.

I need to pull myself together.

I leave Stone sleeping and let myself out of his cabin, crossing the clearing and heading for the school grounds. They are empty. It's early and there was also an attack last night. I imagine the students have been instructed to stay inside.

One of them is choosing not to obey those instructions.

My cousin, Tristan.

I'm not surprised.

I meet him as he walks down the path away from the mansion.

A bandage covers his left cheek and a bruise his right brow.

"What happened?" I ask him, and he snaps out of whatever sick thoughts had been brewing in his mind, and his cool eyes meet mine.

"Azlan." He touches his cheek. "Are you allowed to be here?" His voice isn't friendly.

"Rhianna was attacked last night."

"By a werebeast," Tristan says. "You aren't doing a very good job of looking out for your mate."

I ignore him. He may be efficient at provoking his little friends at this school, but I couldn't give a damn what my little cousin thinks. He's turning into his father. More alike every day. And I certainly don't care what my uncle thinks either.

I examine his cheek and the bruise. "Were you attacked too?" He glares at me and doesn't answer. "Because I understood only the girl was attacked before the beast retreated into the forest."

"That's what I heard too."

"But she says," I stare into those pale eyes of his, devoid of emotion, "something intervened."

"I thought you'd have noticed by now that your girl-friend is several sandwiches short of a picnic, several marbles missing, several screws loose. I wouldn't trust a word that comes out of her mouth."

"She's not my girlfriend. She's my mate."

"And you're so close, right? She tells you everything?"

Maybe he's becoming more adept at irritating me after all. "She wasn't lying about this."

Tristan smiles and takes a step towards me, and I note the slight limp to his gait. He took a beating and neither he, nor the matron, have been able to heal him completely.

"But she does lie, doesn't she? Like I'm guessing she told you she was going back to her dorm last night, and that she'd stay there, nice and safe, all night long. That she certainly wouldn't go out ..." He smiles, all cold sarcasm, and I wonder what happened to that cute kid full of over-brimming excitement. "Wouldn't leave the campus."

My blood runs cold. The gnawing ache in my stomach, so strong I'm grinding my teeth. Strong, like she isn't here, like she's far away.

"If you have something to say, spit it out, Tristan."

His brow furrows and hatred sparks in his eyes. Hatred. He never used to look at me like that. When he was a kid those cold eyes of his would light up every time he saw me. He looked at me with admiration back then.

And while that admiration has faded over the years, he's certainly never looked at me with hate before.

Is it because of the girl? Does he think like them? Does

he see her as a stain on the good old family name? Does he really care about that shit now? Does he think the way our fathers do?

It pains me.

"Me? I don't have anything to say." He stalks off. I think about calling him back, demanding he give me answers. But that ache is deep and painful and I don't like it.

Her dorm room is empty when I arrive a matter of minutes later and when I snoop around, I see her bag is missing and some of her clothes.

She's gone.

For a moment it's like someone's reached into my chest and wrenched out my heart.

I peer down at my chest.

She doesn't trust me. Doesn't want me.

A possessive growl rumbles in my throat. It doesn't matter. She's mine. The bond has been sealed. She can't just run away from it.

I bunch my hands into fists and storm from the dorm building. There are students on the path now and they scatter out of my way, whispering behind their hands and eyeing me with excitement. A werebeast yesterday. The authorities' enforcer today. They can barely disguise their excitement.

I reach the building that houses Tristan's apartment and peer up at the penthouse. Bet he's expecting me.

I sprint up the stairs and pound on his door, so hard the thing wobbles in the frame. When he answers the door, he's dressed in just gray sweatpants, a joint hanging between his lips. His torso is black and blue and another bandage covers one side of his ribs.

He takes a long exaggerated drag, his eyes darting over my face, then blows smoke out of the side of his mouth.

"A second visit in one day? I am honored."

"Where the hell is she?"

"This again." He shakes his head and pads across the room in his bare feet, leaving the door open behind him. I step in after him. If he doesn't tell me in the next five seconds, I'm going to add a considerable number of bruises to his body, pound him until he starts speaking.

"Tell me," I growl through gritted teeth.

He drops down onto a couch, resting his arm on his bent knee, the tip of his spliff smoldering. He looks at me, rolling the spliff between his fingers, then takes another drag.

"Why did you do it?" he asks, his eyes are less hostile now, tempered by the weed. "Why did you claim her?"

I hesitate, debating what will earn me an answer faster, my fists or the truth.

"To save her. To save her life."

He takes another long drag, his eyelids closing as he does. "You think she was worth saving?"

"She's my fated mate."

"That stuff, though, Az, it's fairytales, isn't it? Just because the lines of magic are there pulling you together, doesn't mean it's right, that you belong together. If she's a little bitch–"

"She's not a bitch." A brat maybe, but not a bitch. A brat who has spilled some color into a world that was looking desolate and gray. "She's special."

"I hope so," he says, cutting through the bullshit and sounding earnest for once. "Because my father ..."

"Where is she, Tristan?" Maybe I should have resorted to the fists after all.

"Don't know," he says, leaning over the couch to flick ash into a marble tray. I take a menacing step towards him. "She wouldn't say."

"So help me, Tristan! If you don't start talking some goddamn sense in the next ten sec–"

"I saw her leave the campus. In a car. With her roommate and the pig."

"Were you watching her?" I ask, sinisterly.

"I was walking to the mansion to get these injuries seen to." He points to his cheek and his chest. "She was waiting for her friend on the path. I asked where she was going. She refused to say."

"She had her bag with her?"

He nods.

I go to turn, then hesitate. "Anything else?"

He takes one last drag, then wets his fingers and extinguishes the joint with a sizzle.

"The car was ... different. Modified, I'm guessing."

"Modified?" Where the hell did she get a modified car?

"Where do you think she went?" he asks, interest flickering behind his eyes before the mask of indifference falls back down.

"She has nowhere to go."

"Her home?"

"There are people looking for her."

"People?" He tugs at the bandage on his cheek, ripping it away from his skin. Underneath faint tram-lines run across his flesh.

"The Wolves of Night," I say.

He curses under his breath, that flicker returning to his eyes.

"She killed Marcus Lowsky's brother."

He stands to his feet. "Rhi? Rhianna Blackwaters? Why?"

"To save my life."

He stands there dumbfounded, shock written all over

his face. It's not an expression I've ever seen drawn across my cousin's features before.

"How?"

"Does it matter?"

"You didn't tell our fathers."

"It's none of their business."

"So this is why you did it? This is why you saved her? Your life for hers, hers for yours."

"No." It was more complicated than that. Far more complicated. It was more complicated than the bond, than the pull in my soul. All more complicated. All those things twisted and tangled together, inseparable from the other.

"Why's she running away?" he asks.

I frown. I was the one asking the questions. Now it's him. Why the interest?

I think of what she said. About the thing that attacked her in the forest. About the thing that intervened to save her from the werebeast.

"Are you sure there's nothing you want to tell me, cousin?" I say.

The mask of boredom falls back into place, and he drops back onto the couch.

"Nothing." I turn to the door. "And I hope for your sake you find her dead in a ditch somewhere."

I slam the door hard behind me.

I have to find her before Barone, otherwise there's a good chance that's exactly where she'll end up.

28

R^{hi}

"ARE YOU CRAZY?" Winnie yelps. "We were just attacked by Renzo Barone, and now you can sense another magical around. We need to get the hell out of here."

"Winnie, please, trust me on this. Just stop the car."

She peers at my face, down to Pip's and back up to mine. Then she steps on the brake and we come to a skidding halt.

"Wait here, okay? And if you spot any danger, get the hell out of here."

"Okay, you are crazy, because we're not leaving you to do this on your own."

But I've popped my belt and am jogging back down the road before she can stop me.

The old man with the rose in his jacket watches me as I approach, not moving from his spot.

I slow down as I draw closer. There's a look about him,

one I can't describe. Haunted, skittish, a look of someone who is always looking over their shoulder. The look of an unregistered.

Sometimes, they'd pass through the town, evading the authorities. Sometimes my aunt would let them crash on our sofa for a night or two. Never longer than that. The risk was already too high.

Was he one of them? I search his face. But there's no niggle of recognition.

"Hello?" I say, a little unsure.

"Hello there."

We stand in front of each other silently, in the background I can hear the splutter of the car engine and the whoosh of the wind.

"I'm Rhi," I venture, starting to get cold feet. Is this a trap? Am I being a fool?

"Yes, I know who you are. Mabel's niece."

I nod. "I'm sorry but I don't think I know you."

"You wouldn't. We met when you were small."

"Was it you? You who left the roses?"

"Yes," he says, pinching the flower from his buttonhole. He hooks it out of his jacket and hands it to me. "I remember she had roses growing in her garden. She said they were her favorite. I remember you liked to water them."

I frown. "We had no roses growing in the garden."

"Not here. A different place. You were only little then."

I take the rose from him, lifting it automatically to my nose and inhaling the floral scent.

"I was hoping to speak with you, hoping we might meet." I frown. "You're registered now, Rhianna."

"Y-y-yes."

His eyes flick to the car, that nervous energy coursing through his body, ratcheting up. "You need to be careful."

I lower the rose from my nose. "Why? Why do I need to be careful? Do you know why she was keeping me hidden?"

"They can't be trusted."

"The authorities?"

"Yes, your aunt will have told you that, considering what happened to your mother."

"My mom? What happened to my mom?"

But before he answers, something catches my attention, on the periphery of my senses. I peer over my shoulder. It's not close, not yet.

The man registers the change in my countenance.

"There's someone coming," he says, his body stiff with alarm.

"You feel it too?"

"More than one," he says.

"More than one?" I swing my head around, my mind suddenly buzzing with noise.

"You need to go, Rhianna. If they know who you are–"

He pushes at my shoulder.

"Wait!" I say, "I don't understand."

"Go!" the man says as magical bolts begin to zoom over our heads. He pushes me again, before he ducks down low, covering his head with his arms as more magic cascades our way.

I spin around. It's not Barone. The magic isn't powerful enough, and it's too organized, too orderly. Not like his chaotic, frantic magic. But there are many of them. I can feel them. I just can't damn well see them.

The old man runs for cover, melting into the trees beyond as I sprint towards the car. Magic zooms above my head as Winnie presses down hard on the horn. I fire magic of my own in that direction. Then throw myself on the ground as a ball of fire narrowly misses my head. When I peer up I'm surrounded by a ring of men. They are dressed in army combats, their faces covered by balaclavas and scarves.

I think of the men that surrounded the man in black back in the forest all that time ago. Those were the Wolves of Night. These men are different. More disciplined, better trained. I can feel it in their magic. See it in the way they stand.

I count four. I'm outnumbered. I can't fight them off.

"Stand up!" the tallest one barks.

Slowly, I roll up to my feet, desperately scrabbling for a plan as I do. I don't understand. Who are these men? And what the hell do they want?

"Hands behind your back," the man says next, eyeing my twitching fingers. I note the accent in his voice. He's not from here.

"What do you want?" I ask, but none of them answer. One of the men steps towards me and I flinch. Immediately, they all raise their hands.

"One false move ..." the one in charge says, as if I'm a dangerous animal, as if I'm some kind of threat to them.

I nod my consent. I don't have a lot of choice. I curse myself for being so damn foolish.

The man takes another step toward me, reaching for my arms. He's going to bind my wrists. Panic bubbles in my chest and that magic simmers in my veins. Dark, begging me to use it. Could I? Would it be strong enough?

I close my eyes and hear the sudden roar of an engine, followed by frantic cries of the men, bodies falling on the ground.

I snap open my eyes to find Winnie has driven right at them.

For a split second we gape at each other through the dirty windscreen.

Then I dive into the car as a bolt of magic explodes on the road beside me, creating a crater the size of a bowling ball. Winnie screams as the car rocks from side to side with the blast. Then she floors the accelerator and speeds us the hell away, spinning the car around and yanking on the shift stick.

More magic crashes around us and Winnie stamps on the accelerator again, shooting us forward and away from the men. More magic explodes around us and Winnie weaves the car this way and that, narrowly missing explosion after explosion while Pip whimpers and scrabbles in my lap.

"Barone's men? The Wolves of Night?" Winnie yells over the noise.

"No." I say, "No, not them. They're soldiers," I say in confusion.

"You don't say," Winnie says, her eyes darting to the rear-view mirror. "Shit!"

I turn my head around and find we're being chased. Two cars following us. There's a man leaning out of the window of one, firing magic at us.

A bolt hits the back of the car, jolting us forward, and we both scream.

"What do they want?" Winnie yells and the car shakes again as she battles with the steering wheel to keep us on the road.

"I don't know," I say. "Me, I think– Watch out!" I scream as magic hits a building and rubble tumbles towards us. Winnie swings us left and then right.

"Can't you get us out of here?" I say.

"Not until I find us a decent stretch of straight road."

"Right." I pump down the window and lean right out.

"Rhi, what are you doing?!"

"Fighting back," I shout over the noise. The wind assaults my face and my hair whips about. But I narrow my eyes, waiting for the first car to screech around the corner after us. Then I fire magic of my own. That dark magic sizzles in my veins, desperate to come out and play. But I tamper it down. It scares me. I know it's bad and I don't like the way it makes me feel. Powerful. Destructive. Dangerous. Instead, I send magic that explodes on their car, shattering the wind screen.

Unfortunately that just makes it a hell of a lot easier for the man firing back at me.

I swear and send fire his way, scorching through the air. For a moment the cars are lost in a bellowing flame before they emerge unscathed.

"Winnie!" I cry, "where's that straight bit of road? They're gaining on us!"

"Up ahead! Rhi," she says, "keep firing!"

"Yes, Ma'am," I say, as Winnie yanks on the gear shift and shoots us forward. I fire more magic. It hits the other man's magic head on and explodes into a million shattering colors in the air.

"Rhi, get in!" Winnie says.

I duck back in the car as Winnie punches buttons and I grip Pip tightly in my arms. The car lurches forward. I close my eyes and we explode through space. The car spinning over and over, the two of us thrown around in our seats. I hit my head on the dashboard and then the car roof. But I cling to Pip, not letting him out of my arms, as I'm slammed into the car door and then the roof again.

The car groans and there's the screech of metal scraping along tarmac. Then we skid to a halt.

I open my eyes. I'm hanging upside down, secured in place by my belt. It's deathly quiet, only Winnie's breath and Pip's frightened squeaks. No tires squealing. No exploding magic.

"Did we lose them?" I ask, trying desperately to free myself so I'm ready to fight again.

Winnie doesn't answer me and I twist my head. She's hanging from her seat too, her head limp, blood dripping from her body onto the car ceiling below her.

"Winnie!" I scream, battling with my belt. "Winnie!"

She doesn't respond. I yank on the stupid belt.

"Winnie," I sob, a pain like broken glass in my throat. She can't be. Not Winnie. "No!"

Her eyes flutter open weakly and I almost collapse with relief. But then they droop shut almost immediately. I get a handle on my belt buckle and snap it off, crumpling on the roof below and shuffling through the space to reach her.

"Winnie?" I say, searching her face and her body for signs of a wound. The front of her sweater is drenched in blood. "Oh no!" I say, freezing in terror.

"Rhi?" Winnie says, opening her eyes again.

"We need to get you to a hospital. To a healer!" I back away, trying to find the handle of the door. I need to call for help. I need to run and fetch help.

"No, Rhi," she says, her voice feeble, her face becoming paler and paler before my eyes. "There isn't time."

I know there isn't. I know. But she's my friend. My best friend. I can't watch her die. I need to save her. I need to find someone who can save her.

"Rhi," she says, her eyes swooping in and out of focus. "Heal me."

My entire body shakes. "I … I can't."

I couldn't even heal my damn arm. I can't heal her. Not a wound like that. I don't have the skill or the power.

I can't.

But then Pip nudges at me with angry grunts.

"I can't do it," I tell him. "You know I can't."

He glares at me and snorts as if he's telling me: what choice do you have? Then to drive home the point, he butts my hand with his snout.

He's right. It's my fault Winnie took that hit from Barone. My fault that the protection spell was weakened. And it's my fault she's here injured now.

I jump forward, ripping open her sweater, and assess the damage. Her chest is an open, weeping wound of gore and blood that makes me gag. I swallow down my revulsion, my fear, my nerves, and press my palms firmly against my friend's chest. I feel the beat of her weakening heart beneath my hands. Then I close my eyes and focus.

It's not an easy spell. No matter what Azlan and Stone may say. It requires patience – something I so often lack – and an ability to tune into the other person, to hear their body and their magic, to encourage it to heal.

Blood spills through my fingers. But I keep going, Pip snorting encouragement beside me, his body pressed to mine, and gradually, gradually the blood falters, trickling slower and slower until it stops.

My own heart leaps into my throat and I can't breathe for several seconds.

Did I do it? Did I heal her? Or is she …

Then I feel new skin forming beneath my fingers and tears stream down my face. I've no time to stop, though. I take a steadying breath and keep whispering the words, conjuring the skin and the blood vessels to heal, and new blood to replace the blood lost.

And finally, Winnie takes a deep breath of her own and opens her eyes.

I fall backwards, my arms shaking, my hands covered in blood.

Winnie peers down at her chest, touching it carefully with her fingers. Her skin is still painted with blood but there's no gash there any more. She's healed, the color already returning to her cheeks.

"You did it Rhi! You did it."

I nod. My body's still trembling and I feel lightheaded and sick. I fling myself forward, wrapping her in a tight hug. Then I crawl out of the car on my hands and knees and vomit into the grassy verge.

29

R^{hi}

IT TAKES us several attempts to roll the car back onto its wheels, both of us are weakened – Winnie from her injuries, me from using a large portion of my magic to heal her.

When we finally manage it, Winnie peers at me with curiosity. We're both covered in her dried blood, neither wanting to waste any more of our magic on cleaning ourselves up.

"What?" I ask her.

"I don't know. I'm kind of surprised you have any magic left at all. That was an incredibly tricky healing spell, Rhi."

I flex my fingers and shrug my shoulders. She doesn't need to tell me. My head aches from the effort.

"I guess. But I feel like I have quite a bit left in the tank." Not like the last time when I faced Renzo, and fighting him drained every drop of my magical reserves and left me at death's door.

"Could be the fated-mate bond," Winnie says, walking around the car and inspecting the damage. The car now owns a lot more dents and scrapes than it did previously.

"You think?" I say, staring down at my hands and then my stomach. I can feel the bond humming in there. I can also feel Azlan's concern and his anger but I do my best to block that out.

"I read one article that said bonding to a powerful fated mate would increase your own powers."

"Yes, Azlan said that's why the Chancellor would punish us for our union."

Is my magic stronger? There hasn't been an opportunity to test it since we bonded. But Winnie's right. I should be a hell of a lot more drained than I am right now.

Winnie opens the car door and slides inside. She presses the ignition and to my surprise the car starts.

"Are you up for driving?" I ask.

Winnie smiles at me, although I can see she's more exhausted than she's letting on. "Rhi, I'm fine. You did a really good job."

"And is it safe?" I ask.

Winnie presses more buttons. "Seems there's no damage to the actual system. We're safe to go."

The car looks even more of a death trap than it did before, but after what we've just been through together, I trust my friend implicitly.

Pip seems a little less sure, and it takes the two of us a lot of coaxing and promises of belly rubs and cookies before he'll climb in with us.

"Back to Arrow Hart?" I ask her with a sinking feeling.

I'm not looking forward to facing Azlan or the principal. Neither will be pleased about our little trip.

"Actually I was thinking ..."

"Uh oh," I say. "This sounds dangerous."

Winnie elbows me. "Says the girl who just nearly got us killed. Twice! I was thinking, seeing as we are going to be in a shit-load of trouble when we get back to the academy, there isn't exactly a big hurry to return. Unless, that is, you need to get back to your mate, you know, for the banging."

"I think I'm going to be in even more trouble with the mate than the principal. I doubt there'll be any banging for a long time. A long long long time."

Which has me actually feeling kind of disappointed.

Winnie spots the look on my face. "See, I told you. Once you pop you can't stop."

"Pop what exactly?"

"Your virginity."

"Oh god," I say, covering my face with my hands.

"Anyway, enough about your sex life. It's all you talk about these days." I snort. "What I was thinking is, as there's no hurry to return, how about a little detour?"

"A detour to where?"

"Grandma's."

"Didn't Little Red end up devoured by the wolf after a little detour to Grandma's?"

"No, Little Red's detour ended up saving Grandma from the wolf. It's a good omen, Rhi. Besides," she says, reaching down to tickle Pip's head, "I wouldn't mind my grandma replacing that protection spell seeing as hanging out with you is such a dangerous profession–"

"Winnie, I'm so incredibly sorry–"

Winnie waves her hand through the air. "Rhi, you saved me. There is no reason to apologize."

I stare down at my hands. A sob brews in my chest. "I thought I was going to lose you, Winnie. For a moment, I thought I had."

Winnie breathes in and out, then reaches over to squeeze my hand. "You didn't though. I'm okay. Thanks to you."

I squeeze her hand.

"You saved me too," I point out.

"I did?"

"From Barone, remember?"

"Then we're even."

"I'm not sure your grandma is going to see it that way when we both turn up covered in *your* blood."

"She'll be fine," she says, releasing my hands and pressing away at various buttons.

"Who do you think those men were, Winnie?"

"I don't know."

"You said they were soldiers."

"They were dressed in army combat gear."

"Doesn't mean they were soldiers. Could have been the Wolves of Night after all, or one of the other gangs."

"The man spoke with an accent."

Winnie snaps her head that way. "What kind of accent?"

I try my best to explain, to imitate him.

"Western," Winnie says quietly. "But what would soldiers from the West be doing so far from the border?"

I don't have an answer for that.

"What about that man?" Winnie asks. "The one at the graveyard? Was he part of a trap?"

"I don't think so."

"What did he say?"

"Nothing," I say with irritation. "He knew my aunt. Said he stayed with us one time. But he told me nothing more than that. Just more riddles. I'm sick to death of it. Why can't anyone give me a straight answer?"

"I don't know," Winnie says honestly. Then she nudges me with her elbow. "But Grandma knows everything about everyone. We should ask her about your mum and your aunt. She may know something."

"I doubt it. I've already checked all the library records, remember?"

"My grandma is far more reliable than any encyclopedia. Trust me. Anything she doesn't know, isn't worth knowing."

I'm 100% certain Winnie's grandma won't be able to help me. It's also 100% clear how much Winnie wants to see her.

"Okay, let's go see your grandma."

"Yes!" she says, grinning, turning to look at me and jolting.

"What?"

"Maybe we ought to get rid of all this blood first." She waves her hand through the air and it all disappears. Then she presses some more buttons. "Hold tight," she yells and we're off.

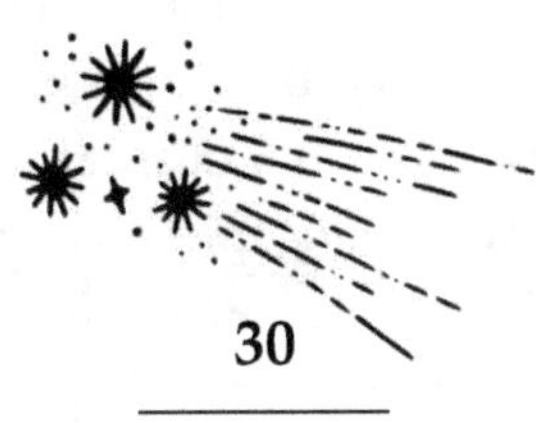

30

R enzo

I OPEN my eyes and stare up at a thick green canopy. A breeze jostles the leaves, and the earth is damp under my back.

I grip my stomach and laugh, kicking my heels against the soft ground as fits of hysteria roll through my body, tears trailing down my cheeks.

That is funny. Fucking comedy genius.

A displacement spell?

My little rabbit and her little friend are hilarious.

I love it.

I swing my arms through the air, rolling up to sit and take a deep inhale, the chuckles still buffeting my body.

So funny.

I swipe away the wetness from my cheeks and stare around.

Now, where the hell am I?

The forest. I recognize the trees and the smell of the place. I'm not far from my little rabbit's home. One I've been watching closely. With the Enforcer locked by her side day and night, there was no chance of speaking to her in the city. But people are like fucking pigeons, they always return home eventually. It was only a matter of time.

I pick myself up off the floor and pat myself down. The knife sits heavy in my pocket, familiar. I'm used to it now. It's like it's always been there. Close to my side, the metal thrumming ever so quietly. So quietly I bet most people don't hear it.

I listen more closely, feel through the air for magic. I can't sense my little rabbit close by. Gone. Fled. That makes me sad and any remaining chuckles die in my throat.

If she was wearing my ring, I'd be able to track her. If she was mine – properly mine – I'd find her instantly.

Marcus will be even more pissed than he already is. He thinks I'm taking too long to catch my rabbit. He thinks it should be easy. But this little rabbit is a clever one, a funny one, a quick and nimble one, maybe even a powerful one.

I hook out the knife and flick up the blade, looking at the cool metal.

I conjure my little rabbit's burrow in my mind's eye, then I bend time and space with my magic, straining the cords of both until I can hear them groaning in my ears. I grit my teeth, pulling with all my might, my brow damp with the effort. I fall and when I land and open my eyes, I'm back where I was at the bottom of the stairs.

The first step is vacant though. No little rabbit perched waiting for me. In fact, the front door flaps open in the breeze and the space occupied by their car is empty.

Yeah, she really had gone.

Shit. Just when things were getting interesting. Just when we'd started to talk. Just when I'd had a glimpse of what my little rabbit is truly capable of.

I peer down at my feet, finding my gift abandoned on the floor. I scoop the boy's teeth into my free palm and jangle them together like loose change. Then I tip them back into my pocket.

She didn't like that gift either. I should have gone with the damn heart after all. I should have dug the knife into his ribs and cracked him open like a walnut.

The knife is still warm in my left hand, light reflecting off the blade and bouncing on the walls. I throw it through the air. Like she did when she killed the man, the memory printed clearly within the knife's magic. It hits the far wall with a twang, the blade stabbing deep into the plaster. I stride through the front room to reclaim it, pulling it from the wall and admiring my handiwork. A deep slit marks the wall. The beginning of a letter. I grin again, sinking the blade into the plaster, adding more cuts to the one that already exists. Over and over again until I've carved out her name and mine.

Side by side. Together, like they should be.

It only takes me a few hours to ride to Lowsky's compound on my bike, deep in the wastelands, far from the authorities' reach. I could slide through time and space again. But it makes me feel nauseous and besides, I like my bike.

The compound is fiercely guarded by patrolling men, by firepower and by dogs, and hidden by complex spells Lowsky paid a fortune to obtain.

However, security's tighter than usual. Twice as many

men, all looking twitchy as hell, eyeing me with suspicion tonight rather than the usual boredom.

I weave my way through the various booby traps – half of them I set myself – and right into the heart of the compound. There are men and trucks everywhere, people rushing from one place to another, shifting arms and shouting orders.

I watch them from my bike. Lowsky's never told me anything beyond what I needed to know. I've always been content with that. I only need to know one thing. Who I'm killing next. The other stuff is boring.

But that little rabbit has burrowed her way under my skin and the killing isn't the only thing I'm hot for now. Maybe I should do what they were always telling me to do as a kid, start paying attention.

I head to the main building, fortified to the fucking nth degree, through to the place where Lowsky likes to hold court.

It's some fuck-off large room, with a jacuzzi at one end, a flat screen TV hanging on the wall and in the other half, Lowsky's leather-backed armchair. I'm surprised the dude didn't buy himself a throne.

He's sitting on it now, his latest girl perched in his lap trying to look seductive and not terrified. Several men stand in a circle around him, regaling information and giving reports. I hover by the door, jiggling my knife in my pocket, whistling to myself. When Lowsky finally spots me, he shoves the girl off his lap and orders everyone out. The girl is so relieved she has to force herself not to sprint out of the room, her eyes trained to the floor.

The other men aren't so intimidated; they all look at me as they pass through the doorway, although no one nods or says hello.

I don't care.

Lowsky's the only one who's ever been prepared to talk to me.

"Renzo," he says, beckoning me forward. "Tell me it's done."

"It's done," I say simply, because that's what he wants me to say, right?

He frowns and exhales, trying to keep his patience. "Is it, though?"

I flop down on the floor, crossing my legs out in front of me and leaning back on one arm.

"No," I say, holding his gaze.

A thunder roars across his face but his voice is quiet when he speaks again.

"Why not? She's just a fucking girl, Renzo. Unregistered. Untrained. Or so you tell me."

I pick at my nails, thick with dirt from the forest.

"Yeah, why exactly am I wasting my time with a girl?" I ask.

"She killed my brother," he hisses.

"He was a little shit," I say.

Marcus is silent again. He can't argue with that. Joey was one hell of a little shit. Couldn't control his temper. Threw his weight and his name around. I spent a lot of my time mopping up his messes.

"She still killed him and now she has to pay."

I lean forward, resting my elbows on my knees.

"What's going on?"

Marcus raises one eyebrow. There's a hickey on his neck. I doubt it was that girl. She doesn't seem the type. Unless of course he made her do it.

"Going on?" he says.

"All the fucking men, equipment. Don't you have a more important job for me to do?"

Marcus rises from his seat, although his hands still grip the armrests. "You think there's a more important job than avenging the spilling of my family's blood?" he shouts.

I lean back and try not to yawn.

Here it comes. I switch off. Let my mind wander back to my little rabbit. What would she feel like to touch? Would she be soft? Tender? Would she purr if I petted her? Would she moan if I fucked her? I'd like to find out.

Marcus's face turns purple with rage, spittle flies from the corners of his mouth, his eyes practically bulge. I guess he's really fucking angry this time.

Wonder if he's going to have me killed.

I smile to myself. Well, that would be fun.

Not today, though. Slowly, the storm blows itself out and Marcus stands there panting, his brow damp with sweat.

I tune back in.

"Nobody escapes a vendetta, Renzo. No one. So either get the job done. Or I'll find someone else to do it for me."

I sit up straight. No. I don't want that. Don't want some other wolf chasing my rabbit. She's mine. I'm doing the chasing.

"I'll get it done," I say casually. "But give me something else to do in the meantime."

He shakes his head. "It's already taken too long. Get it done, then you can have some other job."

I nod and slowly lumber to my feet.

Outside, I stand and watch the busy little bees. What are they preparing for? What is all this for?

There's no point asking. Like I said, no one here talks to me. Not after that incident with the dude and his tongue.

People are so fucking touchy. Especially about their body parts.

I take a walk instead, watching some more. They always said I had the attention span of a flea. But that only applies to the things that bore me. The things that interest me, you know, like stalking, killing, torturing, hey, I've got unbridled attention for those things.

Turns out, I don't need a whole lot of patience today. Because, despite being a dud at math, I put two and two together pretty damn quick.

These are vehicles from the West. Unloading weapons from the West. These are men from the West too.

And then there are the bales of straw and sheep.

Seems Marcus has made himself a little deal.

31

R ^{hi}

DAY PASSES into evening outside the car's windows as we slow down and enter a residential-looking area. I don't know what I expected Winnie's grandma's home to look like – an actual cottage in the woods, maybe – but it turns out to be a bungalow nestled in among a row of about twenty. As we pull into the driveway, the front door opens and an old woman with a pixie-cut hairstyle and big oversized glasses steps out. She stares at our car like something revolting has just washed up on her doorstep.

"Wait here," Winnie says, swinging open her door. "Let me go speak to her before we start with the introductions."

I watch as Winnie walks gingerly towards her grandma and her grandma rests her hands on her hips and frowns.

I decide to give them privacy and, with an inhale to

steady my nerves, pull my phone out of my pocket and switch it on.

The screen immediately lights up and the device pings in my hand with message after message. Fifteen at least, plus several missed-call notifications.

About half of the calls are from the man in black's number, the other from a number that my phone declares belongs to Arrow Hart Academy.

Shit!

I take a look at the messages. Most of these are from Azlan too. All of them asking where I am and what the hell I think I'm doing.

There's also a formally written one from the academy asking that I call as soon as I receive the message and then two more from numbers I don't know.

The first is clearly from Stone. He tells me I'm a dick and a stupid one at that, and need to call in or come home.

Home? Does he seriously think I consider the academy my home? I tsk under my breath and press on the final message.

Where are you, Pig Girl?

That's all it says. Tristan? But I have his number in my phone already. In that case it could be any of the jerks from school. Although why anyone of them care to know where I am is beyond me.

Winnie knocks on the windscreen and I jolt.

"Grandma's making tea. Come say hello."

"Pip?"

"He can come too. Grandma loves animals."

Love is probably an understatement. The woman clearly adores them if her home is anything to go by.

A little dog greets us at the doorway, yapping excitedly at Pip who grunts in annoyance in reply. Three cats sit curled up on the windowsill, each opening their eyes to look our way, then returning to their snoozing when they decide we're nothing of interest. Then there are at least five bird cages positioned around the room, each containing songbirds that chirp away happily, joining in with the noise of the dog.

"Quiet, everyone," Winnie's grandma says, clapping her hands as she enters the front room. The room falls silent.

"Nonny," Winnie says, "this is Rhi. My new roommate."

"Well, you didn't tell me she was stunningly beautiful, Winnifred," the old woman says, stepping forward to take my hands in hers and squeeze them.

"I'm sure I did tell you," Winnie says, dropping onto the couch and letting the dog jump up onto her lap.

"And who is this handsome gentleman?" Winnie's grandma asks, peering down at Pip who's hiding behind my legs. At the compliment, he strolls out, little chest puffed up.

"This is Pip."

The woman ducks down, her back creaking, and ruffles Pip's ears.

"He'll love you forever now you've called him handsome, Mrs. Wence."

"Oh, none of that. Rosa, please. And of course he will. It's how you win all gentlemen over. A few well-placed compliments, a little massage of their ego, and they're putty in your hands." She smiles warmly at me. "Take a seat then, Rhi." She points to the space next to Winnie on the couch, lowering herself carefully onto an armchair. The little dog immediately leaps off Winnie's lap and goes to settle himself on her grandma's instead. "Ahh that's the kettle whistling. Be a good girl, Winnifred, and go make that tea."

When her granddaughter is out of the room, the old

woman says, "Winnie doesn't usually cut class. Are you a bad influence?"

I decide to go with the truth. "Probably."

"Well, good. Winnie's always been too much of a goody-two-shoes for her own good. It's about time she broke loose. I hope you were cutting class to go meet some hot men."

I stare at her. "Winnie has a boyfriend."

"Oh I know that," the old woman says, stroking the dog on her lap, who closes his eyes and starts to dribble. "Doesn't mean she can't have a bit of fun."

"What fun?" Winnie says, walking into the room with a tray balanced in her arms. On top is a bright pink teapot, mismatched tea cups and a plate of cookies.

"The kind that involves more than one boyfriend."

"Because Mom wouldn't have a full-on fit if I dated more than one guy at a time." Winnie places the tea tray on a small coffee table and pours steaming hot liquid into each of the cups.

"Oh, don't you believe a word your mom says. She may preach all this 'be good' nonsense now, but she got up to all sorts when she was your age, I can tell you."

"Do you actually want more than one boyfriend?" I ask Winnie, not willing to acknowledge to myself why I'm asking that question. Yep, refusing to go there at all.

"Me?" Winnie laughs. "It's been hard enough finding myself *one* boyfriend."

"Yes," I say, not wanting to drop the topic of conversation just yet. "But if there was another man ..."

"Do you have a boyfriend?" Winnie's grandma asks with shrewd eyes.

"Rhi has a fated mate!" Winnie says, pouring milk into one of the cups and then passing it to her grandma.

The old woman sinks back into her chair, staring at me.

"Well I never." She glances at Winnie. "The real thing?"

"The real thing." She turns to me. "Do you want milk in your tea, Rhi?"

I shake my head and she hands me my cup. I sip at the hot liquid, certain my cheeks are hotter still.

"And who is the lucky mate?" Winnie's grandma asks.

"The Enforcer," Winnie squeals, obviously delighted to offer this juicy piece of information to her grandma. She picks up her own cup and settles back down on the couch next to me. "He's insanely hot. And dark and brooding and mysterious."

"And an asshole," I remind her, frowning into my tea.

"Oh dear," the older woman says, "some bumps on the road to happiness, huh? Well, the Enforcer and an unregistered. It's only to be expected."

Winnie leans forward, scowling at her grandma. "How do you know Rhi was unregistered? I haven't told Mom. Can you imagine? She'd be demanding I switch rooms faster than you can say 'bad influence'." I choke on my tea. "No offense, Rhi."

"None taken."

"Petunia told me."

"Petunia?" I ask.

"My middle sister. I knew I shouldn't have told that little snitch. Does Mom know?"

"Certainly not. Anyway, I was just telling Rhi here that I think she's a good influence on you." Winnie and I turn to look at each other. The old woman laughs. "I'm assuming this isn't the first time you've broken the rules then."

"Last time it was Pip's fault," I say. Pip looks up from where he's glaring at the cats.

"It wasn't Pip's fault. Someone stole him," Winnie explains to her grandma.

The old woman smiles fondly at her granddaughter, making my ribs ache. "It sounds like you've been having fun. A boyfriend, kidnappings, cutting class. And experimenting with that death trap of a car."

Winnie obviously decides she'd better change the subject. "I brought you something, Nonny." She reaches into her bag and pulls out the three jars she'd taken from my aunt's house – jars that somehow miraculously survived our car crash. The old woman takes them from her hands and examines the contents of each, unscrewing the lid of one and sniffing inside. "Trixie leaves. This is hideously expensive. Where on earth did you get the money for this, Winnifred? You're not robbing banks along with everything else, are you?"

"No, we picked it up from Rhi's aunt's house."

"She used to grow it," I say proudly, remembering Winnie said it was impossible to grow.

"The aunt who was keeping you hidden?" the old woman asks.

"I'm going to kill that Petunia," Winnie mumbles. "She has such a big mouth."

"A big mouth everyone knows she can't keep shut. It's your fault for telling her." The old woman turns back to me. "You were hoping to find some answers? At your aunt's home?"

I glance at Winnie who shrugs. "Not something I told Petunia," she says.

"Something I deduced on my own." Rosa sips her tea. "Pass me a cookie please, Winnifred. Now I'm old I can eat as many as I like." Winnie holds up the plate and her grandma takes two, snapping off a piece and feeding it to her dog. The birds all begin to chirp angrily and she crushes the rest in her hand and uses her magic to toss the crumbs inside the cages.

"Yes. She kept me unregistered and hidden away all my life and I never knew why."

"She must have told you something?"

"That the authorities couldn't be trusted. That she was keeping me safe from them."

"How did she pass, sweetie?"

I look down at the dark liquid in my teacup. My aunt's death is definitely not something I want to discuss. It's too raw. Too painful.

The room is silent except for the low chirping of the birds and the rolling purrs of the three cats.

"Please don't take this the wrong way, Rhianna, but has it ever occurred to you that maybe your aunt was …"

I look up at the old woman and her shrewd brown eyes.

"Wrong?" I venture. "She was always so certain, so adamant. She must have had her reasons."

"I wasn't going to say wrong, my darling, but I've also just met you, rather like you, think you may be a good influence on my favorite granddaughter," Winnie blushes next to me, "and I'd rather not offend you if I can help it."

"It's okay. I'm kind of used to people going out of their way to offend me. I can handle it."

"Okay," the old woman takes a gulp of her tea and holds my gaze, "are you certain she was all there?"

"All there?" I frown.

"Completely sane."

My mouth falls open in astonishment. "Are you asking me if my aunt was mad?"

"It is one of the possibilities. One you ought to consider."

"No, she wasn't. She was one of the most pulled-together, bravest, strongest people I've ever known," I say, raising my chin in defiance. The old woman nods. "And besides, I heard the man in black and Stone talking last night. About my mother. There's something they're not telling me."

"The man in black? Stone?" Rosa asks.

"The Enforcer and Professor Stone from the academy. They're best buddies or something."

"What did your aunt tell you about your mother?"

"Only that she died along with my father when I was a baby. I don't remember them. And the only connection I ever had to them was my father's knife." The knife Renzo Barone still has. I frown harder.

"The knife offers no clues?"

"I no longer have it."

The old woman nods.

"Rhi scoured the academy's library for any records of her parents or her family. She hasn't found anything. Isn't that strange?"

"Not if they were ordinary people, living ordinary lives."

"You think that?" I ask with irritation.

The old woman shrugs. "I think if it was so important to your aunt that you stay hidden and protected she would have left you something to keep you safe. Maybe that was the knife."

"She," I swallow, "passed unexpectedly. I don't think she ever thought she would leave me so suddenly. So soon."

"You said your aunt had it 'pulled-together'. She would have prepared for such an eventuality. Nearly all mothers do."

"Her locket," I say, defeated.

"She was buried with it," Winnie explains. "We went to the cemetery. Tried to retrieve it with a summoning spell. It didn't work."

"Then it wasn't there."

"It was," I say.

The old woman shakes her head, then gently nudges the dog off her lap and stands, walking over to the large cabinet that lines one wall of the room. She opens one of the wooden doors and rummages inside, pulling out a small silver dish.

"We may be able to work out where it is."

Winnie grins at me as if to say, 'isn't she the best?' If she can tell me where the necklace is, then I'll have to agree.

Rosa places the dish on the table next to the teacup and disappears into the kitchen, returning a moment later with crushed herbs in one hand and a small vial of clear liquid in another.

"Summoning spells are mighty useful for lost things, but you need something a little stronger if the object isn't nearby."

She lets the crushed herbs fall into the dish, then pulls out the stopper from the vial with a pop and shakes five drops into the dish. The liquid hisses against the herbs, turning them black and shriveled until they dissolve and the liquid turns jet.

"It tastes pretty foul, I'm afraid, but it does the trick."

"I have to taste it?" I say, alarmed.

"You're the only one who has a connection with this object, who knows what it looks like."

I peer at Winnie.

"It worked when I lost my favorite earring somewhere on campus last year," she says.

"Okay."

"Just dip your finger into the mixture and place it on your tongue." I do as she says and the foul-tasting concoction, like burned tar, stings against my tongue. "Now close your eyes and bring an image of the object into your mind's eye." Again I follow her instructions, conjuring the image of the necklace behind my closed eyelids. "What do you see?"

"The necklace."

"Good. What else?"

I frown. The taste of the mixture catching in my throat. "Nothing, just the necklace."

"Look harder."

I screw up my eyes and focus in on the necklace. "It's not working," I say in irritation.

Winnie rests her hand on my shoulder. "You need to look past the locket, Rhi. At where it is."

I try to relax, letting my mind drift. The necklace is resting on something. At first I think it's my aunt's clavicle, but lines criss-cross the skin.

"Someone is wearing the locket."

"What do they look like? Do you recognize them?"

I stare at it. The skin is old and creased. Tucked beneath an old rumpled shirt. "A man. An old man."

"Do you recognize him? Do you know who he is?"

"No," I say with disappointment. "No, I don't. I can't see their face."

There were no men in our lives. No one I'd recognize.

"Come on, Rhi. Try harder. There is always more to see."

"Nothing." I snap open my eyes. "Damn it."

"At least we know it wasn't buried with her," Winnie says, searching for an obvious silver lining on this fresh gray cloud.

"Which means someone stole it."

"The undertaker?" Winnie suggests.

"Was it valuable?" Rosa asks.

"No, I don't think so."

"Then I doubt it was the undertaker. I assume it was

someone looking for the locket for the same reason as you, Rhianna." The old woman downs the last of her tea and places her cup back on the table. "But I do think your aunt wouldn't have been so cryptic. I think the answer is probably right under your nose." She peers towards my pig. Pip? Has she met the little dude? I love him to bits, but pigs are meant to be intelligent and Pip definitely missed that memo.

I'm about to tell her just that, when my stomach tugs violently. I wince, my hands flying to my belly button.

"What is it?" Winnie says.

"Azlan," I say.

"He's coming?" Winnie asks, her face paling.

"Yes."

"How did he find us?"

I peer down at the table where my phone lies. "I turned my phone on." I sigh dramatically. "He's going to be so angry with me."

"I'm sure if you talk with him about all this," Rosa starts.

"They don't really do talking. They mostly bang," Winnie says helpfully and my cheeks burn.

"Well, that's only to be expected. Are you telling me you aren't banging your boyfriend, young lady, because if–"

"Yes, yes, plenty of banging." She grins at her grandma who nods with satisfaction.

"Good to hear it. You're only young once, girls. Make the most of it while you can, because, as good as eating cookies is, it doesn't compare to a hot man between your legs."

I almost choke but Winnie only laughs.

Laughter that stops dramatically at the sound of a strong fist hammering against the front door.

"Should I get it?" Rosa asks.

I take a deep breath in.

"No," I say, standing up and squaring my shoulders. "I'd better go."

The hook in my stomach practically drags me to the front door and I can feel his presence behind the wooden panel, hear his labored breath, smell that scent of his.

I take another of those steadying breaths and open the door.

He glares at me with so much thunder, I'm surprised I'm not struck by actual lightning.

"Come with me," he growls and grabs my arm.

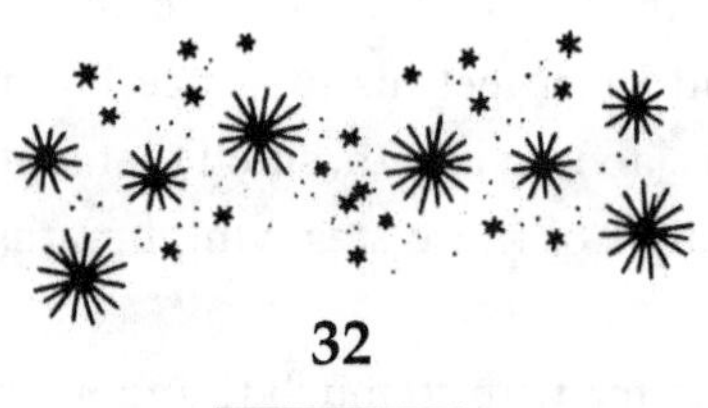

32

R^{hi}

HE DRAGS me down the path before I have a chance to breathe. I pull on his arm.

"What the fuck do you think you're doing?"

He halts. "What am I doing? What am *I* doing?"

"Yes, you can't just turn up at my friend's family home and drag me out without a word. You're not my father."

His eyes flash with more anger. "No, I'm your fated mate. That's meant to mean something, Rhianna."

"Really? Funny because if that was so, you'd think I'd have had a choice in the whole thing."

"It's fate. You don't get a choice. That's the whole damn point." He tugs me closer, growling right in my face. "And I saved your damn life. Maybe it's about time you stopped being such a brat about it and started being grateful."

I stare at him with incredulity written all over my face. "You lied to me."

"I never lied."

"You kept secrets. It's the same thing. And you're still keeping secrets from me."

"Well, so are you. Running away in the middle of the goddamn night." His face cracks, real pain shining in my eyes. "There's a man out there trying to kill you, Rhi. A very dangerous man. How the hell can I protect you if I don't know where you are?"

"It's not your duty to protect me. I can protect myself. I've been doing it a very long time."

"That's where you are wrong. It is my duty. I can't lose you."

"Because I'm your stupid fated mate," I spit back at him.

"No," he says, glaring at me. "Because I care about you."

I stare back at him with even more incredulity. Care about me? Seriously? "Wh-what?"

He sighs, his shoulders and his face softening ever so slightly. "I said I care about you. I care about what happens to you. I care about your safety. I care about where you are. And I care ... about your happiness."

The bond deep in my stomach pirouettes like a spinning top. It makes me giddy.

Is it true? Or more lies? More half truths?

"Do you know how much it hurt to find you gone?" he whispers.

I peek up at his eyes. The raging anger has burned away and I see that hurt shining there instead, like shimmering ashes.

I close my eyes. I'm so confused. So confused about everything. I feel ashamed and guilty. But I'm also so hurt by him too.

"You hurt me too, Azlan. I can't stand all the secrets. I need you to be honest with me. To tell me the truth."

"What secrets am I keeping from you, sweetheart?" he asks with more affection.

I open my eyes and stare up into his. "My mom."

It's fleeting. But it's there. A flicker of something. Alarm? I wait. Will he lie again? Claim he doesn't know what I'm talking about? Is he going to hurt me even more?

"Let me take you home and we'll talk."

I consider his offer and nod.

I say my goodbyes to Winnie and Rosa, and scoop Pip off the floor where he's curled up with the yappy dog, looking far too comfortable. Rosa insists she's taking Winnie back to Arrow Hart herself.

"I'm going to cover for her," she tells me. "Come up with some excuse about how I was seriously unwell and needed her presence immediately." She eyes the man in black with interest. "Want me to cover for you too?"

"No, we'll work something out," I mumble, letting Azlan lead me over to his bike.

Pip looks longingly at the pup by Rosa's feet as I lower him into the box on Azlan's bike but he doesn't make a fuss. Then the two of us are climbing back on his bike, my arms wrapped tightly around his waist and my bond humming all the way up to my chest.

It's easier when it's all physical, when we don't have to talk about the complexities of our feelings, about all the obstacles in our paths, when we can just be, just feel, like now.

It's the early hours of the morning when we pull up outside his house, but I'm not sleepy. I'm wide awake.

"Do you want to head to bed? Talk about this in the morning?" he asks, lifting his helmet from my head and stroking loose strands of my hair from my face, his fingertips tender against my skin.

"No, I want to talk," I tell him.

"Me too," he says resolutely, and I follow him into the dark house, setting Pip down on the floor. Perhaps my little friend senses the tension in the air, or maybe he just doesn't want to witness any banging, because he makes a swift exit out of the room.

"Do you want something to eat? Drink?" Azlan asks me.

I have hardly eaten all day, bar the one cookie at Winnie's grandma's house. I'm light-headed and my stomach aches. But I shake my head. "I want answers, Azlan." I cross my arms over my chest. "I heard you talking to Stone. Last night. I heard you talking about my mom."

He walks to the window and stares out at the darkness, no sign of the dawn yet. "Is that why you ran away?"

"I didn't run away. I went back home. To find my own answers, seeing as no one will give them to me."

"And?" he says, peering over his shoulder.

"How about you answer my questions first? What do you know about my mom?"

"Not a lot."

I huff in irritation and he spins away from the window to face me.

"I've been searching for answers about you since I met you, Rhianna."

"Why?"

"Why do you think?" I shrug stubbornly. "Because I felt

the connection between us and I wanted to know who the hell you were. Why your aunt had kept you hidden all those years. How the hell she'd managed to do it. You know, there were rumors of a girl. An unregistered girl. I followed them up once or twice. It was like chasing wind. I thought they were false. And then I found you and ..."

"You were looking for us?"

"Yes."

"I think I knew it," I say.

He stares at me and the bond between us crackles, begging for us to close the distance between us. But I can't, not until I know everything.

"What did you find out about me?"

"Nothing." I frown. "Honestly, Rhi. There is nothing."

"So I'm just a ghost. A nothing. A nobody," I say repeating those words others have said to me so many times.

"Your aunt kept you well hidden."

"But my mom?"

"I found a file. In the Chancellor's office. A file on a woman I think was your mother."

"The Chancellor? He showed you this file?"

The man in black shifts his weight from one foot to the other. "Not exactly. The Chancellor has never given any hint that he considers you anything but ordinary and of little interest."

"What did the file say?"

"It was incomplete. There were hints there though."

"Hints?" I frown with irritation.

"Reading between the lines, the file seemed to suggest the woman had remarkable gifts. Gifts that would be useful in the authorities' continual struggle with the criminal gangs and the threat from the West. Gifts that could be fatal if they had fallen into the wrong hands."

"What gifts?"

"I don't know, Rhi." He swallows. "What did your aunt tell you about your mother?"

"That she was beautiful. Clever. Kind. That I looked just like her." He nods. "That she loved me. That she'd been so desperate to have me. That I was the ..." my lip trembles and a tear rolls down my cheek, "that I was the light in her life."

The man in black steps forward and cupping my jaw, lifts my face to his and wipes away the tear from my cheek.

"I think you may be the light in mine too, Rhianna," he whispers. I stare at him. I want to believe him so badly. I want to believe that he'd want me despite the bond, despite fate. "I'll help you find your answers, Rhianna. If that's what you want. I'll help you find them."

"Really?" I whisper.

"Yes ..." He hesitates. "As long as you're sure. Sometimes it is better not to know. Sometimes the past is best left untouched."

"Maybe," I say. "But I can't live like this. The not knowing will slowly eat at me until I lose my mind." I take an inhale. "Renzo was at the house."

Azlan's shoulders stiffen. "Did he hurt you?"

"No, Winnie used a displacement spell and we got away."

"You were lucky, Rhi. He's not a man to be toyed with. He's powerful and–"

"Azlan, there's more." I tell him about the men who ambushed me at the cemetery. The men dressed like soldiers.

"Do you think they knew who you were, Rhi?" he says with urgency. "Do you think they were coming after you in particular?"

I shrug. "I don't know. It all happened so quickly."

"I'll find out. There were reports of these incursions. The Chancellor wants me to investigate them."

"It doesn't make sense. Why would they want to capture me?"

"I don't know, Rhi. Maybe you ought to let Stone unlock those memories in your head." His fingers stroke along my jaw and down my throat, setting an ache throbbing between my legs.

"He told you about that?"

"He did."

"I'm scared to open them," I admit in a whisper.

"Then don't."

His finger strokes along my collar bone.

"No," I say. "No, I think I should. I don't want to live in ignorance like this forever. I want to know."

"Then we'll go see the good professor in the morning."

His fingers meander back up my neck and capture my chin. He leans down to kiss me.

"I'm still angry with you," I murmur into his lips.

"Want to show me just how angry you are?" he says, cupping my ass and lifting me onto the nearest available surface.

"This isn't how we should end every fight."

"You want me to stop?" he asks, his fingers already popping open the buttons of my fly.

"No," I confess, rolling down onto the hard, cold counter and lifting my hips so he can peel down my jeans.

I'm wearing the same old underwear I always wear. Low-slung cotton short things that are more about comfort than sex appeal. I decide I need Winnie to take me shopping for an upgrade.

The man in black trails his finger along the waistband of my underwear making me shiver against his touch, all the way along to one hip bone and back to the other, and the need between my legs intensifies.

"We can talk some more if you want to, sweetheart?"

"Enough talking," I pant. "Enough teasing." I capture his hand and guide it inside my panties right where I actually need his touch.

"You are such a brat, sweetheart." He teases me, gliding his fingers along my folds but not dipping inside.

"You sound like Stone," I mutter in frustration.

His hand halts. "Does Phoenix often call you sweetheart?"

Heat sweeps up my cheeks. "No ... I meant ... he's always telling me I'm a brat."

The man in black examines my face. And I'm so damn pleased it's not him who can read my thoughts. How angry would he be? Jealous? Would he care? He says he cares.

I try to read his expression, but there's only curiosity and something a lot darker. Something that has me writhing against his fingers.

"You're so wet," he says. "Always so wet."

"Is it always like this?" I ask him.

"Like what, sweetheart?"

He rings my clit with his thumb, making my legs shake and my core clench.

"I feel like I'm caught up in a whirlwind," I murmur. "Like I'm being thrown from one crazy emotion to the next. Like I want to scream at you and claw your eyes out one minute, and make you moan and fall apart the next. Like I can't stop thinking about the things you do to me."

He stares down at me and doesn't say a word, his eyes turning darker and darker as his thumb flicks against me and he raises me higher and higher.

When I fall apart on his fingers, he grips my thighs and

pulls me to the edge of the counter, ripping away my panties and pulling me right onto his waiting cock. I moan as he thrusts into me and I think Winnie's grandma must be right. Anything that feels this good can't be wrong, and I'm going to enjoy every moment of it while I can. While it lasts.

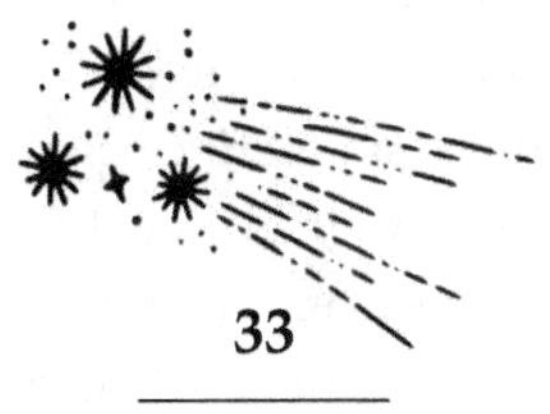

33

S pencer

I LIE ON MY BED, the blind drawn down low, every part of my body aching, my head hammering, my mouth dry, my stomach turning over and over again.

I groan. The pain in my head isn't helped when someone comes banging on my door. The pound of their fist becomes more and more intensive until I give up and yell, "Go the fuck away!" throwing my phone at the door for good goddamn measure.

Instead of doing as I say, the door flings open and Tristan fucking Kennedy swaggers in, the door slamming behind him and making me wince with the whack. No wait, he's not swaggering, he's limping and there are scratch marks down one side of his face, bruises covering the other.

"You're a fucking idiot," I tell him, not even bothering to

attempt to sit up, not if I don't want to spill my guts all over the floor.

"I'm the idiot?" he hisses. A hint of amusement hovers over his face, but I've known the dude long enough. I can see the rage right there, simmering below the surface.

"You could have got yourself killed."

He snorts. "Not a chance. You on the other hand ..."

I certainly feel like I was fucking close. Not that I am going to admit that to the asshole.

He rolls my desk chair across my bedroom floor and drops down on it, kicking his feet up onto my bed. There's a half-smoked joint tucked behind his ear, his eyes are ringed with dark circles, a graze marks his cheek and his hair is a fucking mess.

"You look fucking awful," I tell him.

"I haven't slept. And you don't look so great yourself."

He leans forward, resting his forearms on his knees, his leg jiggling. He's trying to hold back that rage I can see.

"Whatever the fuck you have to say, say it. I'm due a lecture from the principal in half an hour so you can get yours in first."

He stares at me. His leg continues to jiggle.

"Kennedy–"

"He attacked her," he says.

"Her?" I say, like I don't know who the fuck he's talking about.

"Rhianna Blackwaters. Why the fuck would he attack her?"

I roll my gaze away from him and up to the ceiling. "She probably crossed his path."

"Bullshit. He was going to rip her throat out." His voice is so full of tension, I can't help but snap my focus back to him.

"Don't tell me you actually give a damn. The girl is

fucking annoying." The words sound hollow and I wonder if he notices. Because it's clear we're both intrigued by the little thing. The little thing who just happens to be able to wield crimson magic.

The little thing pursued by the werebeast.

I point to his ear and hold out my hand. He drops the joint into my palm and I light it with a flick of my fingers. For a moment, I watch the end smolder, smoke curling up into the air, and then take a long drag.

"You know you'll be in even deeper shit with York if you turn up stinking of weed."

"I'm not going to be in the shit. I'll get a lecture, a slap on the wrist–"

"Rhianna Blackwaters was attacked." That tension is clear in his voice.

I take another long drag, letting the smoke curl around my mouth and down my throat, then breathe it out, the buzz killing some of the pain in my body.

"He wasn't going to hurt her."

"How the hell would you know?"

What do I say? It's not something a magical like Tristan would ever understand, that *any* of the others could ever understand. Living with this monster inside me, constantly clawing to break free, and when he does, trapped inside him, feeling all his emotions and not being able to escape. How could I ever explain it?

What did I feel from him when he had her pinned to the ground, when all I could do was scream in the abyss, spinning in the blackness of nowhere? What had I felt? The same damn emotion the little pig girl evokes from me? Intrigue?

No, more than intrigue. A need to own her. To have her.

I'm not telling Tristan any of that. Not when he looks so

angry. Not when I've seen him look at the girl in the same way.

My eyes automatically fall to my stomach. Thanks to my friend here, the mark is fading, slowly, but it is.

"Do you think that's why it happened?" Tristan asks, his eyes following mine and lingering on my gut.

"Perhaps," I say, because it had been coming long before the girl struck me with her magic. The impact of those pills lessening every day.

I take another puff of the joint and hand it to him. He shakes his head.

"Do you have a hold on it now?" he asks.

The joint hisses, the smoke twists in circles.

"I don't know," I admit.

When Tristan's gone, I drag myself to the shower and wash away all the dirt and dried blood from my body. The warm water eases the ache in my bones but smarts where I'm grazed and cut up.

It's always been strange to peer down at my body, at my arms and my legs, at my hands, and have no idea what they've done, where they've been, or what caused all the marks that line them. The first time, it had left me so disoriented, so dizzy, I'd spent the whole day and night hugging the toilet bowl.

Now I've grown used to it. Now I have better control over it. Or I did.

I cut off the water, and pat myself dry with the towel. Then I put on my uniform, taking special care in front of the mirror, ensuring my hair is neat, my face freshly shaven, my tie straight.

It's the first time I've left my room since the night before and the campus is buzzing with gossip. I knew it would be, the group chats on my phone have been blowing up.

However, despite knowing it would be this way, I still flinch when I hear the words; the awe and the disgust.

I crash through the people, even though it causes my bruised body more pain, and stride towards the mansion. I'm almost there when I feel it in my gut, that sharp tug and the monster inside stirs, suddenly alert, suddenly damn interested.

I swing my gaze around and catch sight of her, walking alongside the Enforcer. Why the fuck is he here? The monster growls. He should be silent. Hardly discernible. He's had his taste of freedom. It should be enough to lay him dormant for weeks, maybe months. But no, he's right here. It's that damn girl.

She twists her head away from the Enforcer and peers towards me, meeting my eyes across the distance. Their caramel color glows in the sunlight and wisps of her dark hair dance in the breeze. She frowns and I frown right back, picking up my feet and jogging up the steps to the mansion, even though it has my guts churning.

The principal is waiting for me in her office, sitting behind her desk. I take a seat on the other side without being asked.

"What happened, Mr. Moreau?" she asks, placing down her pen and closing the letter she was writing.

"I made an error with my medication. It won't happen again."

"You are aware that I would be quite in my rights to expel you. I know your parents sit on the school board – I know you belong to a high-ranking family within the authorities' hierarchy – but if the other students and parents were aware of what you are, they would most definitely demand your expulsion. In fact, the only reason I allowed you to enter the school was the very thorough reassurances I received from you and your family that such an incident like last night's would never happen. I was led to believe you had the matter under your control."

"I do."

"The attack last night would suggest otherwise."

"As I said, it was an error with my medications. I will take steps to ensure such a mistake never happens again."

The principal picks up her pen and taps it on the table-top. "You have my sympathies, Mr. Moreau. I know this situation you find yourself in is a difficult one. The world we live in is a small-minded one with little understanding or empathy for those that are … different. I also have the safety of my students to consider."

"I've been at this school for three years. Nothing like this has ever happened before. And it won't again."

"Good." She pulls her piece of paper back in front of her. "Because I don't want to deprive this school of its greatest dueling asset. Especially when we have the Cross-lantic competition virtually upon us."

Irritation flares in my stomach. Of course, that's the only reason she'll turn a blind eye – no actual concern for my wellbeing – she doesn't even consider asking if I'm okay.

"Good, then let us hope we need never speak of this again," she adds. I nod and stand up. "I look forward to seeing you excel in next week's game Mr. Moreau."

Every step to the door is painful and I wonder if, even with Tristan Kennedy's healing powers, I've any chance of making next week's game.

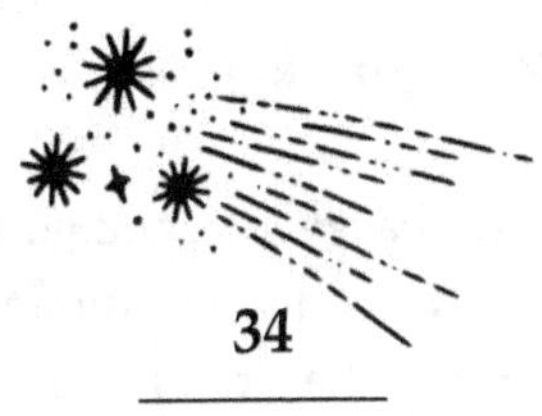

34

S tone

THE LAST PEOPLE I want to see the next morning are, of course, the two people knocking on my door.

I know it's them by the way the hook in my stomach pulls in that direction. I could pretend I'm not in. Make out I'm so deep in sleep I can't hear them, but then Azlan says:

"I know you're in there, Phoenix. Open the door. It's important."

"When is it not?" I mumble, pulling on a pair of pants and stumbling to the door, feeling just as nauseous and crappy as I've been feeling for days now.

He'd messaged me yesterday evening once he'd tracked her down. I didn't respond to his message. Didn't want him to think I cared that he found the little wayward brat. But the fact he messaged me in the first place lets me know he knows how much I do fucking care.

She's all pink cheeks and swollen lips when I open the door, letting me know exactly how the two of them have spent the last few hours. Her hot gaze flirts all over my bare chest and makes the hook in my stomach buzz with excitement.

I take a large pace backwards and go slam on the coffee machine. I need caffeine to dull the stupid sensation.

When I turn back to the two of them, her hot little gaze is dancing around my cabin instead. At all the books scattered over the coffee tables, the kitchen counters and the couch. At the open bottle of scotch resting on the floor by my armchair and the stack of essays I haven't even begun to mark stacked up alongside.

"This place is a mess," she says, wrinkling up her nose.

"You should have seen his dorm room. I think they had to fumigate the place after he moved out."

"Just because I'm not anal with a serious helping of OCD, unlike some people I know."

The girl actually giggles and pokes my friend in the ribs. "I think he means you. I've seen how many times you wipe down the sink."

My friend's lips twitch as if he might actually smile.

I glare at him, conveying just how sickening I find the entire scene. Especially as the girl ran away without telling him where she was going less than twenty-four hours ago. A bit of pussy and all is forgiven.

The half smile drops from Azlan's lips and he glares right back at me.

"We need your help."

"Mine?" I say, pouring myself out a black coffee and downing half the thing. "You know it's Sunday. My day off."

"Rhi wants you to open the memories in her mind."

I take my cup over to my armchair and drop down into the seat. I stare at them both.

"Why the sudden change of heart?"

"I told Rhi what I found in the Chancellor's office about her mother. She wants to know more."

"Can she no longer talk for herself?" I snap.

Rhi rolls her eyes and sends a clear image of a middle finger hurtling my way.

"Do you want my help or not?"

"We do," Azlan says.

"You're doing it again," I hiss. "She can ask me herself."

"Yes, I want your help," she says.

"You're not asking me in a very nice manner, Miss Blackwaters."

Azlan bristles.

"What? Do you want me to get down on my knees and beg?"

If the memories floating around her mind are anything to go by, she's been spending more than enough of her time on her knees, even if the idea is appealing.

You're a pervert, she says loud and clear in her head and I wonder if she made a wild guess at what I was thinking or actually read my thoughts.

I meet her eyes and damn electricity seems to flicker in the air between us.

"Please will you help me, *Sir*?" she says.

Just to antagonize her, I lift my cup to my lips and take a long slow gulp, as if I'm considering her request.

"You're as curious as she is to know what's in those memories. Stop being an asshole," Azlan says.

"I do have essays to mark," I say pointing to the pile of papers on the floor.

"Since when do you actually grade our papers?"

"Phoenix," Azlan growls.

I tear my eyes away from the girl up at him. "I'm only messing. I'll do it. Just let me get dressed first will you. You can barely call this a civilized time of day."

When I return a half an hour later, having taken an especially long shower, I find the girl in my armchair and Azlan frying eggs. I see he's left the bacon in the fridge.

"We'll eat first," he tells me.

"It's probably done best on an empty stomach," I say.

"Because it's going to hurt," she says glaring at me, reminding me of the pain the last time I forcefully tried to rip these memories from her mind.

And in doing so reminds me what I'd seen floating through her mind that night, what had triggered me into wanting to rip them from her in the first place. That wound. That wound that had looked like crimson magic.

I keep my face blank. Now she's inviting me into her mind, I'll be able to see for myself.

"It won't hurt," I tell her. "But it won't be pleasant either. Someone invading your mind can leave you shaken, sick."

"You still want to try?" my friend asks her, sliding eggs onto waiting pieces of toast.

The girl sniffs. "Yes."

"Right. Then follow me to the bedroom."

"Excuse me?" she says.

"I need you lying down."

"I can lie on the floor."

I chuckle. "You're ridiculous, but fine. Suit yourself."

She slides off her seat, eyeing me as she does and rolls down flat on the floor, her hands resting on her stomach. She's wearing jeans that hug her hips and a loose t-shirt that's ridden up to reveal a soft strip of her belly.

I grab a piece of toast and take a large bite, eyeing her.

Then stride towards her, peering all the way down at her, laid out on my hard wooden floor.

"Comfortable?" I ask her.

"Very," she says.

I lick butter off my fingertips and kneel down by her head. Her face is virtually in my lap but she chose the damn floor, not me.

"Now who's on their knees," she whispers.

I can't help a chuckle.

"Close your eyes, Miss Blackwaters." She holds my gaze for one long second, then slowly her lids lower.

I hesitate, knowing Azlan's watching my every move, noting the way her bottom lip quivers as she draws in and out her breath, and her chest rises and dips.

I rest the fingertips of my right hand on her temple and electricity skirts through them.

"What's that?" she says. "Did you start?"

I don't answer and I don't look up at Azlan. My magic rises up through my body, wanting to seek hers out, wanting to make her mine as well.

I force it down, swallowing hard.

"You need to remain quiet and you need to try your best to clear your mind."

I peek inside hers and am met with a mirror, the image of myself lowering to my knees by her head, the same sensation of electricity when I touched her skin.

How can she not know what it means? Or does she know exactly what it means and she's choosing to ignore it like me? Ignore it because she doesn't want it?

I push those thoughts aside. I'm here to help her and, yes, like Azlan said, satisfy my own curiosity too.

"Clear your mind, Rhi." She fidgets slightly and I sense her straining, trying to force the thoughts from her mind and failing. "Don't force it. Relax."

I send calming energy through my fingertips and she sighs, her body going limp. It's erotic and I have to take another of those damn swallows to clear my own stupid thoughts.

Gradually, the thoughts in her mind fade, dissolving away, and without all the noise it's easier to search through them all. I hold back the urge to rifle through them, to dig out that memory of the wound, to learn where and what she was doing yesterday. Instead, I focus in on those thoughts, buried deep, deep down at the very depths of her consciousness. Closed, locked. Impregnable. I nudge at them with my power, testing their durability. Nothing gives. I use a little more force, testing for weaknesses in their binding. Still nothing.

I can hear her breath beneath me, feel the warmth of her skin at my fingertips, and sense the fear, the loneliness, the determination that lies right at the very core of her mind. The pillars of her whole personality, running through her like lines in a stick of rock candy.

I try again, with more force this time. But those memories have been locked tight and no amount of prodding or prying will nudge them free. I'm going to have to rip them apart.

I stare down at her face. Tranquil. Peaceful. Damn beautiful.

I don't want to hurt her. Don't want to hurt her again.

So I try gently at first, gripping the sides of those memories and pulling them open. My magic digs into the sides, and I feel the strain. She murmurs a little beneath me, her eyelids flickering.

"Phoenix?" Azlan whispers with concern.

I hold my left hand up to him, signaling to him to be silent.

Then I try again. I strain harder this time, gripping with my magic and attempting to prize open those memories. She whimpers, her body flinching.

It's no fucking use.

I can't do this, I think, my thoughts sinking into her own mind.

Please, she says in returning. *Please. Just do it.*

I grimace. And her plea echoes around her mind.

Goddamn it! I force my magic deep into the edges of those memories, locked like a safe. I dip them deep, deep down and she moans beneath me.

"Phoenix!" Azlan says.

But it's too late, he can't stop me now.

I grip both sides with the tight vise of my magic and I rip them apart.

She screams, her hands flying to lock around my wrist, her body jolting against the wooden floorboards.

"Phoenix!" Azlan yells. "Stop it, stop it now!"

His words mix with her scream and the loud noise that floods from the broken halves of her memories. She keeps screaming, her grip tight on my wrist as the memories flood through her mind. Dark memories. Nasty memories. Violent memories. Memories that would have been better off locked in her mind forever.

I see them all cascading through her head.

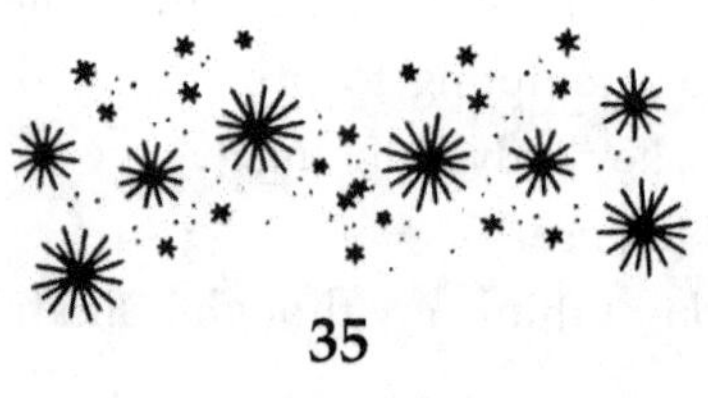

35

———

R^{hi}

WE'RE RUNNING. *Running so fast, grass and brambles scraping against our legs, branches catching our hair.*

Her hand is tight in mine and she's pulling me, forcing me to move my legs.

"I can't," I call out, my little legs so tired, not wanting to run any more.

"Come on, Honey," she urges, "we have to."

But it's no good. I'm too slow and the thunder of heavy boots behind us grows louder and louder.

She swings us to a stop by a tree and lifts me into the branches, beckoning me to climb higher and higher. She follows behind me and I peer down.

"Keep going, Rhi, keep going."

And then she screams and I watch as she falls through the air, down, down to the men waiting for her at the bottom.

I WAKE SCREAMING. *My body shaking. My skin swimming in cold sweat. My nightgown stuck to my tiny body.*

"Rhi," she says, by my bedside, gathering me up in her arms, cradling my body to hers. She kisses my damp cheeks and my forehead, hushing against my skin. "Just a dream, my darling, just a dream."

"They're coming again. They're coming." I sob.

"No, no, just a dream. Just another dream."

I sob harder, as fear racks through my body. "No, Auntie, no."

THE MAN PINS *my arm painfully behind my back. He's huge, a giant, his face cruel and twisted, his breath loud somewhere above my head.*

"Tell us," someone shouts. Another man. Just as big, just as frightening. He's yelling down at my aunt, on her knees in front of us.

"There's nothing to tell. Nothing," she says, her left eye swollen and puffy, blood on her lips.

I struggle against the man's grip, wanting to fly to my aunt's side, wanting to stop all this, wanting to hold her in my arms.

"You're lying." The man smashes his hand across her face and she falls back, meeting the hard floor with a sickening crack.

I'M TREMBLING *in my nightgown. Standing on the landing.*

"Make them stop. Please make them stop." My aunt kneels before me. An old bruise marks her cheek bone and on her lip is a scab where a cut is healing.

"I'm trying to find a way, my darling. I'm trying. You need to be brave for me. You need to be strong."

I bunch my little hands into fists and slam them against the sides of my head. "Make them stop!"

She reaches for my hands, prizes them away from my head.

"They keep us safe, Rhi. They're keeping us safe."

"No they're not. They still come. They still come. And I can't ... make them stop."

"What did you see? What did you see this time?"

A MAN DRESSED IN BLACK. *His face masked in shadow by the dark hood he wears pulled over his head. He lifts his head and magic blasts from his gloved hand.*

ANOTHER MAN, *his face scarred, inks twining up his strong arms, his eyes mismatched colors. He weaves a tight coil around my neck and squeezes and squeezes. I gasp. My lungs burn. The world fades.*

A THIRD MAN. *Lying face down in the dirt. A silver dagger in his skull.*

DEATH AND DESTRUCTION. *Fire engulfing everything. People screaming. People burning.*

Chaos.

❋

"RHI! RHI!" It's not her voice this time. It's louder, stronger, deeper. A voice that tugs me back. That ricochets around my mind and pulls me out of the memories, out of the terrors.

I open my eyes and gasp for air.

I'm shaking, my body caked in sweat. Just like those memories.

And just like those memories, I'm gathered up in strong arms, comforting arms. Arms that hold me close to a solid warm body.

"Rhi. It's okay. It's okay. You're here. You're here." He rocks me back and forth and I cling to him. Cling to him for dear life, frightened that if I let go, I'll be sucked back down into those nightmares. "You're okay now," Stone whispers against my forehead. "You're okay. I've got you."

I swallow, tasting his scent in my mouth; woodsy, bookish, something uniquely his.

"Sweetheart, you're okay," he soothes.

I pull away from him, my entire body still trembling, shaking in his arms, and peer up at him. My vision swims with tears. He stares back at me with concern, none of his usual lazy indifference. His face is as white as I'm sure mine must be and his brow is damp with moisture.

The strange force in my gut, the one I've been trying to deny, the one I've been trying to forget, strains towards him, buzzes at his proximity.

I can feel his heartbeat against my skin. Strong and powerful like his embrace.

"What happened?" I peer up to find Azlan standing above us.

The bond strains for him too and he kneels down next to us.

"It was ..." My voice shakes as violently as my body. I close my eyes, those memories so vivid, so terrifying. The panic rises in my throat and–

Azlan rests his hand on my shoulder and that panic fades away.

I open my eyes and I cup my hand around the back of his neck and pull him in close, pull his mouth right up against mine and kiss him. I kiss him as Stone cradles me in his arms and I hear the professor's breath turn ragged.

I wait to see if the man in black will lift me from Stone's arms and into his.

He doesn't.

I break away from his mouth, and with my body shaking even harder, I turn my head and peer into Stone's eyes.

His eyes are clear and blue like cloudless skies.

I lean forward and press my mouth against his, my heart racing so fast I can hear it in my ears.

I want to know if I'm right. I want to know if this idea I've been harboring is correct. If what I'm feeling is real.

Most of all I want to block those memories from my mind. I don't want to think. I don't want to remember. I just want to feel.

The professor hesitates for a fraction of a second and then he's kissing me back. Pressing his mouth hard against mine and kissing me like he means it, like he wants it, like I'm his.

I shift in his arms turning towards him and I feel another pair of hands at my waist, another pair of lips on my throat.

For a moment I wonder if I'm still trapped inside my mind, if this is all an illusion I'm creating in my own head. My true desires finally manifesting themselves before my eyes.

But it's too real. Too vivid. The strong arms wrapped around my body, the warm hands clasping my waist, the hot mouth sucking at my throat, the soft lips caressing mine.

I rest my palm against Stone's chest, feeling how fast his heart drums, and then I rest my other on Azlan's, his just as frantic.

Does this mean they want this too?

I suck Stone's lower lip into my mouth and rake it through my teeth, making him groan and then I twist my head away, kissing Azlan as Stone drags his teeth down my neck.

A hand reaches under my shirt, calloused fingers brushing against my stomach, over my ribs and cupping my breast. Another hand finds my backside, squeezing through the fabric of my jeans.

That familiar ache strains between my legs and I moan, shifting in Stone's lap until I'm straddling him, something hard pressing against my core. I rock against it as he sucks more desperately on my throat and Azlan lifts my t-shirt over my head.

Stone draws back to stare down at my chest. His eyes turning darker. His hands creeping up to squeeze at my breasts, pinching at my nipples through the material of my bra. My head tips backwards on a long drawn-out sigh and Azlan growls behind me.

"You sure you want to do this?" Stone whispers. And I don't know if he's asking me or Azlan. I don't even know what it is that we're doing. How far this might lead.

I tip my head forward again and meet his eyes.

"No more secrets," I say, trying to sound as determined as I can.

"Secrets?" he says, brow wrinkling in confusion.

I lay my hand on my stomach, where I can feel my bond

with Azlan shimmering, where I can feel that pull towards Stone.

I press my hand to Stone's stomach next.

"Do you feel it?"

He hesitates, peering over my shoulder at Azlan, and for a moment I think maybe I'm wrong, maybe this isn't what I thought it was.

But then he returns his gaze to mine and the look on his face is deadly serious and so real I wonder if I'm finally seeing the true Phoenix Stone.

"Yes."

"And what do you feel?"

He's still pressed against my core, still hard.

"A bond."

"What does it mean?"

"You're not as stupid as you look, Miss Blackwaters," he says, trying some of his usual nonchalance. "You know what it is."

I peer over my shoulder to look at Azlan.

"How is that possible?"

"For one person to have two fated mates? Why wouldn't it be possible?"

"Do you have another?" I ask him. "Do you?" I ask Stone.

They both shake their heads. "Then–"

"You're our core."

"Core?"

"Like the spokes on a wheel. You are our core."

I frown, confused. I have so many questions. Why have they never told me? What are we going to do about it? What it can all mean?

"Are you saying there could be more?" I say. "More fated mates?"

Stone chuckles. "Two not enough for you, Blackwaters?"

"No ... I just ..." I frown because this sensation, the one in my stomach, the one I now know is my bond, I've felt it with others, haven't I? Not as strong, not as powerful, but I have felt it.

But then they're both kissing me again, kissing me like I'm worthy of all their attention, and it feels so special, so different, to be worshiped instead of reviled. To be loved instead of ignored. Everything in my belly and between my legs hums. And I forget all about my doubts and my questions.

"Let's take this to the bedroom," someone says and I'm being lifted into strong arms, two pairs of mouths still on my skin, and carried through the small cabin and lowered onto an unmade bed that smells of Stone.

He lies down beside me, his gaze locked on my tits as Azlan undoes the buttons of my jeans and tugs them down my legs taking my panties with them.

Stone meets my eyes and then his gaze trails slowly down my body, so hot I can almost feel the heat of it on my skin. His eyes linger again at my chest, then meander over my belly, lower and lower until he's staring at the place between my legs.

He glances up at me a second time, then lowers his head and kisses me tenderly, right between my legs, making my entire body shiver with desire.

"Take your clothes off, Phoenix," Azlan says, already shedding his own at the end of the bed.

I lift my head to watch them both. The man in black is taller than his friend and darker, his skin marked only by a handful of stubborn scars. In contrast inks criss cross Stone's muscular frame, his hair and beard are the color of tree bark and his eyes light.

Maybe this is a dream? Maybe they are playing me,

fooling me, tricking me with some kind of deceptive magic? Because how is it possible? How? How can I be the fated mate for these two men? Powerful, strong, beautiful.

"You're all those things too, Rhi," Stone says, hot gaze trailing down my body again and making me blush.

"Me?" I scoff.

"Haven't you escaped the clutches of Renzo Barone twice now?" Azlan says.

"Twice?" Stone says, eyes flicking to his friend.

"Yesterday, at the house," I confess.

"How did you–"

"Winnie used a displacement spell."

Stone chuckles, shaking his head. "A displacement spell."

He stalks towards the bed, shedding his boxers as I unhook my bra, and I get my first look at his cock. Long, thick, curved and pierced at the head with a silver ring.

I gasp and my already-racing heart beats that little bit faster, my pussy making a mess of his sheets already.

I roll up to meet him.

"Is that thing safe?" I ask him.

"My cock," he says with a smirk. "I know I'm bigger than Azlan but–"

Azlan snorts.

"Not your cock, that ring. It looks like–"

"It might make things really good for you? Yeah, it will." He pushes me back down on the mattress. "But not yet. I want to watch as he makes you come first," he says, gesturing to his best friend.

I look between the two of them and raise an eyebrow. "You've done this before, together, haven't you?"

Azlan grunts and Stone chuckles. "The man was practically celibate before he met you."

"Really?" I say. He's been anything but celibate with me. Has he been making up for lost time or is it because he's really into me?

"He had plenty of offers and never took them up, so make what you will of that."

"These private conversations you keep having," Azlan says, opening my legs and settling down between my thighs, "are going to get really old, really quickly."

"So you've really never done this together before?"

"I've never had a desire to see Stone naked before."

"You do now?"

"No, I have a desire to share my mate with her other fated partner. With my best friend. With a man I've always known would share my fate."

"What?"

"Phoenix and I have always shared a connection. A platonic connection," he adds quickly, seeing my eyebrows rise up my forehead. "I knew if I ever found my fated mate, that mate would be Phoenix's too."

"Stone and I are not bonded though ..." I start to say, but my words trail off as he lowers his mouth to the place I'm throbbing and needy.

Stone lies down on his side next to me on the bed, elbow bent, head resting in his hand. He watches my face, then reaches out to touch me, fingers circling my nearest nipple, making the tender skin crinkle and stiffen. Then his gaze drops down to where his friend is sweeping his tongue leisurely through my folds.

"That's how you like it? Slow and gentle." I shake my head, biting down hard on my lip. "Oh he's teasing you is he? Putting on a show for me."

He tweaks my nipple between his finger and thumb,

rolling it back and forth, and I cry out, back arching against the mattress.

"Do you like when he kisses your cunt, Miss Blackwaters?"

"Yessss," I moan.

"Have you been dreaming about me kissing your cunt?" he whispers into my ear. He knows I have. He can see the fantasy right there in my mind. "Ahhh, in the classroom, huh? You wanted me to lie you on my desk and eat you out?"

Azlan groans, his mouth vibrating against my clit and making me moan. I can't help myself, I grind against his mouth and this time it's Stone who groans.

"Shit, such a dirty, little brat."

"I'm not a brat," I whimper as tears begin to trail down my cheeks.

"You are and it's been driving me fucking mad. Do you know how many times you've made me hard? How many times I've *wanted* to bend you over my desk just like you imagined? How much I've wanted you? How much I've wanted to taste your sweet pussy, just like he is doing now? How does it taste, Az?"

The man in black growls possessively.

"Time you were a good girl, Miss Blackwaters," Stone says. "Time for you to do what you're told. Time for you to come."

Then he leans down and kisses me and my world tilts even further than it already has, my breath lost with his, my senses overwhelmed by the feel of Stone's lips and tongue against my mouth, and Azlan's against my pussy.

Stone kisses me deeper, his hand tweaking and kneading at my breast and Azlan spreads me wider, hooking my legs over his shoulders and sucking on my clit.

I cry out again, one hand tight in Azlan's dark hair, the other in Stone's brown.

The sensations in my body build, my magic swirling through me, rising and falling, meeting Azlan's and Stone's, dragging them closer, bringing them into me. My legs shake around Azlan's head and my stomach tightens. Every part of my body tingles with awareness, and just when I don't think I can take any more, when it's all too much, Azlan flicks me hard with his tongue and I come, bliss pouring through my body, from my core all the way to the ends of my toes and tips of my fingers.

Stone draws back to watch my face, holding my gaze with his sky-blue eyes, watching as my body jolts with each of the aftershocks of pleasure.

When it ends and my body is lifeless and limp, Azlan crawls up my body, kissing my thigh and my hip bone, my stomach and my breast. Then he whispers in my ear:

"Do you want him to touch you too?"

"Y-y-yes," I admit. I've been dreaming about him touching me for a very long time.

"Have you now?" Stone says with a smirk, but before I have a chance to whack his shoulder, he's scooting down my body and parting my thighs again. I can tell I'm a mess down there, wet with my arousal and Azlan's spit, but rather than looking disgusted, Stone's eyes seem to darken.

"It's erotic, Miss Blackwaters," he says, sweeping his fingers over me. "Really erotic. Seems like you're a good girl after all, making yourself all nice and wet for us."

He finds my entrance and rings it, again and again until my breath turns needy, then he dips a finger inside, the sound wet when he does.

"Are you sore?" he asks. "Has he been fucking you too much?"

"No, I'm not sore," I say, the words turning into moans as he adds a second finger, exploring until he finds the spot inside that sends me wild. He massages at it, eyes locked on where I'm swallowing his fingers. Azlan watches too. He's right, it is erotic, so much so that it doesn't take long until I'm dancing on the end of his fingers, coming hard and clenching around his digits.

"Well, this is proving a very pleasant way to spend a Sunday morning," he says as he drags his fingers from me, looking at the mess I've made all over them.

I prop up on my elbows, feeling flushed and light-headed. "Better than watching me shovel shit?"

He laughs. "It's a close second." He winks at me, then licks my arousal from his fingers. I stare transfixed.

"Doesn't it taste–"

"Really good?" Azlan says, nuzzling my ear. "Yeah, it does."

I'm not sure I can quite believe that, but I like the way I'm turning them on. I never considered I could do that. Never considered I owned a body or a face that would catch anyone's interest in that way.

"Are you kidding me?" Stone says, grabbing my hands and jerking me up onto my knees. "Have you seen this ass?" He gives my backside a slap that sends a jolt through my pussy, a jolt that has me swallowing down on a moan.

He lifts an eyebrow as if to say, "I know you like that", but keeps that piece of information to himself.

I rest my hands on his shoulders and wriggle my ass. He groans and lands his hand back there, squeezing.

"I'm so fired," he mutters.

And as the words leave his mouth, there's a knock on his front door.

His eyes dart that way and then he's maneuvering me off his lap, and tugging on his jeans, leaving the bedroom and closing the door firmly behind him.

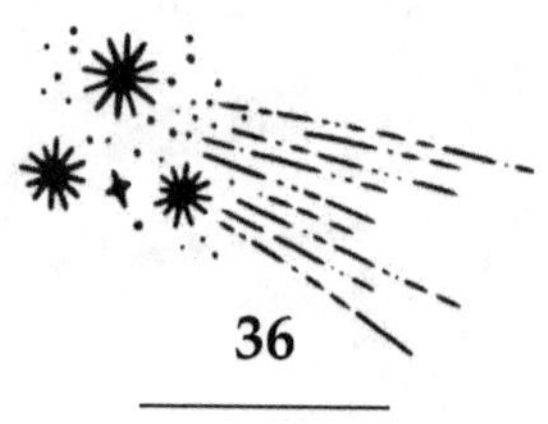

36

S tone

PEOPLE USUALLY KNOW to leave me well alone on a Sunday, so the rap of another pair of knuckles on my cabin door can only be a bad thing.

I'm going to be fired. As soon as they find out about this, because they inevitably will. And I inevitably won't be able to stay away from her. Not when she's my mate. Not when every fiber of my body is straining towards her, not when my magic sang in my body when I made her come with my fingers.

They say it's all the more potent with your mate. That it's addictive. Now I understand the change in my friend. Now I know I'm as doomed as he is.

It's why I fought this thing so vehemently in the first place.

I just didn't expect to be fired quite as quickly as this. Is there some kind of magical surveillance I'm unaware of, one that detects as soon as a teacher lays one finger on a pupil? Is that even possible?

I try to straighten my hair and then I draw back the door.

The principal stands on my porch, dressed in her usual tweed suit, even though it's meant to be her day off too. In fact, I don't think I've ever seen her dressed in anything remotely casual.

I am definitely fired.

"Principal York," I say loudly enough that my companions in the bedroom can hear, "to what do I owe the pleasure?"

"Apparently Rhianna Blackwaters may be missing from campus, again," she says with obvious irritation. "Do you happen to know of her whereabouts? You were the last person to see her."

Is she playing with me? She takes in my half-dressed state, my ruffled hair. Hell, I can smell the girl's arousal on my fingers. I hope to god the principal has a poor sense of smell.

My brain plays through a thousand different scenarios, excuses and explanations for Rhianna's absence. I clutch at the first reasonable one.

"Yes, she's been in my cabin."

The principal frowns. "Excuse me?"

"Rhianna Blackwaters has been recuperating after the werebeast attack in my cabin. I wanted to be able to observe her."

"Phoenix, this is highly inappropriate. Why on Earth was I not informed of her ill-health and why wasn't she taken to the infirmary, where the matron could watch over her?"

"Stella," I say, "we both know Pippa's skills are limited. Miss Blackwater's injuries could have led to a were infection if not treated and monitored with the utmost care and attention."

York narrows her eyes. I don't think she's buying one bit of this story. I've never shown much of an interest in helping my students before, and I've never suggested the matron's talents may be lacking. Shit, I hope that doesn't get back to the woman. She's not half bad really.

The principal's mental shields are too well practiced for me to see what she's thinking, not without force anyway.

"I'd like to talk to Rhianna."

"Miss Blackwaters is sleeping. She had a restless night."

"Is the treatment not working?"

"No, but the attack has caused some disturbing night terrors."

"You were in her room at night!"

I decided I'd better change the subject. "Any further explanation on how the werebeast was able to enter the campus?"

The principal's face remains absolutely passive but I spot her tell, the way she adjusts the collar of her tweed jacket. "No, I'm still looking into it. I've tightened security. Miss Blackwaters can rest assured there will be no further intrusions from such a beast." She peers over my shoulder with suspicion. "I assume she's well enough to return to her own room?"

"Yes, as soon as she wakes up."

"Send her to the matron first. Then on to me." I nod. "And Professor Stone, I understand your concern for the girl but your actions are inappropriate, and given the matron's years of experience, unwarranted. I need not remind you that students are strictly forbidden from entering a member of staff's personal quarters. I am disappointed to say I will have to issue you with a written warning. Do not let this happen again."

"Of course not. I apologize. Ill judgment in trying circumstances."

She hums with suspicion and leaves.

I close the door, not knowing whether I'm relieved or disappointed. Not fired. Just a written warning.

Did I want to be fired? For the principal to force my hand? Perhaps, because having this girl around is going to be a million times harder now.

"You have to go," I say as I open the door and find the two of them perched on the end of my bed. Azlan has his boxers back on and the girl is dressed in her t-shirt and panties, somehow looking even more delicious than she did spread out and naked. Perhaps it's the flushed cheeks and messed up hair, the slight glaze in her eyes like we took her to heaven and back.

She nods her head.

"I told her you've been recovering in my cabin from the werebeast attack, somewhere I could look after you and ensure you were treated right."

"Did she buy that?" the girl asks, nibbling her thumb.

I shrug. "I'm being given a written warning for allowing a pupil into my cabin. But unless you tell her otherwise, I think we're safe."

"I won't tell her otherwise," she says.

"No, because then you'll have to tell her where you really were. As in, not on campus."

"And I don't want you to lose your job."

I sniff, picking up my shirt from the floor and pulling it back over my head. "This job ..."

"Why did you take it if you hate it so much?"

"That," I sigh, "is a long story. And you have to get going. She wants you to go straight to the infirmary to be seen by the matron and then to her office."

"Crap," she says, bending down to fetch her jeans and wiggling them up her long legs.

There isn't really any urgency or hurry, but now I've had a rude awakening from the principal, I'm thinking with my head again and not my dick. This situation is ... difficult. It will become even more so if I sleep with her. And, shit, I was really, very close to doing just that. Her tight, dripping wet pussy hovering right above my cock.

I take a deliberate stride towards the door. My room smells too much like her, her arousal all over my sheets. I'm going to have to wash them, otherwise it will drive me insane.

"We need to talk about this," she says, from behind me.

"This?" I say, hesitating.

"What just happened. Our ... connection. What we're going to do about it."

"We will. Just not now."

I hear her cross the room, her little hand landing on my shoulder.

"I want to have a choice in this. No more surprises. No waking up in a hospital bed to find I'm bonded."

I peer at my friend, who's staring into space with a steely look on his face.

"He saved you," I say in his defense.

"I know. I just ... I just want more control this time."

I nod, even though I don't know how much control I have to give, especially with her warm breath on my neck and my bond thrumming in my core.

"And the memories ..."

I snap my gaze back to hers. "I can search for a way to lock them back up."

"No, no, I don't want that." She takes a steadying inhale, her body shaking ever so slightly. "But," her eyes flicker around my face, "I might need your help to understand them. Both of your help."

"I think that's sensible. Don't be tempted to approach them without us."

She nods and I rest my hand over hers. And for a minute feel as our magic curls around one another's, longing to combine us.

Then I snatch my hand away.

"You need to go." She hesitates. "Rhi–"

"He said he had a gift for me."

"Who?" I say, my brow crinkling.

"Barone." Azlan's spine stiffens. "Teeth."

"Teeth?"

"I think they were human."

"Andrew Playford's?" I ask Azlan.

"Andrew's!" she says, alarmed.

"His body has been found," Azlan says softly.

"Oh." Her gaze falls to the floor.

"He deserved to die," I say through gritted teeth. "He betrayed you. Handed you over to be ..."

"No one deserves to die," she says. Then shakes her head. "You think Barone killed him. Why would he do that?"

"I don't know," Azlan says. "The authorities seem to think Andrew had gotten himself tangled up in gang business."

"Oh," she repeats, picking her shoes up from the floor.

I see her to the door and when it closes behind her, I rest my forehead against the pane of wood and attempt to catch my breath.

"It was always going to happen," Azlan says. "You could only fight it for so long."

And how can I argue with him? He's been through this too. Faced the same temptations. And even my friend, a man I've seen deny himself all manner of pleasures and indulgences, who shunned his family's wealth and luxury for a much harder life, stumbled when it came to this girl.

"If she wasn't so ..."

"Yeah, if she wasn't."

"If I claim her, if I seal the fated bond–"

"We'll find a way to make it work."

"You think we can? That we can live that way?"

"Yes," he says simply.

If the fated-mate bond is rare, the fated-mate bond between one core and many is even rarer. But there have always been cases. Throughout history, throughout time. How I ended twisted up in one is beyond belief to me. Even if, like Azlan, I always knew we'd share the same fated mate if fate ever gave one to us.

She thinks she's unworthy. A nobody. A nothing. She has no idea.

But they've been known to work.

"There was a memory in her head ..." I say, turning slowly to face my friend.

"Yes?" His face is flooded with curiosity. He watched his mate writhe on the floor when I unlocked those memories. He must be dying to know what lay inside.

"Of crimson magic."

"What are you saying, Phoenix?"

"History," I say simply.

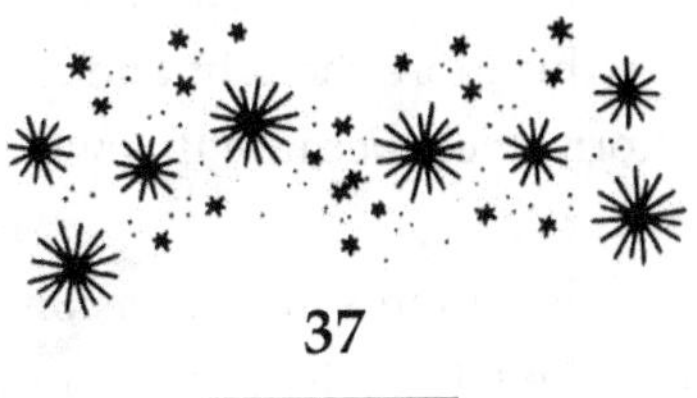

37

R^{hi}

MY BODY DOESN'T WANT me to leave that cabin. The strange sensation in my core, the one I now know to be my bond, doesn't want me to leave either. Both were more than content, cocooned between those two men and it is like ripping off my own skin to leave them. It's that intense, and the fated-mate bond isn't even sealed with Stone yet.

Do I want it to be sealed? My body and the bond both scream yes. But my heart. And my mind. They're less sure.

Stone has hurt me. He tried to rip those memories from my mind on Founders' Night. He chained me to the bed in that motel. He dumped a pile of manure in my face. Not to mention all the times he's laughed in my face too.

So what if he looked at me back there with tenderness, with ... reverence? So what if he pulled me from those nightmares and soothed me in his arms? So what if he pleasured me and never asked for anything in return? So what?

It doesn't undo all the lies. All the cruelness.

I need to give this more thought and more time. I need to stop being a horny mess because that will only land me in trouble.

I weave my way towards the mansion, practicing the story I'm meant to be telling the principal about my whereabouts, and trying my best not to dwell on those newly unlocked memories. As I approach the mansion, I'm so caught up in my own thoughts, I almost walk straight into the solid frame of Spencer Moreau.

"Oh sorry," I mumble, frowning when I realize who it is. Then I frown even harder. He's dressed in his school uniform, even though it's the weekend. But that's not the cause of my frown. He looks awful. His skin has a sickly sheen to it, there are scratches and bruises over his face and down his neck, and a large chunk of hair is missing from the side of his scalp. "Oh my god, what happened to you?" I can't help but yelp.

Did he get into a fight with Tristan? Is that why they're both looking beaten up? Or were the two of them in a fight together with someone else? And why haven't they healed their injuries?

"Nothing," he mutters. He hesitates, eyes flicking over my form. "You were attacked? By the werebeast?"

I guess good news travels fast.

"Yes."

"Were you ... hurt?"

I scowl at him. "If you're asking me if I am now infected with the were curse, I'm sorry to disappoint you, but no."

Is it my imagination or do his shoulders slacken? Probably because he is in fact disappointed by this information.

"And you weren't hurt?" he asks.

I peer up at the mansion, remembering my cover story. "No, I was hurt a little. Professor Stone was treating me all yesterday and I'm feeling better now."

He looks at me with confusion. "Professor Stone?"

I decide I don't want to stick around for anymore interrogation and step around him, hurrying towards the mansion.

He didn't seem convinced by that story. I hope the principal will be.

The infirmary is not somewhere I've ever been. I find it spread out across the whole of the basement floor of the mansion, big enough to be a hospital wing with all its many beds. I don't see why it needs to be so large, especially as the place is completely devoid of any patients. Maybe that's why the matron comes bustling out of her nurse's station with such enthusiasm when I step through the door.

"Are you unwell?" she says eagerly.

"I'm Rhianna Blackwaters. I was attacked by the–"

"Werebeast. Yes, I was expecting to see you much sooner. But I understand Professor Stone saw to your treatment." She says this a little stiffly as if she isn't happy with his obvious interference into her domain.

"Yes, that's right, but the principal asked that I come and get checked out by you."

The matron smiles at me. She has rosy cheeks, and her white starched uniform stretches over her round figure.

"Quite right. Follow me Miss Blackwaters."

She leads me to the last bed on the end row where several machines wait lined up against the wall and draws a blue curtain around us.

"Strip off and pop this on," she hands me a very unattractive-looking hospital gown, "and let's get you checked out. I'll wait out here. Call me when you're done."

I strip down like she requests, noticing I have a collection of love bites on my chest and probably on my neck too. I hope she'll mistake those for injuries and not what they really are.

When I'm dressed in the gown, I call her back in. She spends a long time inspecting the places I tell her the were-beast injured me, reluctantly admiring Stone's handiwork. Then she hooks me up to various machines, testing my blood pressure, temperature and other things I don't understand.

"We don't appear to have your medical record," she mutters as she listens to my heart.

"I don't think I have one."

She lowers her stethoscope. "Why ever not?"

"I rarely went to the doctors."

"You weren't often sick?"

"Well ..." I'm guessing she doesn't know my background. "My aunt tended to keep me away from doctors. We only ever went if it was absolutely necessary."

The older woman lowers the stethoscope to her lap. "Have you been properly vaccinated, Miss Blackwaters?"

I stare at her. "I have no idea."

"Oh my goodness. They should have sent you to me as soon as you entered this school. No vaccinations? My goodness. This school is a breeding ground for all sorts of bugs. Last year we had a bout of flu and every one of these beds was occupied." She shakes her head. "I'd better order some in." She removes a small notebook from her breast pocket and scribbles a note to herself. "Well, despite your lack of formal healthcare and your recent run-in with a werebeast, you appear to be in good health. I'll send you a note when the vaccinations come in and we'll get you all sorted." She pats me on the shoulder. "You can get dressed."

"Thank you," I say, then hesitate.

"Yes?" she asks.

"Erm ..." I say, feeling my cheeks heat.

"What is it, Miss Blackwaters? I can assure you I've heard it all – boils on bottoms, warts on noses, backed-up bowels."

"Contraception," I spit out. "I'd like to get some contraception. Can you help with that?"

"You have a regular partner," she begins, "because if not, I'd suggest you need to protect against STDs and use–"

"Oh no, I don't," I lie, not entirely sure how confidential this information is. I don't want the principal to hear I have a boyfriend and put two and two together. "It's just in case I do get a regular partner."

"Then let me fetch you a leaflet. There are lots of options including hormonal pills, injections, and barrier spells."

"Barrier spells?"

"Yes, a fairly advanced spell but, if performed correctly, almost 100% effective." She pauses. "Do we need to do a pregnancy test too, Miss Blackwaters?"

I guess she isn't buying the no-boyfriend thing. Maybe she spotted the love bites after all.

"No," I say. We've been using rubbers so I'm pretty confident of that but there have been a few occasions when we've almost forgotten and getting myself knocked up is not another problem I want to add to my long list.

The matron disappears behind the curtain and I dress back in my clothes. When she returns, she hands me a leaflet that I bury deep in my pocket.

Then I head for yet another interview with the principal.

✳.

WHEN I RETURN to the dorm about thirty minutes later, having endured an interrogation from the principal, I find Trent just leaving our dorm and Winnie working at her desk, Pip munching on what looks like vegetable peelings.

"Nonny thought he might like them," Winnie explains. "Where have you been?"

"The principal's office."

Winnie grimaces, then examines my face. "You don't look upset. I don't know if that means you are or aren't expelled."

"Not expelled. Stone covered for me."

"Professor Stone covered for you?"

"Erm, yes," I say, coming to sit up on Winnie's desk.

"Because you're bonded to his best friend?" she asks slowly, clearly believing that to be unlikely.

"Not exactly."

"Then why would he be so nice?"

"Because," I say, swinging my legs and nibbling on my lips. I've been such a private person for such a long time, mainly because I only really had Pip to confide in – as much as I loved my aunt, my boy fantasies were not something I wanted to tell her about. It's hard to break a habit of a lifetime and open up to people now. But I made a vow. No more secrets from Winnie. So I'm going to confess. Even though she'll think I'm some sort of hussy. "We were getting it on this morning. And when I say we ..."

"Yes?" Winnie says, mouth falling open in surprise.

"I mean me, the man in black and the professor."

"All three of you!" she shrieks.

I gulp. "Yes."

"Wh-what? ... I mean, seriously? ... I mean, how?" She shuffles back her chair so she can get a better look at me.

"Me and the man in black, we talked last night. And he told me what he knows about my mom."

"Uh uh, hang on, as interested as I am in your mom, back up to the threesome bit, please."

"I'm getting there. Just wait. He doesn't know as much as I hoped."

"You think that's the truth?"

I nod. "So I decided I wanted to open those memories in my mind."

"Wow, Rhi."

"Yeah," I swallow. "We went to see Stone this morning–"

"And somehow you ended up sleeping with them both."

"I didn't technically sleep with them both. It didn't get that far. Stone opened those memories and ..." I shudder really hard, so hard the table shakes underneath me. Winnie reaches out to squeeze my hand.

"Oh, sweetie, I'm sorry."

"He was comforting me, dragging me back, away from the nightmares and then ... then one thing led to another, and maybe I would have slept with them both, but things kind of got interrupted by the principal."

"What the ...?! The principal walked in on you having a threesome? How are you not expelled?"

"She didn't catch us. But that's why Stone was forced to cover for me."

"And your mate was happy with all this? Happy to share you in a threesome? Because the way that man looks at you sometimes – sort of all dark and possessive like–"

"He does not!"

"Erm, yes, he does Rhi. He gives off massive," she lowers her voice, making it all gruff, "she's-mine-don't-touch-her vibes."

"He didn't have a problem with it. He was ... into it."

Winnie whistles. "Wow. Virgin to threesomes in record speed, Rhi."

"I know, is it awful?" I lift my hands to my cheeks. "Am I awful?"

"No, no. If it's what you wanted. If no one was forcing you, or coercing you. If it was your choice–"

"It was. I totally initiated it."

Winnie grins. "Can I be you when I grow up please, Rhi?"

I laugh. "You do not want to be me, Winnie. I have a killer on my tail. A werebeast who wants to eat me. And some scary nightmary memories now circling in my head."

"Plus two hot men who are happy to share you and a really darn, adorable pet pig."

"Adorable is he now?"

"He's growing on me."

We both stare down at Pip who's demolishing potato skins so quickly I'm pretty certain he's going to make himself sick.

My friend stares back up at me, shaking her head in admiration. "I still can't believe the man in black was willing to share. You've cast some crazy-ass spell over that man." I chew at my thumb. "There's more, isn't there? I should know that by now. There's always more."

"Stone is my fated mate as well as Azlan."

I actually feel sorry for my friend. I wish I'd given her some prior warning to this piece of news, because she loses the ability to speak, making strange gurgling noises in her throat instead. I consider slapping her around the face, just to get her to snap out of it.

"You know I've been drawn to him. That I've been developing feelings for him. But it's more than that. There's this pull in my gut to him as well as Azlan and he admitted to me that he feels it too."

"Wow," is all my friend can manage to say, looking utterly bewildered.

"Have you ever heard of it before?" I ask her. "One person having more than one fated mate?"

"Ahhh, now I get it," Winnie says, nodding slowly. "That's what the whole thing about the two boyfriends was about." My cheeks sizzle. "Yeah, I've heard of it," Winnie says, answering my question. "But like in stories and fairy-tales. Never in real life."

"Wow," I say, repeating my friend. "Aren't I the lucky one?"

"Errr, yes," Winnie says. "Both those men are so hot they probably melt tarmac and buildings wherever they go."

I roll my eyes, then ask her the question that's been nagging me. "So in these stories, it's just two fated mates, right? No more than that?"

"Rhi," she says, "what are you asking me?"

I manage a self-abasing eye roll because I'm not certain and I'm not sure I can admit it to myself let alone Winnie – not when they've treated me like dirt.

"I just want to brace myself in case there's some other fated mate out there lurking around the next corner."

"I mean I think I remember one old fairytale from this book Nonny had but I don't remember the details beyond the fact she had several fated mates."

"Several?"

"Four? Or maybe it was five."

"Four. Or five," I mutter, feeling a little sick.

Is that something reserved simply for fairytales like broomstick riding and familiars? Or can that happen in real life too?

"Did you seal it? Seal the bond with Stone?" Winnie says, knocking me out of my reverie.

"No, we haven't had a chance to talk about it yet. To make any decisions."

"Do you want to seal it?"

"He's been a real jerk to me. Way worse than Azlan."

"But he's your fated mate."

"So what? I already have one. Who says I need another?"

"You read all the stuff I printed out for you. Denying your fated mate–"

"Will lead to a lifetime of misery. Say the same stupid magazine with articles about how to make your pussy look baby-face smooth. And how to bake the perfect cake for your man. They're pushing an agenda."

I need to get my hands on the real literature. The books that Stone has been studying in his office. The books I need to quiz him about.

Winnie doesn't look very sure, but she doesn't push me on it. Instead, she tells me about her own encounter with the principal.

"I didn't think I stood a chance. But it turns out my grandma can be a very formidable woman. The principal didn't even try to argue with her or question my story."

"So we're both off the hook."

"Yeah, it seems that way for now."

38

R^{hi}

EXPULSION MAY HAVE BEEN the preferable outcome. Because the next day we arrive in the hall for breakfast and it seems the entire school has heard about the werebeast attacking me. Everybody avoids me like the plague. Taking two steps away from me as I collect my breakfast and go sit at our usual table. Even Trent keeps his distance although at least he talks to me for Winnie's benefit.

"Summer's telling everyone the werebeast bit you and that the school is covering it up. She's saying it went for you because you ..." Trent scratches the back of his neck, "smell like pig shit."

"Delightful," I mutter.

"The werebeast didn't bite her and both Matron and Professor Stone have treated her and checked her over. She's not infected."

I nod profusely, although all this talk is making me a little nervous. Did Stone's magic definitely one hundred percent work? I hope so.

"Yeah, I know Summer's a bitch and everyone knows she's lying, but I guess everyone is on edge too after that attack. Everybody's scared. How the hell did a werebeast get on campus?"

When Trent leaves us, I lean over to whisper to Winnie.

"Was anyone else attacked by the werebeast?"

"No, just lucky old you."

"Hmmm," I say, attempting to swallow a mouthful of lumpy porridge. "I thought maybe Tristan and Spencer had been too."

"Why?" Winnie says, dragging her spoon through the gray gloop.

"I saw them both – Tristan later that night and Spencer Sunday morning. They both looked pretty beaten up."

"Oh," Winnie says, giving up on the porridge and dropping her spoon into the bowl. She leans in a little closer. "Rumor has it most of the cool kids head down to some illegal dueling club in the outskirts of the city most weekends."

"Illegal? In what way?"

"Let's just say, the dueling is pretty unrestricted and there aren't the usual rules that stop folks from seriously hurting one another. That's what I've heard, anyway. It's not like I've ever been." She shrugs. "I bet that's why the two of them were looking beat up. Although, it's pretty stupid so close to their biggest match of the year."

"They are pretty stupid though, aren't they?" I hiss. "I mean, who would want to fight just for the sake of it?" I shake my head, my gaze floating to the two of them sitting at their usual table in the hall. They're looking less beaten up than they did, although I have to say, neither is looking like their usual healthy selves.

I'm not convinced by Winnie's explanation, though. I think of those unhealed gashes, those bruises. Tristan Kennedy, especially, has a permanently flawless face. Any hair out of place has been specifically crafted that way. There's no way he wouldn't heal his face if he could. It would hurt his pride and his massive ego far too much.

I shake my head again.

"So it was just me who was attacked."

"Just you."

"Maybe I'm super paranoid, but it did feel personal." I remember the beast's words. "It was as if it was coming for me."

"Then maybe it was another assassin sent from the Wolves of Night."

"Stone and Azlan don't think so."

"Stone and Azlan, huh?" Winnie waggles her eyebrows. "This next lesson will be fun."

I groan. The more time that's passed since my liaison with the man in black and my professor, the less sure and the more embarrassed I'm feeling about the whole thing.

I keep thinking of the way Stone slid his fingers from inside me and I'd made a horny mess all over his hand. I cringe. That really isn't an image I want in my head when I step into his classroom. I don't want him believing I've been reliving every moment of that encounter. Because I have most definitely *not* been thinking about how good both their mouths felt on my skin, or what a turn on it was to have Stone watch as Azlan made me fall apart.

The problem is, it's either that or the new memories unleashed in my head, and I'm not brave enough to explore those again just yet.

Unfortunately, Stone is a full ten minutes later than he usually is, leaving me to stew in my thoughts, overhearing all the whispered words about my attack bubbling around the classroom.

When he finally shows up, he looks surprisingly pulled together. His hair combed, his suit pressed, his beard trimmed, and he smells of some cologne.

"You look very smart today, Professor Stone," Summer chirps, fluttering her eyelashes at him and making me want to strangle her with my bare hands.

"Thank you," he says, adjusting his collar and giving her a half-smile. "I have a date tonight."

"A date, huh?" Summer teases.

He doesn't look my way. In fact, he seems to be deliberately avoiding my eyes. My stomach drops and my heart strains in my chest.

He frowns, then shakes his head. "Miss Clutton-Brock, my love life is none of your business."

Summer giggles like he's being flirtatious, and he asks us to turn to page 321 of our book and read the passage on rune stones and fortune tellings.

Everybody does as he says, except me. I scowl at him as he busies himself at the front of the classroom. Winnie nudges me in the ribs but I'm tired of his silly games. I lift my hand into the air and call out his name.

"Professor Stone?"

Summer peers over her shoulder at me and makes an exaggerated groan.

"What is it, Miss Blackwaters? Are you incapable of finding the right passage? Page number 321 comes after page 320 and before page 322. I'm sure Miss Wence will help you if you're really struggling."

Half the classroom sniggers and I scowl at him even harder, even though he's refusing to look at me.

"Aren't you meant to be teaching us about fated mates? It's on the curriculum."

"She'd be better off learning about werebeasts, seeing as she's going to be one," Summer sniffs.

The professor straightens a pile of books at the front of the classroom.

"We're covering neither of those things, Miss Blackwaters and Miss Clutton-Brock. Today we are covering the ability to read the future." I huff and he finally lifts his gaze to me. "I think you will find it a lot more useful than either of those other subjects."

"Not if the school experiences another werebeast attack," Summer says.

"Principal York has taken steps to ensure that won't happen. No werebeast will be able to penetrate the campus security again."

"What if they're already in our midst?" Summer asks, making an exaggerated show of spinning around in her seat and staring right at me.

"If you're implying," Stone says in a deadly voice, "that Miss Blackwaters has contracted the were curse, you should know I treated her after the attack myself, so unless you are questioning my abilities..."

Summer shakes her head.

"I suppose that's not giving the students in this classroom much comfort, Professor," I say, "considering it's known that your word is pretty worthless."

His eyes narrow and I scowl right back at him. The room falls so quiet you could hear a pin drop.

"I am not a liar, Miss Blackwaters, and I take offense at such an insinuation."

"You aren't always careful with the truth, though, are you, Professor?"

"I never lie," he growls.

And through my mind, I flash every half truth he's ever told me and every time he's denied me the truth.

"In my office now, Miss Blackwaters," he snaps. "And the rest of you, eyes down and get reading."

He storms through the rows of desks and into his office. Slowly I rise from my seat, aware everyone is watching as I follow him in. He slams the door shut behind us and waves his arm through the air.

"Impregnable spell. No one can hear us and no one can enter," he hisses, before turning slowly to face me, his face full of rage. "You can't talk to me like that in class."

"You're going on a date?" I spit out at him.

He crosses his arms over his chest. "I'm going to visit my mom, Rhianna."

I frown. "Then why did you say–"

"It doesn't hurt if everyone thinks I'm going on a date. Helps to counter any rumors that might start stirring about the two of us. Rumors you just stirred your goddamn self. Acting like my jealous fucking girlfriend in class."

"Don't give me that bullshit, Professor. You did that deliberately. You were trying to provoke me. To hurt me."

"I'm not. I'm trying to protect you."

"You're trying to protect yourself and your job."

"I don't even want this shitty job."

"Then why are you here?"

"People like me and you, Rhianna, aren't offered many choices in life. I don't have the family and connections Azlan does. I may detest this job. But I can't afford to lose it."

I shake my head. "I didn't ask to be your fated mate."

"And I didn't ask to be yours. But here we are."

I point down at all the books scattered across the table. "That's why you've been reading up about it. You've known about this bond as long as Azlan has and you also chose not to tell me." He doesn't answer me, just glares. "What were you searching for in these books, Professor?"

"A way to undo or to remove the fated mate bond," he says with no emotion at all.

I flinch, trying my best not to show it, but his words sting, sting like he just slapped me hard around the face.

"You said no more lies," he says more gently.

"You didn't want to be bonded to me?"

"You just said you didn't want to be bonded to me, Rhianna."

"I said I didn't choose it. I didn't say I didn't want it."

"Do you want it?" he asks, his arms falling to his side as he takes a step towards me. My bond strains for him, quivering and shaking in my core.

"What does it matter? You don't."

"Shit," he says, raking his hand through his hair. "I didn't want it at first. I didn't know you. You were an unregistered. Twelve years younger than me. My student, for Stars' sake, Rhi. So, yes, I was looking for a solution, a way to make it all go away."

"And were you successful? Did you find what you were looking for?"

"No."

"So now you've decided, as you can't remove it, you may as well embrace it?"

"*You* came on to *me* yesterday. I didn't initiate anything. You're with my best friend. You're bonded to him. I didn't even know if you felt this connection."

"How could I not?" I shout back at him. "How could I not? It's there in my core, pulling me, dragging me towards you all the time. It wants you. It wants to make you mine. How could I not feel that, Stone?"

He closes the distance between us, cupping my face in his hand and crushing my mouth against his.

At first I fight, try to push him away, but his kiss only grows stronger, the bond in my core, that hook, swooning with the feel of his skin against mine. I melt into his kiss, resting my hands on his chest, and kiss him back.

When we pause to catch our breath, he rests his forehead against mine.

"I want it and I want you. That's the truth of it."

I look into his eyes. I want to believe him.

He takes a deep inhale.

"We have to go back out there and you have to look suitably chastised, Rhi."

"I haven't forgiven you and you can't keep treating me this way," I whisper. "You can't pretend to go on dates with other women and–"

"I know, I know. Just ..." He exhales and steps away from me, with a groan that suggests it pains him as much as it does me. "No one can know."

39

R ^{hi}

My heart hammers in my chest and as soon as the lesson ends, I head straight for the bathroom to catch my breath. It means I'm going to be late for my next class, but I need a moment to compose myself.

I walk straight to the sink and turn on the tap, splashing cold water over my face and staring into the mirror. My cheeks are flushed, my pupils blown wide, and is it my imagination or do my lips look swollen?

The door swings back as I'm inspecting my reflection and a loud obnoxious groan follows.

I don't need to flick my gaze to the door. I know exactly who's standing in the entrance. Summer.

"Urgh!" she says, strolling towards the sink furthest from mine and stopping to admire herself in the mirror. "Come to cry in the bathroom because the professor has had enough of your cheek and lost his temper with you?" She reaches inside her blazer and pulls out a tube of lip gloss, unscrewing the lid and dipping the applicator into the waiting pink liquid. "You really are pathetic, Pig Girl. The whole bewildered damsel in distress act won't cut it here. Men aren't interested in weak girls like you; no matter how many times you cry. They want a strong, powerful partner. Someone who will stand by them. Someone who will fight with them. Honestly, isn't it about time you admitted defeat and quit? You don't belong here."

I can't help gaping at her. When have I ever cried in front of her? In front of any of them? All the shit they've put me through and I've never curled up and broken down. In fact, I haven't shed one single tear.

"You're so full of bullshit, Summer," I mutter, yanking a handful of paper towels out of the dispenser and patting my face dry.

Summer smiles as she paints her lips pink, tilting her head to the left and then the right to ensure she's happy with her handiwork.

"I know that's your plan, Pig Girl. You're not strong enough or special enough to look after yourself. You're never actually going to make it to graduation, or to the protection forces. So you're hoping to grab yourself a man." She laughs. "As if any dude in this school would be interested in a disgusting little pig like you."

I lean against the wall and toss the paper towels into the basket. I should walk out. I should ignore Summer and her taunts. But this is some seriously deluded stuff, even for Summer.

"Right," I say. "And who have I got my sights set on, then?"

Summer uses her little finger to neaten the edges of her lip gloss, then screws the lid back on the tube.

"Oh, I'm not blind, Pig Girl. I know exactly who you have those beady little eyes of yours trained on. It's so fucking laughable. Can you imagine? Him with you." She chuckles, tossing her hair as she does. "I think he'd rather cut off his own precious Kennedy dick than swing it anywhere near you."

"Tristan?" Now it's my turn to laugh. "You think I'm interested in Tristan?"

"Not just Tristan. Spencer too. It's okay," she says with a fake sympathetic smile. "Most of you virgin girls have a crush on those two. Dreaming that one day they may actually notice you exist. Spoiler alert: they won't." She tucks her lip gloss away inside her blazer and prowls towards me. "So leave them alone, okay? I've seen you stalking them. Hanging about for scraps of their attention. It's really freaking creepy."

"I don't think I'm the one doing the stalking," I say. "I think it's the other way around. They're the ones who can't leave me alone."

"As if! Don't flatter yourself!" she hisses.

"I don't consider it particularly flattering."

"You think because the teachers paired you up a handful of times? You think because you were forced to do helping hand duties? You think because they've spoken to you once or twice, they like you? You really are freaking clueless. It's sort of sad. I'm guessing nobody has ever shown you any attention in the past, which is hardly surprising," she says, looking me up and down with an expression of disdain. "Except that Andrew dude and he was so traumatized by the experience he hasn't been seen since."

Her mention of Andrew has me bristling and I try to walk away. She blocks my path.

"They're not interested in a girl like you. They'll never be interested in a girl like you."

"Are you sure about that?" I ask, not even sure why we're having this stupid argument.

I don't like either of them. They may be hot – really hot – but they are also cruel, vain and arrogant. Even if the pull in my stomach means something – which I'm not convinced it can – I don't care. I could never be with men like that.

It's been hard enough forgiving and trusting Azlan. And Stone?

"Yes, absolutely certain," Summer continues. "You don't move in the right circles. You don't come from the right family. You'll never understand them. You'll never know what it's like to be one of us."

"Such a shame," I say in my best bored tone.

She ignores me. "They're powerful, dangerous, raw. If you'd ever seen them fight you'd know that."

"I've seen them fight plenty." I caught the tail end of countless dueling practices during my time as helping hand to the team.

"No, *really* fight." Her eyes glisten and I think of what Winnie told me earlier about the underground dueling club. "They need someone strong and powerful. A weedy little girl like you – sneaking off to cry in the bathroom – couldn't handle men like them!"

"And I suppose you can?"

"I'm warning you, Pig Girl. Back off and leave them both the hell alone."

"And they couldn't tell me this themselves?" I ask.

"Tristan is too much of a gentleman and so is Spencer."

I laugh again. Gentlemen? Has she actually spent any time in their company?

"Yeah, I think they're anything but." I chuckle.

"I'm telling you, as their girlfriend–"

"Their girlfriend?" I say, the amusement waning away, my stomach twisting instead. "You're dating both of them?"

She smiles like a crocodile at me. "Oh, no. Has that shocked that little puritanical mind of yours? Yes. Both of them. Why not? They're both hot. And so am I. So what if I'm sleeping with them both?"

"Don't you feel used?" I spout out, unable to help voice my own fears.

"Used? No. I couldn't choose between them and so I chose both, and I guess I'm so damn alluring I'm worth sharing."

Surprisingly, I actually find her words comforting (not the result she was hoping for I bet). Stone and Azlan both want me. They're prepared to share to have me. They're both prepared to risk their jobs, their livelihoods and their reputations too. When I come to think about it, it's pretty darn flattering,

"I'm serious, Pig Girl. I don't want you talking to them. I don't want you looking at them. I don't want you even sharing the same air as them."

I shake my head and focus back in on Summer, remembering we're talking about Tristan and Spencer here, not Stone and Azlan. Summer's eyes brim with hatred and malice.

My own hatred seems to multiply in my chest. I would really, really like to slap her hard.

Because, though I hate to admit it, I have been looking at Tristan and Spencer, trying to work out what the hell the pull towards them can mean.

Are they meant to be mine, not hers? And if they are, considering I hate them both and they hate me right back, where the hell does that leave us all?

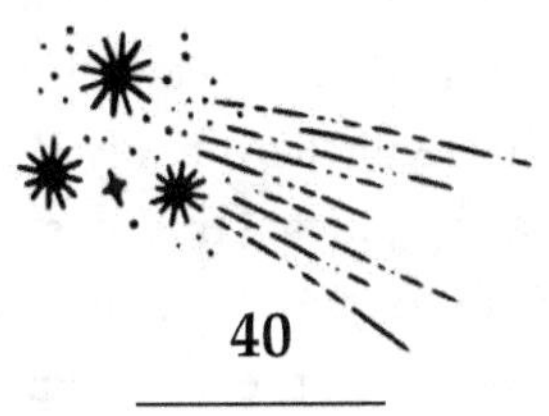

40

T ristan

TWO SUMMONS from my father in as many weeks is not a good sign. But it's not something I can refuse either.

I arrive well after dinner, not wanting to endure a silent meal with my mother and father, her sadness and his temper crackling in the air and affecting my mood.

No, I arrive when I know my mother will have already retired to her room long ago, to drown herself in pills.

My father's long-serving butler opens the doors as I climb the steps and leads me silently into my father's chamber.

What have his sources told him this time? Am I in for a beating? Or is it something else? My father's role on the Council has been to oversee the authorities' ongoing battles with the gangs that rule most of the wastelands, and to keep a watchful eye on the border to the West. The authorities have been trying to undermine the tyrant who's ruled the lands to the West for the last two decades. But he is powerful, well-entrenched and slowly trying to encroach on our lands too. In fact, his tentacles already stretch into our lands – underground dealings, illegal tradings, criminal activities.

Is that what my father wishes to discuss?

The butler knocks on the door and when my father calls, "Enter" holds the door back for me, shutting it ominously behind me as I stride through.

"Tristan," my father says.

He's dressed in old-fashioned dueling robes, a long thin sword in his hand. The man he pays to spar with him stands waiting, his sword hanging limp by his side. My father motions his head to the man who bows and swiftly exits the room.

My father flips off the wire mask that protects his face.

"You're late."

"I had training."

"Ahh, yes." He examines me with his cold, soulless eyes. Calculating, ruthless eyes. "The big game this weekend. You are prepared?"

"Yes, Sir."

"Good, I'm expecting you to crush Aropia."

"We intend to."

My father smiles, but it's the smile of a snake, no warmth in it at all. His smiles used to scare me shitless. They used to turn my blood cold and my tongue to stone. It's been too many years of cold smiles, though, now they brush over me like a light summer's breeze.

I decide to cut to the chase. The less time I can spend in this place the better. Definitely before my mother hears of my visit and appears, high as a kite and provoking my father's temper.

"You wanted to see me, Sir."

"I did." He spins the sword in his hand, enjoying making me wait. Then hangs it alongside the other weapons on the rack on the wall. "There was a werebeast attack at the school."

I keep my features neutral, blank, a skill I've perfected over the years. "There was. On Friday night."

"The school hasn't informed parents of this."

"I believe the principal considers the matter dealt with."

"How was it possible for a werebeast to enter the school grounds?"

I concentrate on maintaining that blank, passive expression. "I don't know."

"You're head of your house, Tristan," he scoffs. "Surely the principal has been keeping you informed?"

"She hasn't told me anything, Sir."

He narrows those eyes of his. "Was anyone hurt?"

I hesitate for a fraction of a second, knowing he's most probably weaving a web for me. One he'll enjoy strangling me in. Does he already know a pupil was attacked? Does he know who? Is that the reason for this meeting?

"Yes," I say, already knowing I've faltered. That hesitation a mistake he'll have spotted. "The Blackwaters girl."

"The Blackwaters girl," he repeats, and I'm almost certain he already knew. "Anyone else?"

There are only two people who know. Spencer and Matron. Spencer wouldn't disclose this information if my father threatened him with decapitation. The matron? I'd reminded her of my age. Of patient confidentiality. But my father is foreboding. Does he know?

I decide to risk it. If I'm wrong and he knows, he'll punish me for it.

"No," I say, forcing myself not to hold my breath. "No one else, only the girl."

My father flicks his hand to me and the tight coils of his magic tighten around my throat. I clutch at my neck, gasping for air.

"Are you lying to me, son?" He squeezes tighter still, black spots appearing at the edges of my vision. I drop to my knees.

I could fight him off. I could blast his magic apart. I could bring *him* to his knees.

But I won't. I won't let him know. Won't let him see the extent of my power.

Not yet.

"No, Sir, I'm not. Only the girl."

"Only the girl," he repeats, releasing me and letting me fall to the ground, spluttering and gasping for air. "But I hear, disappointingly, that she is alive, alive and uninfected?"

I inhale, allowing oxygen to fill my lungs, and wipe away the wetness from my eyes. "Yes, Professor Stone fought the beast off and gave her treatment."

"Professor Stone." He strokes his chin. "Azlan's friend."

I nod.

"Why did it attack her, Tristan?"

"I don't know," I say honestly, although I have my damn suspicions. "Wrong place, wrong time."

"This girl has a habit of placing herself right in the center of trouble. I want you to keep a watchful eye on her."

"I believe Azlan is already doing that, Sir," I say bitterly.

He scoffs. "I want you to watch her and report anything else unusual back to me."

"You asked me to avoid her. Not to speak with her."

"You don't need to talk to her, Tristan. Only watch. You understand." He turns towards the weapons, straightening them on their hooks. "Your cousin may not be my son. But his bloodline is pure. His powers strong. He owns our family name. And this girl ... this nobody appears out of nowhere destined to be his mate. It makes no sense. There is more to this situation than your cousin is divulging, more, perhaps, than he is even aware. I want to know what that story is, Tristan. You know I've never liked to be kept in the dark."

"Yes, Sir."

"Good," he says. "Then I will see you at the weekend's game. Will you see your mother?"

I peer up at the ceiling. "Is she coming to the game?"

"Of course, the whole Kennedy clan will be there to cheer you on," he says so coolly I almost shiver.

"I'll see her then."

I HAVE no intention of telling my father anything about the girl. Nothing at all. I want nothing to do with her.

And yet here I am, fist pounding on my cousin's door, hoping none of my father's little spies have followed me here. I took a deviating route though the busy city center, blended in with the crowded traffic. But maybe he has one watching Azlan's house.

I thud again. I don't even know if he's home or off on one of his assignments. But then I hear the heavy thud of his boots, the swivel of the eye hole and the door swings back.

"Tristan." He sounds neither surprised nor happy to see me.

"We need to talk," I say sternly.

"Have you come to deliver another of your riddles?" He frowns at me.

"You found her, didn't you?" I say, pushing past him and into the house. I want to ask him where she was. What she had been doing. But I'm done with her. Done with this obsession. She's his now. "In one piece, unfortunately."

He slams the door shut hard behind me.

"I've no time for petty insults, Tristan. Spit out whatever you have come here to say. But," he lowers his voice to a sinister growl, "know if you speak like that about her again, I'll snap your neck in two."

I scoff at him. It's been a long time since we battled out in the forest behind my father's house. I was much younger then, he far stronger. He may think he could break my neck, but I'd snap his before the idea even crossed his mind.

"You really are fucked, aren't you?" I say.

"Being a part of this family means I always was. With or without Rhianna."

The way he says her name, so familiarly, has jealousy rolling through my stomach. It's hard to imagine them together. My cousin has worn this mask of stone on his face for a long time, concealing the softer side I know lurks beneath. The mask is so effective, I'd begun to wonder if the man I'd known before – the one who made me laugh, who carried me on his shoulders, who turned leaves into butterflies just to see my wonderment – had gone forever. But does that man reappear for her? Is he all butterflies and fucking giggles?

"My father sent for me this evening." I walk through into his kitchen, trying not to search for signs of her here. Signs of domesticity. The thought making me sick. "He's heard about the werebeast. Knows it attacked Rhianna."

"You told him?"

"He already knew."

"You told him anything else?"

I spin around to face him. "No." We may no longer be allies but we both know the less my father knows the better. Every piece of information he'd only use against us anyway. "But he has his suspicions about the girl."

"What suspicions?"

I shrug. "Believes there must be something special about her." I stare at my cousin's face. I wait for him to tell me there isn't.

But there is. There is something special about her – and it isn't the hole she blasted in Spencer's stomach. It isn't the way her magic matched mine pace for pace out there in the meadow.

No, it's something more.

The way my magic wanted to combine with hers.

The way I'm pulled towards her by that hook in my stomach.

The way she's captured my goddamn attention. The way she's invaded my mind. The way I'm here telling him all this when I shouldn't be.

Azlan is silent. If he thinks there is something special about the girl, if he knows about the crimson magic, he's not telling me.

"He's asked me to watch her. To report back to him with any information."

"I see." He holds my gaze. "And will you?"

"I have better things to do with my time." Which probably sounds fucking unconvincing considering I'm standing in his house telling him all this.

"You'll have to tell him something."

"I know," I say with irritation, as if I don't know my

father better than anyone, better even than my mother. "I just thought you should know. He's watching."

"I ... I appreciate it."

I nod, curtly. Then I make my way to the front door. I can smell her scent, barely there, but I can smell it.

I need to get the hell out of here.

I have my hand on the doorknob when he says,

"She is special, Tristan. Just not in the way you think."

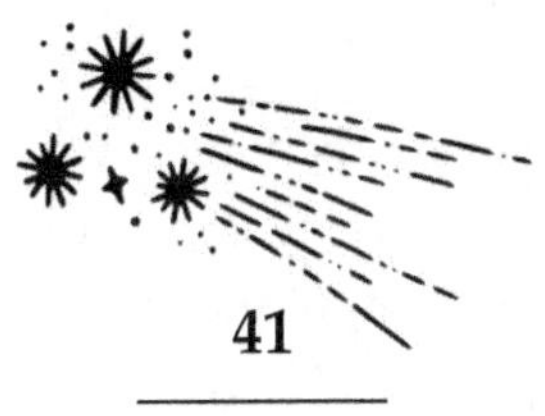

41

S pencer

It's late but I can't sleep. Haven't been able to sleep for days. Partly it's the upcoming match. The biggest of the academic year. The one everyone is counting on me to win for them.

Partly it's what happened. The fear that it will happen again. I'm taking double the tablets I should and pushing my body to the physical limit. Despite that, the thing still stirs inside me. Won't leave me damn alone. And those black clouds have been looming over me, turning all my thoughts dark.

Usually, I'd go fuck some girl. Let them suck my cock. A way of releasing the tension, soothing my mind, and distracting me from my worries.

That shit isn't working anymore. I've tried. I just end up thinking about Pig Girl, comparing the girl in front of me to the girl that won't get out of my head. It's the fucking anthesis of a turn on and my cock won't play ball.

Instead, I'm here in the gym, lifting weights until my arms shake.

I'm about to increase the weight I'm lifting even further, when the door creaks open and Tristan strides through, wearing nothing but a pair of shorts.

"You can't sleep, either?" I say.

He spots me on the bench.

"I just went to see my father."

"You want to hit something?"

"Your face."

I rub my jaw. I'm almost healed. Though that ache won't go. I still feel like shit.

"I was thinking more about the punch bag. But if you want to go a round and get yourself knocked out before Saturday's game ..."

"I'd like to go down to the warehouse," he says, cracking his knuckles and rolling his shoulders. "Blow off some steam."

"Yeah," I say. I wouldn't mind doing that myself. But the match is days away and neither of us can risk an injury.

"Let's do the bag," Tristan says.

We're silent as we strap up our hands, and then I hold the punchbag in my arms, throwing my weight against it and letting him volley his fists into its depth. Anger spits in his eyes, his brow is drawn low, and it doesn't take long for sweat to slide down his face.

"What did he want?" I ask.

"Asking questions about the werebeast attack," he huffs out, punching at the bag with all his force.

"Right." I know he won't have told him. I also know that will have cost him; even in the dull light of the gym, the faint marks on his neck are visible. They'll be gone by the morning. Tristan will heal them himself.

"Asking questions about the pig girl too. Thinks she's special."

My eyes automatically fall to my stomach. The mark's gone now. "I think we should talk to her again."

He frowns harder, smacking the punch bag so hard, I'm tousled backwards. "It's impossible. She won't talk to us."

I regain my balance. "Then we'll make her."

He glances at me, then his watch. It's midnight. "She'll be asleep."

"Then we'll wake her." I've been trying my best to avoid her. That pull in my stomach is becoming more and more insistent, though. It wants to be as close to her as is physically possible. I'm damn tired of fighting it.

Tristan thinks about it, then nods, wiping his brow with the back of his wrist.

At her dorm, I try to blast her door open, but there's some protection spell on it that I can't penetrate.

"How the hell did she do that?" I say. The girl may have wielded crimson magic, but that was some damn fluke. She can't handle even the most basic of spells.

"The roommate?" Tristan suggests, hammering his hand against the door.

It's the roommate who opens the door looking fucking terrified.

"Where is she?" Tristan demands.

"It's the middle of the night. You can't be here," the roommate insists, shutting the door in our faces. Tristan simply forces it open and we push our way inside, ignoring the outraged protests of the other girl and some snorts from the pet pig, running circles around our feet. The pig girl is sliding off a top bunk, dressed in sleep shorts and a tank, her dark hair braided over her shoulder.

"We need to talk to her," Tristan says, striding right over to the pig girl and grabbing her upper arm.

"What the hell do you think you're doing?" she hisses. She doesn't seem like someone who's just woken up. Is she also unable to sleep?

"I said, we need to talk to you," Tristan says.

"In the middle of the night?"

He glares at her, holding her angry gaze in a way that feels personal. I look between the two of them.

"You can't simply barge into our room and drag Rhi out of bed. I don't know who you think you are–"

"You don't know who we are?" I growl at the roommate. "Are you stupid? We can do whatever we like in this school. And if we want to talk to her, then we will. So go back to sleep and stop screeching in my ear!"

"Don't talk to her like that," Pig Girl says, directing her attention at me.

"I'll stop talking to her, if you move your goddamn feet and come with us."

The roommate grabs Tristan's arm and tries to pull his grip from the girl.

"Don't make me hurt your roommate," Tristan says darkly.

The pig girl scowls some more, then relents. "Fine."

Tristan forces her forward and the three of us walk towards the door.

"Should I fetch Professor Stone?" the roommate asks in desperation.

Professor Stone? Again? I look at her, sure I see her cheeks pinken in the darkness. "It's okay, Winnie. Let me find out what these dickheads want, and then I'll be back."

The roommate wags her finger at the two of us. "If she's not back in twenty minutes …"

"We'll return her safe and sound," Tristan says with sarcasm, forcing the pig girl out of the door.

"This couldn't wait until the morning?" she says, sounding bored as we march her out of the dorm and into the woods. Somewhere our conversation won't be overheard.

"Too many pairs of ears listening in during the day," Tristan says.

"Like the pair belonging to your girlfriend Summer? Does she know you have a penchant for dragging girls out of their beds in the middle of the night?"

"No, usually, they're trying to drag me in with them. And she is not my girlfriend."

The pig girl rolls her eyes and snatches her elbow away from Tristan, folding her arms over her body. It's cool out here in the night's air below the canopy of trees, and goosebumps thread across her skin.

"Funny, that's not what she told me."

"Are you jealous, little Pig?" Tristan says with a smirk.

"No," she says firmly, scowling at us both. "You can date who the hell you like. I couldn't care less."

"I don't date," I say, spitting out the last word like it's dirty. The last thing I need is some annoying girl hanging around my neck, pawing at me.

"Sleeping with, then," she says, meeting my eyes.

I hold her gaze. I can see her pulse pounding in her throat, see her breath cloud faintly in front of her mouth. That pull wants me on top of her. "I'm not sleeping with her anymore."

She swallows, then looks away. "What do you want?"

"You mean apart from you to disappear and never be seen again?" Tristan asks.

"I'm not going anywhere. And last time I checked, you weren't allowed to talk to me. For someone who is meant to be ignoring me, you are going out of your way to speak with me, Tristan Kennedy."

He smiles in that lazy way. "You should know by now I don't always do as I'm told. Something we have in common."

"I'm nothing like you," she spits.

"Are the two of you done?" I snap.

They both look at me. The girl's cheeks are flushed and his eyes are shining.

I can't deny that there's some kind of fire between them. A fire that would burn them both to ashes if either one let it. I don't know how I feel about that.

I step towards her.

"Everyone says you have the were curse."

"By everyone, I'm guessing you mean Summer. I already told you, I don't. Professor Stone–"

"You seem pretty close to the professor."

Tristan shifts his weight from one foot to the other, fiddling with the bandages on his hands.

The monster inside me stirs. He's always been better at reading situations, at reading people, and he can sense something now.

"There's something you're not telling me," I say lowly, the darkness dangerous in my veins.

Tristan ties the bandages and flexes his fingers.

"She's bonded to my cousin," he whispers. "He's best friends with the professor."

I stare at him, and he looks up from his hands and meets her eyes. She glares at him so ferociously, I see him flinch.

"You weren't meant to tell anyone."

"What?" I say, gripping her elbow and shaking her. "What the fuck? You're bonded? Are you fucking insane?"

She snaps her head around to me.

"No more than you are."

"You're nineteen."

"Twenty," she corrects.

"He's twice your age."

"He's not, and I didn't have much say in the process."

The monster inside me roars and I feel my bones begin to snap. "He forced you," we say together.

Her eyes widen in horror and I stumble back from her, closing my eyes and struggling to contain it.

"What's wrong with him?" I hear her say.

"Nothing," Tristan says, his voice retaining that bored tone, "just revolted by your confession, and the thought that anyone would want to be with a girl like you."

Her attention snaps back to him. "Your cousin does."

Tristan takes a step towards her. "Because he doesn't know what you're capable of? Doesn't know who you really are?"

Her face falls. "I ... I don't know what you mean."

"The crimson magic," I spit, finding my voice again. "Does your mate know about it?"

She shakes her head.

"Has it happened again?" Tristan asks carefully.

Her gaze shoots up to his.

"Shit, it has," I say.

She twists her head to look at me.

"When?" I ask.

"I'm done talking with the two of you. My life is none of your business. Go back to your dueling, and your cheerleaders, and your boring little friends, and leave me alone." She starts to walk away. I block her path.

"Your business will always be our business, Pig Girl. We rule this school and we own everyone and everything in it. Including you. If we tell you to get the hell out of your bed and come see us in the middle of the night. You do it. If we ask you questions, you answer them. Understand?"

"You're so full of shit!" she snaps.

And something snaps inside me too. I slam her against the nearest tree.

"Don't make me burn another hole in your stomach, Spencer," she says, struggling against my body as I pin her to the trunk.

"Do it, little pig, and I won't be so nice. This time I'll tell the principal, who will tell the authorities, and before you can say, "Oh Spencer, I'm so very, very sorry," you'll be locked away in some cell, with no hope of ever emerging. They won't even consider the Northern Labor Camps for you."

"Like I said, you're full of shit."

"He's not," Tristan says, coming to lean against the tree trunk beside us. "You really don't know what you're dealing with, do you?"

"So tell us: when else has it happened?" I add.

Her breaths come in panicked little pants, her chest rising and falling beneath me. "When my life was in danger."

"Because the werebeast attacked you?" I say, frowning.

"No. I don't think the werebeast was out to hurt me." Tristan glances at me and I meet his eye for a fraction of a second.

"Who was trying to kill you then, little pig?" I ask.

"Renzo Barone," she says.

42

R^{hi}

THERE'S A SHOCKED SILENCE, and I can hear the rustle of the branches above our heads, and the distant squeak of bats through the trees. I guess whatever they were expecting me to say, it wasn't that.

"What the fuck kind of trouble have you got yourself tangled up in, little pig?" Spencer says, still pressing the full weight of his body against mine.

The bond in my gut spins frantically and I just want to be away. Away from these two men. Their proximity is confusing. I hate them; I really do. I don't care if fate has other ideas. I don't care if it's trying to pull me towards them. I don't care if their strong bodies so close to mine has little thrills of anticipation racing up and down every nerve. I don't want them. I don't want them to be mine. And they clearly don't want me to be theirs.

"Maybe you ought to ask his cousin?" I say through gritted teeth. I don't want Azlan to fight my battles for me, but I also know he is the one thing that might keep these dickheads from bothering me. I send a blast of my magic Spencer's way. Not enough to hurt him, just enough to let him know I'm not playing.

He flinches, stepping backwards, and shaking out his hands.

"Little bitch," he mutters.

"I'd rather you told us yourself," Tristan says, still leaning against the tree trunk, his breath warm by my ear, making my body wilt ever so slightly towards him.

"How about you answer some of my questions instead? How about you tell me why the two of you were walking round like someone beat the shit out of you? And why you didn't heal those injuries?"

Tristan leans in closer to me so his mouth is hot by my ear. "You tell us your secrets and we'll tell you ours."

"And let me guess, you want me to tell first."

"Ladies first," Spencer says, then chuckles. "Wait, is she actually a lady? After all, she does sleep with pigs."

I give him the finger and push off the tree. I'm done playing games with these two. They may be bigger and stronger than me, but if they hurt me again, I will hurt them back.

"I'm going back to bed." I start walking, pushing right past Spencer.

"We're not done talking to you yet, Pig Girl," Tristan calls after me.

"Tell someone who cares, like ... erm ... your cousin."

I keep one eye over my shoulder the entire way back to the dorm, half expecting a bolt of magic to send me flying, but I make it in one piece.

Winnie's sitting on her chair with Pip in her lap when I open the door.

They both start talking at once and I bend down to scoop Pip up and let him lick my face.

"I'm fine," I tell them both. "Nothing happened."

"What did they want?"

I frown. "Hmmm, I don't actually know."

The bad mood rolling off the two of them had been palpable and I half suspect they were just looking for someone to take those moods out on. And, hey, guess what? That lucky someone seems to be me more days than not.

The other half of me suspects more though. That I'm not the only one feeling the pull. Are they feeling it too? Is that why the pair of them can't seem to leave me alone despite telling me on a regular basis how much they despise me, how revolting I am? They really are one fucked up pair.

"Can we forget about those jerks and go to sleep?" I add.

Not that I've been sleeping much these last few days. I've been too frightened to close my eyes and drift away, petrified those memories set loose in my head will haunt me.

"Sure," Winnie says, "but I warn you, it's going to be hard to escape those two jerks in the next few days. With the Cross-lantic match on Saturday, they are all anyone is going to be talking about."

43

R^{hi}

IF I'D HOPED the run up to this big match would mean Spencer and Tristan's attention is diverted away from me for a short time, well, I'm wrong.

When I step out of my dorm the next morning, one half of the deadly duo is blocking the path, feet planted wide, arms crossed tightly across his giant frame.

I hope for one fleeting moment that he isn't waiting for me. But with his eyes locked on my face, I know he is.

"Really?" I say, with irritation. "It's been what? Six hours."

"Come with me," he says.

Winnie steps in front of me. "No way. You dragged her out of bed last night. You're not hassling her again this morning." She hesitates, then straightens her shoulders.

"Get lost, Spencer, or I'll report you to Principal York for harassment."

Spencer pays no attention to my irate roommate, peering straight over her head and speaking directly to me.

"We're going to the gym. I have thirty minutes free."

"Excuse me?" I say.

"Your self defense skills are woeful. I'm going to help you."

My jaw slackens and I stare at him in utter disbelief.

"You have to be kidding me," I finally manage to splutter.

"You've been a dickhead about helping Rhi out all term and now all of a sudd–"

"If you have someone like Renzo Barone on your tail, you need to know how to defend yourself," he hisses lowly.

Winnie glances over her shoulder at me, then back up at Spencer. "Rhi's faced him twice already and is still here to tell the tale," she says, sounding proud. "She doesn't need your help."

"She does," Spencer says, clearly losing patience with my roommate and stepping around her to grab my arm. "Come on, we're losing time here."

"Well, perhaps this isn't a very convenient time for me," I say, "I haven't eaten breakfast and–"

"I picked us up bagels from the hall. You can eat afterwards. Come on." He yanks on my arm and I stare at Winnie in disbelief. She shrugs.

This is probably a trap or some kind of sick scheme he's organized with Tristan or Summer or both. Then again, if it's not, if he really is prepared to help me, can I afford to turn the offer down? I'm in desperate need of learning.

"Fine," I mutter.

He pulls me along the path, leaving Winnie gaping at us both, only dropping his hand from my arm when other people appear on the path. Then he makes a deliberate thing of walking three paces ahead of me, although I don't miss how he keeps glancing over his shoulder to ensure I'm still following him.

At the gymnasium, I turn towards the girls' locker room.

"We don't have time for you to change," he says, smacking back the gymnasium doors.

"I'm not fighting you in this," I say, glancing down at my stupid skirt and socks.

"You think Renzo Barone is going to wait around while you change into more suitable attire, Pig Girl?"

"No," I concede, following him through into the empty gymnasium. The mats are already set up. Was that simply luck or did he do that?

He tosses his bag to the ground and toes off his shoes. Then he meets my gaze and my bond shimmers. Does he feel it too? Or am I reading this all wrong?

"You've been approaching this all wrong. Making it far too easy for me," he says.

"If you'd actually tried to–"

"Would you just shut up for one micro-second and listen?"

I harrumph, resting my hand on my hip and giving him my best deathly stare.

"You've been trying to meet me head on, trying to fight me as an equal," he continues, ignoring my look. "I'm much bigger than you." His eyes meander down my body and that hum in my stomach grows more violent. "That's never going to work."

"Then what should I be doing?" I ask in irritation.

"I'm coming to that," he snaps back. Then takes an inhale like he's trying to regain his calm. "You need to use my size and my weight against me. Use it to your advantage.

You're lighter than me, more nimble, quicker. Get me off my balance and, whatever you do, don't let me ..." he swallows, "get a hold of you."

I remember his lips on mine, his hand around my throat and I'm forced to look away from him.

"Why are you doing this?" I ask. "Why the change of heart?"

"Renzo Barone."

I don't think that answers my question. What does he care if Barone is chasing me? What does he care if the assassin slits my throat?

"How do I get you off your balance?"

"I can show you a few moves, little things you can use. Come here." He beckons towards me and my feet take me to the center of the mat where he is waiting.

His gaze does that thing down my body again, although this time he's much closer and I can smell his scent, feel the heat of his body.

He reaches out and takes a fistful of my shirt.

"I thought I wasn't meant to let you get a hold of me."

"I'm showing you the move. Ready?"

"Yes."

"When I'm lunging for you like this, my weight is all forward. Use that to your advantage. Twist to the side and then slam me down."

"I've tried that a million times," I mutter. "You always end up on top of me."

"Your timing's off. You always move too soon, always signal to me what you're going to try. Wait until I'm committed. Until I have no chance of righting my balance. Okay?" I nod. "Let's go then."

With his grip on my shirt, he lunges toward me. I repress the urge to wriggle free and let myself begin to topple, taking him down with me. Then at the very last minute, I yank away, rolling across the mat and letting Spencer land face down on the ground.

I can't help a little yelp of triumph, before jumping onto his back.

"Got you!" I say.

He twists his head to peer at me.

"I don't think so, Pig Girl," he says, all of a sudden turning his body, grabbing my waist and rolling us over, pinning me onto the mat with his vast body.

"Asshole," I mutter.

He grins, his face millimeters from mine. We've been here a million times before. His weight pressing me down into the ground. His grip tight on my body.

His eyes drift down to my mouth. Then he frowns.

"That was a stupid move on your part. Stop trying to fight someone so much bigger than you. If I'm flat on my back, you strike me, take me out. Either that, or you run like hell. You don't climb on top of me."

"Right," I say, my cheeks flushing with embarrassment.

He goes to roll off me but I grab onto his bicep.

"Wait, what should I do if I do mess up and an attacker has me like this, pinned to the ground?"

"Unless you can use your magic, there's nothing you can do."

I think of how the werebeast had pinned me to the ground like this. How I hadn't been able to fight back.

"There must be something," I say in desperation.

He pauses, thinking. "If your life really is in danger, then you fight with everything you've got, okay? Spit in their eye, bite their fucking nose, gouge out their eyes. Fuck, head butt them if you have to."

"Head butt?"

He grins. "It's pretty effective, especially if the other person isn't expecting it." The smile fades again. "Just don't give up, okay, Rhi?"

"Giving up isn't exactly something I do."

"Yeah," he says. Taking my hand, he yanks us onto our feet. "Come on," he says, "I'll show you some other moves."

44

R^{hi}

Winnie's right, dueling *is* all anyone in the school can talk about for the next three days. It turns out this match is some massive grudge affair that only happens every other year between the academy and some prestigious magical school based over in Aropia. Last time, the match took place over there. This time it's happening on home soil and everyone seems determined the Arrow Hart team will send them packing with their tails between their legs.

Sport has never been my thing but, with everyone's attention diverted, at least they stop talking about me and the werebeast attack and I'm no longer avoided like the plague. Well, no more than usual, anyway.

On the downside, with no interest in this stupid match and the dueling team, I have plenty of time to think. Plenty of time for those memories to stroll into my head and leave me trembling. It doesn't help that there's been no opportunity for me and Stone to talk again and Azlan has been sent off on his mission to the West. He sends me brief, perfunctory messages, and it's hard to believe he is the same man who did very enthusiastic things between my thighs.

Worse yet, I'm back on helping-hand duties and with the team practicing every minute they can get, I'm up late every night, washing kits, clearing up the locker room and avoiding Spencer and Tristan at all opportunities. They're too occupied with the match anyway and for once leave me in peace with only those haunting memories for company.

By the time Saturday finally rolls by, I don't want to see another kit, boot, or stinky jockstrap again in my life. As helping hand, you'd think I wouldn't have a choice and would be required the day of the big match. However, the cheerleading squad wants to prepare the dressing room and kits themselves. And Summer makes it abundantly clear I won't be needed.

Oh, boo hoo. I plan to laze around in bed all day, snuggling with Pip, perhaps catching up on all my missed assignments and staying the hell away from the dueling pitch, no matter how many times Winnie insists it will be fun and I should 'get in the school spirit'.

Unfortunately, my bumming-around plans are rudely interrupted by a message from Stone.

I sit bolt upright on my bunk, staring down at my screen as Winnie stands in front of the mirror, painting the Arrow Hart crest on her face in green paint.

"What is it?" she says.

"A message from Stone."

"What does he want?"

I press my thumb on the message and read.

· · ·

Stone: Come to my cabin as soon as you can.

"Is it a booty call?"

I snort. "He's barely said a word to me in four days."

"Maybe he's going to make it up to you now."

I shake my head and type my reply.

Rhi: Are you sure that's sensible, Professor?

Stone: Don't be a brat. Azlan is here.

"Oh," I say out loud.

"Your cheeks are flushing," Winnie says, standing on her tiptoes to try to read my message. "Is he sexting you?"

"No," I say, snatching my phone away. "Azlan's there too."

I nudge Pip out of the way and jump down onto the floor.

"Maybe they're hoping to pick up where they left off last weekend," Winnie says with a wink.

I peer down at my body. I'm wearing my pajamas, no makeup and my braid is coming loose. At least I showered last night.

"I'm sure it's not that," I say, strolling to our wardrobe. I wish I'd already forced Winnie to help me find some better underwear and some better outfits. The only clothes I have to wear are jeans, jeans shorts, t-shirts and Winnie's little black dress that she adjusted to fit me. A dress I'm not even sure will fit me anymore now I actually have some curves. "I don't know what to wear."

"It doesn't matter," Winnie says. "They'll have you out of your clothes in a matter of minutes anyway."

I elbow her and she chuckles.

"Here," she says, reaching around me to fish out a light summer dress from the back of the wardrobe. "I was going to suggest you wear this to the match anyway. Everyone always dresses up. It'll probably come down to your knees but I think it will fit."

I smooth my hand over the skirt as my phone chirps in my hand.

STONE: Hurry up and make sure you aren't seen.

"WHAT'S HE SAYING?" Winnie asks, taking the dress off the hanger.

"He's being a dick."

"You should punish him then. Take a photo of yourself in your underwear and tell him you may be awhile."

"Winnie! I am not doing that." Although the thought of teasing Stone like that is kind of hot.

"You should," Winnie insists.

"Hmmm," I consider, then type out a reply.

RHI: If you want me to walk across the campus naked, I can come right away.

THERE'S a pause and then his message flashes up.

. . .

STONE: Can you not read, Blackwaters? Stop being a brat and put some damn clothes on.

I GROAN. "I don't think sexting works on Stone."

"That's because you're not doing it right." Winnie snatches my phone from my hand. "Take off your pajamas."

"Woah, Winnie. I can see why Trent walks around with such a smile on his face."

"Just do it, Rhianna. You're twenty years old and you've never done the sexting thing. It's fun, trust me." Pip snorts from my bed. "You stay out of it, young man. She's allowed to get laid."

I realize Winnie isn't going to back down on this and Stone's messages have left me pissed off. I do want to make him suffer. Okay, I'm not sure 'sexy' pictures of me will actually make him suffer. But I'm sick of him either bossing me around or ignoring me.

I step out of my PJs and stand in front of Winnie.

I'm wearing my usual boy-short panties and a plain white bra. At least the panties look a little more sexy now I have more of an ass, and I think I may have gone up a bra size too, judging by the way my tits are almost spilling out of it.

"We need to get you some new underwear," Winnie says.

"This is stupid," I say, trying to snatch my phone back.

"No, it's not," she says, raising my phone over her head so I can't reach it. "Just try not to look like you're posing for your mugshot. Try and look sexy."

"How?" I say with exasperation.

"Rhi, you're pretty stunning. It isn't hard."

"Me? Sexy?"

"Says the girl who was having a threesome with two

very hot men last week." Winnie gestures towards me. "Now turn to the side, thrust your chest forward and your butt out and then peer back at me all seductively over your shoulder."

"I am not doing that, Winnie."

"Rhianna Blackwaters, yes you are."

"Winnifred Wence—"

"Do it!" Winnie barks in her most authoritative voice.

I huff but turn to the side and look over my shoulder at her.

"That's it, now stick your butt out."

"No," I say firmly.

"Okay, then look down at the floor ... then up at me." She snaps away, then examines the screen. She presses a few buttons.

"What are you doing?"

"Adding some filters to make the lighting look more seductive. And ... there!"

She flips the phone my way and I peek at the photo. "Oh," I say, because the picture isn't half bad. She's caught me just as I was looking up, and the effect has me peering through my eyelashes, and with my hair all messed up, it does look ... kind of ... sexy.

"I can't send him that!" I say.

"Yes, you can," Winnie says and before I can do anything about it, she flips the phone back around towards her, typing away and hitting send.

"Oh shit. What did you write?"

"I wrote: I'll be right along, Professor."

"He's going to kill me."

"He's going to pound you into the nearest mattress. Him and the man in black together."

"I don't even know if I want him to touch me, let alone

..." I gulp, the image Winnie's just created in my head scorching hot. "He's a giant asshole."

"One you just tortured," Winnie says, handing me back my phone and returning to the mirror. "Now take your time getting dressed and make him suffer. He deserves it for being such an assy asshole."

I nod half-heartedly and tug the dress over my head.

Forty-five minutes later, with no more messages from Stone received, I'm knocking on his cabin door.

It swings back, and he's there glaring at me like I just indulged in torturing a litter of kittens.

"What the fuck?" he growls, hauling me inside. Azlan lurks in a corner, his arms crossed, his face thunder.

"It was Winnie," I squeak.

"Funny, it didn't look like Winnie in that photo."

"She thought you deserved to be tortured."

"And why would she think that, Miss Blackwaters?"

"Because she knows what an asshole you've been."

"I thought we agreed to keep details of our private lives private."

"Winnie is my best friend. You have Azlan to talk with about things. I need someone too."

"I thought you had the pig for that."

"Delete the photo," Azlan growls from his corner, where he's doing a very good impression of looking like the grim reaper himself. Certainly, like he might be about to take a life.

"No," I say automatically. I don't really care if I keep it or not but he's not ruling my life.

"Hand the phone over, Blackwaters." Stone holds out his hand to me.

"No, it's my body and my phone."

"You know how easy phones are to hack into? You want that photo shared around the school?"

I shrug. "Most of the school have seen my tits."

"What?" Azlan growls, stepping out of the shadows.

"Courtesy of your lovely, little cousin."

I glare at them both. So much for seduction. The picture obviously wasn't as enticing as I thought it was.

"The photo was very fucking enticing, Miss Blackwaters, which is why it needs to be deleted. And as for seduction–"

"Can you not stay out of my head for more than two seconds?"

"As for seduction," he repeats, in a low voice, "that isn't why we asked you over."

I fiddle with the hem of my dress. I'm guessing they've invited me over for the 'serious' talk. Where Azlan tells me we need more time apart and Stone tells me last weekend was all a mistake. One he regrets.

"I don't regret it," he says softly. "It wasn't a mistake. But we're not rushing into anything here either, remember? And the three of us have limited time to talk. The match starts in less than an hour and they'll be expecting me there."

"Then what do you want to talk about?"

"What Azlan found out West," Stone says.

"And those memories in your head, Rhi," the man in black adds.

I lean back against the door and close my eyes. The wood is smooth and cool against my palms. I don't want to think about those memories.

"You're asking me now?" I whisper. "You haven't asked me once this week."

"I told you to leave them well alone," Azlan says, "until we could talk again."

"But they've been creeping into my awareness anyway." I suck air down into my lungs. "Every time I close my eyes. Every time I try to sleep. And it's getting harder to tell which ones are memories and which ones are bad dreams invading my head."

"Some of those memories were dreams, Rhi," Stone says, and I open my eyes.

"And the funny thing is I don't remember dreaming like that. I rarely ever dream you see. Once, twice a year maybe and now my sleep is flooded with them."

"The dreams in your memories, what were they of?" Azlan asks.

"Men chasing us, coming to find us, hurting us." I bring my fists to my head, just like I did in that memory, feeling those memories crawl into my mind and I'm sucked back down, down into them.

"Rhi," Stone says, "stay with us." He rests his hand on my shoulder, grounding me, keeping me from falling into their depths.

"Rhi," Azlan says with concern.

"Of you," I say, shaking my head. "I dreamed of you. Of the man in black. I can see you raising your hand, the bolts of magic spiraling towards me. Just like it happened. Just like that night in the clearing."

"That's not possible. You couldn't have dreamed that. Memories can corrupt, become twisted and distorted."

"They were locked in her mind, Azlan," Stone says quietly. "There was no chance for them to corrupt like that."

"Why? Why were they locked away?" Azlan says.

"Can't you see how much they terrorize her? Wouldn't you lock such memories away if it were your child?"

"It doesn't make any sense," he says stubbornly. "I thought they would tell us something. Show us who Rhianna is. Who her parents were."

"Maybe there is something in there. Buried," I say. I swallow, my body trembling, despite the warmth of Stone's hand. "I could search them."

"No, Rhi," Stone says. "Don't do that."

I take a deep breath, focussing back on the two men in the room and letting the memories slowly fade away.

"It's easier to forget them when I'm with the two of you," I admit, the bond in my core purring like a cat.

Azlan steps forward and rests his hand on my other shoulder. "If you ever need me, I'll be here. All you have to do is call me, Rhi. You don't have to do this alone."

I try to believe him. I try really hard. But it's hard to trust either of them. After all, the friend I did trust led me straight to the man attempting to kill me.

"She doesn't believe you," Stone scoffs.

"Stay out of my–"

"Because trust has to be earned," Azlan says. "But you also have to be willing to give me the opportunity to earn it, Rhi. And it works both ways. You want me to trust you, show me I can."

"Okay," I say.

I peer at Stone.

He opens his mouth, then closes it.

"What did you find out West?" I ask Azlan.

"The rumors are right. Forces have been coming over the border."

"Why?"

Azlan shakes his head. "That I'm not so sure of. There are reports of some magicals being kidnapped, but if they were, they were unregistereds, on the run. We don't know for sure who they took."

"Why would they be stealing unregistered magicals?"

"To boost their forces," Stone says.

"They're planning on attacking?" I say in alarm. The supposed threat from the West has existed for such a long time and never materialized, I had assumed it was never going to.

"Possibly," Azlan says. "The Chancellor is upping our forces at the border."

"And what about, Rhi?" Stone asks. "Any intelligence on why those soldiers attacked her?"

"No. But if they were there hoping to pick up stray magicals, I'm assuming it was a matter of wrong place, wrong time."

"It wasn't targeted?" Stone asks.

"I can't be sure, but I don't think so."

I feel Stone's body relax next to mine and he exhales a puff of air. He squeezes my shoulder.

"I have to go," he says.

"Already?" I say, unable to hide my disappointment. I was hoping for more time together.

"The match will be starting shortly and I'm meant to be meeting with the contingency from Aropia."

"Right," I say flatly.

"I have to be there. If I'm missing, then–"

"Sure." I look away from him.

He lowers his hand from my shoulder and I sense his posture stiffen.

"Blackwaters," his tone is no longer tender, "delete that damn photo."

"Have you deleted it from your phone, Professor?" I say snarkily.

He leans forward so his mouth is by my ear. "No. I'm keeping it."

Then he pushes me away from the door and leaves.

45

R^{hi}

Azlan strokes along my jaw.

"Give him time," he says as we hear Stone's footsteps clatter across the porch.

"You think time will stop him being a massive jerk? Because he's had thirty years."

"I think you have a way of confusing the hell out of him. You confuse the hell out of me."

"Is that meant to be a compliment? Is it meant to make me feel better?"

"It's an explanation. Stone is a good man, Rhi, and trust me there aren't as many as there should be out there. He may be an asshole sometimes, but he will always do the right thing by you when it counts."

Would he think that if he knew what Stone tried to do on Founders' Night? Then again maybe he'd think he was justified if he knew about the crimson magic. Tristan and Spencer said the authorities would lock me away if they knew. Is that true, or are they trying to scare me? I consider telling him. He said I should trust him. But can I?

"I missed you," he says, sliding his hand into my hair.

"Really? It didn't seem like it." He frowns quizzically. "Your messages weren't exactly …"

"I'm not good with words. But next time I'm away, if you want to send me one of those photos, I could send you one of my own."

"I didn't think you approved."

"There are ways of sending me a photo, Rhi, without using a phone."

"There are?"

He closes his eyes, our bond shimmers between us and an image appears before my eyes. One of the photo I just sent Stone.

"I can't read minds," he says. "But the bond allows some limited communication as long as you keep it open. If you do, I'll always know when you're in trouble."

"Okay," I say, although I don't know if I'm ready for him to feel every one of my emotions, especially when so many of them are screwed up.

He keeps stroking along my jaw as his hand finds the hem of my dress.

"I didn't want to leave you. I didn't want to be away from you. You know the only place I want to be is here."

He trails his hands up my thighs.

"You seem pretty good with your words to me," I sigh.

"It's easier when I'm standing right in front of you."

He strokes along the gusset of my panties, probably aware of just how wet I am.

"It's been too long," he says.

"Yes," I mutter. Way too long. It feels like an age since he was last inside me. "I talked to the matron."

"Oh kay," he says, clearly puzzled why I'm talking about the school nurse while he's busy sliding my panties down my legs. He follows them right down to the floor, helping me to step out of them, and kissing my foot, then my knee and then the sensitive skin on the inside of my thigh.

"About contraception."

"We can keep using–"

"She talked about a barrier spell."

He stands and looks down into my face. "It stops pregnancy," he says, "but it would mean–"

"You'd come inside me," I whimper.

His eyes darken and the bond between us smolders. "Come inside you," he growls. "You'd like that, pretty girl?"

I nod, biting my lip and feeling my cheeks sizzle.

"Shit," he mumbles, raising his hand and muttering words under his breath, his magic shimmering all around me. "Done," he says, opening his eyes, his pupils blazing.

And then everything turns frantic. My fingers scrabble at his fly, his yanking my dress over my head. I grapple at his shirt, he rips away my bra.

Then he walks me back against the door, taking a hold of my backside and hoisting me upwards so I can wrap my legs around him. He kisses my mouth and thrusts his cock into me and we both groan, the bond thrumming so violently now I can feel it in my chest.

"Sh-sh-shit," he says, as he plunges all the way inside me. Here he pauses, kissing my mouth and my neck, my cheeks and my tits.

Then with a pained groan he slides out and fucks me hard.

"Does it feel ..." I ask.

"Yes, it does, I can feel everything, all of you. So tight, so warm, so soft."

The bond glows at his words, like it's pleased with his praise, and I make a note to go fishing for more of it, if it generates that feeling inside me.

He grunts. "Fuck, pretty girl, I'm going to pump you full of my come. Pump you so full of it, that belly of yours bulges."

And it's not only the bond glowing. Now it's all of me. I like it when he talks dirty like this. The man in black always has a handle on his emotions. But not when he's with me. When he's fucking me, he loses all restraint and that tongue of his runs wild.

"You want it?" he asks.

"Hmmm," I murmur.

"Rhianna, do you want it?" he says, fucking me so hard the entire cabin seems to rock.

Each thrust has my eyes rolling around in their sockets, moans and whimpers flying from my mouth. It feels so good. He makes me feel so good.

"Rhianna," he growls. "Tell me: do you want my come? Do you want me pumping you full of it?"

"Yes," I whimper.

"Yes," he repeats, his voice so deep, so low, it's almost lost to a rumble in his broad chest. "Yes, you do, don't you? Because you're mine. All mine. My mate. My pretty girl. And my cock is just what you need."

He braces one of his hands by my head, leaning back to deepen the angle, and with the other hand he rubs at my clit. The sensation is overwhelming, the combination in my pussy and where he is touching me divine, and when I come, I scream so loud, I swear they must hear me all the way out in the dueling ground.

My cunt clenches and convulses around him as I ride the after-waves of pleasure.

"See how much you want it? See how your pussy is milking me for it? Shit, Rhi, You're so... so ..." With a grunt he comes, hot liquid flooding inside me. My bond goes wild for it, vibrating so violently inside my belly I crash over the edge with him, and we collapse down on the floor, panting, me still jolting in his arms.

I stroke the damp hair from his neck and kiss his cheeks, wrapping my legs around him. Not wanting him to go, even as he rocks gently and his cock softens.

Slowly, he slips out of me, examining my thighs as he does.

"Don't waste it," he says, trailing his fingers up my thigh to capture the come that's dribbling down my leg. He scoops it up in his fingers and thrusts it up inside my still-thrumming pussy. "I want you to have it all."

I gaze at his face, his eyes so dark like that first moment we met, like my dream. His own gaze is fixated on his fingers, buried inside my pussy. He looks entranced, beautiful. I know I'm falling for him. I always was, regardless of the bond.

"I wish we could be together like this all the time," I whisper, even though I know it's my fault we're apart. That I chose it, chose to return to the school.

"We will be," he whispers, nuzzling my neck. "We will be eventually. You, me, and Stone too. Together."

And his words make that strange sensation in my core spin like a carousel.

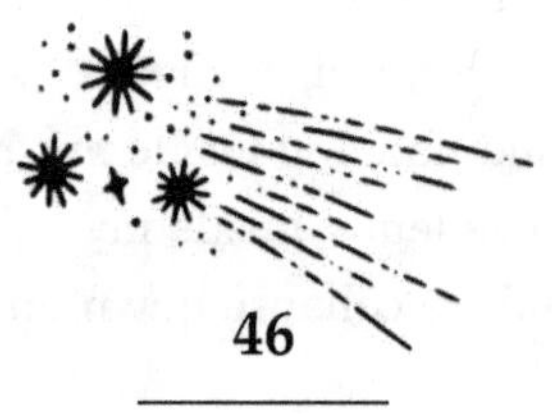

46

S pencer

"WHERE'S THE PIG GIRL?" I ask.

I thought she'd be here, doing her duty as our team's helping hand, lining up to kiss our cheeks and wish us luck. Instead, it's Summer and her girls, so fucking buzzed, I'm surprised they're not wetting their panties.

"Her?" Summer says. "I told her to stay away. I didn't think you'd want her polluting the air with her bad smell before the match."

"Not to mention her bad attitude," Aysha says. "Only positive vibes. We wanted you boys to know how much we're rooting for you."

So much so, half these girls were 'helping' my team-mates to relieve stress yesterday evening, even though Coach insists on a strict no-sex ban before a match this big.

"Hey," Dan said, when I reminded him of this, "a blowie isn't technically sex."

"It's still blowing your load."

"It helps me sleep."

Maybe it's something I should have gone for too. Five different members of the cheerleading squad knocked on my door last night offering their services. I'd sent them all away. Choosing instead to toss and turn in my bed all night. Not from nerves, from fucking adrenaline, the plays and our game plan buzzing around my head like a swarm of crazed hornets.

"Who wants a good luck kiss first?" Summer asks, fake eyelashes fluttering. She's in her element today. This is as much about her performance as it is ours. She loves the limelight and as head of the cheerleading squad it will be all hers.

"I'd rather sit back and watch you make out with Aysha," Dan says with a smirk. "That will definitely give me the encouragement I need."

Chloe scowls at him and he grabs her by the waist and drags her down onto his lap. "You know it's my favorite type of porn, sweetheart. Gets me in the mood." He nuzzles her neck.

"You're meant to be gearing yourself up for this match," I grind out between my teeth. "Not gearing up for an orgy."

"I'm just kidding, man," Dan says, kissing Chloe's cheek and placing her back on her feet, slapping her ass as she trots back towards the other girls. "I'm ready. And a little bit of light entertainment never hurt anyone before a match."

I glare at Tristan, waiting for him to back me up here, but he's lost in his thoughts, staring into space. Something he's been doing a lot of recently. Either that or disappearing into thin air. If it wasn't for Summer moaning about his

absence, I'd take it personally and believe he was deliberately avoiding me.

"You're becoming such a fucking bore, man," Dan says
rolling his eyes. Maybe that's true. Maybe a few months ago,
it would've been me encouraging Summer and Aysha to
make out. Hell, I'd probably have got right in the middle of
that and had them both making out with me at the same
time.

It's the dark cloud. It's there constantly. Unmoving. My
head pounding from the pressure of it.

"I just want to win this match."

"Are your parents coming to watch?" Tristan asks.

I stare down at my boots, lifting my foot to retie my laces.
"No fucking clue."

I haven't seen my parents since the winter holidays. And
only then because I had nowhere else to go but home.
They're not like Tristan's parents, stepping into the limelight
at every opportunity. They may be powerful, but it's a power
wielded in a different way, and they have their reasons for
clinging to the shadows.

"Mommy and Daddy coming," Dan jokes, "is that why
you're so wound up? You want to impress them?" He presses
his hand to his chest, mocking me. "How adorable."

If we didn't need him for the match, I'd blast him across
the fucking changing room.

Instead, I manage one of my easy smiles, dazzling all the
cheerleaders lined up for us. "No, planning to score for your
mom. Always makes her hot for me."

Dan leaps to his feet as the changing room erupts into
laughter.

"Don't speak about my mom–"

"Come on, man, don't worry about it. I doubt she'd be
able to fit me into her very busy schedule."

"What the fuck does that mean?"

I wink at him and he looks like he might want to murder me. But then the changing room door opens and Coach walks in. He takes one unamused look at the girls and they flee before he says a word.

"You should be swotting up on last-minute plays, not chasing skirt," he says, shaking his head.

"Kisses from cheerleaders are known to bring good luck," Dan says.

"We don't need luck. We're going to crush them," Coach says, with a glint of triumph in his eye. He lifts his fist and crunches it tight. "No mercy, boys. Give this everything you got." He sticks his fist out in front of him and we gather around, laying our hands one on top of the other. I take the opportunity to squeeze Dan's hand, grinning at him widely.

"This is the biggest match you'll ever play as seniors, boys. Are you ready?"

"Hell, yeah," we yell.

"What are you? A bunch of choir boys. I said, are you ready?!"

"Hell, yeah!!" we all shout.

"Then let's do this."

I punch my fist up in the air, adrenaline pumping through every muscle in my body.

Coach draws me in close. "I'm counting on you. Never had a dueler like you, Spencer. Go out there and show everyone just what you can do."

I nod and he gestures for me to go first.

I pick up my feet and jog down the tunnel, out towards the light of the ground. The cheerleaders are lined up out there now, shaking their pom-poms and bouncing up and down.

The ground is alive with noise and movement, the roar

of hundreds of people, the drone of the band, the yells of the cheerleading squad. Banners bristle in the wind, and arms wave. The helmet is tight on my head, my mouth guard rough against my gums, the taste plastic and sterile.

I rub my fingers together, damp with anticipation and try to block out all the sound, all the stimulation from my mind. But I can't help scanning the stands. I already know she's not here. I'd feel it deep in my gut if she were. I look anyway, spying her roommate, her dark hair tied around her head, her cheeks painted the same color as my jersey. No Pig Girl.

I shouldn't be surprised. When has she ever done what she's supposed to do? Coming to this match is unofficially mandatory. No one misses it. No one wants to. Everybody wants to see us compete against the Aropia fuckers. For us to show them who's best.

Not her.

I roll my shoulders, jumping up and down on the spot. Waking up my body.

I need to focus, concentrate. This is my moment to shine. The one where I get to show all the world just how fucking good Spencer Moreau is. Better than them. Not something to be sneered at, disgusted, reviled. I may be different, but I am also superior.

"Are you ready to grind these fuckers into the dust?" Dan says, whacking his hand against my shoulder, his eyes wild with adrenaline.

"Fuck, yes," I grunt.

The day is clear, the wind light, and I can smell the grass and the dirt in my nose. I am more than ready.

The other team emerges from the tunnel, dressed in a golden kit that glistens in the sunlight. Idiots. It will make it ten times easier to spot them and blast them out of the game. They're all tall, well-built like us, the same determined glint in their eyes. I keep my eyes on their captain. He's been their champion for several years now. He alone took out five members of our team last time we met. But I wasn't a senior back then. I was on the bench more often than the field.

This time things will be different.

The referee beckons me over and his words float through my head unheard. Then I'm shaking the other captain's hand, both our grips so freaking tight, we might snap bones. I look him hard in the eyes, noticing their peculiar green color and the freckles across the bridge of his nose, a nose I can see has been broken and repaired numerous times.

As I stroll back into my own half, taking my position, my teammates around me, the stadium falls quiet, five hundred breaths held. Then the whistle pierces the silence. For a moment no one moves and my heart clatters against my rib cage.

Then the opposing captain raises his hands and his team mates scatter across the field. I smile. I am ready for this, fucking ready for it.

Magic flashes around me, multiple colors. It hisses and crackles, booms and whines. I'm oblivious to it all, eyes still fixed on that captain as I begin to move towards him, deflecting magic, swerving attacks, as I move across the field. I'm too quick for them all and on my path I toss one opponent straight over my shoulder. As he hits the ground, his uniform fades a dull gray. He's out of the match and our score just jumped 50 points. Another kid I hit mid-chest as he rises in front of me and he stumbles to the ground. Another 50.

My shoulders loosen, my heart beats more steadily. I

settle into my stride, beginning to enjoy the match, especially when the crowd starts chanting my name.

I'm dueling some of the best I ever have, when I feel it. The moment she steps into the stadium. I feel it in my core. A sharp tug. If I turn my head, she'll be there somewhere in the crowd. She's already missed the first quarter, missed me take out three of their players and dodge a combined attack aimed right at me.

She missed all that, but now she's here.

And I have a desire to impress her. To show that I am the best.

I focus my eyes on that captain and sprint as fast as I can. He hears me coming, spinning around to face me. Our eyes lock again. The other players freeze around us. They know it's between the two of us now.

The captain sweeps his arms in circles in front of his body and a tornado of magic blasts my way. I knock half of it away with my own magic and battle through the rest, the force of it making my eyes stream and my hair whip backwards.

I fire magic of my own at him and he grins ducking and diving it all. I curse, determined to get closer. Like Tristan, his magic is good. But one on one, physically, he doesn't stand a chance. He must know it, because next he slices his hands through the air and arrows of magic litter down on me like rain. I shield myself, gritting my teeth against the few that make it through and hit my skin.

I'm gaining on him. He glances over his shoulder as if he's debating whether to retreat. But Dan and Tristan are right there, blocking his way and his teammates have been too complacent to protect their captain.

We fire magic at each other. It explodes as it collides, lighting up the stadium in a boom of color. Then I'm crashing through, my hands grabbing at his shirt. I land a punch to his gut, and the gold of his kit flickers. I hit him again, just for good measure as he attempts to zap me with his magic, and then I lift the fucker above my head and throw him to the ground. His uniform fades to gray. He's out.

The stadium erupts. They chant my name. My teammates rush towards me, high-fiving me, slapping me on the shoulder, hugging me.

The atmosphere is electric and my magic feeds off it, fizzes in my veins.

I spin around, arms raised, soaking up the adoration. Everyone is cheering, worshiping me.

Everyone but her.

She stares at me from her seat, her eyes connecting with mine like an electrical current, the sensation in my body tugging hard.

Fuck her.

Fuck her.

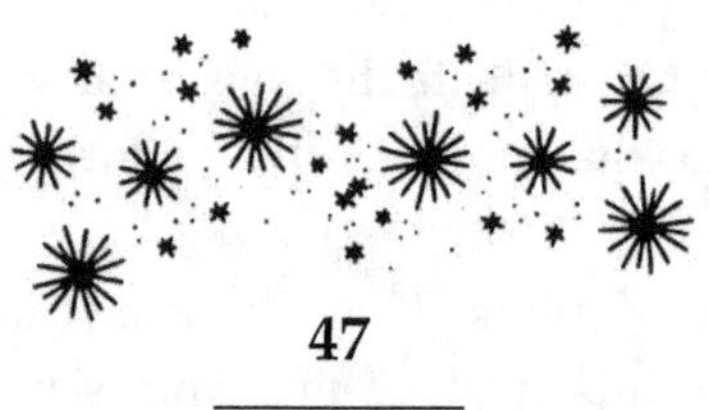

47

R^{hi}

Everybody goes mad around me. Even Winnie, jumping up and down and hugging Trent tightly. Banners sway, someone two rows below is actually sniffling, and the noise is deafening.

Not me. I'm standing statue still, my heart pounding, because the way he moved, his eyes. It's so familiar. Like ... like a wolf. But that can't be right, can it? I shake my head. The werebeast came from outside. They're highly dangerous creatures. There's no way in hell one would be living among us in this school. I must be mistaken.

"Rhi," Winnie says, squeezing me next now Trent has released her from his jubilant hug. "We're going to win!"

"Aren't there like ... erm ... another two quarters to go?"

"Yeah, but we're crushing them. Spencer is on fire." I

pull a face. "We can forgive him for being a dickhead for a few minutes if he brings the cup home to Arrow Hart."

"He'll be an even more insufferable dickhead if we all worship him like a god!"

"He is a dueling god," Trent says in a way that would have me thinking he had a crush on the guy if he wasn't so clearly nuts about Winnie.

"You didn't even see half his takedowns," Winnie says, "you were too busy off doing whatever you were doing."

My cheeks sizzle and I decide to change the subject.

"How is this game even legal?" I say, grimacing as a player is thrown across the ground.

"Because the magical and physical strikes are restricted," Trent tells me, eyes locked on the match. "Plus they're wearing protective clothing. Their kits protect them from any real damage but register a deadly strike. Nobody actually ends up seriously hurt."

"Really?" I say, watching one of our players hobbling off the pitch, his emerald kit now a muted gray.

"Well, occasionally, but it's rare."

"Hmm," I say, wincing a second time as violent magic smacks Spencer's helmet and explodes into sparks. "And how do we win?"

"You really never watched dueling before?" Trent says, finally swinging his gaze to me in amazement.

"Nope."

Trent gapes at me until Winnie nudges him and points to the field.

"The winning team is the one with the most points at the end of the match or the final team standing if they manage to knock out all the opposing team's duelers. And," Winnie says, anticipating my next question, "you earn points by knocking players out of the game."

The crowd start to cheer as Tristan and Spencer pin two of the opposition between them, battering them with their magic.

I can't watch, not as more magic crashes against Spencer's helmet and then Tristan's.

I look away.

The man in black said his family would be here watching Tristan play, but he was adamant he wouldn't be joining them. I search the elegant-looking boxes on the far side of the stands. The Chancellor occupies one with Principal York, several of the councilmen and women I recognize from the night I was brought to Los Magicos, and a man I assume is the Aropia Magical University's headmaster. In the next box sit two well-dressed men who look remarkably alike, along with a blonde woman who can only be Tristan's mother, the likeness uncanny. Which means the men must be Azlan's father and uncle. I try to find the likeness between the two men and my mate, but I can't. Mostly because the taller man in particular gives me the creeps, his eyes cold, his demeanor – his every movement – seeming calculated. There's one other person in the box, a younger woman.

As I stare, the younger woman looks up from the pitch and meets my eye. She smiles for a fraction of a second before glancing the taller man's way. I smile back, even though she's no longer looking my way and my heart drops a little. How different things could have been if my fated mate had been from a family like Winnie's. A family who would have welcomed me with open arms. Would I be sitting with them now if they had? What would that be like, to be surrounded by family? People who love and care for you? But Azlan's family look about as capable of love and care as a pool of crocodiles.

I shake my head, trying to dispel the sadness, and run my gaze further along the boxes, ignoring the way Winnie grabs my hand and squeezes it with excitement.

The box next to Azlan's family is empty. But as I squint, I notice a family crest painted on a banner hanging over the box. A moon and a crossbow. It's a crest I've seen pinned to Spencer's chest on more than one occasion, although I'd assumed it was some fashion brand. Is this his family box? Empty. I frown. He's the star of this show. They're all screaming his name. Why wouldn't his family be here to watch his moment of glory? What can that mean?

I don't linger on his box though, my eye is drawn onward, as if of its own accord, and I scan my eyes over the other spectators, examining with interest the large group of Aropia supporters. It's as I'm doing so that I spot him, sitting in the crowd for everyone to see, a red rose pinned to the lapel of his jacket.

I jolt.

"Don't worry," Winnie says, "Tristan will take him down ... See?" she says, pointing to the pitch.

"No," I say, "it's not that." I tug my hand free of hers. "I need to ..."

I turn and start pushing my way along the row, people cursing me, and Winnie calling after me. I keep my eyes on the man and when I reach the steps, hurry down them three at a time.

Why is he here, an unregistered among all these magicals? Does he want to get caught? Has he come to speak with me? Or am I mistaken again? Am I imagining things?

As soon as I'm out of the stadium gate, I sprint around the stands, hearing the loud roars from within, and seeing magic soar high up into the air. I calculate roughly where the man was, slowing my steps as I make it right round to the other side of the stadium. I go to push my way inside, but then I hear a voice call me.

"Rhianna."

I spin around and find the older man standing right behind me. It's him. The man from the cemetery.

He beckons to me and I follow him away from the stadium and into a copse of trees that lie to the west.

"What are you doing here?" I gasp. "Are you crazy? Do you want to get caught?" Maybe he does. Maybe he's tired of running and has come to hand himself in. He must have been running for years, decades.

"I'm perfectly safe. Only you can see me."

My brow crinkles in confusion. "What?" I say. Am I dreaming? Am I dreaming this?

He lifts his hand from his pocket and opens his fist. In his palm lies a silver locket.

"My aunt's locket."

"Yes." He steps a little closer. "I'm sorry. I never intended to steal it from you."

"Then why did you take it?"

"I came looking for you and your aunt. To see what she had heard. To tell of what I knew."

I screw up my brow in confusion. "There's war brewing, Rhianna Blackwaters. I can feel it in the air." He tips his head to one side, looking at me intently. "Do you feel it too?"

I simply stare back at him in confusion. He shakes his head, clearly disappointed by my response.

"In the town, they told me your aunt had died – buried in the cemetery – and that you had left town with two older men. I assumed either the authorities or the gangs had taken you."

"The authorities."

"I went to pay my respects to your aunt and standing

there I sensed it – the locket." He adjusts his glasses on his nose, the locket still shining in his other hand. "I assume you know what it is?"

"What it is?"

"Yes, what it can do."

"N-n-no. I didn't know it could do anything. I thought it was just a necklace."

"It is a cloaker."

I shake my head in frustration. "I don't know what that is."

"A powerful charm that can keep you hidden. Hidden from anyone you choose. How else do you think I could stand here among all these magicals and not be seen?"

"I saw you."

"Yes, strange that." He tilts his head, examining me. "How do you think your aunt kept you so well hidden from the magicals all those years?"

"She never ..." I trail off.

"I took it because I didn't think you had need of it. I thought you were never coming back. But then there you were, at the cemetery, and I intended to hand it over to you then but–"

"Those men."

"Yes, I lost my chance."

"Then why give it to me now?"

"It belongs to you, Rhianna Blackwaters. It was your aunt's and your mother's before hers. I have no business owning what is yours."

"You knew my aunt."

"As well as anyone living underground can know another."

"Do you know why she was keeping me hidden?"

He closes his fist around the necklace and lets his arm fall to his side. "She never told you?"

"Never explicitly. She just said I wasn't safe with the authorities. I'm sure she would have told me, but she was taken so suddenly and ..."

"I suspect she thought you were safer not knowing."

"Yes, but she was wrong. Not knowing, not understanding, not being able to face whatever danger she feared with understanding, is far far more dangerous."

He considers me, his eyes traveling back and forth over my face as if he's deciding what he should do for the best.

"Please," I say, my voice breaking.

"Very well. I have to say, I agree with you. I think she should have told you from the start."

"Perhaps," I say, not wanting to criticize the woman who cared for me with all her heart all those years.

"Your aunt was a talented witch, Rhianna. But your mother, she ... she was something else."

"What do you mean?"

He takes another step closer, lowering his voice, even though there is no one around us to hear. "She was a seer."

"A seer," I repeat.

"She could see the future. Read it. Predict it."

"So ..." I say, unsure what this can mean.

"There haven't been any seers in centuries, Rhianna. And being able to see the future is both a gift, a blessing, a tool in the right hands. And a deadly weapon in the wrong."

"My mother, she wouldn't have–"

"No, but there were those who wished to use her gift in their battles, in their wars."

"The authorities," I say.

"And the gangs. The leaders in the West. They all wanted your mother. They all wanted her gift."

"A weapon," I whisper.

"Yes, that's right. A weapon to destroy their enemies."

"What happened to her?"

"That I don't know. I'm not sure your aunt even did. But she knew that with your mother gone, they'd come looking for you."

"Me?"

"To check whether you possessed your mother's gift. She feared you too would be lost in the battle between the authorities and the gangs, the authorities and the West. Collateral damage."

"I don't," I say quickly.

"No, I didn't think you did. You would be far too valuable an asset to allow you out of the Chancellor's sight." He smiles. "It seems your aunt's fears were unfounded. You are an ordinary girl. Perfectly safe. Of no real interest."

"Yes," I say, a shiver trailing down my spine.

"But, even so, this necklace belongs to you, and perhaps it will come in handy to you one day."

"How does it work?" I ask.

"It will make you unseeable to those you don't wish to see you. There are, of course, always some with the power to see through it, but those people are rare." He meets my eye and holds out his hand. "There is war coming, Rhianna Blackwaters. Maybe you can't feel it, but I can. Your aunt was very kind to me. Aided me when I was most in need of help. I wished to warn her and repay the favor. Now I have passed the warning to you instead, ensured you have her cloaker. My debt, I think, is repaid."

I nod.

He hesitates, then continues.

"Remember, no matter what they tell you, Rhianna, no matter what they say, you are free to choose your side in the fight. If you choose to fight at all. We all have the freedom to choose. No matter who we are." He motions with his hand. "Here, take your locket."

"But if I take it from you ..." I say, peering over my shoulder.

"They'll be able to see me. Yes, well, beg your pardon, if I don't hang around for a long goodbye. It was good to see you again. I'm sure both your aunt and your mother would be proud of you. And I am glad I could return this to you."

He opens his fist and the necklace falls through the air. I reach out and catch it, the metal warm against my palm.

"Thank you," I say, but when I look up, he is already gone.

I bring the locket up to my face, eyes racing over the intricate carving, twines and flowers following the oval outline. I realize I forgot to ask him if he opened it. If there was anything inside – a message, a note, a photo?

The stadium erupts behind me, the sound so loud, the ground under my feet shakes.

I catch my thumbnail in the join of the locket and pull. It clicks open easily with no resistance, no special lock, no spell to keep it shut.

I prize open the two shells and examine the inside.

A small photo lies within, a picture of a woman and a man. They are both staring down at a small baby cradled in their arms. The woman looks like me. Just like me. My mother.

Carefully, I remove the photo and check the back, check behind.

Nothing. No words. No secret clue.

Nothing more.

48

R^{hi}

I DON'T REMEMBER where my feet take me after that, or how long I wander, lost in my thoughts, my mind swimming with the old man's revelations, with the memories still threatening to haunt me, and with the image of the photo inside the locket.

I try not to feel the hurt deep in my heart. She would have wanted me to have the locket, of that I am sure. A gift to keep me safe and hidden. A gift to show me I was loved. But even so I feel the pain. No note, no words, no message. How could she leave me so unprepared?

Because she was struggling every day to keep us alive.

I know it is the truth, yet it does little to numb the pain.

I keep walking, unaware of where I am, the day darkening around me, the air turning cool, until I'm snapped rudely from my trance by Summer freaking Clutton-Brock.

"Look what the cat dragged in," she says, and I blink finding myself in the gardens outside Venus common room, right in the middle of what looks like a victory party. Music thumps, paper streamers hang limply from the trees and the air smells of weed and alcohol.

I reach for my aunt's necklace. But I don't know how to use it and there are already dozens of pairs of eyes observing me like I'm a fresh meal to be devoured. That or tortured.

The people around me are swaying and grinding to the music. The dueling team have lost their shirts, their ripped chests gleaming with sweat in the light from the lanterns, and half-dressed cheerleaders paw over them.

Summer steps in front of me blocking my path. She's dressed only in her cheerleading skirt and her bra and a massive love bite marks her neck.

Actually maybe this isn't a party. Maybe it's a freaking orgy. I can see one girl down on her knees with some jock's dick in her mouth. And another dude has a girl pressed up against the trunk of a tree, his hand up her skirt.

"You're NOT invited to this party, piggie," Summer says. "Nobody's keen to catch something off you. Especially as you're riddled with the were-infection now as well as all those swine STDs."

I take a step backwards. I'm absolutely fine with that. I don't want to be here. But the dancers have moved in behind me and I'm trapped. I spin around, colliding immediately with the hard body of Spencer Moreau. He's clutching the Cross-lantic trophy in his hand, a girl hovers at his side, and there's a second girl hovering behind him.

His eyes alight on mine.

"You weren't at the match," he growls.

"No," I say, "I don't like fighting."

The girls around him laugh like I've made the most hilarious joke.

"You should have been there anyway. Everyone else was there showing their support, cheering on our team."

"I don't remember hearing it was compulsory."

"It is. Everybody knows it." He shakes the second girl off his shoulder as she reaches out to touch him, and leans forward. "What's wrong? You think this school isn't good enough for you, little pig?"

I'm not interested in his bullshit. I'm not going to play his games and beg for forgiveness, because that is clearly what he wants.

"Oh sorry, did I hurt your feelings? Are you upset I wasn't there worshiping at the Spencer Moreau shrine?"

I smile at him, but it's quickly wiped away as a hand pulls at my hair, forcing me backwards. I scream, hands flying to my scalp and look up through tears into Summer's face. She leans down towards me and, as if these people can smell a fight brewing, heads snap our way.

"You have no fucking respect, Pig. For this school, or for us. Maybe it's about time we taught you a bit of school spirit."

"Let me go," I hiss at her, my eyes smarting with tears.

"No, not until you learn some manners."

"I'm warning you, Summer," I say, raising my hand towards her. I've been wanting to blast this bitch since the day I met her and this seems like the perfect opportunity.

"Are you? How cute. Go ahead, Pig. I'd like nothing more than for you to use your magic on me, because then you'll be out of here faster than I will be able to smile. Expelled. We all want you gone. You pollute the fucking air."

I scowl at her, lowering my hand. She's not bluffing and

there are at least fifty witnesses here. She tugs sharply on my hair, making me yelp. I pull on her hand, trying to shake her off, but her grip only tightens.

"Now, how shall we start?" she says. "Maybe by worshiping at the feet of Spencer Moreau. He just won us the cup. He just took out more of the opposition than any player has ever done for this school. You should be grateful. You should be honored to be in his presence." She grins at me with a wicked wildness in her eyes. The girl really is a bitch. "Down on your knees."

"No!"

We tussle on the grass; Summer trying to drag me down, me refusing to let her. The people around us leer at me, some hissing, "Knees."

I peer up at Spencer. His face is blank, devoid of all emotion as he watches us both.

"Aysha, Chloe!" Summer screams in frustration. Several of the girls from the cheerleading team step towards us, but Spencer holds out his hand to stop them.

"Fight your own battles, Summer," he says quietly, meeting my eyes, his eyebrow twerking over so slightly as if he's saying, "What you waiting for? Fight."

Summer scowls at him, then shakes my head, the pain in my scalp making me gasp.

"Kiss his feet!" she yells, and lights blind my eyes. I squint. People are filming us on their cell phones.

"No!" I yell back.

We tussle some more, both falling to the ground and she manages to shove down hard on the back of my skull, forcing my face down into the soft ground beneath me. Instantly, my mouth and nose fill with earth and I struggle back up, unable to breathe. It only makes Summer push down harder.

"You need to learn, Pig Girl," Summer hisses in my ear. "That I'm in charge here, not you. What I say goes. So get in fucking line or I will break you."

I gasp for air, my lungs starting to burn, my head screaming with pain.

"Look," Summer says, "down in the dirt where the little pig belongs."

I can't breathe. I can't breathe. Dark spots dance across my vision. I writhe on the ground. My lungs desperate for oxygen.

I grab Summer's wrist. I'm going to blast the bitch to the next continent.

"That's enough!" Spencer says firmly. "You've had your fun, Summer. We don't need anymore unconscious girls at this party. They're a fucking trip hazard."

Summer's grip loosens, and I manage to lift my head enough to suck in air, coughing and spluttering as dirt flies down my windpipe.

"But–" Summer says with an obvious pout.

"I said, that's enough," Spencer says, anger in his tone. "I don't want her lips on my skin. Not when she's probably been making out with her pig with those same lips."

Laughter breaks out around us.

But I don't care what Spencer has to say. I don't care if half the school is filming us. I've had about as much of this girl as I can take.

"Fine," Summer says, rolling me over to face her and staring down into my eyes with a cold look, "I think she learned her lesson anyway–"

She doesn't finish her words because I slam the front of my skull hard against her face. She screams, falling backwards and I climb on top of her, pinning her arms by her sides. Her nose is all busted, blood streaming down her face.

My fingertips buzz with magic. My stomach spins with excitement. I want to make her hurt so badly.

"You're not in charge, Summer Clutton-Brock. You're a bully and a bitch. And if you ever touch me again, I will mess up that pretty face of yours so badly you'll weep every time you look in the mirror."

There is stunned silence all around us. No one dares move.

"Rhianna," Spencer finally says, softly.

I jolt. Then I climb to my feet, my legs shaking, my heart hammering. I take a step away and then another.

Summer whimpers on the floor and in the next minute, she's surrounded by a group of cheerleaders, helping her to her feet and leading her away towards the Venus common room.

The people gathered around us move away too, the sound of their voices fading away and the music rising again.

I wipe my hand over my mouth and spit dirt onto the ground.

Spencer doesn't move. He simply watches me and I can feel that familiar pull towards him.

"So blasting holes in stomachs is a treat you reserve purely for me," he says.

"Would you have preferred a broken nose?"

"It was a good move. And it seems you do actually listen to me."

I rub at my scalp. There's a small bald patch and I'm pretty sure Summer took a handful of my hair with her.

"You could have stopped it though. Instead, you all just watched," I snarl.

"If you actually acted like you should, little piggie. If you showed respect, if you did what you're meant to do–"

"Spencer, you had hundreds of people cheering out there for you today, chanting your goddamn name. Who cares if I was there or not?"

"I care," he says, holding my eyes, his chestnut gaze softening. "I wanted you there."

"Why?" I ask incredulously.

He opens his mouth, "I ..." I tilt my head to the side, waiting for his explanation, that hook wanting me closer to him. Then he closes his mouth, his jaw stiffens, and that same steely expression returns. "Where were you?"

I hesitate. I'm not telling the truth. Not the whole of it anyway. "I was with Azlan."

His lip curls and disgust fills his eyes. "He's old enough to be–"

"We had this conversation already, remember? He's also my fated mate. Remember that bit too?"

"Then why aren't you with him, little pig?" His eyes flit down my body. One strap of my dress is broken, the hem is ripped and there's blood on the skirt. "If I found my fated mate, I wouldn't let her out of my sight. I'd have her by my side every minute of every day. I wouldn't let any fucker hurt her. I wouldn't let anyone lay one single finger on her ever!"

"Really?" I say, feeling that sensation in my stomach. I'm so damn confused.

"Really," he says.

"And yet you stood and watched while she–"

"You're not my–"

"No, I'm his."

He growls, the noise low and rumbling in his chest. I stare at him, that earlier thought from the match flitting through my mind again.

Wolf.

I shake my head.

"Spencer?" a female voice calls out from the party, and when his head turns that way, I take my chance and hurry away, not waiting for him to finish the job Summer started.

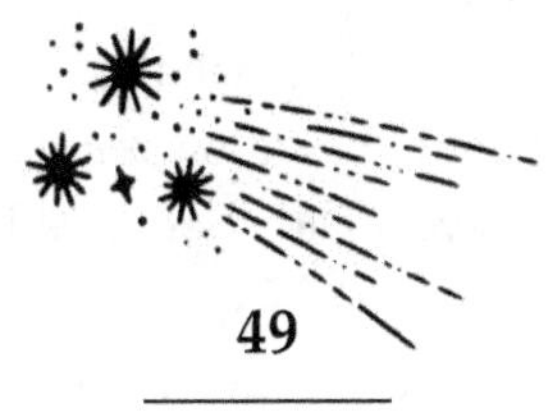

49

S tone

IN THE DISTANCE I can hear music and laughter, cheering and chanting. The entire campus is celebrating the Arrow Hart victory. But I ducked the formal dinner with the Aropia Magical University congregation, choosing instead to sit out here on the steps of my cabin, nursing a beer and gazing out across the meadow.

Maybe because I know she'll come. I have that feeling.

I sense her far across the meadow before I see her, before I hear her.

"Rhi," I call out and she crosses the meadow. As she comes nearer, I see there's mud smeared across her face, her hair is a mess, her dress ripped, blood on her hands. I bolt up onto my feet and sprint towards her.

"What the fuck happened?" I say, skidding to a halt in front of her and twisting her towards me.

"I don't want to talk about it."

"I do," I say, alarm and anger colliding together in my gut. "What happened?"

"Just some assholes being assholes."

"Did they hurt you?" I swallow and lift her chin so she's forced to meet my eye. "Did they ... Where the fuck was Azlan?"

"It was Summer and her girls. And I'm fine," she says, touching her scalp. A clump of hair is missing.

"I'm going to fucking kill her," I say, taking a decided pace in the direction of the campus. "I'm going to pluck every strand of hair from that stupid girl's head."

She tugs on my arm. "You're not. You're going to let me fight my own battles."

I yank on her grip, the anger white hot in my veins. "She's a little–"

"Bitch, I know." She places her palm on my chest, blocking my path. "But you're going to have to beat up an awful lot of people in this academy if you want to avenge every wrong ever done to me. And that includes yourself." The anger rushes from me in a sudden gush and in its place I feel the weight of guilt. She examines my face. "What you did to me ... on Founders' Night."

"I'm sorry," I whisper. "I'm really sorry for it. If I could ..."

"Rewind time. Yeah, well."

I take her hands in mine. "I am truly sorry."

"You know that isn't enough, though, right? Anyone can say sorry." She swallows. "Andrew said he was sorry. He bought me flowers and everything. And then ..."

"Yes, I know. I know I have a lot of making up to do to you, Rhi. An awful lot." I've treated her like shit. I've treated her worse than shit. I am no better than the spoiled, self-entitled jerks in this academy. She's my fated mate. I should have been falling at her feet and dedicating my life to her. Fuck, I should probably be falling at her feet now.

"You can start by fetching me a drink." She points to my bottle of beer resting on the decking behind us.

"You're underage," I say.

She scowls at me and sends a picture of the pain she'll cause to my balls if I don't hand the drink over.

I chuckle and take her hand in mine, leading her over to the decking and passing her my drink.

"If you'd used similar force on Summer perhaps–"

"Oh, I was tempted, but she's just waiting for the opportunity where I attack her with my magic, then she'll be straight to York, demanding I'm expelled."

"I thought expulsion was what you wanted."

She sighs. "I don't know anymore."

She chugs a long mouthful of beer and I snatch the bottle back.

"Easy, we all remember what happened the last time you drank." She wipes her hand over her mouth and I trace my knuckles down her cheek. "I don't want you to go. I want you to stay here with me."

She stares at me.

"Half the time I think you hate me, Professor."

"I don't hate you. I think you know it's quite the opposite."

"Do I? You've never said it."

I take a deep inhale. "It's not a word that comes easily to me, Rhianna. You have to understand that. My past ... my life ..." She nods.

"It's just a word. Like sorry."

"It isn't, it's a hell of a lot more than that. And it scares the shit out of me if I'm honest. That's why I never told you ... that's why I've been fighting it. I was afraid."

"You? Afraid?" she scoffs.

"Me." I sigh, dropping down to perch on the edge of the decking. "My dad ..." I take a long gulp of my beer, the bottle bumping against my lips as the bottle shakes. I peer up at her and she's watching me, waiting.

I sigh again and close my eyes, bringing the memory in front of my eyes and projecting it into her mind.

A YOUNG MAN. His chestnut hair clipped short against his scalp, dressed in the dark uniform of the authorities, a soldier's cap balanced on his head.

He reaches down and lifts the small boy from the ground, holds him in his arms, kisses his cheeks and his forehead, hugging him tight. The boy squeezes him, refuses to let him go, and the man peers towards a young woman, concern etched all over her features, tears in her eyes.

She peels the boy from the man. Kissing him longingly, hangs onto his hand. But then he's slinging his kit bag over his shoulder, walking away, waving to them as he goes, all the way to the end of the road. Then he steps around the corner and he's gone.

"WHAT HAPPENED?" she whispers as the memory fades and I open my eyes.

"He was sent to fight in the Western border lands." I stare up at the darkening sky. "And he never came home. When the time came, when he was asked, he gave his life to protect us, to defend us. While others ..."

I drop my gaze to hers.

"While others?" she says.

"Shirked their duty."

"You think that's what I was doing? What my aunt was doing?"

"When I first met you, yes, yes, I did."

"It should be a choice. It shouldn't be forced, mandatory."

"And what would you choose now, Rhi?" I ask.

She meets my gaze with her steely one.

"I hope you know me well enough by now, Phoenix, to know I fight for the people I love."

"I do. I was wrong."

"What happened afterwards? To you and your mom?" she asks.

"My parents ... they were ..."

She squeezes my hand. "Fated mates?"

I peer up at her. I hate telling this story. Hate the way people's eyes flood with sympathy. I hate that. But hers don't. They're steady. She's faced her own loss in life. She knows sympathy is as worthless as unfelt words of apology.

"Yes. My mom never recovered the loss of her mate. It ripped the soul from her body and she lost her mind."

"But you were meeting her for lunch? The other day–"

"At the home, Rhi. Where she's been locked away for the last twenty-five years."

She doesn't bother telling me she's sorry. She leans over me and presses her lips to mine, and it's exactly what I need.

"It won't happen to us," she says against my mouth.

"No," I say. I'm damn determined it won't. Because, damn it, I do love this girl. For all her brattiness and snark, for her sharp tongue and her naivety. I love her.

I love her for her smile, her laugh, for the way her cheeks fill with color and her eyes dance with excitement.

Fuck, I love her.

I pull her into my arms and carry her into the dark cabin, kicking the door shut behind me and striding through to the bathroom. She frowns as I lower her onto the closed toilet seat.

"This wasn't exactly where I thought you were going to take me."

I simply smile at her, using my magic to turn on the taps and let the bath fill with warm, bubbly water.

Then I peel off her dress, pausing to heal the grazes on her skin, the missing hair on her head, the cut over her eyebrow, relieved, and not a bit surprised, to find the blood on her skin is not her own. She climbs into the bath, sighing with relief as the warm water swallows her up and I kneel by the tub.

"You aren't coming in?" she asks.

"No," I tell her, picking up the sponge from the shelf and running it softly over her face, wiping away the mud and the grime.

"I could do it myself," she says.

"I want to do it, Rhianna, so don't be a brat for once and let me."

She shrugs her shoulders and leans back her head allowing me to trace the sponge over her shoulders. Then I reach into the bath, lifting each of her arms in turn and sliding the sponge across her skin. When I'm satisfied, I reach up on my knees and plunge my arms into the water, caressing her chest, her soft tits and her stomach next, wiping away all that mud.

"Lift your leg," I tell her, and with her eyes still closed, she raises her left. I tickle the sponge over her foot, a smile appearing on her lips, and then I glide the sponge up her long legs, all the way up the soft skin on her thighs.

"Now the other one too, sweetheart." She lowers her leg and lifts her right and I repeat my care.

When I'm done, she peeks open one eye.

"Aren't you cleaning any higher, Professor?" she asks. "You're always saying we should complete our work thoroughly." She grins, lowering her voice in an attempt to emulate mine. "No cutting corners." She frowns and wags her forefinger at me.

"Well, Miss Blackwaters, if that's what I said, I'd better live by my words. Wouldn't want to gain a reputation for being less than liberal with the truth now, would I?"

"You? Liberal with the truth? Never! You're an epitome of rule-following and respect."

"Exactly. You'd certainly never catch me stripping the clothes off my most bratty student and touching her," I run my knuckles up her thigh, finding her pussy, "here."

She sighs. "That would most definitely be considered scandalous."

"And very naughty," I growl against her ear. "Especially if that naughty, bratty student let me touch her there, especially if she opened her legs when I told her: part your thighs for me, Miss Blackwaters."

"I'm not sure such a bratty student would do as she was told."

"Oh, she would," I say, stroking along her seam, "when she knew how good I'd make her feel." I use my magic to make the water vibrate against her and, with an even louder sigh, her legs fall open. "See," I say, "just like that."

I explore her more intimately, finding her entrance and circling it, then her clit and pressing against it.

I sweep my tongue around her earlobe, then plunge my tongue into her earhole, mirroring the actions with my fingers and making her gasp.

Water splashes against the sides of the bath as she raises her hips in an attempt to grind against my fingers.

"Such a brat. Such a needy brat," I say, pumping my fingers in and out of her and watching as her body writhes in the water. "Such a goddamn beautiful, fucking irresistible brat." She moans and I think she likes my words as much as she likes my fingers. "Would you like your professor to make you come?"

"Yes," she gasps.

"Manners, Miss Blackwaters," I say, using my magic to have the water sparking against her clit again. A promise of what's coming if she plays nice.

Her body jolts. But when I cut my magic, she frowns.

"Come on, sweetheart. Use your manners and I'll make you feel so fucking good."

"Yes ..." she hesitates, catching her breath, "yes, please. Please make me come, Professor."

"That's better," I say, rewarding her with a kiss to her shoulder.

I reignite my magic, using it to thrum the water against her clit.

"Is this how you used to get yourself off, Miss Blackwaters? In that shack of a house of yours, all alone in the woods. Did you touch yourself and make yourself come in the bath?"

"In the shower," she confesses.

I can see the picture of it in her mind, running the flow from the shower-head over her clit and making herself come.

Damn.

"And who did you imagine while you did it? Who were you imagining?" I say, as I work my fingers inside her pussy and my magic against her sensitive little nub. "A man like me?"

She opens her eyes to stare up into mine. Her mouth falls open, color sweeps over her face and she moans. She looks so vulnerable when she comes, that steely mask of hers falling away and revealing the true girl beneath. The one I want to know.

"Yes," she says. "A man like you."

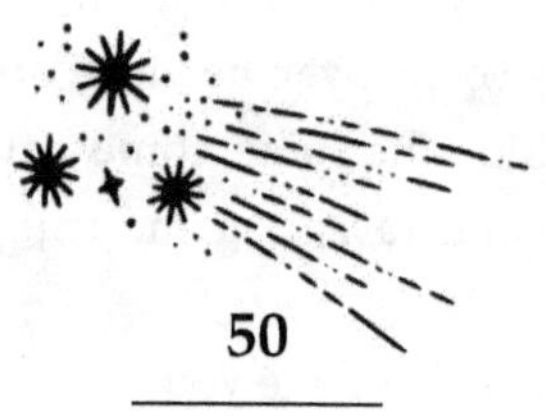

50

S tone

"WILL YOU FUCK ME NOW, PROFESSOR?" she asks.

I splash water at her face.

"You're so impatient, Miss Blackwaters. Did you never learn, good things come to those who wait? Now lean forward."

She huffs but folds over, wrapping her hands around her legs and resting her cheek on her knees. She watches me, her eyes swimming with satisfaction and her cheeks still flushed from her orgasm. I swim the sponge across the skin of her beautiful back.

"I was looking for you this evening," I say. "I was debating whether to call Azlan. Thought you may have run away again."

"I was walking. Thinking and walking. It's how I ended up ambushed by Summer and her gang."

I frown. I'm going to find my own way to deal with that girl. "Thinking? Sounds serious."

"I wasn't thinking about you, Jerk-face," she mutters.

"Miss Blackwaters," I say, ignoring the insult, "let's not pretend you aren't always thinking about me, when we both know you are."

"Just because you can't stop thinking about me, Professor, does not mean I'm thinking of you."

"When you send me pictures like you did this afternoon, can you blame me?" Fuck, that picture. It's all I've been thinking of.

Her scent is tantalizing in my senses, like I'm already drowning in her and her soft hair tickles against my face as I rub her shoulders.

Fuck, I can't help myself anymore.

Her magic hums in the air and mine rises to meet it, twisting and twirling with hers in some seductive dance I want to emulate.

"I am thinking about you," I say. "I am thinking about you all the time."

I reach into the bath and gather her, sopping wet, into my arms again. Her breath hitching.

"Wh-wh-what are you doing?" she whispers.

"Fuck the waiting. I'm taking you to bed," I say, my voice so dark, it makes her shiver. And fuck, if that doesn't make me harder still.

I stumble through the doorway, and into my bedroom. I can hear the thump of her heart and the whistle of her breath. I drop her down onto the mattress. Her hair spreads out in a fan around her head, and my eyes fall to the milky skin of her soft thighs.

I lean down and kiss her there, her skin damp, trailing

my hands up her long legs, feel as she squirms beneath me, her breaths turning needy.

At the apex of her legs, I pause. I smell something different. Something masculine. I dip my finger inside her again. Now she's no longer in the water, I can feel her better. She's wet and sticky.

"Azlan," I mutter.

"Yes," she says, "we ... we used a barrier spell. You ..." Her fingers stroke through my hair. "You could use one too. You could come inside me."

I close my eyes. The want is so fierce, it's almost painful. I want that. I want what he has. I want to come deep inside her beautiful pussy.

I strip off my shirt and my pants. She's all bare and spread out beneath me, her eyes wide and gleaming in the darkness. She looks even better than that photo and I can't deny myself this anymore.

I was always fucked. Always doomed. The moment I answered that call from Azlan. The moment I agreed to help him bring the girl in. The moment I laid eyes on her. From that moment, I was set on a path, my fate, and it was always leading right here. Into my bed, between her legs. This was always where I was meant to be.

So damn the consequences. Damn all of it. She's my mate, my fated mate, and I'm done fighting it. I'm letting go. Falling.

"You know what happens if we do this?" I say, hoping with everything I possess, she doesn't change her mind, that she won't refuse me.

"Yes," she says. "The bond will seal."

Yes, if I give myself to her – either by magic or by body – that fated-mate bond will be sealed. Forever.

"And you want that?"

"I want you, Stone. I want you really badly."

Her pussy's all pink and swollen. I can see just how much she wants me and it makes my blood heat so high, I think I might boil in my own skin.

"You can have me other ways," I whisper. "We don't have to–"

"I want you this way. I want it really badly," she says.

"You're not going to–"

"Regret it? No, no. We still have a hell of a lot to work out, Professor, and you are not done groveling by any stretch of the imagination." I nod, earnestly. Fuck, I'll happily grovel for the rest of my life. "But the three of us, we belong together, don't you think?"

I lower myself down, cradling her precious head with my arms, my cock nudging between her legs.

"Yes, we do."

And then with my eyes locked with hers, I thrust into her, her warmth and softness swallowing me whole.

"Ohhhh," she moans, her head tipping backward. She's tight and I lower my mouth, sucking and nibbling her throat, her pulse leaping against my lips, until she relaxes, loosening around me and I sink further inside. All the way, until my hips are flush with hers. I groan, pausing for just a moment, savoring the feel of her, the warmth of her, and then I'm sliding out.

The friction, the feel of my cock ring, sends moans racing from her lips. And I do it again and again, just to hear more of those noises, just to make her feel good.

"Can you come this way, sweetheart?"

"Yes," she moans, "yes, it feels so good."

I smile. Best way to tame this wild little cat was always going to be with my cock.

I give her more force, more pressure, hold her in my arms as she writhes in the sensations.

I fuck her harder, and she wraps her legs around me, forcing her heels into my backside and pleading for more. The bed shakes, banging against the wall.

"Phoenix!" she calls out and then she's falling, color racing up her neck and into her cheeks, her mouth falling open on one long sigh, her body stilling, then jolting beneath me as she's struck by wave after wave of pleasure, her pussy clenching and sucking around me.

No wonder he's half mad, obsessed. Why he can't leave her alone.

This ... this is ...

I'm on the verge of coming myself, but then she's pushing at my shoulder and I see in her mind what she wants. I let her roll me over onto my back and watch as she hooks her knee over my lap, hands resting on my shoulders, then sinks slowly, slowly, so fucking slowly, onto my waiting cock.

We groan when she swallows me whole, and then she's riding me, grinding her hips around and around at first, getting herself off on the feel of my cock. But then I grab her by the waist and bounce her up and down, up and down, up and down, until I can't take any more.

It's like lightning. Like lightning in my body, starting right in my core and streaking through every limb.

I come with a groan so loud it makes the walls of my cabin shake, and then I'm pumping seed inside her as she follows me for a second time.

When she collapses down on top of me, her skin is coated in sweat like mine and I hold her close and lick the salt from her neck.

"Okay?" I ask her, still catching my breath.

"Yes," she says, snuggling into my chest. "Can you feel it?"

"Yes," I say, the bond, shimmering like sunlight deep in my belly, my entire body thrumming with it, our magic curling around us like an embrace.

We lie, catching our breaths, basking in the sensation, moonlight falling through the open curtain.

I smooth damp hair from her face and stroke her cheeks, her jaw, her mouth.

"So, what were you thinking about earlier? How to shake off the pig?"

"No." She tucks her hand between us and draws out the necklace she's wearing, lifting a locket.

"It was my aunt's. My mother's before her."

"It's very pretty."

"An old friend of my aunt's just gave it to me. He was in the stadium. He came to find me."

My spine stiffens. Will this girl ever learn? Is she trying to get herself killed? "What?"

"He's a friend. It's okay."

"Remember the last time you went off with a friend?"

She swallows. "Yeah, well, this one had information about my mom."

"Accurate information?" I say slowly, examining her face. "Real information?"

"I think so," she says, "but I guess I can't be sure."

I eye the necklace in her hand. "Give it to me."

"No! Why?"

"To check it's not cursed."

"Oh," she squeals, lifting it over her head and passing it to me. "I don't think it is though."

"You know what a curse looks like?"

She chews her lip. "No."

"Exactly, it doesn't look like anything."

She huffs and punches my shoulder.

I turn the locket over in my fingers, admiring the engraving on its shell, feeling for magic with dark intents on its surface. I can't feel anything. "Have you opened it?"

"Yes," she says, shoulders slumping. "There's a photo inside. Of my parents and a baby. I'm guessing me."

I look up at her face. Her eyes are full of sadness. "You have us now, Rhi." I know what it's like to lose your family. To have no one.

"It's not that," she says.

"What is it?"

"It's just ..." She inhales, her bottom lip quivering. She's on the verge of tears. This girl, so fucking young, has been through so much, and though she's spat and hissed like a cat, I've never seen her cry. It fucking cracks my heart in two.

I lift her chin.

"I thought there would be words, you know," she continues." A note, a letter, a clue even. But there was nothing. She left me nothing at all." A fat tear rolls down her cheek. "I miss her. I miss her so much."

"What else, Rhi?" I say softly, swiping the tear away gently with the pad of my thumb. "What did he tell you?"

"My mom was a seer."

I stare into those strangely honey eyes of hers. "A seer?"

"Yes, the authorities wanted her and so did the gangs and the West. Wanted to make use of her gift. He didn't know what happened to her, but that was why he said my aunt was keeping me hidden. She didn't want the same fate to befall me as my mom."

"It won't," I say firmly, my jaw tightening.

"But those dreams, Phoenix? The ones from my memories. They were predictions, weren't they? Dreams of the fut–"

"In the past. You haven't had any in years, years and years. Maybe you had the gift in the past, but you don't have it now, Rhi. And you, me and Azlan are the only ones who know. You're safe."

Her mouth falls open on an "oh."

I can feel her emotion through the bond. Alarm.

"What, Rhi?" I say, ice running through my veins. "Did you tell anyone else about those dreams? Winnie?" She shakes her head. "Then what? What is it, Rhi?"

She meets my eyes and I see that image again. A wound. A wound that looked like it had been made by crimson magic.

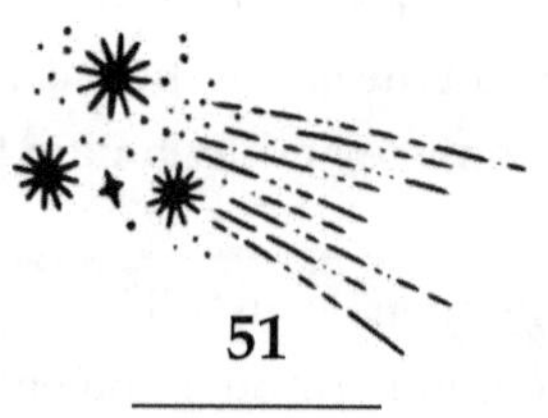

51

R enzo

CRIMSON MAGIC.

I've heard about it. Heard the tales when I was a boy. Listened to men long for it. Watched magicals battle to grasp it.

I've never seen it wielded. Never felt it crackle through the air. Never heard it sizzle on the ends of fingertips.

Never tasted all the damage and destruction it could do.

Fuck, it was tantalizing.

My precious little rabbit. Who knew?

Such big round innocent eyes. Such a pretty porcelain face. Such an aura of innocence about her. So tempting to corrupt her.

Yet, underneath it all, deep inside her, darkness.

Crimson magic.

Is that why?

Because we are alike the two of us. I saw the glint in those eyes. Hidden and repressed. She wanted to hurt me. She wanted to kill me. She has a lust for it, just like me.

I spin the knife in my hands.

Lowsky wants her dead. That hasn't changed. And he's growing impatient for me to finish the job.

There's something afoot. Plans brewing with the West.

He wants this done before he initiates whatever he's planning to start.

But the girl. She's far more valuable alive than dead. And not just because I want to make her mine.

The two of us, the two of us together, we could be unstoppable. Hell, we could destroy the whole damn world.

Read Book Three next, *Shattered Stars*

Want to read a bonus scene from this story? You can find all my bonus material on my website here

For sneaky previews, spoilers and all the latest news, join Hannah's reader group

Thank you so much for reading. If you enjoyed this book, please consider leaving a review or rating — it's a great help to indie authors like me!

ALSO BY HANNAH HAZE

All available on Amazon and Kindle Unlimited.

Fantasy Romance RH
The Arrow Hart Academy
Fractured Fates
Twisted Ties
Shattered Stars
Burdened Bonds
Destined Dawn

The Firestone Academy
Storm of Shadows
Spark of Sorcery
Taste of Thorns
Lure of Lightning

Contemporary RH omegaverse
The Rockview Omegaverse
Pack Rivals Part I

Pack Rivals Part II
Pack Choice
Pack Gamble Part I
Pack Gamble Part II
Pack Education Part I
Pack Education Part II

In With The Pack
In Deep - Rosie's story
In Trouble - Connie's story
In Knots - Alexa's story
In Doubt - Giorgie's story
In Control - Sophia's story
In Stockings (Christmas Novella)

Contemporary MF omegaverse series
The Alpha Rock Stars
The Rockstar's Omega
Rocked by the Alpha
Fourth Base with the Alpha

Contemporary MF omegaverse standalones
Oxford Heat
The Alpha Escort Agency
Omega's Forbidden Heat

Contemporary MF omegaverse novellas
The Omega Chase
Online Heat
Christmas Heat

Alien omegaverse MF romance series

The Alpha Prince of Astia
<u>Alien Desire</u>
<u>Alien Passion</u>

ABOUT THE AUTHOR

A recovering cynic, Hannah grew up swearing she would never marry. Then in 2001, she met her husband and has been a card-carrying romantic ever since. Despite being an avid writer and reader, Hannah decided to do the sensible thing and study science at university, putting authoring ideas to one side.This all changed when she discovered the joys of a good romance book and came to the realisation that love stories are always the best ones.

She now uses her knowledge of chemical bonds and reactions to ensure her books are full of sparks. In fact the electricity between her characters is sure to set your pulse racing and your heart fluttering.

Hannah loves reading to her three children, including doing all the silly voices, and going for long walks in the countryside (the muddier the better). Her head is always full of new story ideas and you are most likely to find her avoiding the demands of her very naughty cat as she attempts to write them all down.

Sign up to my newsletter:
www.hannahhaze.com/about

Join my reader groups:

https://www.facebook.com/groups/hannahhazehotromancereads

https://www.facebook.com/groups/softandsteamyomegaverse

Visit my website:
www.hannahhaze.com

Catch me on TikTok:
www.tiktok.com/@hannahhaze_author

ACKNOWLEDGMENTS

Firstly, a massive thank you to all my readers. I know I have kept you waiting for this next book and I really, truly hope it delivers. Do not fear: the next book is in progress!

My wonderful beta readers have kept me on track as always and I am super grateful for all their feedback — good and back. Aimee, Alanys, Courtney, Jenna, Jessie, Kiki, Leandri, Lili, Morgan and Sara — you all rock!

Thank you to Christian for another beautiful cover and James for editing my smutty words.

And lastly and always, big kisses to Mr. D and Stephy for their continued support, and my children for their never-ending patience and cheerleading!

www.ingramcontent.com/pod-product-compliance
Lightning Source LLC
Chambersburg PA
CBHW070744120726
47910CB00001B/167